WISSAHICKON SOULS

A WISSAHICKON CREEK STORY

PJ DEVLIN

Benezet Street Press

Copyright © 2014, 2017, 2020 PJ Devlin
Cover Photo: John M Devlin
Cover Design: Kathy Butterfield, Artovation

ISBN: 978-1-7340801-0-0

Benezet Street Press

DEDICATION

For my parents, Peg and Mike Jeffers, who brought us to the Wissahickon
and set us free

AUTHOR'S NOTE

Wissahickon Souls is a work of fiction set in and around Philadelphia and Haiti from 1806 through 1836. Claire Penniman and her family, and Lawrence Williams and his family, are characters constructed from my imagination.

Names, characters, businesses, places, events, and incidents are used in a fictitious manner. Resemblance to actual persons, living or dead, is coincidental. Allusions to historic persons and descriptions of religious ceremonies identified as Voodoo were modified to suit the story. French or Haitian Creole phrases may stray from correct spelling and usage. I modified actual events to serve the story and made up the rest as I went along.

With honor and respect,

PJ Devlin

PROLOGUE

THE ECLIPSE JUNE 16, 1806

On Germantown Road, merchants and workers, tailors and sailors, white and black men, women and children stood shoulder to shoulder as the sky changed from blue to yellow. The day dawned cloudy, but as noon approached the sun flared in fiery splendor as if preparing for its role in the upcoming spectacle. Suddenly, chirping birds swept through the sky in great dark clouds, like children running home before dark. The people watched in fear and dread as the moon devoured the sun.

In the brick house in the alley, Elizabeth Penniman lay on her side, legs drawn against her swollen belly. The cramps worsened, coming every few minutes. She stuffed her fist in her mouth to hold back her screams – of pain, of fear the pain would never end, that the work of getting this baby into the world would take her from it.

"There now, Elizabeth, this baby coming. Push big next time that pain hit and we soon see who causing this trouble," her mother-in-law, Dinah said.

In the noon hour, the room became dark and Elizabeth's moans grew louder.

"Moses, bring the lamps, light those candles, this baby coming, eclipse or no eclipse. We ain't stopping to watch the sight," Dinah called to her son.

Moses, dusky skin beaded with sweat, placed candles around the room as if it were an altar. It shouldn't be so hard. At twenty-six, his wife was still a young woman.

"You go on now, this women's work," Dinah said.

"She be all right?"

"She be right as right can be once the baby come."

As day turned dark as night, Moses stood on the porch with his son, Samuel, in his arms. The three-year-old watched the eclipse through the piece of glass Moses had smoked over a candle. Samuel gazed at the black sky.

"Daddy, stars."

"The stars make a dipper, like a soup ladle. The stars at the edge point to the North Star, our star."

A huge black ball covered the sun and white flames flared around it through smoky yellow clouds. The air grew cold. On the tip of the black ring in the sky, a tiny light shone like a diamond.

Elizabeth's scream, long and primal, pierced Moses' heart. Samuel leaned his head against Moses' shoulder and whimpered.

As pink and yellow shimmers heralded the return of day, Dinah carried a screaming baby onto the porch.

"The Lord give you a daughter, a fine baby – and loud."

Moses cradled the delicate bundle in one arm with Samuel in the other. "And Elizabeth?"

"Elizabeth done herself in, but proud to give you this girl child. It sure be good to see the light."

Inside, Elizabeth leaned against pillows, her brown skin wan. Moses put the baby to her breast and sat beside her while Samuel stroked the baby's fingers.

"You done good, Elizabeth," Moses said, tears in his eyes. "That eclipse a powerful wondrous sight."

"This baby girl's a powerful wondrous sight to me," Elizabeth said. "I want to name her Claire, after Clara, Anna William's mother."

"Claire Penniman," Moses said, "born on the total eclipse of the sun."

At Wissahickon Farm, Raymond and Anna Williams watched the eclipse with their young son, Reuben. Earlier in the day, the sky surrounded the red-gold sun like a blue blanket. Now, a black cloud of starlings swooped across the dimming sky and cows lowed for their calves. When the sky turned dull yellow, cows lay down, front legs tucked under their chests. Along the Wissahickon Creek, birds roosted in trees. Like a stain, the shadow of the moon crept across the sun until day became night. Reuben watched the solar eclipse through a colored glass jar and called, "Look at the stars."

When the sun disappeared, a white ring encircled the void and beyond that, a miasma of yellow clouds dissipated like milk poured in water. Later, sunbeams broke from the moon's shadow, and a loud fluttering noise marked the rising of hundreds of wings flying west.

"An awesome spectacle, Anna," Raymond said.

Anna's eyes swept the sky. She quoted Amos —

> *And it shall come to pass in that day, says the Lord God, that I will make the sun go down at noon and I will darken the Earth in broad daylight; I will turn your feasts into mourning; and your songs into lamentation. I will make it like mourning for a son and its end like a bitter day.*

THE INDENTURE

This INDENTURE Witnesses that Claire Penniman, a Negro female of six years, with consent of her father, Moses Penniman, a carter, Voluntarily Indentures herself to Raymond Williams of Wissahickon Farm in Montgomery County near Philadelphia to serve Raymond Williams and his Assigns for the Term of twelve Years from the first day of Claire's arrival to Wissahickon Farm during which time Raymond Williams or his Assigns shall give her two hours of schooling all days but the Sabbath in the months of October through April to educate this child in letters, cipher, and agriculture, and will supply her with sufficient Food, Apparel, Lodging, and other necessaries. At the expiration of her term, Claire will be released from obligation, and receive payment according to the Custom of the County. Provided on this Condition, that Claire shall be transported and returned to her family, Moses and Elizabeth Penniman, no fewer than thirty days each year, to be determined according to the requirements of Raymond Williams and Assigns.

August 14, 1812

PART 1

GERMANTOWN and
WISSAHICKON FARM

1812 - 1824

CHAPTER ONE

The Wissahickon Creek ran high after days of rain. Claire Penniman, six-years-old, jumped off a boulder into the shimmering green water of Devil's Pool. She paddled to the middle then back to the flat granite rocks along the bank. Her father, Moses Penniman, a free-born Negro, fished nearby, keeping his eyes on her. A cool breeze rustled the branches of hickory trees. Green-husked nuts dropped onto boulders and bounced into the creek.

Moses loved the tranquility of the woods along the Wissahickon Creek. Pine smells suffused the air. Dapples of sunlight flickered on the water. Overhead, he heard a distinctive trill and caught a glimpse of a blue warbler.

"Daddy, look, there goes a catfish," Claire called.

Creek water glistened on his baby's hair. Her round eyes gazed at him with expectation and trust. Moses raised his pole. The hook and weight swayed over the water.

"How about you find a fat worm for that catfish?"

Claire dug into mud near Moses' feet. "Got one!"

While Moses hooked the wiggling worm, Claire hopped and jiggled. He handed her the pole. She grinned up at him, and her sweet baby smile brought tears to his eyes. This morning, his little girl made her mark on her indenture agreement. On Sunday, Raymond Williams, the owner of Wissahickon Farm, would arrive at the Penniman's house to collect Claire and her older brother, Samuel. Moses sighed.

Three years ago, Moses and his wife, Elizabeth, indentured Samuel to Wissahickon Farm. Now nine-years-old, Samuel loved farm life. Moses wanted both children to experience life away from the city, to thrive in clean air with good food, and learn to read, write and cipher. He wanted to shield them from the slurs black people absorbed like biscuits in tea.

Raymond and Anna Williams were good white folks. Moses' wife, Elizabeth, had known Anna since childhood. Claire would be treated kindly. Besides, the children's agreements included an unusual clause – Claire and Samuel received thirty days to visit home each year.

Footsteps crunched over fallen branches. Moses turned.

"There you be, Moses," Old Caesar, an elderly black man, called. "I been looking for Claire."

The man's buff-colored spaniel, Peanut, scurried to the creek bank while the old man sidled down.

"Claire wanted to play in the creek afore she go to Wissahickon Farm," Moses said.

"You know I can't let this little child go on without she tell Old Caesar good-bye."

Claire gave Moses the fishing pole, then hugged the old man's legs. Eight years before, Moses found Old Caesar, a runaway from slavery, shivering in Mystics Cave, cut into the ridge above the creek. For a hundred years, runaways had been directed to Mystics Cave to wait for help. Ever since the time of Jack Penniman, freed by William Penn, the family business was helping slaves escape to freedom. Since childhood, Moses worked in the family business. Many runaways continued to New York, Boston, or Canada, but Old Caesar built himself a well-hidden shack along the Wissahickon Creek. Over the years, he became family.

"I don't like white people," Claire said.

"Can't say I blame you, but Samuel done fine at that farm," Old Caesar said.

Moses took a deep breath. "Claire, you know Mr. Raymond and Miss Anna treat you fair. You know you been fussing to learn to read and write. Wissahickon Farm's the best place for you until you grown up."

"Daddy!" Samuel's voice.

After he burst through the trees and brush, he crouched to catch his breath. Sweat trickled down his face. His calico shirt hung off his shoulders, unbuttoned and torn. He smelled like burned tar.

"Slave catchers come for Joe! Mama say come home. Tell Old Caesar disappear."

Moses stiffened. His eyes grew wide, and his hands quivered.

"Caesar, take Claire and stay out of sight until it's safe."

Moses wiped his brow and followed Samuel. His wife, Elizabeth, and his mother, Dinah, were in the house alone. His heart raced. No telling what a slaver might do.

"Samuel, go home. I'll take a look down the road."

But Samuel raced past with Old Caesar's dog at his heels.

Claire tugged Old Caesar's hand. "Peanut chasing Samuel."

Old Caesar made a circle of his thumb and forefinger, held them against his tongue and whistled. He whistled again.

"Lord, Lord," he said, "where that little dog go?"

"He gone to Germantown," Claire said. "Come on. We go find him."

"Your daddy say hide from the slavers, Child," Old Caesar said between labored breaths. "But, oh Lord, I can't lose my little dog."

"Don't worry," Claire said. "I ain't scared of no slave catchers."

Claire marched ahead and waited for Old Caesar at the edge of the woods in bright sunlight. I sure will miss Old Caesar when I go to Wissahickon Farm, she thought, I sure will miss Mama and Daddy and Granny.

Moses pushed through the back door of his house. At the front windows, Elizabeth and Dinah, who everyone called Granny, peeked outside from behind muslin curtains.

"Where the slavers?" Moses asked.

"They're down the alley," Elizabeth said. "They caught Joe Johnson in the livery stable, hiding behind feed bags. The poor boy. People say someone gave him up."

"Them slave catchers be devils," Granny said. "I like to tell them go back to hell."

"Where's Claire?" Elizabeth's eyes darted around the room.

"I left her with Old Caesar down the creek," Moses said. "She don't need to see none of this." He paused. "Where Samuel go? I told him get inside and stay inside, but he kept running."

Elizabeth caught her breath. "Find him, Moses. Bring him home."

Moses trembled. He crossed the porch and front yard to search for Samuel. Six black men huddled on one side of the alley.

Someone shouted, "Let that boy be!"

A white man in a wide-brimmed black hat astride a horse brandished a long barrel gun. The other white man tied Joe Johnson's wrists. A Negro hurled a stone that struck the standing white man's hat. The mounted slave catcher lowered his gun and pulled the trigger. With a loud crack, alley dirt exploded in a yellow cloud. Smoke spiraled from the rifle barrel. The crowd backed away.

"You niggers stay back," the slaver yelled, "This ain't none of your business."

Moses spied Samuel with the black men, and ran for his son. Another gunshot deafened him.

"You, Nig, stop there or I'll shoot you dead," the mounted man shouted.

"I come for my son," Moses said, "he just a boy."

The slaver fired. A tree branch shattered. Smells of gun smoke, horses, and the sweat of frightened men thickened the air. Moses raised his hands and stumbled back.

"Here I be, Daddy." Samuel gripped his arm.

Elizabeth, skirt in hand, eyes wide, crossed the alley to her husband and son.

"We want no trouble," she called.

While they backed toward their house, Moses kept his eyes fixed on the men and horses. The mounted slaver held his long gun ready.

"Look here, Niggers. We got the right by law to capture fugitives. Tiny Joe Johnson run away from Captain Edward's farm. We aim to bring him back to Talbot County where he belongs."

The Pennsylvania law for the gradual abolition of slavery didn't apply to escaped slaves from other states. Even though he and his family were born free, Moses was terrified. Slavers paid no mind to stealing free people off the street and sending them south into slavery.

The Penniman family helped runaways to freedom since Jack Penniman's time. Someone gave up Joe, Moses suspected, or the slavers got lucky.

After Elizabeth and Samuel climbed the porch steps, Moses motioned for them to go inside.

"I need to see this," he said.

From behind a porch pillar, Moses watched the slaver tighten the rope around Joe's wrists. The mounted white man waited, rifle ready. The horses snuffed and pawed the ground. A dog barked, and a horse reared.

Moses narrowed his eyes. Old Caesar's spaniel, Peanut, growled and snapped at the horses' legs.

The unmounted slaver lunged at the dog. Peanut scurried away, then stopped and growled. Moses feared if he whistled or called the dog, the slavers would turn on him. He turned to go inside but a sound drew him back.

His baby, his Claire, marched up to the slavers and grabbed Old Caesar's dog. His stomach lurched. He stepped off the porch and started towards Claire, palms up and steps slow and steady.

"I get this dog out the way your horses," Claire said, voice direct and high-pitched. "You hurting Joe."

The mounted man grunted and spat at Claire's feet, but the other slaver loosened the rope. Both men laughed.

"Get out the road, Pickaninny, this ain't no place for babies," the mounted slaver said.

"We going."

Peanut weighed almost as much as Claire, but she wrapped her arms around the dog and dragged him across the alley. Moses held his breath, aware of his own skunky smell.

Elizabeth called, "What's happening?"

Moses gestured for her to stay back while Claire led Old Caesar, hugging Peanut to his chest, toward the house. Every few steps, Claire looked at the slave catchers. Moses wanted to shout, *Keep coming, don't look back*, but he kept silent, afraid to draw the slavers' attention. When Claire and Old Caesar finally reached the house, he ushered them onto the porch. Elizabeth glared at him.

"You told me Claire was safe down the creek."

"Peanut run away, Mama. I had to get him. Don't cry," Claire said.

A dark spot hovered across Moses' vision. No, not now, he told himself. Sharp pain struck behind his left ear. His stomach lurched. He staggered to a chair as the spot grew blindingly large. Flashes – yellow, blue, green, red – zigzagged in a crescent along the left side of his vision.

"Daddy, you got the sick headache?" Claire asked.

Moses let Elizabeth lead him inside to the settee. She propped a pillow against the sofa arm and helped him ease back. Claire draped a wet rag over his eyes, and water dribbled past his ears. The flashing zigzag subsided. The smell of turnip greens and onions simmering with a ham bone drifted from the kitchen, along with Granny's voice.

"This a free state. Peoples make it to freedom, they ought to be free. It ain't right they take Joe to Talbot County."

Moses opened an eye. Old Caesar sat in a rocking chair, observing him.

"Caesar, why you let Claire near the slavers?" Moses' voice was weak.

"We ain't 'tend go nowhere near them. Peanut run away and Claire go after him. I most fall over dead I see my little dog at they horses. I keep my head down and pray. Claire brave. She snatch up Peanut, never you mind."

Claire tugged Old Caesar's hand. "Peanut want to bite the slave catchers, and I want to shoot them."

"You keep clear of slavers, you hear?" Moses said.

Old Caesar rested his hand on Claire's head. "I sure gone miss my little child when you go off to that big farm." He sighed. "I best get Peanut home."

Granny handed Old Caesar a sack. "Beans, onions, squash from my garden and fresh boiled eggs."

"Amen," Old Caesar said, "Thank you, Dinah."

The following day, as Moses entered the kitchen, sweat beaded on his brow. After William Penn granted him freedom, his great-great-grandfather Jack built this brick house, where Jack and his second wife, Verily, raised four boys and two girls. For the past hundred years, the house sheltered generations of Pennimans, born free.

"Are you feeling better?" Elizabeth asked.

"Mostly." Moses rubbed his temples.

Elizabeth dropped potatoes in a pot. Steam reddened her cheeks.

"Open the door, let out the steam," Moses said.

He whisked the heat toward the back door, to little avail. Elizabeth shuffled a loaf of rye bread out of the oven and set it on the bread board. As always after a sick headache, he felt ravenous. After yesterday's terror, he cherished the comfort of his family in the refuge of their home. The salty smell of boiled oysters made his mouth water. Elizabeth undid her bandana and tied it again.

"Will you get the jar of cold tea?"

While Elizabeth stirred the stew, Moses stepped outside, opened the cellar door, and climbed down the steps. Dank air cooled his face. Before he grabbed a pot of cold tea, he circled the room, scrutinizing dark pockets behind stored foodstuffs, calculating how many runaways might hide there. He bit his lower lip. During the day, his delivery business kept the family well-provided. At night, the family business delivered runaways along the path to freedom. If only Joe Johnson had gone to Canada.

Back inside, the smell of oyster stew brought to mind the sea, and the years he worked on the wharves in James Forten's sail-making factory. Since he lost his thumb, he earned his living as a carter and messenger. Elizabeth sewed and washed clothes for wealthy whites. His mother, Dinah, once a glove maker, now worked on quilts and helped Elizabeth.

"Call the family. Supper's ready," Elizabeth said.

Samuel was nowhere to be found, but Dinah and Claire came at his call. They took their places at the table. Claire sat by his side, crumbling a corn cake and arranging the crumbs in the shape of the crescent moon. Although Moses' heart ached at the thought of sending away his little girl, August was the month yellow fever vapors saturated city air. When he looked at Claire, he saw the baby face of their first child, Tabitha, lost seven years ago to the strangling cough. He and Elizabeth swore to keep another child from succumbing to an untimely death. To do that, this little child, like Samuel, must leave them for healthier surroundings. Moses wiped his eyes. Under Mr. Raymond and Miss Anna's care, Claire would breathe clean air and learn to read, write, and cipher – skills to let her make her way in the world.

Moses was grateful that Raymond and Anna Williams, white people he trusted, agreed to indenture his children. Elizabeth had known Anna for more than twenty years – since her mother, Ruby, a freed slave, cooked at Anna's parents' Hansel and Gretel Inn. Later, Anna married Raymond and moved to Wissahickon Farm. In 1793, while the yellow fever ravished Philadelphia, Anna invited thirteen-year-old Elizabeth to stay at the farm until the deadly illness ran its course. There, Anna taught Elizabeth to read and write.

The kitchen door slammed. Samuel stood in the doorway, clothes soggy, nose bloody, and shirt torn.

"Lord, Lord, what now?" Moses said.

"I been swinging on vines across the Wissahickon. Might be I slip off," Samuel said.

Elizabeth wiped her hands on her apron. She ran her fingers along the bridge of Samuel's nose.

"It's not broken. Does it hurt? No? Wash up and change into the calico shirt on the clothesline before you join us for supper," Elizabeth said.

"Bring my basket of mulberries," Granny said.

At the buffet server, Elizabeth ladled creamy oyster stew into five porcelain bowls. Moses moved close and wrapped his arms around her.

"You smell like honeysuckle," he said.

"And you'll smell like oyster stew if you don't get out of my way."

After Samuel returned, and soup bowls were set at each place, the family sat in silence with their heads down and hands folded.

"Thank you, Lord, for the food we eat," Granny said, "and for keeping the devil outside our door."

Moses wiped unexpected tears from his eyes. He glanced at Elizabeth. Today, his family was together, enjoying supper, chatting happily. Tomorrow, his children would leave for Wissahickon Farm, away from the killing vapors of late summer, and the jeers of foreigners who thought themselves better than Africans born free in Philadelphia.

After supper, Moses sat in the front room on the rocking chair with Claire on his lap. A welcome breeze fluttered the curtains. As soon as Samuel came into the room, Claire wiggled down to play pickup sticks with him. With her head propped on her right fist, Claire lay on her stomach, kicking her legs one at a time. She took a stick.

Granny, white hair escaping her green bandana, came stiff-legged from the kitchen. She dropped onto the blue-striped settee. Elizabeth settled next to her, pulled up her skirt, and fanned her face. Smells of horses and cook-smoke, and sounds of people arriving home came from the alley.

From her sewing basket, Elizabeth retrieved the pantalets she made for Claire from remnants of corduroy and calico. The moment Claire learned she'd join Samuel at Wissahickon Farm, she begged for trousers so she could run and work unencumbered, like a boy. When Elizabeth remembered her own days at Wissahickon Farm, she agreed trousers were more practical than skirts but wondered what Miss Anna would think. Elizabeth trimmed the bottoms with lace. At least the pantalets were pretty.

Granny held at arm's length the quilt she made for Claire. Ever since she gave her spectacles to an elderly runaway, Granny sewed by touch as much as sight. Elizabeth placed Granny's finger on the quilt's border to sew the final stitches. After she tied the last threads, Granny caught Claire's eye and motioned for her.

"Baby, you ready to make this quilt your own?"

Claire nodded, eyes wide and tongue between her teeth. She squeezed her eyes shut and held out her hand. Granny glanced at Elizabeth before she pricked Claire's index finger with the needle. A drop of bright blood blossomed on the fingertip. Claire opened her eyes while Granny pressed her finger onto the quilt.

"By your blood, this quilt protect you," Granny said.

"Amen." Claire put her finger in her mouth.

"You've had a busy day, Child. Time to put these trousers in your trunk and put you in your bed," Elizabeth said. "You have an even busier day tomorrow."

As soon as Claire settled, Elizabeth called Moses.

"Claire, you got your whole life in front of you. What you seen, those slavers, that's hard. That's why we sending you to Mr. Raymond and Miss Anna. You going to learn to read, write, and cipher. No man can steal what you got in your head. Work hard, do your best, and soon you come home for a visit. Samuel be there to look after you." Moses kissed Claire's forehead. "Sweet dreams, Baby."

Elizabeth looked into Claire's eyes. "You know Miss Anna took me to Wissahickon Farm when I was a girl, not much older than you, in the days when people all over the city got sick from yellow fever. She taught me to read and write, and let me ride the horses. You're going to Wissahickon Farm to work, but you are not a slave. You are a free-born African. You have a home and family who loves you. Now close your eyes and sleep, my darling."

Claire listened to her parents' footsteps on the stairs. She yawned and snuggled into her pillow that smelled like lavender. She wondered what Wissahickon Farm was like. She worried about the white people, but Samuel said they were good white people. Claire thought about the slave catchers and wrinkled her nose.

I'm not a slave. I'm a free-born African.

She fell asleep and dreamed of horses.

The sun struggled to rise in the eastern sky. Moses paced the alley. He listened for horse hooves and watched for Mr. Raymond's wagon. His right ear buzzed. He swatted at a fly. For a moment, his head spun, but he took a breath and returned to the porch. He sat in the shade and pulled the rim of his hat over his eyes.

Minutes later he heard soft footsteps, felt his hat lifted, and opened his eyes to Claire's forehead touching his.

"You sleeping, Daddy?"

"Resting my eyes, Baby. You smell so good. Mama fix your hair pretty. You ready for your big day?"

"I'm sad. Why don't you come with us?"

Claire pressed her hands on his cheeks. He covered her hands with his.

"Little Girl, I'm going to miss you sorely, but I know you be fine. And you come home to visit before you know it."

Horse hooves clopped down the alley. Raymond Williams, a gaunt man with a sparse grey beard, halted his two horses at Moses' house. The small Conestoga wagon was filled with boxes, barrels, crackers, molasses, rum, coffee, tea, sugar, chocolate, beer, whale oil, rolls of fabric, candles, soap, and a jingling bucket filled with nails and bolts. Raymond smiled when Samuel lugged over water buckets for the horses. He hopped down and handed the reins to the boy.

"Thank you, Samuel. Good morning, Moses." Raymond placed a jug of rum at Moses' feet. "I imagine you enjoy a drop at the end of a long day. Are my charges ready for the farm?"

"Ready as ready can be." Granny hugged a thick quilt, rolled and ready for Claire.

On the porch, Elizabeth pulled Claire close and smelled the rose water she used to bathe her.

"Do your work cheerfully and learn as much as you can. We'll think about you every day."

After Claire climbed into the wagon, Granny reached for her hand and gave her lemon suckets wrapped in a hanky.

"I save these for you. Soon's you learn to read, my bible be waiting. You strong and you good. I carry you in my heart."

After he returned the reins to Mr. Raymond, Samuel hugged his parents and grandmother.

"I take care of her," he said, his voice deep.

Samuel helped Claire settle in the back of the wagon then swung onto the bench next to Mr. Raymond.

"Are you fine back there, Lassie?" Mr. Raymond called.

Claire shrugged but said nothing.

Moses, Elizabeth, and Granny held out their hands to touch Claire one last time. Claire wanted to cry, but bit her tongue. She was brave.

Mr. Raymond clicked his tongue and shook the reins. The wagon jolted forward. Claire watched her parents grow smaller. Granny's trembling voice reached her.

*Old Zion's children marching along, marching along, marching along. Old
Zion's children marching along, talking about the welcome day.*

Claire sang back, her voice high and sweet, and Samuel joined in.

*I called my mother in the morning, marching along, marching along. I
called my mother in the morning, talking about the welcome day.*

As the wagon rocked over the road, Claire gazed at the shops, homes,
and the red-brick church that had made up her days. She waved to the
Negroes they passed but lowered her eyes when white people looked
her way.

When they came to the shanties where poor white folks lived, Claire
watched two boys and a girl kick a corn husk ball. Their clothes were
tattered and dingy – the younger boy wore a long shirt that showed his
bum, and the older boy wore striped pants that flapped around his calves
and a faded shirt with a torn sleeve. I could sew that tear, Claire thought.
The girl wore a mud-colored shift that hung below her knees. Claire
peeked at her.

The girl, with stringy yellow hair that needed a ribbon, stuck out her
tongue and yelled, "What you looking at, Nigger Girl?"

Claire reached into Mr. Raymond's bucket of nails and picked out a
wing-shaped bolt. As the wagon drew close, Claire threw the bolt then
ducked when the girl cried out, 'Hey!' Her brothers stepped forward and
raised their fists.

"Claire, did you throw something at the children?" Mr. Raymond
asked. "Samuel?"

"The white girl call Claire a nigger girl. They ain't much to call names."
Claire tried to make Mr. Raymond invisible.

"My mama say that ugly talk," she whispered.

"Your mama is right, that is ugly talk. I don't allow it on the farm. Still,
we don't throw stones at the poor."

Mr. Raymond tossed a couple pennies, and the shanty children leapt
for the coins. Claire raised her head above the sideboard and stuck out her
tongue. As Mr. Raymond looked back, the white girl stuck out hers.

"That's a fine example of the riffraff off the boats," he said, and handed
Samuel the reins. "Now, Young Man, show me what a fine driver you are."
Mr. Raymond turned to Claire. "Let me tell you about Wissahickon Farm.
My great-great-grandfather, Cyrus Williams, received our land from
William Penn in payment for a debt. In those days, the Delaware Indians

lived along the ridge and sometimes visited with gifts of corn and sturgeon. The stones used to build the house, the servants' quarters, and the bridge that crosses the Wissahickon were dragged from the land to clear it for fields and pastures. Those early settlers turned the Indian wilderness into a fruitful farm."

"My great-great-great-grandfather, Jack Penniman, bought hisself from William Penn," Claire said, remembering the story her father told her. "We been free a hundred years."

"You certainly have."

Mr. Raymond continued to drone on about the history of his farm. As he spoke, Claire fell asleep to the rocking of the wagon and the buzzing of cicadas that hummed through the trees.

CHAPTER TWO

WISSAHICKON FARM AUGUST 1812

Samuel's voice shattered Claire's deep sleep.

"We here, Claire, we here!"

The wagon wheels crunched over gravel beneath a tunnel of trees that reached to each other like Mama and Daddy when they embraced. Crows cawed. A shiny black wing glinted on a high branch.

When the horses approached a stone bridge over a wide creek, Claire clenched her fists and shut her eyes until the clattering of hooves softened and the wagon bumped onto gravel. She opened her eyes to the vision of a house as grand as rich men's houses in Germantown. Claire inhaled strong but agreeable smells — animals, green fields, wood, and honeysuckle's sweet fragrance — so different from Germantown's tarry stench.

The main house was built of rough-cut stone in irregular courses, two stories high. On its gabled roof, smooth slate shingles shone in the sun. Stone chimneys rose from each corner. Along the upper level, four dormer windows popped out, shutters painted black. A wooden porch wrapped around the front.

As soon as the wagon pulled up, a tall yellow-haired woman stepped into the yard. A tiny boy clung to the woman's dress, staring at Claire from wide-set green eyes. That boy look like the skink Daddy show me down the creek, Claire thought. She jumped from the wagon into Samuel's arms and hid behind his legs to peek at the boy.

"This is Elizabeth's daughter," Mr. Raymond told the yellow-haired woman.

With eyes as blue as a summer sky, Miss Anna bent to study Claire.

"You are the image of your mother when she was a young girl. I suppose you're hungry. The men had their supper and are back in the fields, but Molly saved portions for the three of you."

Samuel handed Claire the package wrapped in brown paper and tied with a purple ribbon, her mother's gift for Miss Anna.

"My mama told me give this to you," Claire squeaked.

"Told me. How nice. Thank you."

Claire frowned. "She didn't tell you, she told me."

Mr. Raymond coughed. Samuel poked Claire's shoulder. Miss Anna opened her mouth, but before she spoke, a craggy man with stringy white hair and prickly stubble on his cheeks hurried to join them.

"Here's the little lass. I was here when your mother came the summer of the yellow fever, a scared young girl much like yourself. Never you mind, you'll soon get used to us."

Mr. Raymond cleared his throat. "Hamish, please have the wagon unloaded. Samuel will bring Claire's chest to Molly's room. I purchased *Robinson Crusoe* from the book seller. We'll all vie to read it, I'm certain."

A short, freckled girl with thick red hair and blue eyes emerged from the front door and hopped down the porch steps — Molly, the Irish girl who helped Miss Anna with cooking, cleaning, sewing, and whatever needed doing.

"Is this young Claire? It's with me you'll be spending your time straight off. I've set up a pallet in my room. I see you have a chest for your things. That's well and fine."

Claire touched Molly's hair. She'd never seen red hair up close. It felt like puppy fur. Then she turned to Samuel.

"Put my chest in your room, Samuel," she said.

Samuel put his hand on Claire's shoulder. "Your room's with Molly. She be all right, Molly. She just scared."

Claire stayed close to Samuel, who led the way to the wash basin outside the kitchen door. The sky was blue, bluer than Claire ever imagined. If she could touch it, she knew it would feel like blueberry jelly. She watched a cloud the shape of a sailing ship cross the sun. She didn't see the skinky boy until she bumped into him and he dropped to the ground.

Claire shut her eyes, waiting for his wail and a slap on the face. On the streets of Philadelphia, some white people struck their servants and, although she wasn't a slave, she wasn't exactly sure what she was. But she knew the little boy sprawled on his bum was Mr. Raymond and Miss

Anna's son. The silent boy rubbed his dusty hands on his britches and stared at Claire. Samuel came looking for her.

"What you doing down there, Lawrence?"

Samuel helped the boy up and brushed him off.

Claire shrugged. "He knocked hisself down."

"You all right, Lawrence. We go inside soon's we wash up," Samuel said.

The silent child, with eyes too wide for his face, white wispy hair like a dandelion gone to seed, and a small, straight nose, stood and stared. He stood, and he stood, and then ran to the back door and disappeared inside.

"What wrong with him?" Claire asked.

"He don't talk," Samuel said. "Nobody know if he can."

"He's a wee boy, like Mama's song." Claire sang softly into the wash trough as she rinsed her hands and face.

> Oh, where are you going? asked the false knight on the road. I'm going to the school, said the wee boy, and he stood. What is that upon your back? asked the false knight on the road. And well it is my books, said the wee boy, and he stood.

Hamish set a barrel of whale oil by the cellar door to join Samuel and Claire.

"It was I who taught your mother that ballad —

> Oh, I think I hear a bell, said the false knight on the road. It's ringing you to hell, said the wee boy, and he stood. And he stood, and he stood, and he stood, and he stood. I wish you to go to hell, said the wee boy, and he stood."

After Samuel and Claire splashed water on their faces and rinsed their hands, they climbed the back steps and entered the house.

"There's a cushion on the chair next to Mr. Raymond to raise you up, Claire," Miss Anna said.

After Mr. Raymond's prayer of thanks, Claire bowed her head and whispered, "Amen."

Molly placed a hard biscuit and a bowl of pea soup in front of Claire. She watched Mr. Raymond, then dipped her biscuit in the soup and tasted it — bland and grainy, not good and spicy like Mama's, but she was hungry. The spoon Molly set for her was too big. When she reached for it, it slipped out of her hand and dropped to the floor. Her eyes shot to Miss

Anna, but Miss Anna's attention was on Mr. Raymond, who talked about market prices and the beggars on every corner of the city. Samuel's eyes were fixed on his plate of waffles and bacon.

Claire leaned sideways to search under the table, and the spoon's cold silver handle brushed her palm. Green lizard eyes stared up at her. She nodded her thanks. After she made sure neither Mr. Raymond or Miss Anna were watching, she popped a pickled beet in the boy's mouth.

Mr. Raymond's voice called her to attention.

"Claire, you met Lawrence, our youngest son. At supper you'll meet Reuben, our older boy, who's working in the fields. Now, I believe it would be well for Samuel to show you about Wissahickon Farm. Will you do it, Samuel?"

"Yes, Sir." Samuel winked at Claire.

Lawrence followed Samuel and Claire to the front of the main house. Its variegated grey stones glittered in the sun. Claire stared at the windows on the upper floor.

"I want my room there." Claire pointed to the far-right window. "I want to look out and see the whole world."

"They the family rooms up there. When you bigger, you get your own room in the quarters out back. Ain't nobody but Hamish, me, and Molly sleep outside the quarters. I got my room behind the stables so's I'm near the horses."

Samuel swept sweat from his brow. A dark cloud passed over the sun, giving a moment's relief from the August heat. A brisk breeze hinted of rain.

"Let's go on."

They headed to the paddocks and whitewashed barns. A dozen chickens squawked in a fenced-in yard. One had a bright red crest with mottled black and white feathers, like a ribboned rock Claire found in the Wissahickon Creek near Old Caesar's cabin. Another hen was speckled brown, black, and white. A black and red rooster raced toward the fence where the children stood, crowed, puffed out its chest and flapped its wings. Claire backed away while Lawrence watched silently.

"Roosters can be mean, but he can't fly over the fence," Samuel said.

Southeast of the house, white and black lambs grazed in a pasture. The sheep watched the children from dumb eyes. Their wool looked brown and heavy. Claire leaned through the lowest rung of the split rail fence and held out her hands.

"Come here, Lambie, I won't hurt you." The nearest lambs moved away. "They lazy all right."

"They hot," Samuel said. "Soon enough we shear them. Then they look like scrawny goats."

Behind a barn, mud-covered hogs huddled in the pigpen. A black sow lay on her side in the shade. While piglets squirmed at her teats, the sow's chest rose and fell.

Claire wrinkled her nose and sneezed. "Why so many piggies? Why they different colors — red, black, mixed up, and covered in mud? They stink like the scavenger's wagon on clean-up night."

"Those hogs Mr. Raymond's pride," Samuel told her. "Each time he go to Lancaster, he come back with one or two new breeders. When we get a litter, we feed 'em 'til they nice and fat. Eight months later, we drive hogs to Market Street to sell whole, except the ones we keep for ham and bacon."

"I want one of the babies. They look just like a baby child."

Claire climbed the fence, teetered, and swung her arms for balance. Lawrence grabbed her ankle and made a squeaky noise until Samuel lifted her down.

"Claire, don't never go in the pigpen. Sheep, goats, cows, horses let you be, but pigs gone eat you up." Samuel patted Lawrence's arm. "You a good boy, Lawrence. You know nobody go in the pigpen."

Tears welled in Claire's eyes. "Nobody tell me. Why didn't you tell me?" she asked Lawrence, who stared at the ground.

Arms out, Claire spun in a circle, looking at the sky.

"I have to pee," she said.

Lawrence put his hand over his mouth and giggled. Samuel pointed toward bushes behind a fence.

"Don't you come with," Claire told Lawrence.

She skipped down to the fence, scurried under, made sure the boys couldn't see, then squatted. On her way back, she plucked a creamy yellow flower from sweet smelling honeysuckle vines wrapped around the fence rails. With her thumb and finger, she pinched the green bud, pulled its white string, and a bead of sweet nectar dropped on her tongue, like Old Caesar showed her down the Wissahickon. Poor Old Caesar. She missed him already. Claire stomped up to Samuel.

"I don't like it here. I want to go home."

"Mama and Daddy want you to read and write and live in the country. You know the sickness coming. This place fine once you learn your work."

"I'm plain worn out." Claire sounded like Granny. "This place wears on me."

"You want to go down the creek?" Samuel glanced at the darkening sky.

Lawrence ran down the hill toward the creek, and Claire and Samuel followed. Trees lined the creek as far as Claire could see, bordering tall stalks of green corn that swayed in the intensifying breeze.

"My feet hurt," Claire said.

Samuel swung her to his shoulders and carried her to the bank. Claire hopped on a rock at the edge of the creek and dipped her feet in the cool water. With a roar, Lawrence jumped from behind a tree, fingers curled into paws. Samuel plopped the little boy next to Claire. He smelled like dirt. He put his thumb in his mouth.

"You know what this creek's called?" Samuel asked.

"Course not, guess it's the old cow creek," Claire said.

"It's the Wissahickon Creek, same creek where Daddy take us fishing. It go all the way past Old Caesar's shack and on to the river."

Claire leaned back to splash Samuel, lost her balance, and tumbled in. When the back of her head clunked against a rock at the bottom, she gasped and choked. Water filled her mouth and throat. Claire felt herself spinning. She crossed her arms over her chest to spin faster. Her right arm erupted in pain as Samuel pulled her out.

Samuel laid her over his knees and thumped her back – pound, pound, pound. Claire wanted to scream for Mama to tell him to stop, but Mama's voice whispered, 'Be brave, be proud, be strong.' Creek water gushed from her mouth and nose.

"Lordy, Claire, you can't drown your first day on the farm."

Claire slid off Samuel's lap. On her knees, she coughed and gagged. The wind came up, sudden and harsh like Samuel's voice, and black clouds churned the sky. Hard raindrops pelted them. Samuel grabbed Claire's hand and pulled her toward the main house, but Claire dragged her feet and wrenched free. She pointed to Lawrence, whimpering down by the creek.

Lawrence, yellow hair matted and eyes huge, stood rooted by the bank. Claire ran back, took his hand, and pulled him to Samuel. As they ran to the farmhouse, they held hands, like the game of whip they played in the alley. Miss Anna raced from the house toward them. A bolt of lightning struck a tree, and its branches sparked and smoked. After she swept up Lawrence, Samuel and Claire followed Miss Anna to the porch.

In the pasture, cows stood like statues, heads down and rumps turned toward the beating rain.

Claire pulled Samuel's sleeve, nodded toward Lawrence and whispered, "That boy don't know we black."

CHAPTER THREE

WISSAHICKON FARM OCTOBER 1812

Anna fingered the pocketbook Elizabeth sent with Claire in August. Elizabeth was a gentle soul – mannerly, quiet and unassuming even as a child, never contradictory or challenging, always knew her place. But Claire! After two months on the farm, Anna considered her a terror.

As she sat near the window, Anna admired Elizabeth's intricate needlework and the embroidery embellished with beads. The fabric was soft and silky, pale gold, with one side depicting the Hansel and Gretel Inn – the inn Gustaf and Clara, Anna's parents, owned, where she first met nine-year-old Elizabeth and her mother, Ruby. The pocketbook, useful as well as pretty, closed with a drawstring. It had a long strap so Anna could wear it under her blouse or let it hang in view.

Inside, Elizabeth had tucked a small sewing kit. When Anna unfolded the blue calico, she found three needles, two horn buttons, and sturdy white thread – perfect for quick repairs. As she held the purse to her heart, Anna felt wistful and a little sad, remembering the happy years after the War for Independence, when her parents were alive and people were kinder, full of hope for the future. Her thoughts drifted to those times.

Anna was eighteen in 1789 when Ruby Morris and her child, Elizabeth, presented themselves at the kitchen door of the Hansel and Gretel Inn. After Ruby's enslaved husband, Samuel Morris, bought her freedom, she and little Elizabeth lived in a boarding house less than a mile from the Inn. What a cook Ruby was! Her beer-batter fried catfish, stewed oysters, and the crisp scrapple from leftover pork scraps and cornmeal drew customers like flies. There were plenty of those, too. The sweet smell of baking rhubarb and strawberry pies attracted dozens of neighborhood people, but the stench of green tomatoes and onions stewing in vinegar kept away the faint of heart until the pot cooled in the backyard and bowls of green tomato pickle garnished every table.

'I hear you need a cook,' Ruby had said that day to Anna's mother, Clara. 'I'm the best cook you'll ever find, and I sew and clean and keep accounts.'

Mutti looked startled. No black ever worked in a permanent position inside the inn. The well-spoken African woman at the door wore a white apron over a blue-and-white-striped cotton dress and a turban of the same material. Over Mutti's shoulder, Anna noticed the young girl twirling one of her braids while smoothing the yellow ribbon belt of her green calico dress. When the girl saw Anna staring, she smiled and lowered her eyes. Anna followed Clara outside.

Although Anna's mother arrived in Philadelphia as a girl, the sounds of Germany abided in her speech. 'Vell,' Clara said, 've do need a cook, but ve always hire men. My husband, Gustaf, vill return in a few hours. Come back then.'

'If it's no trouble, Miss, we'll wait in your yard, or, as it's getting near time for supper, I could start a sauce for the salt cod I see there. Those apples look too soft for biting, but they'll work fine in pancakes. When I cooked for Miss Chew, she surely loved my apple pancakes,' Ruby had said.

Without knowing how it happened, Anna and Clara stepped aside, and Ruby entered the kitchen. The room thrummed with eggs cracking, butter melting, and Ruby's finger tapping the iron fry pan to make sure it was hot. Soon, the smells of codfish in cream sauce and sweet yeasty pancakes floated from the serving area to the road, and the tables filled with neighborhood merchants and soldiers. Until well into the afternoon, Anna couldn't take a moment to eat herself. By the time she sat for supper, hardly any food remained. With a cold pancake, she sopped up every drop of the sauce on her plate.

An hour later, Anna's father, Gustaf, drove up with a loaded cart. Ruby and Elizabeth were washing dishes in the back yard. When Clara and Anna heard his gruff demanding voice – 'Who are you? What are you doing there? You, Child, out of the way' — they rushed outside in time to see Ruby dry her hands and turn to Papa.

'Mr. Gus, I cooked dinner for your customers and now I'm washing the dishes. This child is mine," Ruby said, with courtesy and confidence.

Clara held the horses' reins while Gustaf hopped down from the wagon. Anna smiled at the memory of resting her hand on Elizabeth's shoulder so she wouldn't be frightened. Anna heard Mutti's words even now.

'She's a cook, Gustaf, good food. Ve had so many for dinner, no food left but the plate I kept for you. You eat. You decide.'

How Anna missed her mother! Papa had frowned and grunted but followed Mutti inside.

'She's African,' Anna heard him say, certain Ruby and the child heard too. 'Who will come to a German tavern with an African cook? Is she owned or free? What is Anna doing with that child? I leave for one day to buy our week's supplies and you go crazy?'

'Eat,' Clara had said.

Ruby moved close to the kitchen door to eavesdrop, and Elizabeth looked up at Anna with a wide smile and crooked teeth. Anna noticed her almond-shaped eyes, and long fingers and toes. Some may have thought the girl homely, but Anna was drawn to her. Anna had asked, 'What's your name?' The child lowered her eyes.

'Elizabeth. I'm nine-years-old, and I can write my name.' As she spoke, she inched away. 'I got work to do, Miss, if you don't mind.'

Anna glanced at Ruby as she returned inside. Gustaf was scraping his finger across his plate while Clara stacked the coins from supper. Mutti took two coins, stepped outside, handed them to Ruby, and said, 'Ve open at dawn.'

Until the day she died, Ruby cooked for the inn, driving Anna's father mad but filling seats day after day. No one ever complained about an African in the kitchen.

Anna smiled to think back to those times. Brassy and confident, Claire took after Ruby, her maternal grandmother, rather than her quietly competent mother, Elizabeth, whom Anna cherished. She sighed and tucked the sewing kit into the pocketbook.

At the sound of a goose honking and the sheep dog barking, Anna rose and walked outside to investigate. Claire slammed into her thighs, knocking her back a step.

In the front yard, Raymond and Reuben, pitchforks held against their shoulders like guns, shook with laughter. Molly came out from the kitchen. Farm hands working nearby dropped their hoes and shovels and moved toward the house.

With goose feathers fluttering from her braids and face streaked with green muck, Claire held out hands dripping with yellow goo. Slimy pieces of eggshell slid from Anna's apron to the ground like canoes wending their way through a muddy stream.

"I find a goose egg down the creek for you, Miss Anna. That bad goose chase me but I don't let it get your egg. Now look what happen."

Eyes wide with disappointment, Claire gazed up at Anna. Behind Claire stood little Lawrence, face bright with glee. Across the yard, Raymond, Reuben, and the farmhands looked pleased. This tinker of a girl will be the end of me, Anna thought. She caught sight of Samuel near the barn, shaking his head.

"To the wash tub with you," Anna said, brushing her hands and hiding a smile.

The children walked hand-in-hand to the back yard, and as she followed, Anna contemplated the change in Lawrence since Claire's arrival. He'd never been one to smile. In fact, he'd hardly left her apron strings. Now he followed the girl like a gosling, though he neither honked nor spoke a word.

CHAPTER FOUR

WISSAHICKON FARM MARCH 1813

Raymond ran his fingers through his beard while he studied the livestock ledger. Outside, Claire's voice rose, shrill and confident. 'Lawrence, get the ball! Throw it! Not in the pigpen!' Raymond looked out the window at the children – Claire with her hand on her hip and poor little Lawrence in a frenzy running back and forth alongside the pen. Raymond started out the door, but Claire raced over to the boy, took his hand, and led him away. 'Don't worry, Lawrence, we'll make another ball. The piggies can keep that one,' he heard her say. She and Lawrence skipped away. He shook his head and smiled. Babies.

Sometimes, Raymond worried he accepted Claire too young. In 1809, when Samuel was indentured at the age of six, he was a sturdy boy, serious and eager, quicker to learn the ways of farm life than the alphabet and ciphering. Raymond's decision to give Samuel over to Hamish's care proved brilliant.

Early that year, Hamish's fourteen-year-old son left for work at a grist mill in Ohio. A month later, Hamish's young wife, Maude, died in child-birth and the infant with her. Hamish was devastated. After so much loss, Hamish's spark returned when Raymond and Anna assigned Samuel to him. The boy followed Hamish everywhere and soon learned to muck the stalls, curry the horses, and lead the animals to pasture. Within three months, Hamish had Samuel riding bareback through the training ring along the northwest section of the farm. Now, Hamish dearly loved Samuel and depended on him.

As if he'd been dreaming, Raymond looked up from his ledger. Anna placed her hands on his shoulders while Molly cleared the dining table and set out slates and slate pencils.

"I'll be teaching the children now, Raymond. Will it bother you?"

"Not at all. I'm considering adding to our goat herd, Anna. Do you think we can manage another dozen?"

"There's little risk, Raymond. The milk, and cheese, and young bucks have sold well. I think it's a wise decision."

"Well, then." As soon as Raymond put away his ledger, the children came inside. Raymond walked into the dining room, picked up a slate, rubbed it on Lawrence's hair and said, "Best slate cleaning head on this farm."

He slid the slate in front of Lawrence and rested one hand on the boy's head and the other on Claire's. The feel of the girl's hair was different from the wispy softness of Lawrence's – stiffer and stronger, like the girl herself. Raymond pulled on his jacket and went outdoors.

While Molly wiped the children's hands and faces, Anna waited with hands in her apron pockets. Anna always had Molly put out a slate and pencil for Lawrence, hoping he might learn to write since he didn't speak. She lost sleep most nights fretting over her young son.

Sometimes, she wondered if the boy was feeble-minded and worried about who would care for him when she and Raymond passed away. But perhaps there was hope. Since Claire came to the farm, Lawrence seemed brighter. Now, evenings after supper, Lawrence rushed to the back kitchen to sit with Claire, trying to form letters with his fingers in flour Molly spread on the floor for them.

Claire would draw a letter and say, 'This is A. You try.' And Lawrence would move his fingers through the dust until Claire dismissed him with, 'They squiggly lines, not letters.' Yet the next evening, there he'd be under Claire's strict eye, running his fingers through the flour. If Claire told him, 'Now, that look like A,' he smiled. He seemed to understand. Why didn't he speak?

Reuben, their thirteen-year-old, slammed the kitchen door and dropped into his seat, smelling of manure and damp wool. Next year, Reuben would enter the University of Pennsylvania to advance his studies. Anna planned for him to become a physician – he had a quick mind and a knack for inventing. With dark hair, brown eyes, and high cheekbones, their eldest took after Raymond. Blond-haired Lawrence favored Anna.

Elizabeth's children's features were also quite different from one another. At ten, Samuel was broad and stocky, with a wide face and umber skin, his hair in tight curls. Claire was skin and bones, no matter how much Anna fed her, with sticks for legs and arms. Her round eyes protruded a bit, giving her a quizzical look.

After Anna took her seat at the head of the table, she noticed Claire had lost her front tooth. The girl pushed her pink tongue through the gap.

"Are we ready for lessons?" Anna asked.

"Yes, Mutti. Yes, Miss Anna."

"Today we will start *Robinson Crusoe*. Reuben, please read the first page."

Reuben stood, cleared his throat, and took the book in his hands. Anna frowned at Claire, who poked her tongue through the gap at Lawrence and giggled as Reuben began to read.

> *I was born in the year 1632, in the city of York, of a good family, though not of that country, my father being a foreigner of Bremen, who settled first at Hull; he got a good estate by merchandise, and leaving off his trade, lived afterwards at York, from when he had married my mother, whose relations were named Robinson, a very good family in that country, and from whom I was called Robinson Kreutznaer —*

"Robinson? But your name is Reuben," Claire blurted.

"Enough," Anna said. "Reuben, please continue."

> *I had two elder brothers, one of which was lieutenant-colonel to an English regiment of foot in Flanders, formerly commanded by the famous Colonel Lockhart, and was killed at the battle near Dunkirk against the Spaniards —*

"I never met those brothers. Which one got hisself killed?"

"Claire, you know Reuben's only brother is Lawrence," Anna said.

"I want to read." Claire reached for the book.

"You haven't learned enough words yet," Anna told her.

"I can read."

Reuben shrugged and handed Claire the book.

She held it upside down. "When I was borned, I had my brother Samuel and he was not killed but my sister Tabitha was killed by a strangled cough but that was afore I was borned and I'm from a good family what worked for Billy Penn and that's why my name is Claire Penniman."

Claire returned the book to Reuben and pushed her tongue through the gap.

"Claire Penniman," Anna started, but her words were cut short by Raymond's laughter from the doorway. She turned so Claire couldn't see her smile.

Samuel hung his head. "Sorry, Miss Anna. She know better."

"White Socks is ready to foal. Samuel, I need you at the stable. Come along, now," Raymond said. "Reuben, please bring in the cows and oversee the milking."

After Raymond and the boys hustled off, Claire turned to Miss Anna.

"I want to see White Socks have her baby."

Anna sighed. "Mr. Raymond and Samuel are well on their way. Perhaps in an hour, Molly or I can take you. "

"I can take Claire," Lawrence said.

Anna blanched. The little boy's voice was high-pitched but strong, his words clear.

"Lawrence? Was that you?"

When he nodded, Anna took him in her arms and swung him in the air. She found herself laughing and crying, unable to speak. She pulled him close and held him tight.

"I teached him," Claire said. "He's learning good."

Lawrence nodded and smiled.

"I can take Claire," he said again.

As she watched the little ones run toward the stone bridge across the Wissahickon, Lawrence's words swirled through Anna's brain like a cyclone. She wiped away tears and crossed her hands over her heart. Claire, she thought, Claire. Lawrence's first words included Claire.

As they ran through the chilly March air, Claire's face stung, but Lawrence's hand in hers felt warm. Her heart raced. Their footsteps clopped across the stone bridge like hooves. At the stable door they met Mr. Raymond.

"Lawrence can talk now," Claire said, "I teached him."

Raymond tipped his head. "Is that so?"

Lawrence shrugged. Claire nudged him.

"Yes, Papa. Claire teached me."

Raymond knelt and placed his hands on Lawrence's shoulders. He leaned over and kissed his son's forehead.

"I knew you had it in you." He wiped away a tear. "Has Mutti heard the news?"

"She throw Lawrence topsy-turvy," Claire said, and Lawrence nodded vigorously.

At the sound of thrashing, Raymond turned his attention to the stall, where White Socks, the Chestnut with a white star on her forehead, a black tail, and white from her knees to her hooves – 'Such markings are called socks,' Hamish told Claire – huffed and snorted. She lay on the ground and writhed, then rolled to standing. Samuel gestured for Claire and Lawrence to keep back.

Hamish helped them climb to the loft to watch from above. White Socks groaned and heaved. Under her black tail, a sack appeared, followed by what looked like a stick covered in gauze. The horse stamped her front hoof, then sprawled down in a heap. The stick thing, sheathed in white, poked out farther, and Claire realized it was the baby's legs.

White Socks rolled as if to get up, then collapsed back and huffed. The gauze got thicker but seemed stuck, and Claire wanted to run to White Socks, kneel alongside her, pull out the bundle, and stop her pain. The air smelled ripe with blood, piss, and wet straw. Mr. Raymond and Hamish watched as Samuel tended to the mare.

"Samuel, what will you do next?" Hamish inched closer to the boy and the writhing horse.

Samuel licked his lips and spoke softly to White Socks.

"There now, you be fine." On his knees, Samuel examined the sack under the mare's haunches. "The head coming. Whoa, now, soon enough."

As Claire watched her brother, a feeling of ownership and pride welled in her chest. The dark lump of the foal's head poked out behind the stick legs, then slipped back.

"It went back in, Samuel, pull it out," she cried.

Samuel kept his eyes on the mare's middle. When the horse groaned, he placed both hands on the re-emerging head and tugged gently until more dark showed beneath the gauzy sheen. He waited. When the mare tensed again, he tugged, and the body slid out with the back legs still inside. After he stripped away the white coating, Samuel eased out the back legs. Blood from the mare trickled down his arms. Samuel looked under the baby's tail.

"A filly."

A meaty smell, salty and buttery, hit Claire when the afterbirth whooshed out. The foal was dark and wet, her mane plastered to her head. She tried to stand on skinny legs but stumbled. White Socks licked and nuzzled her baby's pelt and, after a bit, heaved herself to standing. Soon, the filly managed to rise and, balanced on splayed wobbly legs, root for her dam's teats.

"Well done, Samuel, my boy," Hamish said, his wrinkly mouth drawn up in a smile.

Lawrence crawled to the ladder, climbed down a few rungs then jumped into Mr. Raymond's arms. After Claire climbed down, Mr. Raymond knelt to face the children.

"My brother borned that baby horse," Claire said.

"And so he did," Mr. Raymond agreed.

"What you name it?" Lawrence asked, words clear and sweet.

Mr. Raymond swung Lawrence onto his shoulders.

"By my stars, this is a day to remember. And by stars this filly will be named. Wissahickon Farm names its black fillies, Star of Night. This is the fourth Star of Night."

Somehow, even then, Claire felt that Star was hers.

That evening, Anna and Raymond knelt as Lawrence said the bedtime prayer aloud for the first time.

> Come great spirit, heavenly dove, with light and comfort from above. Be
>   our guardian and our guide and ever watchful at my side.

After Lawrence snuggled under the linen sheet, Anna leaned down to kiss him. Her hand skimmed under the pillow. She pulled out a little white tooth – Claire's – and showed it to Raymond before replacing it.

Later, as Raymond blew out the candle by their bed, Anna turned to him.

"What do you make of Lawrence talking?"

"I think Claire unlocked his tongue."

"How can it be?"

"It's been good for Lawrence to have a playmate, and Claire is full of life. I think of the words of Isaiah —

> The wolf shall dwell with the lamb and the leopard shall lie down with the
>   kid, the lion and the sheep shall abide together, and a little child shall
>   lead them."

"Are you calling Lawrence a lamb and Claire the wolf who abides with him?" There was a smile in Anna's voice.

"I meant the part about a little child shall lead them."

"And what of the tooth?"

"What of it? Children love to collect things. From what I know of Claire, she gave it to Lawrence to put under his pillow in hopes of receiving a penny. I'll put two there before he wakes up."

The sounds of night – a hoot owl, a branch brushing against the house, Raymond's wheezy breathing – kept Anna wakeful. She stared into the dark, wondering what the future held for her little son and where Claire Penniman might lead him.

CHAPTER FIVE

E ven though it was June, frost covered the ground. No one remembered a year being as cold for so long. Snow, wind, and freezing rain had continued into May. June wasn't much warmer. Early each morning, the farm hands headed to the fields to salvage what they could and replant wheat, barley, corn, and alfalfa. Mr. Raymond and Miss Anna spent each evening going over accounts. 'Thank God we delayed shearing the sheep so the beasts at least have the warmth of their wool,' Claire had heard Mr. Raymond say.

During the few days in early April without snow and punishing winds, Claire and Molly's efforts to plant the vegetable garden would have been for naught, except that Reuben insisted they cover the plants with sheets and blankets. Now, despite the terrible weather, Molly had scrawny vegetables to put in soups. The air smelled empty and dead, and the land remained colorless. Never had it been so cold on Claire's birthday. Today, June 16th, she turned ten, and was no longer a child.

Brown speckled eggs, warm from the hens that scurried out of the coop as soon as Claire sprinkled feed in the yard, nestled in two baskets. She crunched over frozen ground to the cellar to store the eggs before she went inside for breakfast.

Despite the chill, Claire smiled as she imagined the beef-heart soup and prune cake with chopped walnuts Molly would make. Miss Anna always made birthdays, she called them *kinderfests,* special, even this year, when food was sparse. She wondered if Mama, Daddy, and Granny remembered her birthday. The bad weather made for extra work for everyone, and Claire wondered when she and Samuel would visit home again.

In the cellar, she placed the baskets on the egg shelf. The dank chill from the stone walls felt even colder than outside. Steam rose from the milk cistern – Mr. Raymond and Reuben had gotten to the cows early.

In the fruit corner, the pear and apple barrels were empty, waiting for this year's crops to ripen, if ever. Thank goodness, other shelves were stacked with dried fruit, jams and jellies, green-tomato pickle, pickled squash, and the jars of preserved peaches and plums Molly put up last year. On the meat side, hams and mutton legs hung from hooks. Slabs of bacon wrapped in paper sat on shelves.

Claire's stomach rumbled. She rushed up the cellar steps without looking, and bumped into Lawrence. Goat milk splashed from his pail.

"Sorry," Claire said.

"No matter."

Lawrence's green eyes appeared grey in the muted morning light. The world is grey, Claire thought, it even smells grey.

Outside the kitchen door, Molly clanged the bell for breakfast. Claire rinsed her hands and face in icy water from the wash basin. Molly waited on the steps, and pulled Claire into a hug.

"Sure and you're growing up lovely, My Heart."

Lawrence appeared with goat milk splotches on his boots.

"And there's the lad. Leave your boots by the door, Master Lawrence. In honor of Claire's birthday, I plucked the sad small strawberries that dared to ripen. As my Mam used to say, 'Take the little potato with the big potato.'" Molly shivered. "A cold summer day chills a body more than the coldest day of winter."

Claire and Lawrence glanced at each other and giggled. Now nine-years-old, Lawrence was slender and almost Claire's height, with blond dandelion hair his mother cut with a bowl.

A cup of tiny strawberries sat on the dining table. Claire avoided the temptation to take a few before she sat down. At the head of the table, Miss Anna filled Mr. Raymond's cup from a pot of sweet-smelling coffee.

"Ah, you decided to join us," Mr. Raymond said. "Eat well. We have a full day ahead of us." He winked at Claire. "With the promise of a special supper after chores are done."

"Thank goodness we had a good harvest in the fall. Is there hope for the corn and oats we planted last month?" Miss Anna's eyes looked hollow and tired.

"There is hope, though we should expect low yields. Whatever crops we manage to bring to harvest are thanks to Reuben. Before the frost and freeze last week, he insisted we cover the plants with straw during the night and rake it aside after the sun appeared."

Lawrence bit his small finger nail and spit it on the ground.

"Papa, what's that machine Reuben made? I watched him hitch it to the brown horses and drag it across the field."

"Another one of his contraptions. Reuben attached iron claws to a board, set precisely to unearth weeds between the rows without damaging the crops. And the glory is, it works. That boy is filled with ideas."

"Reuben is a modern man and great thinker," Miss Anna said.

Mr. Raymond nodded. "As Matthew says,

> *His winnowing fork is in his hand and he will clear his threshing floor and gather his wheat into the barn, but the chaff he will burn with unquenchable fire.*

I best see to the fields."

When Mr. Raymond rose to leave, Lawrence grabbed his sleeve. "What was that terrible noise last night, Papa?"

Miss Anna glanced at Raymond. She pursed her lips.

"A pack of dogs killed three sheep before Honey scared them away. They'll return tonight, and we'll be waiting for them." As he headed for the door, Mr. Raymond patted Claire's shoulder. "Ten-years-old today?"

Claire nodded and smiled.

Anna stirred sugar into her cup, sat back, and observed the children. Claire added applesauce to a bowl of porridge and ate with fervor, stealing glances at Lawrence and giggling. Lawrence toyed with a boiled egg. He cracked the bottom and top. Then he picked off one small shell chip and sighed. Claire watched while he picked off another chip. Anna knew Lawrence's slow and systematic ways frustrated Claire – so quick of mind and movement that she leapt before she looked.

Claire put out her hand for the egg, and quickly peeled the remaining shell. Then she crushed it and put it in a bowl for Molly to spread in the garden.

"Crush an eggshell, save a sailor," Claire said.

Lawrence took tiny bites of egg white until only the yolk remained. This he put in a biscuit with a slice of scrapple.

"Molly, did you make ketchup?" Lawrence called.

"I did not. There are no early tomatoes this foul year. I'll make ketchup when I have tomatoes."

Lawrence frowned, squeezed the biscuit, and nibbled the edges like a mouse.

"Don't play with your food, Lawrence." Anna sighed, went to the window, and stared out at the gloom.

After breakfast, Claire returned to her tiny room in the quarters, the one she moved into on New Year's Day despite Molly's fuss about waiting until she turned twelve. Claire straightened Granny's quilt — a garden of calico, homespun silk, and linen patches — over the fine mattress her mother made. Its surface was pale-yellow linen. The inside was stuffed with wool from Wissahickon Farm. Claire's mattress was as fine as those in the big house, and Molly spent many afternoons studying the workmanship.

Claire raised the quilt and inhaled the familiar smell of her own sweat mingled with odors of hay, horses, and leather. She pressed it against her cheeks, anxious for her next visit home. The constant bad weather changed the cycle of work on the farm. Everyone worked extra hard to save the crops and protect the livestock. Even Molly spent time in the barns, clearing out dirty hay and beating her broom at mice nested in corners.

Claire and Samuel hadn't been home since Christmas, at first because of bad weather, and now because of the added workload the bad weather created. Back in April, Lawrence was happy they stayed on the farm for Easter because his birthday fell that day. For Lawrence's *kinderfest* cake, Molly made a carrot cake sprinkled with sugar. Today, June 16th, was Claire's birthday.

On top of her walnut chest, Claire propped up her mirror. With her hair parted in the middle and brushed back, Claire looked like her mother, except her complexion was darker. Still, she had her mother's high forehead, short nose, long lashed round eyes, and full pink lips. Her dark eyes protruded a bit, as did her front teeth.

Claire tightened a yellow bandana across her forehead, drew it behind her ears, and tied it in back. Next time she visited home, Mama would braid her hair in tight rows. Claire's nails had cracked over her pink fingertips, and her palms were hard and calloused. From a small jar, she scooped out beeswax and rubbed it on her hands. Before she left the room, she pulled on a wool sweater which no longer fit Reuben, then headed to the stables, swinging her arms and humming.

Across the Wissahickon Creek, Claire entered the stables where the Williams kept their racehorses separate from the workaday steeds. Most horses were in the pasture grazing on meager patches of grass. Star of Night, still in her stall, whinnied when Claire entered. Three-years-old, Claire's favorite horse stood fifteen-hands high. She checked Star's coat for ticks and burrs.

When Claire led Star outside, Hamish greeted her.

"The horses need running, but the ground's spongy. I can't remember another year it stayed so cold into June." Hamish blew on his hands then clapped them.

"Is this the worst year ever?" Claire asked.

"Ach, Lassie, my father spoke of the winter of 1741 when he was a lad of six. The snow fell until it was deeper than his head and people starved. My granddad picked dead starlings off the snow and my granny boiled them to stave their hunger. Then, in 1765, on the day I was born, March 24th, three feet of snow fell and my father had to deliver me himself, since nary a midwife could make it through."

"Still that was March, not June."

"Nor was it the day of the great solar eclipse ten years ago, the day you were born."

Hamish looked at Claire, still a little girl in some ways, yet growing strong and confident. The horses did as she said – the best test of a horse trainer, in Hamish's opinion.

"Star's tired of this cold weather and wants me to take her for a ride," Claire said.

"Samuel rode Lightning Strike to the practice ring. Mind the ground. I don't like the feel of it. Still, the beasts must be exercised."

"Star's not a beast, she's a person."

Claire held the reins while Hamish put a light saddle on Star, then stepped into his cupped hands to mount.

"If Star's a person, what are you, Lassie?" Hamish asked.

"I'm a human."

Claire rode Star across the pasture to the trail, watching for soft spots. I'm a human, same as Lawrence, same as Miss Anna. A crisp wind came up. Claire tightened her sweater.

"I'm ten years old, almost grown," she said out loud.

In the mushy ground, Star's feet made a sucking sound. The filly's muscles felt tense as she trotted toward the track, and Claire smelled Star's cold sweat. Along the pasture's edge, mountain laurel flowers clung desperately to their branches. Overhead, a redheaded turkey-vulture road the wind. Star's ears twitched and she raised her head. From the direction of the track, Claire heard barks and growls. Star halted, then stepped back.

Claire rubbed Star's neck and said in a soothing voice, "Whoa, Girl, easy."

At the sound of Samuel's shouts, even louder than the barks, Claire urged Star forward, but the horse refused to move. She slid down and continued on foot. As she went, she gathered stones and wrapped them in her sweater. Behind her, Star snorted and pawed.

At the edge of the clearing, Samuel crouched in front of Lightning Strike. Outside the wooden fence, four dogs snarled and barked. Samuel cracked his riding whip.

"Stay back," he called in a low voice.

Lightning reared and snorted, ears back. Claire saw the whites of the stallion's eyes.

"Easy, Boy," Samuel said.

She crept closer. A dog growled menacingly.

"Claire, don't look in they eyes," Samuel whispered.

People say dogs smell fear, and if they smell me, they smell fear, Claire thought. She heard Star approach. The filly huffed and nudged Claire as if wanting her to come away.

The biggest dog, thick and tawny, squeezed under the fence and charged Lightning. The stallion reared and squealed. Samuel cracked the dog's snout. It bared its teeth, lips curled and ears forward.

Lightning bucked, kicked the dog with his rear legs, then galloped onto the practice track. Before she could grab her reins, Star of Night followed. Claire's stomach lurched.

The other three dogs crawled under the fence, and Claire forgot the horses. She pelted the dogs with the stones she gathered. She hit one on the snout, another in the ribs, and the third on its haunch. Growls turned to whines. She struck them again and again until they crawled under the fence and ran.

Samuel circled the tawny dog, which lay on its side, panting, saliva spilling from its mouth. Its front legs splayed awkwardly. Though it couldn't get up, it snapped and snarled.

"Kill it," Claire screamed, "before it gets up."

"It ain't going nowhere."

Samuel's eyes were wide and his whip hand twitched. Claire trembled but searched until she found a heavy rock. She drew near the dog.

"Don't you hurt my brother or my horses, or Mr. Raymond's sheep," she yelled, and dropped the rock on the dog's skull.

"I don't think it hear you. It's good and dead. Where those horses? Lord, there be trouble if they come back lame."

Samuel tried to whistle but couldn't control his breathing. Claire pressed her thumb and finger against her tongue and blew a shrill note. Star of Night whinnied. The horses trotted towards them, but shied away at the bloody smell of death.

"We got to walk them. They too skittish to ride," Samuel said.

As they led the horses toward the stable, Claire and Samuel spoke softly, their heartbeats slowing, and their breathing less labored.

"Where those dogs come from?" Claire asked.

"I think they from the Schmidt farm up Plymouth Meeting. Old Schmidt die from lung fever, and his widow gone bust. With this hard weather, I expect she let the dogs run when she gave up the farm. Lucky you come by."

Star nuzzled Claire. She warmed her hands in the horse's mane. The soft ground made the going slow.

"You think those dogs killed Mr. Raymond's sheep?"

"Might be. They act like wolfs in the wild," Samuel said.

"I hate those dogs, and I hate being cold, and sometimes, I hate Miss Anna."

"Watch what you say, Claire. Mama don't like that talk."

Along the pasture's edge, tree branches rustled from gusts of wind. Behind patches of clouds, a dull sun hung in the sky like a ring of steel. Overhead, the turkey-vulture spread its wings in a six-foot fan of silvery feathers, paused as if suspended in time, then dove at the ground.

"I hope the buzzards eat that bad dog," Claire said.

"Every creature hungry this year," Samuel said.

Hamish waited by the stable, a wide white building with black trim, twelve stalls, and a tack room. Directly behind the stable was the cottage where Hamish lived, as had his father, grandfather, and great-grandfather. At fifty-one, Hamish was weathered yet robust, with white hair and baggy eyes. He was short of stature with sinewy muscles and ropey veins.

"So the two of you met up, did you?"

"Four dogs went after Samuel and Lightning Strike. Samuel whipped

the baddest dog, and Lightning kicked it. I threw stones at the others,"
Claire reported, voice shaky.

Hamish frowned as he took the horses' reins. Lightning had a bloody
scrape inside his left rear leg. He inspected Claire and Samuel.

"I'm fine," Claire said, "But Samuel's bleeding."

Dirt, grass, and blood oozed from a crescent-shaped gash on Samuel's
calf.

"Was the dog mad, Samuel?" Hamish asked.

"I ain't seen no foam."

"I killed that dog," Claire said. "It ain't mad no more."

"Claire, walk to the house with Samuel so Miss Anna can clean and
stitch his wound. I'll tend to Lightning."

Claire and Samuel trudged across the stone bridge toward the house. She
watched Samuel for signs of pain but he didn't limp. Despite the extended
cold, clover grew in random spots. As they walked, Claire picked a leaf
and bit into it, relishing the sharp sour taste. Branches rustled in a breeze
too cool for June. She thought Samuel should wear a jacket, but sweat
beaded on her brother's face. He often waited until December to don the
lined corduroy jacket Mama made — not likely he'd wear it in June.

The smell of beef-heart soup, and the rumble in her stomach told Claire
it was supper time. In twos and threes, men walked from the fields toward
the house. Outside the kitchen, Molly hung clothes on the line.

"What brings the rarely seen Samuel to the big house?"

"Samuel saved Lightning from a pack of dogs," Claire said with enthusiasm. "Now Samuel has a bite on his leg. Miss Anna and me need to
fix it."

Anna stepped out from the kitchen, wiping her hands in her apron. She
raised her right eyebrow.

"Come, Boy, I'll take a look."

Samuel showed her the bite.

"Does it hurt?"

"Naw. Not much it don't, Miss Anna."

"We say, it doesn't hurt much," Anna said.

Claire spied Mr. Raymond crossing the wooden bridge and ran down
the hill to meet him. Her voice carried to the back yard.

"A bad dog bit Samuel. He saved Lightning."

"Come along then, Samuel," Anna said, heading toward the kitchen. "That wound needs cleaning."

"Clean it outside, Miss Anna. No one want to see my bloody leg before they eat."

The boy smells particularly strong, Anna thought as she returned with a curved needle and silk thread to stitch the oozing wound. First, it had to be cleaned. She added drops of iodine to a bowl of water, swished it, then dipped in a rag.

Lawrence, a streak of dirt across the bridge of his nose, arrived from the pigsty, and Claire raced back to Samuel.

"I told Mr. Raymond you saved Lightning," she reported, breathless. "I can sew Samuel, Miss Anna."

"Wash your hands." Anna handed Claire the cleaning rag. "Be gentle.

Samuel looked peaked. With fists clenched on the seat of a ladder-back chair, the boy grimaced when Claire dabbed the wound, stopping to ask, "Does that hurt?"

"It doesn't hurt much," he said and glanced at Miss Anna.

"Lawrence, have Molly make Samuel a cup of tea with molasses and a few drops of rum." Anna smiled at Samuel. "You can use some shoring up."

When Raymond arrived, he knelt beside Samuel and looked in his eyes. "You faced the pack of dogs, did you? Brave boy."

"I did too," Claire said.

"They'll be back tonight. Those dogs are running wild, attacking farms. Better the Schmidts shot them than leave them to ravage the neighbors. This is the result." Raymond bent close to Samuel's ear. "Your sister tells me you saved Lightning. Indeed, she tells me *she* saved Lightning."

"Samuel's wound is good and clean, Claire. Now, line up the skin so it fits together," Anna said.

Claire's eyes stung from salty sweat. She pushed the needle through Samuel's skin like Mama taught her, tied a tight knot, cut it with her teeth, and began again. The wound took twenty-two stitches, the most Claire ever did. By the time she tied the last knot, she trembled.

"You have a good hand, Miss ten-year-old Claire Penniman. Your mother taught you well. No one could do better," Anna said.

Field hands, fed and ready to return to work, gathered around Samuel, shaking their heads and muttering, "Damn dogs. I'd a killed the lot of 'em, I swear."

"I'm hungry," Claire said, "Let's have our supper."

Inside, Raymond, Reuben, Lawrence, and Hamish sat at the table. Steaming bowls of beef-heart soup thick with barley sat at each place, along with biscuits, and mugs of tea. Hamish waved Samuel to take the chair next to him.

After supper, while Claire cleared the dishes, Molly put a prune cake with sugared walnuts on the table. Mr. Raymond lit a thick candle in the center of the cake.

"Now, Claire Penniman, make a wish and blow out the candle so the smoke carries your wish to God," Miss Anna said. "Tell no one, or the smoke will carry it to the devil."

Claire took in the people gathered at the table. Except for Samuel, they were not her family, but they shared her life. Not her family, but her pack, like a pack of dogs. Not the kind to bite, she hoped. After she blew out the candle, she glanced at Lawrence but kept her secret – that someday, after her indenture, she would have a farm with horses and goats, and live forever free.

Molly served Claire the first slice. She savored the sticky dried plums and sugared walnuts.

"Thank you, Miss Anna. Thank you, Molly. This cake is delicious."

"A birthday to remember," Mr. Raymond said. "You saddled Star, slew a dog, and stitched Samuel."

"And last, you'll sleep," Lawrence added.

"But first, we have to slay the savage beasts that attacked the sheep. I can help," Claire said. "I'm not afraid."

Miss Anna shook her head, no.

Mr. Raymond scratched his chin. "I'll keep her close, Anna. Claire, you may come along."

"I'm coming, too," Lawrence piped up.

Raymond nodded, avoiding Anna's eyes.

At dusk, they herded the livestock into the barns. Angry bleats and moos resounded throughout the piss-stinking stalls. The hay would be awful to rake tomorrow, with more animals inside than usual. The goats and cows would yield little milk, and the hens would lay fewer eggs. Animals did not like changes to their routines, but it was better than being attacked by a pack of dogs. Four old sheep stayed in the paddock as bait.

Mr. Raymond, Reuben, and Hamish, along with Claire and Lawrence, gathered downwind from the paddock, behind a barricade of logs. Mr. Raymond and Reuben took practice aim with the musket and hand gun. Hamish's quiver of arrows hugged his back. He plucked the bowstring to test its tension.

"I can load and fire an arrow faster than fiddling with a firearm," Hamish said.

Reuben leaned two stout chestnut spears with sharp points against the barrier. Claire and Lawrence put rocks and stones in piles. Claire stayed close to Hamish.

"Do you think the dogs remember I killed their brother?"

"Those curs have four things on their minds, that being the four sheep," Hamish answered. "Unless you flock with the sheep and say, *bah, bah,* you won't interest them."

When the sun dropped below the horizon, Claire wished she had a blanket like Miss Anna sent with Lawrence. When Raymond noticed Claire shivering, he draped the blanket over both children.

"Are you afraid?" Claire whispered.

"A little," Lawrence said.

A flock of geese rose to the sky, and sounds of anxious animals carried from the barn. The four bleating sheep moved to a corner in the paddock. Three dark shapes appeared outside the paddock fence.

"There they are!" Reuben raised the musket to his shoulder.

"Let them come closer," Mr. Raymond whispered.

He knelt on one knee with the barrel of the hand gun resting on the barricade. He fixed his eyes on the dogs.

Hamish pulled an arrow from the quiver and nocked it on the bow string. In the dimming light, they watched the dogs, tongues out and huffing, linger outside the pen while the sheep's bleats grew urgent. One dog crawled under the post-and-rail fence, snarling, and leapt at the sheep. The other dogs followed.

"Now!" Mr. Raymond aimed and shot. "Damnation."

The blast hurt Claire's ears, and her eyes watered from the acrid smoke. The dogs cowered at the blast, then in a frenzy went for the nearest sheep's throat. Lawrence shrugged off the blanket. Claire and he pelted the dogs with stones.

Reuben hopped over the barricade and raced to the paddock. At the fence, he raised the musket and fired. The ball struck a sheep's head, and the blast knocked him backward off his feet. As soon as he was down, a mottled dog growled and came at him. Reuben shimmied toward the barricade, using the musket as a shield.

Hamish raised his bow, drew the arrow to his chin, and released. It struck the mottled dog in the haunch. Mr. Raymond fired the hand gun and struck the dog's neck. The dog dropped on Reuben's legs, and he shoved it away with the musket.

Claire and Lawrence threw stones at the two other snarling dogs. Hamish felled a scruffy brown dog with an arrow through its heart. When Reuben got to his feet and ran for the barricade, the last dog, its coat black, left the sheep to chase him. The dog dashed to the end of the barricade and came around, barking ferociously. Hamish's arrow tore a furrow in its side.

As he reloaded the hand gun, Mr. Raymond's hands shook. The dog, ears back and teeth bared, stopped six feet from Lawrence, and growled. Lawrence pitched his handful of stones at it, then ran. The dog raced after him.

Claire stepped in the dog's path with one of Reuben's spears clenched in both hands. The dog snarled and leapt at her. She jammed the spear in its mouth, and the impact threw her backwards. She rolled away, palms burning. A blast deafened her. The dog's skull exploded in fur, bone and blood.

Claire lay on the ground with an arm over her face until Mr. Raymond picked her up and set her upright. Two yards away, the black dog's body twitched. Reuben, Hamish, and Lawrence joined them.

"How can three dogs wreak such havoc?" Hamish asked. "I feared they'd never die." He turned to Claire. "You're the bravest little lassie I know. And you're a brave lad, Lawrence."

"Reuben, while you and Hamish bury the curs, I'll dispose of the poor old sheep." Mr. Raymond knelt to speak to Claire and Lawrence. "You, my dears, are most wonderful children. Go inside, and be mindful of what you tell Miss Anna."

As Claire and Lawrence walked away, breathless and giddy, she held Lawrence's hand, unable to let go.

CHAPTER SIX

A t the sound of commotion, Anna rose from her chair to look out the window. Claire and Lawrence, as thick as thieves at thirteen and twelve as they were at six and five, huddled together in the front yard, their backs to the house. In the breezy March morning, Claire's red scarf fluttered like a flag. As if they felt her eyes on them, they turned and skipped to the porch steps.

"Go around back," Anna said. "I'll have no muddy boots in my parlor."

Anna placed *The Last of the Mohicans* on the table, and joined Molly in the kitchen to wait for the scamps, certain they were up to no good.

With red cheeks and runny noses, Claire and Lawrence, stumbled inside. They smelled like winter – of well-worn clothing and damp wool. Molly poured boiling water over tea leaves, and pulled a pan of Brown Betty from the oven. The rich scent of apples baked with butter and brown sugar warmed the house.

Anna closed the kitchen door and frowned at the muddy clumps on the floor. A puppy yelped and wriggled in Claire's arms. Anna took the tiny dog. She examined its eyes, and ran her fingers over his teeth.

"A small male, but healthy. Why, might I ask, have you taken this pup from his mother?"

Claire's radiant smile took Anna aback.

"Mama's letter said Old Caesar's little dog, Peanut, got trampled under the stage coach. He needs a new puppy to keep him company. Honey has five more puppies. She don't need this one."

"She doesn't need this one," Anna corrected.

"No, she don't," Claire said.

Anna raised her eyebrow. "It's proper to say, Honey doesn't need this one."

"Honey doesn't need this one," Claire said, "but Old Caesar sure do."

"Old Caesar sure does need this one."

Anna handed the squirming puppy to Claire.

"I told you Miss Anna would let me give you to Old Caesar. He be so happy," Claire said.

"Old Caesar will be so happy."

Claire nodded. "Yes he will."

Anna folded her arms and glanced at Molly, who pressed her lips together. When Claire wasn't engaged in tomfoolery, her spoken grammar was almost as good as her own.

In the entryway, Raymond leaned against a chestnut pillar. Anna loved the merriment on his weather-beaten face. His mouth, a touch of red almost lost within his grey beard, curled open in a grin, and his dark eyes crinkled.

"Did Miss Anna give you the pup for Old Caesar?"

"She did, and I'll take good care of him until I bring him home," Claire answered, voice joyful.

"I'll help train him," Lawrence said. "Pretty Boy will be the best herding dog in Germantown."

"Pretty Boy is it?" Raymond took the pup. "He's most certainly pretty. Now, return Pretty Boy to Honey. The pups need each other's warmth."

"Thank you, Miss Anna," Claire called, as she ran out into the cold with Lawrence.

Molly mopped the floor behind them, tsking to herself.

Anna sighed. "Those scalawags will have their way."

"They will, Anna, but I neglected to tell you I promised Claire one of the litter. The girl does not forget a pledge," Raymond said. "It's better to give her the pup than to drown it in the Wissahickon. We don't need another mouth to feed, not even a dog's. That one's the runt. I may be able to sell or trade the others."

"We'll be fortunate to sell anything this year," Anna said.

"With prices down and dirt poor immigrants flooding into Phil-adelphia every week, I've not in my lifetime seen such despair. It's well we can feed ourselves and our workers," Raymond said.

"I wonder how others get by. We've had hard times before, but now there's so much need." Anna paused. "The Society for Supplying the Poor with Soup runs out every day, I'm told, and the poor house is filled to brimming."

"Yes, and the nature of commerce is changing. Robert Fulton's steam ships have injured the sail-making trade, but they carry goods to markets more quickly than wagons. Now there's talk of steam-powered vehicles that roll over roads on iron rails. What's next? Are we to tie sacks to the legs of hawks so they can fly our wheat to the West?"

Anna looked out the window, as if she could see delivery hawks sailing through the sky.

"The children are gathering for lessons," she said.

Raymond followed her gaze. "How pretty the snowflakes are, sprinkled along the banks of the Wissahickon. While you teach your lessons, Hamish and I will forge into the cold to check the horses."

Slates and slate pencils rested on the table. Anna kept her hands in her apron pockets while Molly poured tea and served Brown Betty. Claire sat next to Lawrence and across from Samuel. When Anna eased herself into the chair at the head of the table, Claire smiled. The girl loved to read.

"Today we'll continue reading *The Last of the Mohicans*. Claire, will you pick up where we left off?"

Claire stood with the book in her hands. She glanced at Lawrence and cleared her throat to start the second chapter. With her voice strong and dramatic, Claire read of fair Alice's fear of the Indian runner. She raised her voice as she delivered Alice's comments.

> *If he has been my father's enemy, I like him still less!* — a few sentences later — *Should we distrust the man because his manners are not our manners and that his skin is dark?*

Claire glanced at Miss Anna.

"Thank you, Claire. That's a good place to stop. We will resume reading tomorrow. It's time to work on weights and measures. Everyone, slates and pencils. If Mr. Raymond buys a new milk barrel that is four feet high and two feet across, how many gallons of milk will it hold?"

While the students worked out the sums on their slates, Anna sipped her tea and studied Claire, whose tongue poked from the corner of her mouth as she concentrated. *The Last of the Mohicans* was proving an awkward story. Claire read herself into every passage, and what words had Anna to explain?

Claire called, "Miss Anna, I got the answer. Ninety-four gallons."

"And what does that mean, Claire?"

"It means we gonna need more cows."

CHAPTER SEVEN

WISSAHICKON FARM MAY 1820

E ver since she witnessed Star's birth, Claire knew she belonged at the stables. As she brushed the horse's coat, she practiced piano scales in her mind. Almost fourteen, she was tall and slender, with thin legs, and arms, and long fingers Miss Anna said were made for the piano. Claire liked to play in the evenings after supper.

Miss Anna drilled Claire until she memorized Benjamin Carr's *Federal Overture* – a piece of music Miss Anna and Mr. Raymond favored. Claire preferred to play gospel songs and the ballads Hamish taught her. Yet out of love for Molly, who still looked after her although Claire surpassed her in height, most often she played the sad, lonely songs of Ireland.

Last night, when Molly heard Claire at the piano, above the clanking of pots and pans she'd called, 'Will it be *The Lass of Aughrim* this evening?' Then Molly left the kitchen to stand behind Claire, singing the last lines with tears in her eyes. The words and melody played in Claire's mind.

She took her young son in her arms, and turned from that cold cold place,
saying, my lovely son, in the sea will we find our peace.

Claire untangled Star's mane and worked it into braids, much like the braids Molly wove into Claire's hair on Sundays – not as tight as Mama's, but good enough until her next visit home. She wondered why Molly never married or had a suitor. Molly was kind and humorous and a good cook. A year ago when Claire asked, Molly answered, 'Well and there's no

Catlicks to be found on the farm for a girl like me.' That puzzled Claire, but Molly went on with her work, disinclined to discuss the matter further.

After chores that day, Claire and Lawrence looked for catlicks down by the Wissahickon, thinking it some magical plant like catnip. They picked a bouquet of purple-headed thistles but dropped them when the spikes stung their fingers. Lawrence was covered with a red, oozy rash and Claire's hands itched for days. Only when Miss Anna overheard Claire and Lawrence discussing the absence of catlicks on the farm did they learn Molly would marry only an Irish-Catholic man.

Star nudged Claire. After examining her hooves, Claire threw a soft blanket across the horse's back and covered it with a pad and saddle. Today would be an easy ride, long but slow, to make up from yesterday's bad weather that kept the horses from exercising. Samuel, out of breath and nervous, with bits of leaves in his hair, entered the stable.

"You look like the devil chasing you." Claire glanced out the stable door.

Last time she and Samuel went home to Germantown, Claire learned Samuel had joined the secret family business – helping runaways escape from slavery. Soon, she hoped, she'd help too.

"Peddler come by yesterday with a message, and I headed to the cave this morning. Now I got to catch up all my work." Samuel looked over his shoulder.

"You see anyone from home?" Claire asked.

"Just Old Caesar. Then I climb to the cave with food, and tell the runaways, hold fast, someone be coming for you tonight. I ran back here fast as lightning."

At seventeen, Samuel looked like Moses, broad shouldered and dark, though not as tall. His corduroy britches reached below his knees, and his enormous calves tapered into sturdy ankles over scarred and battered feet. From the dog bite years ago, a jagged pink half-moon cupped Samuel's right calf. Because he sweated so much, Samuel liked to wear his hair close-cropped. The tight curls glistening on his head now were the best measure that a visit home – and to the barber – was due.

As Samuel inspected the tack equipment, Claire sighed. Each time he took off to deliver a message to runaways, she worried. Most of the time, like today, she didn't even know he'd gone until he returned.

"I miss Mama, Daddy, and Granny, and I'm worried. Mama's last letter said Daddy's sick headaches seem worse." Claire sighed. "I'm ready to go home."

"Two more weeks, soon as planting done, long as the weather hold," Samuel said.

"Mr. Raymond says since there's little money to pay for help, we all have to carry the burden," Claire said.

"Look to me like Lawrence helps carry your burden. He's one peculiar white boy."

"He's not peculiar. He's . . . a *culchie*." Claire used Molly's word for a country boy.

Claire ran her hands along Star's neck. She inhaled the rich, horsey smell of alfalfa, leather, and sweat, a scent that penetrated Claire and Samuel's clothes and clung to their skin even after they bathed.

When Claire led Star out of the stable, Samuel followed. He stared upwards, as if gauging the days until a vessel at sea would land in port.

Yesterday, Samuel and Hamish rounded up the horses when angry clouds blackened the sky, minutes before thunder as loud as cannon fire shook the ground. Great bolts of lightning crackled through the clouds like fiery whips and charged the air like a red-hot iron. Finally, today dawned bright and dry.

"I'm going to ride Star to Germantown Road," Claire said.

"Don't get this horse all tired out."

"Don't get yourself all tired out."

Samuel stooped and cupped his hands, and Claire stepped onto them to mount. She clucked at Star as her body rocked in time to the horse's trot. Most days, work on the farm exhilarated Claire. But some days, like today, she felt a deep longing for her parents, her granny, and her little bed at the top of the stairs. A few weeks ago, spots of blood appeared on her chemise. When Molly noticed the stains while doing laundry, her reaction troubled Claire, as if she'd done something wrong. 'Ah, it's the women's curse, Claire, and you so young to be afflicted. I'll make you a moon apron to hold the rags and catch the flow.'

Claire loved Molly, but she needed to talk to her mother about the blood, the belly cramps, the change in her bosom, and how Miss Anna always seemed angry with her. Nearly every day, Claire felt like she couldn't do anything right. As she rode Star down the driveway toward the road, from the corner of her eye she saw a flutter of wispy yellow hair like wheat chaff blown in the breeze. A white elbow jutted from behind an oak tree.

"Lawrence?"

But before she heard an answer, she'd ridden past. Overhead, she glimpsed a flash of red on a branch – a cardinal. The bird chirped, *hurry, hurry, go home, go home.*

At the end of the long gravel path, Claire let Star ramble toward Germantown Road and the sounds of men working on the highway to Reading. Men worked on roads constantly – clearing paths through trees, brush, and rocks; leveling the surface with rakes and shovels; laying broad stones; pounding those stones into gravel; and covering the gravel with sludge made from clay and mud. As soon as they completed one section, they moved on to the next. Then, in a month or so, the road men would appear again to rake and level, fill-in ruts, pound rocks, and re-cover the surface until rain, and the piss and pods of hundreds of horses pulling wagons and carts gouged new ruts into the road. 'At least it keeps the rabble in the rubble,' Mr. Raymond liked to say.

Claire felt free as Star moved well off the Williams' property, southeastward in the direction of Germantown. Each step brought her closer to her mother. Knowing this made her lighter, as if a burden fell from her shoulders. She sat high in the saddle and imagined she was the daughter of a wealthy African like James Forten, riding through the countryside to a garden party.

When she passed Abraham Rex's Great Store, she waved to the gristly men sitting outside. From the corncob pipes they clenched in their teeth, sweet tobacco clouds hung then disappeared like ripples in the wind. Housewives swept their stoops, indifferent to the black girl on a horse. On a flat stretch of road, soiled children rolled twine balls toward carved wooden figures, trying to knock them down.

Star needed to drink, and they stopped at a water trough outside the Mermaid Inn in Chestnut Hill Village. With a sharp breath, Claire realized she'd ridden Star more than halfway to her family's home. Her stomach knotted when she thought of the trouble to come, and she wondered how long it would take to ride back to the farm. As soon as Star had water, they must turn back.

"Aren't you Raymond Williams' girl? Why are you so far from the farm on his good mare?"

A thin man in wool pants and a white shirt squinted at her from his right eye. His left eye socket was a bed of scars and when he turned, the left side of his face flared red and angry, with the hair on that side flopping over his skull, and no ear to be seen. Claire swallowed and thought hard.

"Mr. Raymond sent me with a message for . . . Robert Bogle."

"The fine foods man?"

Claire let out her breath. "Mr. Raymond wants Robert Bogle to provide refreshments for a gathering at the farm. Sometimes my mother, Elizabeth Penniman, works for him. That's why Mr. Raymond sent me."

A sturdy white woman, her dark hair mostly covered by a bonnet, walked out of the Mermaid Inn. With hands on her hips she stared at Claire while the scarred man continued his inquisition.

"Raymond Williams allowed you to take this horse? Why didn't he send you in a cart with a draft horse? That mare looks purebred."

Claire answered in the easy way her mother told her to use around white folks who didn't like Africans to sound too well-spoken or uppity.

"Because he want me to hurry, and he don't want me getting caught up in road ruts or lose a wheel. I need be getting along now, Mister. Star and I thank you for the water."

"Wait a moment, Missy," the woman said. "Did you say the Williams are planning a ball?"

Claire rolled her eyes and looked down. She hoped the woman couldn't see her hands shake.

"Not a ball, Mrs. They planning a barn raising. After the new barn get built, Mr. Raymond and Miss Anna want to serve special food."

"Here, now." The woman stepped in front of the man. "That horse needs feed. You look like you could use a bite too. There's fresh fodder around back."

The woman disappeared inside and returned a few minutes later with a pewter cup of cider and a biscuit, halved and filled with bacon. Claire choked when she took a bite.

"You tell Raymond Williams that Mr. and Mrs. Harold Longfellow took care of you and his horse, and that we are great at raising barns."

Claire mounted Star and waved when she reached the road. She wanted to ride to Wissahickon Farm, but Harold Longfellow and his wife stood outside their inn, watching. If she turned back toward the farm, she feared the man would suspect she was a liar and call the constable. She had no choice but to ride Star in the direction of home.

CHAPTER EIGHT

GERMANTOWN MAY 1820

The sun began its descent by the time Claire turned Star off the main road and onto the alley. At the Penniman home, she walked Star through the gate to the shed where Moses kept his two-wheeled cart and whatever broken-down horse the livery man let him borrow. In the back yard, Granny hung clothes on the rope Daddy strung from the house to a chestnut tree. As soon as she spied Claire, she hurried over.

"Child, what you doing with that fine horse? Your Daddy say there too much work on Wissahickon Farm for you and Samuel to visit home."

Claire rested her head against Granny's shoulder, took deep breaths, and trembled. She didn't know how it was she'd ridden Star all the way home, or how she could ever go back to the farm. Granny stepped back to look at her.

"Elizabeth's letter worry you about your Daddy?"

Claire raised her head, eyes wide. "How is Daddy?"

"Got the sick headache again. Can't stand the light and keeps a vomit bucket by his bed. He so poorly, can't hardly take a sip of tea."

In April, when Reuben returned to the farm for a break from his studies at the University of Pennsylvania Medical School, Claire questioned him about sick headaches, and what could be done for them.

'When people get sick headaches, they see lights in their brains, like lightning flashes. Dr. Nottingham reported success with the use of feverfew, but it must be used sparingly. Too much can lead to muscle apoplexy,' he told her.

She was glad Reuben was such a know-it-all.

After she saw Daddy, she'd go to the apothecary and tell the chemist that Reuben Williams sent her for feverfew. Star ambled across the yard to join an ancient mare nibbling honeysuckle vines.

Claire rinsed her hands and face at the water barrel, then headed inside. She felt sick about Daddy's headaches, sick about riding Star of Night all the way home, sick about what Mama would say, and sick about what Mr. Raymond, Miss Anna, and Samuel would think. She wished she could start the day over, but despite her fear, she felt relieved to be home. She crept into her parents' room.

"Daddy," she whispered. "It's me."

The room smelled sour, like onion grass. Daddy lay on the bed with a rag over his eyes. The curtains were drawn, and the room was dark. Claire reached for her father's hand. He squeezed it but turned away.

"Sick," he said. "Sick, sick headache."

"Can I get you something?"

"Sick," Daddy said.

"Claire?" Her mother's voice rose up the stairs.

"I have a sick headache too," Claire whispered.

Elizabeth sat at the table across from Mr. Raymond and Miss Anna. The upstairs floor creaked whenever Moses moved.

"She said God told her to come home because her Daddy was sick," Elizabeth said.

Elizabeth wrung her hands, a habit since childhood. Anna had the urge to reach across the table and hold those hands, to assure Elizabeth all would be fine, like she did when Elizabeth spent the summer and fall of 1793 at Wissahickon Farm, away from the galloping yellow fever.

"Perhaps God spoke to Claire, but He neglected to include us in the message," Anna said. "When she didn't appear for supper, the whole farm was in an uproar. After Lawrence told us he saw her ride off on Star like she was going to tea, Hamish paced circles in the front yard, muttering, 'The slave catchers got our Claire!'"

"I don't believe Claire meant to run away," Elizabeth said. "And yet, her explanations don't entirely make sense."

"Samuel told us she planned only a short ride down to the road and back. We checked the stables, barns, and far pastures to no avail. Hamish hitched up the carriage for us, and we drove here with Samuel, our hearts in our throats."

"She's been trouble to you." Worry lines creased Elizabeth's brow. "What have we done?"

Anna fingered the beaded pocketbook Elizabeth sent with Claire all those years ago.

"Claire's never ill-mannered or spiteful. But she's rambunctious, like a young filly taken from her mother too soon, impossible to break. I had reckoned Claire would be more like you."

"She's like my mother, Ruby — bold and brash, but true to death. I hope Claire learns there's a time to be bold, and a time to be humble, a time to stand up, and a time to sit down, like Ecclesiastes — *To every thing there is a season, and a time to every purpose under the heaven.*"

"Ruby was one to speak her mind. Smart too, like Claire. Elizabeth, that child can read any book I put before her. When Reuben's home, she studies his medical books and makes drawings of the muscles, bones, and intestines. Then she tries to teach Lawrence. Sometimes I fear for her," Anna said.

They heard Moses' footsteps. He entered the kitchen squinting.

"Feeling better, Moses? I'll bring the tea." Elizabeth turned to Anna. "These headaches steal his days."

"Miss Anna, we mighty sorry for the trouble." Moses pressed his fingers against his temples. "Claire's a good girl, but she sometime dance with the devil."

"Thank the Lord she arrived home safely. We feared the worst," Raymond said as Elizabeth placed a teapot and cups on the table.

The kitchen door swung open. Claire stopped at the threshold, frozen.

"Mr. Raymond and Miss Anna have been waiting more than an hour to speak with you," Elizabeth said.

She touched Moses' arm, and they left the kitchen.

Claire dropped her eyes and inched inside. Raymond met her, put his hand on her shoulder, and walked her to Anna.

"Star, she's fine, Mr. Raymond. I took care of her. We didn't ride fast. I stopped for water and feed. She's grazing in the back yard."

"I'll join Samuel outside to check Star over. Miss Anna would like a word."

The door slammed shut behind him.

Before Anna opened her mouth, Claire blurted, "I wanted to ride Star back to the farm but the man at the Mermaid Inn watched me, and I didn't know what to do, and Daddy's sick, and Mama and Granny get sad when I stay away so long."

The child looked sorrowful, waiting for the punishment she knew she deserved. But instead of an apology, she gave a scatterbrained explanation that made no sense. Anna remembered Elizabeth as a child at Wissahickon Farm — separated from Ruby because of the yellow fever and frightened, but brave and obedient. Anna thought of her own mother, Clara, and Gustaf, her father, both stricken by a winter cold that turned to pneumonia and killed them before she knew they were ill. How she missed them still!

"What do you think we should do about this?" Anna asked.

"I don't know, Miss Anna."

"I want you to think about it."

"Make me clean the chamber pots and privies."

"Worth consideration. More to the point, until we trust you to be where we expect you to be, you aren't to visit the stables or horses."

"But the horses need me," Claire said.

"It's true the horses need you, but we need you, too. We need to know you're doing your chores without fear you've run off, or gotten lost, or, God save us, been stolen away. For now, you and Samuel will have your visit home. Too much time passed since you last saw your family. In two weeks you'll return to the farm, and show us we can depend on you."

"Yes, Miss Anna," Claire said.

Elizabeth and Moses returned to the kitchen.

"Claire and I understand each other," Anna said. "Claire, will you ask Samuel to hitch up the horses? And tell Mr. Raymond I'm ready to start back."

"I believe Claire intended to return to the farm, but got caught in the lies she told the Longfellows. Moses and I will discuss her obligations to you," Elizabeth said.

Anna took Elizabeth's hands. "Claire's certainly mischievous, but this escapade exceeds her wildest antics. I agree she got herself in a situation she didn't know how to escape. What provoked Raymond and me was fear she came to harm. Thank God, she's safe."

On the front porch, Claire and Elizabeth watched the Williams' cart roll out of sight, both thinking of the day Claire first left for Wissahickon Farm. Elizabeth led Claire to the glider chair. There, with her head against her mother's chest, Claire wept.

She felt like a pot boiling over. Her upper lip quivered, and her entire body shook. As the glider moved back and forth, Claire breathed in shallow gulps. Her mother's scent – soap and sweat, bread and butter, earth and air – comforted her. She fell into a deep sleep.

When she felt Mama shimmy out from under her, Claire opened her eyes, confused, mouth dry. In the late afternoon, sweat trickled down her forehead.

"Are you leaving me?" Claire asked.

"For a moment. I thought you'd never wake up."

"Stay."

"I wish my mother, Ruby, lived long enough to know you. Miss Anna thinks you favor her. She was a slave to the Morris family until my father bought her freedom and mine, since she carried me in her womb." Elizabeth tilted her head and considered Claire. "Tell me why you're sad."

"I don't know what's wrong with me. Sometimes, I want to go down to the creek and scream," Claire said. "Two weeks ago, my stomach hurt like a goat butted it, and blood trickled down my legs. I was scared and tried to hide it, but Molly saw blood on my britches. She said it's the women's curse and made me a moon apron. I remembered you told me when girls become women they get their monthly courses. But I'm not a woman, I'm a girl. I want you to make my moon apron and tell me not to worry, not Molly, and not Miss Anna. She doesn't like me."

"Oh, Claire, I'm sorry. I didn't get my courses until I was fifteen and you won't be fourteen for a month. I supposed next spring was time enough to prepare you for the changes. When I'm indisposed I get stomach cramps, too. During the day when I'm busy I ignore them, but at night your father brings me a heated brick to lay above my womb. These are hard times, Claire. We miss you every day, but Miss Anna is a wonderful teacher. You're learning skills to take care of yourself and your family, and you're away from rowdy city boys and their trouble."

Claire sucked her index finger. "I miss Granny, Daddy, and you. I miss our house."

"Only four more years and you come home for good. Is life unbearable on the farm?"

"Mostly, I like it." Claire's voice grew excited. "I want us to live on a farm. Daddy, Samuel, and me, we can work it. You and Granny can tend the house and the chickens. That's what I want, Mama. I want my own farm."

Elizabeth ran her fingers through Claire's hair.

"Your own farm? Who knows, Child, anything is possible. This hair is a mess. Come around back so I can clean it, oil it, and put it in rows. Then we'll see about making you a Penniman moon apron."

CHAPTER NINE

GERMANTOWN AUGUST 1820

C laire crouched behind a mulberry bush outside the Ram's Head Tavern to spy on the men who stole Old Caesar's pup, Pretty Boy. Burning cigar embers flared on the young dog's fur. The puppy's whine pierced her heart, but the smell touched her nerves. She wanted to confront the terrible men, swat the cigar out of the tall one's hand, grab Pretty Boy, salve his burns, and bring him to Old Caesar. Claire willed herself to be invisible.

"If the dog dead tomorrow, Billy, what good it do us?"

The squat slave catcher nudged the whimpering dog. Pretty Boy bared his teeth and took a kick to the ribs.

"Nah, it'll live. Tomorrow, we'll bring it to Nigger Alley, get us a bucket of water, and dip this black mutt's head under 'til Caesar come out to beg mercy for his dog."

The tall man spit tobacco. "I might could take a drink and have me some supper."

Caesar, now in his sixties, lived in freedom since Claire was a little girl. She wondered why the slave catchers were after him now, what sort of bounty an old man might fetch from his former master.

The slavers sauntered toward the tavern door, past a white kitchen boy carrying a bucket of wash water. When they passed, the short man smacked the boy's bottom. The boy dropped the bucket, and dirty water splashed his clothes and spilled across the courtyard.

After the men disappeared into the dim building, their coarse laughter and the lingering smell of moldy leather choked Claire like fingers around her neck. Pretty Boy whimpered and gnawed the rope tying him to an oak tree.

At dusk, the courtyard was clear. Claire crawled toward Pretty Boy with an eye on the tavern windows, straining her ears for the sound of men.

The tight knot binding Pretty Boy to the tree didn't budge. Claire cursed herself for rushing after the men without a plan for how she'd steal back the dog. A Negro girl could hide a small knife under her skirt or pick up sharp stones as she walked along, yet Claire thought to do neither.

"I'll be back, Pretty Boy," she whispered.

Along the post-and-rail fence that enclosed the tavern yard, lush honeysuckle vines grew. If Claire was careful, no one would see her crawl under the vines. The slavers had tethered their horses to hitching posts on the side of the tavern. Their leather saddles and saddlebags hung on rails. Claire gathered hay from a lean-to and tossed it to the horses. She rummaged through the saddlebags and found a thin wallet she tucked in her belt, but nothing to cut Pretty Boy's rope. There must be a knife in the kitchen, she thought. Men's loud voices demanding bread, oysters, and beer rippled through the tavern windows. Dishes clattered in the kitchen, and pans rattled on the cook stove.

Claire peeked inside. The kitchen boy hung pots on hooks, stacked dishes on a wooden tray, lined up cups, set cooking knives in a block, and snuck a biscuit under his shirt. His yellow hair formed sweaty ringlets that spiraled over his ears. He heaved a bucket of garbage against his chest.

"*Monsieur*, I will dump the debris in the scavenger's bin," he called to the cook, and headed out the door.

After the cook swigged the last drops of a bottle of spirits, he swaggered into the dining room. Claire took her chance. She waited until the boy took a few more steps away from the building, then shot inside like a bullet and grabbed a chicken-gutting knife from the block. Outside, she couched and crawled through the sweet-smelling vines. When she reached the oak tree, the kitchen boy knelt beside Pretty Boy, feeding him a biscuit.

"I won't hurt you," the boy whispered.

Claire held her breath.

"*Mademoiselle*, come out of the shadows. The men are occupied with cards and rum."

The knife's wooden handle was damp in her palm. Would the kitchen boy grab her? Turn her over to the slave catchers? Pretty Boy yipped and tugged the rope. Claire edged closer.

"Come quickly. I can't be seen to help you," the boy said.

Something about the boy was different – yellow hair, fair skin, but Africa in his nose and mouth, and the sound of the islands in his voice. Desperate to free Pretty Boy, Claire drew close, knife clutched tight.

"Give me the knife," the boy said.

Suspicious but unafraid, she handed it over. With a flick of the wrist, the boy cut the tether and shoved Pretty Boy toward Claire. He tucked the knife in his apron.

"Go. I will return this to the kitchen."

"Thank you." Claire scooped up Pretty Boy but hesitated. "What's your name?"

"Felix Bonnet — a mulatto come by ship from Haiti. You?"

"Claire Penniman, born free, indentured to Wissahickon Farm."

"Claire Penniman, we will meet again," Felix said. "Hurry. Warn the dog's owner the slavers are after him. *Au revoir*. No fear."

With Pretty Boy hugged to her chest, Claire raced across the yard to the cobblestones of Germantown Road. A few steps off tavern grounds, she heard a hard slap and a vulgar voice. She dodged into a dark doorway, shaking.

"You, Boy, where's my dog? This rope's cut." The slave catcher's voice. Another slap and a grunt.

"What have you done?" A harsh voice Claire didn't recognize. A whip crack.

Felix's voice, high-pitched and terrified. "I found the *petit* dog choking. I did not think he would be of use to you dead. But when I cut the rope, he escaped. Please, *Monsieur*, no more."

Another crack. Claire's stomach lurched. She crept deeper into shadows where Pretty Boy's whine wouldn't alert the men. The stolen wallet rubbed her waist, and she wondered if she should throw it in a garbage pile. Lights flickered from windows above storefronts where tailors bent over their stitches, and potters painted flowers on their wares. At the count of three, Claire took a breath, then ran, arms straining from Pretty Boy's weight.

Gasping, with sweat spilling down her chest and blood pounding in her ears, Claire entered the alley. After a final look back, Claire bounded up the front porch steps and burst inside. The faces of her family quivered in the flickering candlelight. She set down Pretty Boy and bent to catch her breath.

"Where you been, Girl?" Moses asked. "You and Samuel due back at Wissahickon Farm in three days. You need be spending nights with your family, not running the streets. We been worried."

"Why do you have Pretty Boy?" Elizabeth took the puppy.

"The slave catchers stole him, Mama, they burned him. Look, his poor ear."

"They see you, Child? They get a look at you? Why they steal this dog?" Granny asked.

"Somebody must of give up Old Caesar," Moses said. "Got to be for money. A hungry man sell his soul to feed his family. Old Caesar knows the woods and creek for hiding out. But Pretty Boy been sniffing 'round the wrong place."

"I saw Pretty Boy down Germantown Road playing with the pepper pot woman's little boy. The slavers lured Pretty Boy with a meaty bone. I followed them to the Ram's Head. They tied Pretty Boy to a tree. After they went inside, the kitchen boy cut the rope and I grabbed Pretty Boy. Daddy, they whipped the poor boy, but I was scared and ran. No one saw me." A drop of sweat spilled from Claire's forehead, crossed her eye, and landed, salty, on her lip. "I found this." She slapped the wallet on the table.

Moses embraced Claire, gazing at his child from eyes as dark and deep as Devil's Pool.

"That kitchen boy African? He give you up?"

"He looks white, but he's a mulatto from Haiti. He never gave me up. He took the blame."

Moses' face relaxed. Pretty Boy whimpered while Elizabeth examined his burns. Granny gave him a carrot.

"The pup's ear most off," Granny said.

"Claire, get the balm of Gilead from the cabinet for the burns. I'll stitch his ear after he settles. My brave girl," Elizabeth said.

Moses sighed. "You brave but you too young for this trouble. How can a man hurt a harmless puppy?"

"Same way they hurts harmless men. Child, you put your own self in danger and this house, too, if the slave catchers see you." Granny put her hand on Claire's arm. "Old Caesar love that pup like a baby. Come and eat, we save your supper."

"Why they chasing Caesar? He's too old to work." Claire frowned. "Why don't they leave us be? We got to warn Caesar, Daddy."

"You done your part. I'll tell Caesar," Samuel said.

Claire's stomach rumbled at the earthy scent of tomatoes, carrots, cucumbers, and cold bacon. She wrapped bacon around a tomato slice and savored the salty meat and sweet fruit. After she finished, she wrapped the left-over bacon in brown paper and stored it in the cellar for tomorrow's breakfast.

When she returned inside, she drained a glass of cold tea sweetened with molasses and worried about the kitchen boy. Did Felix have a bite to eat, a place to go, someone to salve his wounds like Elizabeth did Pretty Boy's? White skin and yellow curls did not save Felix's back from the whip. The slave catchers must have recognized, as Claire had, that African blood ran through Felix's veins.

Elizabeth held Pretty Boy in her right arm and took Claire's hand with her left. "Mix a teaspoon of rum with water, then bring me my silk thread and curved needle. Time to stitch Pretty Boy's ear."

Elizabeth taught Claire the secret of healing – be kind, hold a hand, soothe a brow. A baby will let you lance a boil if she's held to her mother's breast. These worked for animals as well as humans.

Elizabeth handed the pup to Claire and lit the precious oil lamp. Pretty Boy sighed and yawned, stretched out his legs like an infant, and fell asleep on Claire's lap. When Elizabeth pulled the needle through his ear, the puppy jerked, but with Claire's hands cradling his head, he stayed still. It took only a few stitches to close the tear.

In dim candle light, Moses checked his deliveries for the next day, then closed the roll-top desk. He checked outside before he opened the slaver's wallet. He took out a folded document and a Philadelphia map. He spread both on the floor.

"This the warrant to claim Old Caesar, after all these years. Those men be madder than hornets they find this paper gone. I think it's time this warrant, map, and wallet go where they belong." Moses rose. "You think the night cool enough for a fire in the hearth, Elizabeth?"

Moses stacked kindling wood in a tent, and set the papers aflame. The leather wallet curled in the flames, smelling like bad meat burning.

Soon, Claire rested her head against a settee arm. She shut her eyes, her breaths matching Pretty Boy's. She was deeply asleep when scuffling, whispering, and a sharp bark brought her to consciousness, though all she wanted was to sleep, ignore her terror of the slave catchers, and her guilt at the whip's crack and Felix's cry.

She opened her eyes to the smell of dirt and the feel of Old Caesar's calloused fingers on her cheek. She felt disoriented, then came to herself. Caesar took Pretty Boy from her lap.

"My little Claire save Old Caesar's baby from the clutches of evil men." Pretty Boy squirmed in the old man's arms.

"Caesar, they're coming for you," she said, sitting bolt upright. "You got to hide."

The elderly man, with a ring of white hair around his bald head, a thin white mustache, and clothes that flapped like a scarecrow's, smiled.

"I be on my way to the caves above the Wissy 'til those slave catchers far away. They gone think Caesar dead. A black body from the poor house be lying in a new pine box, wearing Caesar's clothes, waiting for eternal rest. Cry at my grave, Little Girl, and I see you on the other side."

Caesar patted her leg and chuckled, then, with Pretty Boy clutched to his chest, slipped into the night.

Morning dawned hot and pink. Claire woke to the smell of corn biscuits. Before she remembered she was home, she bolted up, worried she forgot to feed the goats on Wissahickon Farm. As she passed through the kitchen, she smiled at her mother.

Outside at the water barrel, she splashed her face and rinsed her mouth. In the chicken coop, she gathered four warm eggs, cleaned them, and gave them to Elizabeth to boil. Samuel and Moses sat at the table with mugs of black tea. Claire set a bowl of milk toast at Granny's empty place.

"Where's Granny?"

"She be coming along," Moses said, "soon as she gathers the plums what dropped overnight."

Despite the heat and humidity that raised beads of sweat on Claire's forehead, the hot tea tasted good.

Elizabeth placed a bowl of boiled eggs on the table next to the remains of last night's bacon. She added a loaf of rye bread, cut into cubes to soften in tea. Before she sat, she dropped pigs' feet, onions, tomatoes, parsnips, and a splash of vinegar into a pot of boiling water to start soup for dinner.

From the alley, pounding horses' hooves and a gunshot startled the family. Shouts from the slavers made Claire's heart pound. Her parents and brother sat with wide eyes and concerned looks on their faces. The slave catchers were back. Claire's eyes widened.

"Granny's out there!"

She followed Moses and Samuel onto the porch. Her father's broad face glistened with sweat. Samuel clenched his fists, ready to fight. The slavers stopped their horses in front of the Pennimans.

"We come to collect that old nigger, Caesar. You best not be hiding him, less you want your sorry houses burned down."

Three black women watched silently from a nearby yard. Across the alley, Granny stood under a plum tree, hickory cane in her right hand, a basket in her left. Samuel leapt off the porch and dashed to Granny's side.

"Don't move!" a slave catcher yelled, and fired into the air.

The basket dropped. Plums rolled across the alley. Granny took Samuel's arm and waved her cane at the white men.

"Leave these peoples be," she shouted.

The short man aimed his rifle.

"Stop." Claire grabbed the horses' reins and glared.

"My old grandmother's born free. She can't do you harm. And Caesar died yesterday. You're too late."

The tall slave catcher and Claire locked eyes. The man laughed, and spit a black glob out the corner of his mouth.

"You mighty uppity for a pickaninny bitch. That old nigger dead? You swear to Jesus?"

"His heart broke after he lose his little dog. Go see for yourself. Caesar lying in a pine box up the meeting house waiting until his songs be sung and his grave be dug."

"You niggers move out the way afore we run you down," the tall man shouted. He tipped his hat to Claire. "I don't find that runaway dead in a pine box like you say, I'll come back for you."

After they rode away, Moses pulled Claire inside. He gathered the plums while Samuel led her to the porch.

"You damn lucky, Boy, that man don't shoot you dead. But you make me proud, taking care of Granny."

"That slaver scare the living daylight out of me," Samuel said.

"The boy done good," Granny said. "Like Isaiah say, *No weapon form against you shall prosper, and every tongue rise against you be condemned.* Now I say we eat these plums, sweeter 'cause they hard fought come by. It ain't right, taking the pup and coming after Caesar. Weren't Claire the end all?"

"I hope the dead man looks like Caesar," Moses said.

In the kitchen, plum juice dripping down her chin, Claire longed for the peace of Wissahickon Farm, the goats, the horses, the smell of ripening grain, and the cool water of the Wissahickon Creek to soak her legs with Lawrence. Claire would shoot those slave catchers if she had a gun. And she knew where to get one. Lawrence.

∾

A frantic knock on the back door startled Claire. She nearly choked on her plum pit. When Moses opened the door, the boy from the Ram's Head Inn, Felix, tottered in, then fell forward in a swoon. Dried blood marked an X on the back of his blouse. Samuel jumped up, right arm raised, ready to strike. Claire grabbed his wrist and drew him away.

"It's Felix. He helped Pretty Boy."

Samuel's broad face glistened with sweat and rage.

"He work for the slavers?"

"No. He cut Pretty Boy loose. Look what they did to him. Still, he told them nothing."

Samuel and Moses carried Felix into the front room and laid him on a quilt on the floor. When the boy opened his eyes, Claire saw they were blue. His face was mottled from bruising, and his yellow hair was filthy and matted against his scalp.

"*Excusez-moi de tu déranger.*"

Felix's eyes were wild, and saliva dripped from his mouth. When Elizabeth held a cool rag against his forehead, he closed his eyes. The word, Mami, escaped his lips. Claire leaned against her mother and watched him twitch.

"What do you know of this poor boy?" Elizabeth asked.

"His name is Felix. He works in the Ram's Head kitchen. He cut Pretty Boy's rope. After I ran away with Pretty Boy, the slavers whipped him. But I kept running."

"We'll let him sleep."

Elizabeth lingered to watch the boy's chest rise and fall, like she watched her babies breathe. The boy was skin and bones, as delicate as a girl. Waves of sorrow crashed over her – for Felix, for Claire and Samuel, for herself and Moses, for Granny. Philadelphia was a refuge for slaves but hardly a safe haven for anyone with African blood, not even those born free.

The few steps to the kitchen felt to Elizabeth like a long journey. She wanted to sit, rest her head on the table, and garner the strength to go on. How close had Claire come to such danger? How much must we bear?

On the porch, Claire and Samuel knelt with pick-up sticks, playing silently without their normal teasing, while Granny and Moses sat and rocked. Puffs of smoke drifted like clouds from Moses' pipe. A fly buzzed near Claire's ear. She rose and joined her mother inside.

"What will we do with Felix, Mama?"

"The Lord knows, but I surely do not."

"Are you sick?"

"I'm tired, Child. Bone tired. Will you stir the soup? I'm going to sit on the porch with Daddy and Granny."

The broth simmered with vegetables from Granny's garden. After Claire dropped in pork and a handful of coarse salt, the flame sparked and the pot sizzled. She dribbled in a mix of flour and water and stirred the thick paste into the brown liquid.

When Claire returned to the front room, Felix stirred. Although wan and weak, he appeared clear-eyed. Claire took his hand and sat beside him on the settee. Samuel loomed over them, eyes narrowed.

"Why you come here, Boy?"

At the sound of Samuel's voice, Elizabeth, Granny, and Moses came inside and surrounded the yellow boy.

Elizabeth spoke first. "How do you feel, Young Man?"

Granny rested her hand on his forehead. "No fever. He get better once he eat and rest."

Felix gazed around the room, then lowered his head and covered his eyes. The settee shook with his sobs. Claire glanced at her father.

"You're safe now, Boy," Moses said. Sweat trickled down his face, his skin the color of freshly brewed coffee. "No one hurt you in this house."

Felix dropped his hands. His cheeks were flushed.

"I am sorry to cause you trouble, but I knew not where to go. After those terrible men beat me, the cook sent me away, shouting, 'Good riddance to bad rubbish.' I hid through the night among the graves behind St. Michael's church. As day broke, I wandered the streets until I came upon a man from Saint Dominique who told me where to find Claire Penniman."

Felix's words seemed to glide from his mouth like skaters on a frozen pond. He had the diction of the West Indies, silky and somber, a lilting pause in his articulation as he searched for English words. But he smelled rank, like moldy potatoes. Dried blood plastered his threadbare shirt to his skin.

Moses stroked his chin. "I got to ask, Boy, you a runaway?"

"No, *Monsieur*. In spring, I arrive from Haiti where we are free. Soon after I landed on your shores, I found work at the Ram's Head, but now I am useless. It is difficult to find employment when you are neither black nor white and wear a bloody shirt. I mean no trouble, but I held hope you might know someone who would hire me."

"Felix, come outside to the washtub," Elizabeth said. "Samuel, you come, too. First things first."

In the backyard, Elizabeth and Samuel removed Felix's bloodstained clothes, doused him, washed his hair and body, and rinsed his wounds. Twenty minutes later, Samuel led a restored Felix to the table. Samuel's church shirt hung from Felix's emaciated body. The boy's yellow hair fell in wet ringlets around his almost white face. The lines of blue that ran under his skin reminded Claire of a rock she once found along the Wissahickon.

Elizabeth dried her hands in her apron and passed glasses of cooled tea. Claire passed porcelain bowls of soup to each of them, then placed a loaf of corn-rye bread on the table next to a pot of butter. Felix smiled when Samuel cut a thick slice of bread and buttered it for him. From her seat across from the boys, Claire watched tension release from Felix's shoulders and heard him sigh when Granny bowed her head and prayed.

"Good Lord, bless this food and these peoples and keep us safe from wicked men. Amen."

"How old are you, Felix?" Elizabeth's voice was gentle.

"I have seventeen years, *Madame*."

Claire raised her eyebrows. She thought he was younger.

Felix stirred spirals in his soup. "I was born on the first of January, 1803. A French soldier, who arrived with General LeClerc to reclaim Saint Dominique as a French colony, put me in Mami's belly. She would never tell me the soldier's name or what power he held over her, only that he died in the Battle at *Vertières* when the Haitian army defeated Napoleon. My mother's man, Jacques Bonnet, a free *gens de couleur*, raised me as his son in the hat-maker's trade. My mother was a weaver. When she took to bed last year with a tumor, Jacques took to rum. He died in the street, his neck slashed, in a fight all men say he started. When Mami learned of his death, she told me to find a ship bound for America. One month later, she died. I landed in Philadelphia this spring."

Claire heard music in Felix's voice, music of the islands and of France, music of hot summer breezes and cool blue water, music that captivated her. Claire wanted to stare at Felix, study his blue eyes, examine his yellow skin, touch his hair. What is he? Negro? Colored? White?

Always, it was African heritage which determined a person's place in the world. Claire understood that, but she didn't understand why. On Wissahickon Farm, a person's strength and ability determined where Mr. Raymond assigned him or her to work. For Claire, it was outside with the cows, chickens, sheep, and her beloved horses and goats; for the groomsmen, Hamish and Samuel, the stables and the horses; for Reuben and Lawrence, the fields and orchards; for Molly, the house and kitchen.

When Felix finished his soup, his face was flushed, but his expression was calm. He seemed younger than Samuel, though they were close in age. Moses ducked outside the kitchen door but returned in a moment with a basket of fruit – apples, pears, peaches, and plums. He offered the basket to Felix, who chose an apple before passing the basket to Claire. While everyone else ate their fruit, Felix held his apple with both hands, studying it.

"It ain't gonna eat itself." Samuel said.

"Taste the apple, Felix. It's mighty fine, come from Wissahickon Farm," Moses said.

Felix bit into the apple with a loud crunch and chewed with a thoughtful expression.

"American apples – we do not have these in Haiti, and I like them very much. They are good to eat from the tree. At the Ram's Head, I helped the cook make confections with sliced apples – pies and tarts and apple sauce. The cook's wife taught me to make Brown Betty, have you tasted it?"

After Granny sucked plum juice off her fingers, she said, "I been baking Brown Betty my whole life every September when apples so plentiful people happy to give them away."

"Perhaps next month you will allow me to bake with you. So simple to make, so delectable to eat. In Haiti, we eat bananas, mango, the coco, you call it, coconut? And *zorang*, the orange. Every day in Haiti I eat three, even four *zorang*. But here, *zorang* are not common. One day, I will send a letter to my Uncle Henri to ask him to ship oranges to me, and I will give them to you to thank you for your kindness."

Granny patted the boy's hand and placed a tin of candied ginger on the table. She chose a sugary piece, popped it in her mouth, and slid the tin across the table.

"I sure do like a taste of orange. We sometime get one at Christmas. What you say about mango fruit?"

"Oh, mango is, one may say, like your muskmelon or peaches, sweet with juice." Felix's eyes watered as he sucked a ginger candy. "An ancient mango tree grew near the Catholic church and the priests allowed all to pluck the fruit. Mango finds its way into many foods, like apples do."

"Claire and Samuel's indenture holders are generous. We enjoy many fresh foods from the farm where they work." Elizabeth fanned her face. "Let's move outside. It's too hot in here."

"I like it hot, like Haiti. Here, I am never warm."

On the glider, Elizabeth's hands flew over pieces of corduroy –
remnants from trousers she'd made for Moses and Samuel – to fashion
britches for Felix. Beside her, Claire put the finishing stitches on a yellow
calico shirt while Granny stitched binding onto a quilt.

"Here, now, Child," Granny said to Claire, "finish this corner for me."

Claire took the quilting needle, tucked the fabric at the corner and
anchored it.

"That fine," Granny said.

"May I try?" Felix asked from the steps where he sat with Samuel.

"Quilting women's work," Samuel said.

"Samuel." Felix accented the last syllable. "No skill is women's work or
men's work other than childbirth. All skills have their use. How is this
different from Jacque Bonnet's work as a hatter or the work of a shoemaker or tailor?"

"Or sailmaker." Moses shuffled a well-used set of playing cards that
Billey Gardner, once a slave to James Madison, gave Moses when he was a
young man working at James Forten's sail-making factory.

Moses held up his left hand with a short stump for a thumb. "I lost the
top of my thumb when a boom fly off the gooseneck joint on the ship I
tended. Bent my thumb until it most broke off. The ship doctor took out
the shattered bone and sew the skin shut. That shows a man should have a
strong stitch."

"And strong stomach," Samuel said.

Felix squeezed next to Granny and accepted the quilt as if it were an
infant. He stroked the cloth and inspected the seams.

"*Madame*, you use colorful fabrics of different textures and, here, a
picture of a child and a tree with apples. What work! Show me how you
do it."

Claire watched Felix's nimble fingers work through the binding. With
an intent expression, he seemed at ease. After he returned the quilt to
Granny, Elizabeth held up corduroy britches, shook them, and gave them
to the boy. Claire handed him the calico shirt. Felix stepped into the
kitchen and returned moments later in his new clothes. He raised his arms
and turned in a circle.

"*Merci, Madame, Mademoiselle*, a perfect fit. Your kindness . . ."

Tears welled in his eyes. A light breeze carried the scent of honeysuckle
from the vine that laced through the porch railings.

"What will Felix do for work, Daddy?" Claire asked.

"I been giving that some thought, Child. Seems I heard Chauncey, the
barber, say he need help. He been looking for a lad to clean up, wash hair,

shave faces, and shine shoes," Moses said. "Patrons might like that Frenchy talk."

"*Oui, Monsieur.*" Felix's hands trembled. "I believe Mami will find her rest in the deep waters, now that her son has found his way." He turned to Claire. "And you forever have a friend."

CHAPTER TEN

WISSAHICKON FARM JANUARY 1821

New Year's Day dawned cold and grey. Lawrence burrowed beneath his quilt. The heating brick had cooled and his wool socks offered scant comfort against temperatures hovering near zero. Last night he had the disturbing dream about Claire again. Reuben assured him such dreams were normal for a thirteen-year-old boy, and the stuff of manhood. When he was a bit older there were women in the city who would attend to his needs. For now, Reuben urged him to enjoy the dreams but direct his thoughts to his studies and chores.

The smell of coffee, yeasty cinnamon buns, roasted chestnuts, and bacon rose up the staircase. Lawrence poked at dying embers in his fireplace and shimmied into the under-drawers Molly knit for him, then pulled on his buckskin leggings and a second pair of wool socks. He buttoned his shirt as he stomped downstairs.

"Happy New Year, Lawrence," Molly called, face red from steam.

She poured him a cup of black tea cooled with a splash of goat milk. After he gulped his tea and snuck a sweet bun from the basket, he pulled on his boots, warm from their place near the stove.

In the crisp morning air, he crunched over a layer of frozen snow to the barn. Inside, Reuben milked a red cow.

"Slept in, did you?" Reuben asked. "Claire and I milked all but those two. Sheep Hill looks fine for sleigh-riding."

"I was hoping to shoot the small handgun Papa gave me," Lawrence said. "The dead hickory down the creek a ways will make a good target if Papa allows me the powder."

"I don't see why not. You're man enough for that little weapon. I'll mention it to Papa when I go in."

Reuben lifted the bucket with ease and dumped steaming milk into the large barrel by the door. Lawrence took the milking stool, and rested his head against a cow's flank.

"Happy New Year, Mrs. Cow."

He firmly tugged the teats from top to bottom until milk came in a steady stream. After he drained the udders, he emptied the bucket into the barrel and went to the next cow. In this cold, there was no chance of spoilage. The greater likelihood was the milk would freeze solid. Ice cream, Lawrence thought, welcome even in the coldest weather.

Where's Claire? Until he saw her each morning, he found it difficult to focus, like trying to read a book without sufficient light. He wondered how he would get through each day without her after he entered Germantown Academy in a few days.

Each time Reuben or his parents reminded him how fortunate he was to study under newly hired John M. Brewer from Harvard, his stomach lurched, though he couldn't deny he was looking forward to Charles Wister's course on geology. The school term lasted eleven weeks, but Lawrence would return home many weekends.

After he finished milking, he crunched to the side barn where the nanny goats' palsied bleating and their kids' high-pitched cries created an ear-splitting clamor like the discordant notes of an orchestra tuning instruments. Outside in the paddock, Claire, in a red blanket cape with the hood up, walked among the goats. Lawrence stood silent as the rising sun flared behind her and ice sparkled around her feet, and he felt glad.

"Happy New Year, Claire," he finally called.

Claire turned, face hidden by the cape, but Lawrence felt her smile.

"Happy New Year. Come hold Ruby's head while I clean out the debris in her hooves."

"After we finish our chores, I hoped we could take the sleigh up to Sheep Hill. Reuben says it's good for sledding, and the Wissahickon's frozen solid. If the sun stays bright, the snow may melt and we'll lose the chance."

"Mr. Raymond gave us the day off, as long we take care of the animals. We can go after breakfast."

"Let's hurry before the cinnamon buns are gone."

While Claire helped Molly with the dishes, Lawrence, small pistol in hand, tapped his foot while he watched his father. Raymond poured gunpowder into a pewter powder flask and dropped lead balls into a leather pouch like marbles.

"I'm trusting you, Lawrence. I want no tomfoolery. This weapon is small, but it can do great harm. Henry Deringer has been experimenting with these smaller pieces, and though he's one of the best gunsmiths in America, it's a new design. He urged me to buy it along with my new flintlock rifle."

Lawrence took a breath and forced his foot to stop tapping. "I'll be careful. I remember the directions. Twenty grains of gunpowder into the barrel, then ram down a lead ball. When I'm ready to shoot, cock the hammer and squeeze."

"Before you shoot, call out a warning in case someone's within range." Raymond patted the boy's shoulders. "You're a good lad. That's DuPont gunpowder, Son, the best made."

Anna, coughing like a barking dog, entered the study, nose red and dripping copiously. She eyed the gun. Her voice was a strained whisper.

"Do you think that's wise, Raymond?"

"Lawrence assures me he'll be careful. You should be in bed, Anna. I'll have Molly bring you a strong cup of tea and a hot mustard compress."

"Happy New Year, Mutti. I hope you feel better."

Lawrence tucked the gun in his belt and slung a leather pouch over his shoulder. He stretched his arms into Reuben's old oil-coated jacket and pulled a beaver hat over his ears. His heart raced while Molly wrapped two baked potatoes and the last cinnamon buns in a piece of linen and slid them in a canvas purse.

From the doorway he called, "I'm taking the sleigh to Sheep Hill. I'll be home in time for evening chores. . . Claire's coming along."

Outside, Claire, wearing Lawrence's outgrown corduroy britches tucked into his last year's boots, clapped her hands. Molly poked her head out the door and tossed Claire the warm food purse. Claire looped it around her neck, tightened her blanket cape, flipped up her hood, and slid her hands into wool mittens.

Lawrence retrieved the sleigh from the barn, untangled the pull rope, and dragged it behind him. The gun's hard bore pressed against his thigh. He and Claire crunched over snow-covered fields, their breaths smoky clouds. The sky was steel grey. The sun glinted off the snow, and they raised their hands to shield their eyes.

Claire's voice broke the silence that felt sacred to Lawrence. He joined her in song, wary that his changing voice might crack and make her laugh.

> Molly, lovely Molly, I delight in your charms, many the night I held you in my arms. If ever I return, it will be in the spring, when the mavis and turtledoves and nightingales sing.

When they reached the top of Sheep Hill, Lawrence straddled the sleigh and leaned against the seat.

"Sit here. Are you afraid?"

"No, though it's a tight fit."

Claire sat with her knees drawn up and her back against Lawrence's chest. He wrapped his arms around her, and inhaled the damp wooly scent of her cape tinged with the musky smell of her body. They rocked the sleigh forward until it tipped down the crest of the hill. As they gained momentum, icy wind blew up his sleeves and whipped his cheeks raw. Claire screamed and he laughed, heart banging in his chest. The sleigh bumped and lurched and made fast for the creek.

"Jump!" he yelled.

He dragged her off with him, and they stopped just inches from the frozen creek. After he untangled himself and got to his feet, he stepped toward the creek bank to retrieve the sled, but Claire leapt on him, knocked him down, and rubbed snow in his face. Before he rose again, she was gone, slipping and sliding and scrambling up the hill.

"Beat you to the top!" Her voice echoed against the hills and trees in the cold, still air.

~

Under a maple tree, Claire and Lawrence sat on the sleigh, breathing heavily after their dozen rides down Sheep Hill. From under her cape, she brought out the potatoes and cinnamon buns, still warm from her body, and unwrapped them.

Lawrence's potato's skin was soft. He tasted the dirt it grew in and a hint of salt he knew was the taste of Claire, and he relished it. The sweet buns were thick and soft from melted butter. He took a bite, then another, then popped the rest in his mouth.

"Chew slowly and taste every bite," Claire said.

Sugared cinnamon sparkled on Claire's lips, and Lawrence wanted to taste it. Instead, he broke the quiet that stretched between them.

"Molly makes the best cinnamon buns," he said.

"She'd make a fine wife for someone, but she rarely leaves the farm," Claire said.

"No one keeps her here. It's her choice."

"I know. But she has nowhere to go. Did you know she has a sister, Bridget?"

"I've heard talk about her family, but I don't remember it."

"She and Bridget crossed the ocean together but became separated when the ship docked in Philadelphia."

Lawrence frowned, forehead creased with concern.

"Did Mutti choose Molly and leave her sister behind?"

Claire swallowed the last sweet bite before she answered. "Molly told me that after they docked, she waited on the wharf, but Bridget never came. Molly was confused and frightened. She expected that she and Bridget would be together in America. When your mother noticed Molly alone and crying, she paid the captain for her passage and brought her home to the farm. Molly says your mother saved her, since she was a wee girl not fit for heavy work."

"What happened to the sister?" Lawrence's breath clouded.

"Your mother left word with the captain to tell Bridget where to find Molly, but in all these years, Molly never heard from her."

"That's sad. Do you think Molly's ever been in love? Will she ever find a man to marry?"

"She's only twenty-three. Not too old to find someone yet."

"Do you think she's ever been kissed?" Lawrence asked.

"How would I know?"

"Have you?"

"Have I what?"

"Been kissed."

Claire scoffed. "No."

"Me neither. Do you want to, so if someone asks, we can say we have?"

"Lawrence, your mother. I don't think . . ."

Lawrence put an arm around Claire's shoulder, pulled her close, and brushed his lips against hers. She stiffened and pulled away. He dropped his arm. Had he misread their closeness? Didn't she feel the way he felt?

"Claire?"

When she said nothing, he held her hand and sighed. She slipped out her hand. His heart broke. But as soon as he got to his feet, she wrapped her arms around him and closed her eyes. He put his mouth on hers with gentle pressure, touched his tongue to her lips, and tasted cinnamon. Her lips were soft. He wanted to stay in the cold with his mouth on hers and his arms around her. He searched her lips with his tongue. His rod swelled and he hoped she couldn't feel it through his clothes. When he slid his hand under her cape, she pulled it out.

"Don't. No one can know we kissed. Not your mother or your father. Not your brother or mine."

"I won't tell," he said, breathless.

"Swear."

"I swear. But did you like it?"

A hint of a smile crossed Claire's face. "What's in your coat? I felt something."

Lawrence was aghast. But she pointed to the bulge from the gun, and he exhaled all the air in his lungs.

"I brought the pistol my father gave me."

After he handed her the gun, she studied it. She took off her mittens to hold the pistol in her right hand with her finger on the trigger.

"I'll kiss you again if you show me how to shoot it."

Lawrence took her hand. They walked along the frozen creek to a toppled hickory, ice-covered with its roots exposed. Claire returned the gun.

"It's small, so it won't shoot a great distance. Stand back," Lawrence said.

More confidently than he felt, Lawrence dropped powder down the barrel and rammed in the lead ball. He stepped forward, raised his arm and steadied his hand. The shot boomed, and a piece of bark flew off the tree. A puff of acrid smoke escaped the barrel.

"You did it!" Claire clapped. Her eyes were wild. "Can I try?"

Lawrence held the gun behind his back. "Pay me."

Claire narrowed her eyes. She leaned in and kissed him, a short, hard kiss. He pulled her close and kissed back, lingering. When her tongue explored his lips Lawrence couldn't breathe.

"My turn," Claire said.

As he reloaded, Lawrence felt her eyes studying each step so she could do it herself next time.

"Take your stance and aim. Keep your eyes on the spot you want to hit. Don't look at the pistol, look at the tree. When you're ready, pull the trigger."

The gun's blast threw back Claire's arm. Dead leaves swirled in the air. The gun powder smell made her queasy, but she felt powerful and unafraid. She would learn to hold her hand steady. She would learn to shoot the gun.

"How do you make the bullet go where you want?"

"Keep your eyes on the target. Aim with both hands."

On the walk back, snow flurries whirled around them. Lawrence's feet felt frozen and painful, but the gun warmed his hip and thoughts of Claire warmed his heart. He wanted to kiss her again, to press his body against hers, to feel his blood pulse. As they approached the farm house, his mother waited in the kitchen doorway, her straw-colored hair wind-blown and glistening with snow, a patchwork quilt wrapped around her shoulders.

"She's in a grand pucker," Claire said. "I'm going to the barn to tend the goats and pigs." She dropped her voice to a whisper. "Never tell."

Lawrence dragged the sleigh to the barn before he confronted his mother.

"You'll catch your death, Mutti. What are you doing out in the cold?"

"Were you with Claire the whole day?"

Lawrence took his mother's arm and led her inside. He closed the kitchen door.

"I told you this morning Claire and I were going to Sheep Hill to sleigh ride. Does Papa know you're out of bed?"

"Claire is a servant, Lawrence. You and she are no longer children. Friendship has limitations." Anna's voice was gravelly and deep.

"Mutti, we had the day off. We went sleigh riding. Who else would go with me? I know who Claire is, and I know who I am, and I know you need to get back to bed."

CHAPTER ELEVEN

WISSAHICKON FARM JULY 1821

The July afternoon promised to be a scorcher. As the farm hands prepared to return to work after the mid-day meal, Mr. Raymond and Hamish returned from the wharves. They brought with them an awkward, gangly boy. Hamish was getting no younger, and Samuel's indenture would end in a couple years. Since Reuben and Lawrence were often away for their studies, Mr. Raymond decided to bring on a boy to help with the work.

Mr. Raymond called the workers to gather around and meet the new lad. Claire bit into a green apple and tilted her head to observe him. The boy stood almost six feet tall, with ruddy sunburned skin, unkempt dark hair that fell past his shoulders, and eyes as black as an Indian's. His thin trousers barely reached his knees. He stole a glance at Claire and their eyes locked. Sweat trickled down Claire's back. She longed to cool off in the Wissahickon Creek. She took another bite and spit out a seed.

"Save the seeds for the seed bucket."

Lawrence had crept up right behind her.

"As if I don't know that."

In the summer heat, little pustules appeared on Lawrence's forehead and around his chin. His hair lay damp on his head like a horse's coat under a saddle and smelled as bad. Claire found it a relief when he left for Germantown Academy. Yet once he was gone, she missed him. Whenever he returned from his studies, they worked side-by-side while he told funny stories about classmates and teachers. Her feelings confused her.

When Lawrence ignored her, she desperately wanted his attention. Once she got it, she ignored him. Every day, she thought of the kisses they shared when they were alone and out of sight. Her longing for Lawrence frightened her. Miss Anna must never know. Lawrence's breath felt hot on her neck.

"Please welcome young Duff MacDonald." Mr. Raymond rested a hand on the boy's shoulder. "The lad is thirteen-years-old, arrived on our shores from Scotland. He'll help Hamish and Samuel with the horses. Now, time to return to the fields."

"Claire!" Miss Anna's hands were on her hips. Her face was red and sweaty.

Claire raised her hand. "Here I am."

"Missy, show Duff the empty room in the quarters. After he settles, bring him to the stables. Show him how we muck the stalls and treat the leather."

As Claire approached the Scottish boy, she felt Lawrence's eyes on her. She feigned indifference and motioned Duff to hoist his bag and follow her. The boy's bare feet struck the ground like a full-grown bull.

When they reached the servants' quarters, Claire opened the door to the middle room. Like all the rooms, a high, narrow window let in light from the rising sun – an effective wake-up call on all but the deepest days of winter. The room contained a wooden pallet, a pine chest with three drawers, a bedside table, and a hurricane lamp in need of a candle. An old rag-rug lay on the floor by the pallet.

"This is your room."

The boy stared at Claire, blinking his dark owl eyes.

"Whatta eye due wid me steuff?"

He sounded like his mouth was full of pebbles.

Claire sat on the pallet and regarded him. "You'll have to learn to speak English if you're going to work on the farm. No one understands bog talk."

A deep red burned on Duff's cheeks. He dropped his bag on the floor and stomped outside.

"Mr. Duff, come in here and get settled. We have work to do before supper."

"Duff," he said, "Duff, nay Mr. Duff."

"I'll have to teach you to speak properly along with everything else. Come back inside."

He certainly thinks well of himself, Claire thought as she emptied the boy's bag. When he reappeared, a snub of candle, a flint, a biscuit hard as a rock, and a pointy sailor cap lay on the pallet. Claire waved Duff's tattered blanket.

"We're expected to bring our own mattresses, quilts, candles, and combs. The horses have better blankets than this ratty piece of wool. You should burn it."

In a rage, Duff yanked the blanket, and it tore in half. Slowly, he sank to the floor, a piece in each hand. He covered his eyes. Claire knit her brows at the boy's swallowed sobs.

"You don't need to weep over that rag. Molly will find you better bedding."

"It's me tartan, given by me da when he put me on the boat. It's all I have of home."

Claire held out her hand for the pieces, and Duff surrendered them.

"I'll ask Molly to find you a blanket and mattress, a shirt, and trousers." Claire stared at his ankles and feet, black with tar. "Miss Anna will make a trace of your feet to send to the shoemaker. No shoes here will fit those big feet, so you'll go barefoot until autumn." She smoothed the remnants of his tartan. "If you like, when I visit my family, I'll ask my mother if there's hope of mending it."

"Is it possible? I trust it to ye then."

He circled the dust with his toe.

Claire felt sorry for the ungainly boy. She was beginning to understand the cadences of his speech.

"What do you know of horses?" she asked.

"I know enough. Are ye a slave to this plantation? Are ye ordered to wear men's clothes?"

Claire clenched her jaw. "I am a free African born in Philadelphia to free parents of free parents. Like you, I'm serving an indenture in order to be educated and learn skills. As well, the air on the farm is more healthful than in the city. I choose the clothes I wear, and a woman's skirt is fit for neither farm work nor tending animals. I'll be on my own long before you, Scottish Boy." She turned in a huff. "I'm going to the stables. Come if you like."

Claire left the room and started across the field. *Who is this boy, dressed like riffraff, smelling of rotten potatoes, crying over his torn blanket, to look down on me?*

As she ran toward the stone bridge to the stables, she imagined herself as Star of Night, black and sleek, pulling at the bit, begging for free rein to race to the finish, oblivious to other horses, other riders, oblivious to all but the call of the Earth and her muscles, flying now, breath rhythmic, unstoppable. Granny's treasured Wedgwood medallion appeared in Claire's mind – the image of an African in chains and the words, *Am I Not A Man And A Brother?* engraved around the edge. She imagined asking Duff, Am I not as good as the likes of you?

When she reached the creek, she slowed. Sweat trickled down her face, back, and chest. Instead of crossing the bridge, she hopped to a flat stone in the middle of the Wissahickon and let water run over her legs. She burned with fury. A slave to the plantation. A servant. My blood, sweat, and life are on this land, no different than Lawrence or Reuben or Hamish or Molly. What gives that big galoot, not one full day on the farm, the right to call me a slave?

Footsteps pounded over the field and stopped at the bank. Claire wet her face. Duff stared, awkward and unsure.

"Are you afraid of water?" she asked.

"A'm fine, thenk ye."

He splashed in and knelt on the creek bottom, facing her. Still, she had to look up to meet his eyes.

"It's few girls I knew in Scotland and none of them brown like ye. None who wear men's knickers." He scrubbed his feet with sandy gravel until lighter skin appeared. "In Scotland, all gab about American blacks is of slaves."

"Not all Negroes in America are slaves, though many are in bondage. What matters on this farm is the work we do, not the color of our skin."

And that was true, at least for Mr. Raymond, Reuben, Lawrence, Molly, and Hamish. But as for Miss Anna, although she treated her and Samuel fairly, Claire sensed a wariness. Miss Anna must never learn of her special friendship with Lawrence.

After Duff splashed water on his chest, he lay back and let water run over his ruddy face and black hair. When he sat up, he doused Claire with a mouthful of water. She shook her head like Star of Night, then splashed Duff and grinned.

He was a young boy far away from his home. She forgave him, then took a strand of his long hair in her fingers and examined it. It felt slick. Even wet from the creek, it smelled foul. It hadn't been washed for a long time.

"It will take a good scrubbing and a sharp pair of scissors to make you presentable. Tonight, Molly will cut your hair and sew by candlelight to put you in decent clothes."

Duff touched Claire's braids, then gestured for her hand. When she gave it, he looked first at the back, then turned it over and compared her palm to his own. He returned her hand to her lap and ran a finger over her lips. Claire felt strangely moved.

"Yer hair is coarse like sheep and yer skin is brown like earth. But our hands are the same, though yours are smaller. In my village, I was a shepherd afore the rich took our land. I ken sheep and lambs. I dunna ken horses."

"Well, come along then," Claire said, feeling drawn to this boy with his tears and awkward touch. "A strong back will do for now."

CHAPTER TWELVE

WISSAHICKON FARM AUGUST 1821

L ast night's fearsome thunderstorm cooled the summer air. Farmhands waited in the front yard for the day's announcements. Raymond adjusted his felt hat. He coughed and spat. Catarrhal bronchitis waylaid him in July, and still each morning he woke coughing up phlegm. Reuben, home from the University of Pennsylvania to help with the harvest, told his father to rest another week, perhaps two. But Raymond would devote no more time to this infernal ailment.

"Lads and lass, it's harvest time. After we bring in the barley, Miss Anna will take the choicest grain to brew beer from her mother's recipe."

Anna's pudgy cheeks shone red as the rising sun's rays angled across her face. Workers murmured and shifted from foot to foot in anticipation of days of backbreaking labor that would result in tankards of beer and thick barley porridge covered with cream.

Raymond continued, voice hoarse. "After breakfast, we'll organize the work teams. Eat hearty, and pray God the weather holds."

The men and Claire followed Raymond into the dining room. At the head of the table, he sat with Anna on his right, and Reuben and Lawrence on his left. He sipped tea and covered his cornmeal mush with thick molasses.

"It's well you're eating again, Dear, to build your strength," Anna said.

At the long table, workers drank coffee, cider, or tea from pewter cups and sopped up bacon grease with crumbling corn cakes. The smell of strong coffee and fried bread filled the room. Raymond thought that

Lawrence, also home for the harvest, seemed uncommonly quiet. Anna thrust her elbow into his arm, and nodded toward Claire and Duff at the far end of the table, head-to-head in conversation.

Duff shoved biscuits in his mouth so his cheeks puffed out like a frog's. When he choked, pieces of biscuit spewed over Claire's plate, to her amusement. Anna grimaced.

"What's the harm of it, Anna?" Raymond whispered. "They're like colts and fillies romping in the pasture. Both are hard workers."

Anna's face flushed as she glared at the young indentured workers leaning against one another, laughing. She cleared her throat, loud enough for all to hear. When Duff and Claire looked her way, she frowned, pursed her lips, and shook her head ever so slightly. She turned to Raymond.

"Duff's a simple boy off the boat, but I expect more from her. She's with us almost ten years, and her parents are good Christian people. Perhaps I should bring her in from the stables and have her work in the house."

"Oh, Anna, don't bother yourself. There will be little time for tomfoolery once the workday begins."

"I don't like the way those two carry on, Raymond. I certainly believe Africans should read and write and be free to earn their livings in the trades, but too much familiarity with whites is a recipe for trouble."

"Anna, what you see is youthful exuberance, nothing more."

Anna shrugged. Raymond always saw the best in people. It was the trait that drew her to him, but she sometimes thought he was too easy on the workers and too ready to find excuses for them.

There was rustling at the table as Molly and Claire cleared the plates.

Raymond cleared his throat. "Gather by the wooden bridge. Reuben will divide the work teams."

~

Lawrence got to his feet. Now fourteen, he favored his father's thin frame, though his hair and features resembled his mother's. When flushed from anger as he was now, his wide-set eyes glowed green like the Wissahickon on a sunny day.

How can Claire behave so shamefully? Lawrence wondered. He dug his upper teeth into his lower lip. Didn't she know she belonged with him? Hadn't they shared their first kiss? Didn't the lingering kisses and touches in secret places prove she loved him? He came home with the expectation of spending time alone with her. Instead, she cavorted with the coarse stable boy. He shot an angry look her way. When Claire caught his eye and smiled, he resented her mockery.

"Where shall I work today, Papa?" Lawrence struggled to control his voice.

"The far field. You wield a scythe as well as any man."

Lawrence dropped an apple in his pocket. As he watched Duff and Claire, laughing, hustle from the kitchen, heat rose from his throat to his cheeks. They were laughing at him. He thought of the gun he taught Claire to shoot and wished he could shoot Duff with it right now.

"Lawrence, I asked you a question," Anna said.

He tore his eyes away and looked at his mother as if awakened from a deep sleep.

"On your return to Germantown Academy, will you deliver six barrels of apples to the Green Tree Tavern?"

"Of course," he said.

He grabbed his hat and went out the door.

By the time Lawrence trudged to the far field where golden barley swayed in the breeze, the sun had burned off the morning mist and shimmered in a turquoise sky. He chewed barley seeds, then spit them out as he watched Hamish and Duff cross the wooden bridge over the rain-swollen Wissahickon.

Duff led the red-coated Morgan horse that was hitched to a two-wheeled wagon. At three years, the colt was settling down but could be difficult when fillies were around. Hamish led Old Cyclone, hitched to the smaller cart. Old Cyclone and Old Hamish were a pair. Both suffered arthritic joints and had round black growths around their eyelids.

Simultaneously, the grooms pulled their hat brims forward. Hamish wore an ancient tricorn hat he swore General Nathanael Greene gave him when the Continental Army stopped at Wissahickon Farm before the Battle for Germantown. Duff wore the wide-brimmed felt hat Mr. Raymond gave him his first week on the farm after his skin blistered.

As the morning wore on, Lawrence's shoulders ached. He slashed, gathered, and bundled barley into sheaves, then tossed them to the edge of the plot. Three young boys were hired to collect the sheaves and drag them to the two Scotsmen to load in the wagons.

Lawrence's dove-grey pants darkened with sweat. He took off his hat and rubbed his sleeve across his brow. His face shone from exertion and his body stank like onion grass.

While he labored to cut and bind the barley, down by the creek Duff and Hamish – hired men, servants – did nothing but stand by the horses. Duff's face had the rough look of a peasant. His speech was garbled and his manners, atrocious. At meals, he reached across other workers to grab biscuits. He chewed with his mouth open and held his fist ready to stab baked apples when the dishes were passed around.

And I'm a better horseman, Lawrence thought. What does Claire see in him?

He slapped on his hat and returned to work. After another hour, the youngest hired boy brought Lawrence a sack with dried venison, a pumpkin tart, and a jug of apple cider. He sat on a long, flat rock jutting from the woods, took a gulp of cider, and chewed strips of venison. When he finished, he lay on the granite and put his hat over his eyes. He listened to the slashes of men cutting barley, and warblers singing in trees at the edge of the woods. He swatted a black fly that buzzed near his ear. A branch dropped on his leg. As he sat up to get back to work, he pushed it off his thigh and grunted when it slithered across his legs. A thick black snake tumbled off his lap to the ground. He leapt up, heart racing.

With the scythe held high, he readied himself to cut off the head of the six-foot snake. The snake folded its shiny black body – with a white chin and mottled belly – into a tight coil. A rat snake. Not poisonous.

"Scared the daylights out of me," he said aloud.

He tipped the cider jug, sucked the last drops, and tried to stop trembling. The sound of voices down by the bridge drew his attention. Duff sat on the ground with one boot off, shaking out pebbles. To the amusement of Hamish and the young boys, he moved his huge hands through the air like an outdoor preacher. He should have been packing the wagon. The black snake raised its head and Lawrence smiled. We'll see how long Duff sits idle.

Lawrence prodded the snake with the end of his scythe, keeping his distance to avoid its musk spray. Before it slithered away, he snagged the snake on the scythe and dropped it in a pile of cut barley. He packed the snake in the middle of a barley bundle, and carried it to the wagons.

"You boys get back to collecting the barley if you want to get paid," he called to the youngsters. He turned to Duff. "If you're not too exhausted from all your hard work, you might find it in you to load the wagon."

Lawrence jogged back to the field, and immediately swung the scythe through a row. He glanced toward the wagons. Duff said something.

Hamish shook his head. Lawrence took another swing but kept his eyes on Duff. Duff hoisted the barley bundle to the wagon bed. Lawrence rolled his eyes. I guess my joke didn't work, he thought, and sliced through more barley. A deep bellow echoed through the fields. Lawrence looked up in time to see Duff stumble backwards and fall on his rump. He laughed so hard he bent over to catch his breath.

A terrible squeal stopped his laughter. The Morgan horse reared. Duff tried and missed and tried again to grab the colt's reins, but the horse, dragging the wagon, bolted toward the creek.

"Stop!" Duff yelled, chasing after the horse.

The wagon leaned left, then righted itself. A few yards away, Old Cyclone jerked his head up and down. Hamish held tight to the reins, but the frightened old horse bolted after the Morgan. The wagon smashed into Hamish and tipped over. Lawrence vomited. Old Cyclone dragged the wagon on its side a few more yards until the weight stopped him. The old horse heaved and pawed the ground but stayed in place.

The Morgan horse dashed toward the bridge. Two farm hands flailed their arms and yelled, "Stop!" The horse shied away and galloped along the Wissahickon with the wagon rocking behind. When the colt, strapped to the wagon, tumbled into the rocky creek, its leg broke with a crack so loud, Lawrence heard it in the barley field.

All along the creek was chaos – broken carts, broken horses, broken men. Uncut barley swayed in the breeze. The black snake slithered toward the woods with unimaginable speed.

Lawrence turned in a circle. He searched the land for accusers, anyone who saw what he did. But men and boys ran toward Hamish or the colt screaming in the creek. No one looked his way.

He played a little joke to give Duff a start. Who could imagine the stupid Scot would holler, terrify the horses, drop the reins and let them run amok? All because of a harmless black snake.

Lawrence's knees wobbled as he trudged toward the mayhem and Hamish. He shaded Hamish's eyes with his hat and took the old man's hands, bloodied by the reins. Please God, don't let Hamish suffer.

"Are you with me, Hamish?"

"The horses, Lawrence. What of the horses?"

Hamish breathed in short gasps. His deeply wrinkled face lost all color.

"Something spooked them." A bead of sweat dropped from Lawrence's forehead onto Hamish. "Old Cyclone settled down, but the Morgan went in the creek."

"No," Hamish whispered and shut his eyes. "And Duff. Is the boy injured?"

"Duff's fine."

Lawrence stared at the dark stain spreading on Hamish's filthy britches. Reuben, dirt-streaked and sweaty, stinking of blood and horse piss, reached them and knelt on one knee.

"How's the old man?"

"He's taken a blow. His hands are sliced, but his leg looks really bad."

"Bad enough," Reuben said. "Keep his leg higher than his heart while I make a tourniquet." He turned to Hamish. "Hamish, after I slow the bleeding, we'll move you to the house. You'll have women fussing over you before you know it."

Hamish shut his eyes. Lawrence turned his gaze to the bridge. A hired boy held Old Cyclone's reins. In the creek, men struggled to unhitch the wagon from the Morgan horse. Duff stood on the bridge, hat in hands, and head hung low.

From the farm house, Raymond, rifle shouldered, marched to the creek like a soldier. When the shot rang out, Hamish moaned. Lawrence shut his eyes.

With the farmhands and grooms working on the barley and Samuel on an errand off the farm, Claire tended the horses alone. She loved the stables, loved when the horses nuzzled her and begged for carrots. To be by herself with these animals was a rare opportunity she treasured.

Claire felt happy that Lawrence was home, but worried too. At breakfast, he seemed cold and distant. She lingered at the kitchen door, hoping to catch him before he left for the fields, but he must have gone out the front. As she released the horses to pasture, filled water troughs, and mucked out the stalls, she wondered if he met a girl in the city – a white girl with round blue eyes and soft blonde curls cascading around her face. That would explain his deliberate avoidance and demeaning stares. She wanted to vomit. If only Samuel were here, but he'd driven a wagon to the grist mill in Flourtown to have wheat ground into flour.

Claire leaned against the fence. A cloud passed in front of the sun. She hugged herself. Two young horses played – feigning nips and running away with the other chasing. They were too young to ride, but Claire worked with them on stable manners and accepting the bit and reins. Soon she would put blankets on their backs to get them used to the feel of a load. Star of Night crossed the pasture and nudged her. She examined the mare's eyes, ears, and coat, then patted her haunches.

"I'll take you for a ride when Hamish and Duff get back."

Then she remembered Lawrence's slight. Her chest tightened. The sharp crack of gunshot startled her. Her heart raced. Star backed away – eyes wide and nose twitching. Claire spoke gently.

"There now, it's far from here, whatever it is."

The other horses pawed nervously. Claire felt frightened and anxious. The rifle was rarely fired, never in the middle of the day. Had wild dogs or wolves threatened the livestock? Hadn't they had enough of them?

As shouts carried in the breeze, Claire exited the paddock and locked the gate. She looked toward the farm house where people rushed here and there, like children playing tag. What on Earth was going on? Slave catchers? The thought nauseated her. She wanted to hide in the stables, but her legs carried her toward the turmoil. Despite fear that strangled her with each step, she ran as fast as she could, oblivious to rocks, roots, and burrs that dug into her bare feet. Tears spilled down her cheeks.

In the midst of men and boys who jerked like they were hauling lumber in short, quick yanks, Claire picked out Duff's gangly form.

"Duff!" she yelled.

He turned at his name. Claire feared he was hurt and bleeding, so wan was his face and so languid his step. When she reached him, she took his hand. Tears ran down his face in dirty tracks. She hadn't seen him cry since the day his tartan tore.

"What happened? Are you injured?"

"Leave me be. Help Hamish and the horses."

Duff collapsed against an oak tree, and Claire knelt facing him. He trembled, though she observed no wounds.

"Go," he said.

Reuben and two hired men approached the farm house, carrying Hamish on a litter. Lawrence walked alongside holding up Hamish's leg, but Hamish's hand dragged on the ground, and blood seeped from a rag tied around his thigh. Claire shuddered and couldn't speak.

As soon as he saw her, Reuben called, "Claire! Wash up. Bring Mutti clean water, vinegar, and bandages. Bring your needle and silk thread. Hamish's wound is deep."

From her room, Claire grabbed the needle and thread, then raced to the fresh water tubs outside the kitchen. She pulled off her filthy work blouse and in only a vest, scrubbed her hands, arms, and face. Behind her, Miss Anna held a towel and a fresh cotton apron. After she dried herself, Miss Anna tied the apron around her.

"Molly mixed a bucket of water and vinegar. I gathered a basket of bandages, and I see you brought your needle and thread." Miss Anna put her hands on Claire's shoulders. "Remember you are your mother's daughter, Claire. Use the skills she taught you to close Hamish's wound. No one has a better hand than you."

"What happened?" Claire asked, but Miss Anna already stepped inside.

Hamish lay on the dining table. Claire never saw such a grave injury. She tried to still her quivering hands. Hamish needed her. Miss Anna held Hamish's head as Lawrence dripped West Indian rum between his lips. After Hamish swallowed and coughed, narrow streams the muddy color of the creek dribbled from the sides of his mouth. Claire dabbed his face and gave him a tight smile.

"Well, Hamish, looks like you near did yourself in."

"I'm an old fool to be felled by a horse and cart."

His rheumy blue eyes rolled back. Claire kissed his forehead.

"You'll live the life of luxury for a few months while Samuel, Duff, and I take care of the horses."

"Sure, you and the boys," he slurred, head lolling.

Reuben cut off Hamish's pants and told Lawrence, "Clean the wound with plenty of water, not too cold, not too hot. Mutti, stay by his head and drip rum in his mouth, since we have no camphor. It's Hamish's good fortune the wheel didn't sever the artery."

Claire stood at Reuben's side as they examined the damage. The wound ran inside and across the front of his the right thigh. When Lawrence poured vinegar water over it, Hamish lurched then fell unconscious.

"Lawrence, replace the tourniquet with a clean one. Claire, wash the skin around the wound. Yes, up there too. We can determine the extent of the injury once the blood and dirt are wiped away. Many of my colleagues consider cleaning wounds to be time wasted, but I've found a good cleaning leads to less infection and better outcomes."

Reuben's knowledge and confidence reassured Claire. Together, they would save Hamish.

After she cleaned Hamish's leg, Reuben pulled the skin apart to examine the wound. Reuben had taught Claire to identify major muscles through touch on flesh. Now, they were exposed.

"Part of the sartorius is severed. I'm concerned at the loss of blood. You need to work fast."

Reuben propped Hamish's leg on his shoulder to stabilize it. Claire poured vinegar water over the wound, dabbed it dry, and ran her fingers over the torn muscle. Oozing blood made stitching difficult, but she took a deep breath and set to it. Her sweat dripped onto Hamish's wound. Lawrence pressed against her and wiped sweat from her forehead.

With Lawrence behind her, Claire felt lighter. His touch was gentle and kind, the Lawrence she loved. When he pinched Hamish's skin together, the stitching went easier and quicker. After she tied the thirty-third knot, she was exhausted. Her thumb and forefinger prickled. The metallic smell of blood mixed with the acrid odor of vinegar, nauseated her.

"You have as steady a hand as the best instructors at the university," Reuben said while he wrapped clean strips of linen around Hamish's leg.

Spit bubbled from Hamish's mouth. Anna wiped his face. Reuben and Lawrence carried Hamish to Molly's room off the kitchen where she'd care for him night and day.

Claire slipped out the door to escape the gore and anguish. She dropped the bloody apron, and pulled on her dingy work blouse. Streaks of blood coated her face and arms, and spattered her hand-me-down britches. All she could think of was the waters of the Wissahickon. She staggered to the creek bank and stepped in. The current carried watery traces of Hamish's blood to the city.

She took off her blouse to rinse while she splashed her arms and face. In the ripples, her hair's reflection made a fuzzy halo. Alongside shimmered dandelion hair. Claire covered her chest.

"Thank you for saving Hamish," Lawrence said, then turned and walked toward the house.

A pebble dropped from the stone bridge — Duff. Claire pulled on her wet blouse and ran to catch him. He smelled sour and skunky. His shoulders sagged and his movements were hunched, like an elderly man.

"Tell me what happened," she said.

As they walked toward the stables, she put her arm around his waist. From the corner of her eye, she saw Lawrence, halfway to the house, watching.

CHAPTER THIRTEEN

WISSAHICKON FARM SEPTEMBER 1821

Harsh winds and driving rain pounded the farmhouse and barns, saturated the fields, and drenched the beasts. Claire raised her face so the wind would blow away her tears. The Wissahickon Creek's turbid brown water rushed past, awash with leaves, branches, and swirling corpses of small animals. A baby duck opened its beak in a silent scream, sinking then bobbing to the surface of the swift-running water. She watched a twig float by, and wished she could float in the torrent all the way to the ocean, so far away no one would ever see her again. That would serve them right. It would serve Miss Anna right.

At a sound like a bone breaking, Claire turned toward the barn. The copper weather vane – a four-foot-high horse running across an arrow – swung wildly, tipped to one side, and spun to the ground in a series of crashes until the arrow jammed in the ground and stopped. In the blink of an eye, the cupola followed, banging and snapping before it shattered to pieces, like Miss Anna's stoneware beer stein only an hour before.

Claire didn't know which scared her more, being outside with gale winds and rain stinging her face like needles, or being in the house with Miss Anna, whose anger and disappointment shamed her. In her palm, she squeezed a rough-edged piece of stein decorated with the image of a deer in flight.

~

Because the raging storm limited her chores to milking and feeding, Claire got it in her head to read further into *Mansfield Park* by Jane Austen – the book Miss Anna was using for their lessons. In a way, Fanny Price, who was sent to live with wealthy relatives to get a good education and better her state in life, reminded Claire of herself – except Fanny was white and Claire was black. Still, Claire understood Fanny – never as good as her cousins, tolerated but not accepted, and, against all bounds of propriety, attracted to her benefactor's son.

The book sat on the top shelf of the bookcase in Mr. Raymond's library. Claire couldn't find Miss Anna to ask if she could borrow *Mansfield Park*, so she dragged a leather footrest to the bookcase, climbed on it, and stretched to reach the book, but only brushed it. She hopped to get hold of the book, but when she landed, the footrest slid away. As she flailed to right herself, she knocked the beer stein off its shelf.

The porcelain mug shattered on the hardwood floor. The bottom, with *Deutschland* etched into it, ended up next to a palm-sized piece of white stoneware on which a blue deer leapt through glazed leaves. When Miss Anna and Molly burst into the library, *Mansfield Park* lay splayed on a chair, and Claire sat on the floor with the blue deer clenched in one hand, fitting together broken stoneware like a puzzle without all the pieces.

"Are you hurt, Lass?" Molly asked, kneeling to gather shards.

Miss Anna bent forward, checked Claire's arms and legs for blood, then pulled her to her feet. Claire's elbow burned from scraping the shelf, but she ignored the pain and faced Miss Anna.

"Would you care to tell me what happened here, Missy?"

"I fell."

"I see that."

I wanted to read *Mansfield Park*. I'm sorry I broke your stein." Claire squeezed the deer piece so hard her hand stung.

When Miss Anna's eyes grew red and her lower lip trembled, Claire's stomach lurched.

"My mother brought this stein from Germany. It's the only thing I have from the Inn. You know better than to enter family rooms without permission. Go to the quarters. Leave the book."

As she checked the spine and smoothed *Mansfield Park*'s pages, Miss Anna's hands trembled.

"I'm sorry. I'll make it up to you."

"Go, now," Miss Anna whispered.

In her room in the quarters, Claire lay on her mattress while wind rattled the windows and rain pelted the roof. Outside, lightning cracked, followed by an explosion like a cannon's roar. Claire peered outside and watched black smoke spiral from the big elm on the creek bank. A huge branch teetered and crashed to the ground. The fallen branch, thick with dark leaves, danced like a tipsy tent while tendrils of smoke blew sideways. Moments later, Mr. Raymond and Lawrence, wearing oil-coated jackets, clumped through the yard and across the wooden bridge to herd the goats to the barn.

Storm or no storm, Claire would not spend another minute banished to her room like a child. She pulled on a rough wool sweater, stomped barefoot into the gale, and slid on her rump down the slick grass toward the creek. The air reeked of electricity and mud. The elm's dangling branch created a shelter from the rain, and Claire crawled under it. Splinters sprawled on the ground like debris from the dynamite explosions that shattered bedrock to make roads. With its bark shorn, the elm looked as vulnerable as a naked man.

Now, as Claire huddled under the branch, a slate shingle blew off the farmhouse roof and clanged against the fallen weather vane. Wind roiled the Wissahickon. She shivered. As soon as Mr. Raymond and Lawrence got the goats across the bridge, Claire would follow them to the barn. The storm's wrath scared her more than Miss Anna.

Despite the shepherd dog's barks and nips, the goats hesitated to cross the creaking bridge. It took hat waving and shouting before they finally crossed, their bleats smothered by the wind. In a great gust, Mr. Raymond's black hat blew off and was swept away in the current.

By the time Claire looked away from the goat-herding commotion, the creek had overflowed its banks. Water fast approached her refuge. When she got to her feet, she slid toward the creek. Heart racing, she dropped to her knees and crawled. The farmhouse was lost in the onslaught of rain, but she focused on the sound of bleating goats to guide her through the storm.

As she staggered toward Lawrence and Mr. Raymond, a high-pitched, garbled cry came from the creek. In water already ankle deep, Claire shielded her eyes and stared at the creek. She heard the cry again, and stepped closer. There. A black kid born in the spring bobbed in the rushing water.

Without thought, she plunged in, arms outstretched to grab the animal. She pitched under. Coughing and gagging, she broke the surface with an arm wrapped around the kid's chest. Although it thrashed and butted, she held tight — this helpless creature would not drown. She narrowed her eyes, searching for the bridge.

The goat kicked her. Rain and creek water blinded her. A bolt of lightning crackled across the sky, illuminating the farmhouse and stick figures running from the barn. Lawrence? Samuel? Mr. Raymond? *Help*, she screamed in her head.

A moment later, she collided with the submerged bridge and took the impact in her hip. She lost hold of the kid, but grabbed its leg before the current carried it beyond salvation. The bridge barrier was their only hope against being swept downstream, certain to drown. With all her might, Claire wrapped her legs around a railing and hugged the young goat close. It bleated and thrashed. It took all her strength to hold on.

Gabriel, blow your horn. Jesus, save me and this kid, she prayed. Her thoughts drifted to Germantown and the brick house in the alley. Mama, Daddy, Granny, Samuel. Please, Lord, let me see them again. She squeezed her eyes shut and imagined she and Granny were on the porch, rocking. From yellow eyes, the goat stared at Claire, issued a quiet bleat, and fell limp. Claire struggled to keep its head above water as the goat surrendered. She would never surrender. She spit out a mouthful of creek water.

"Claire, we're coming. Let the goat go," Mr. Raymond shouted, voice distant and garbled.

"Claire!" Samuel's voice.

Mama, Granny, Daddy, I believe. The goat's head lolled on her shoulder. Water swirled around her face — her baptism. Claire wore the white dress Mama made, and the congregation sang for her soul – Granny's voice loudest.

Take me to the water, take me to the water, like John did Jesus one day. Take
me to the water, take me to the water, baptize my sins away.

Her head dipped under. She came up sputtering with a baby goat for sacrifice, like Abraham slew instead of Isaac. I will not sacrifice this kid. Claire shouted with the congregation —

Glory, glory, hallelujah,
When I lay my burden down, Lord.

No! Not me! I will not lay my burden down.

Mr. Raymond and Samuel tied a rope to an oak tree, then slipped the rope harness over Lawrence's shoulders. Samuel moved halfway down the line and eased Lawrence toward the creek a few feet at a time. As the specter of Lawrence approached the bank, lightning lit the field like Independence Day fireworks.

Wade in the water, children. Claire's heart lurched with hope but her brain filled with cotton. It would be easy to let go, let the current carry them down the creek to the Schuylkill River, into the Delaware, and out to sea. *God's gonna trouble the water.*

With interest but not emotion, Claire observed Lawrence splash in the creek, buffeted by the rushing water. Samuel controlled Lawrence like a marionette. Soon, face, dripping and anxious, he was so close she could kiss him. His arms wrapped around her like her arms wrapped around the little goat. She unhooked her legs from the bridge railing and closed her eyes.

"You scare the daylights out of me."

At the sound of Samuel's voice, Claire forced her eyes open. Rain pelted her face. She lay on muddy ground under the oak tree, not knowing how she got there.

Mr. Raymond took Claire in his arms and carried her through the pounding rain to the farmhouse. She tried to ask what happened, but no words escaped her raw throat.

"There, there," he said. "It was brave and reckless to hazard the creek to save the doeling. Lawrence is looking after it. It will be fine. The whole farm's in an uproar worrying about you."

Claire woke warm and dry in Molly's bed, with an aching head and sick stomach. Through swollen eyes she peered toward the tick of knitting needles and the creak of the rocking chair — Miss Anna. At Mr. Raymond's footsteps, she closed her eyes.

"The girl near drowned, Anna, to save the beast."

"A fool thing to do, Raymond. How could we ever face Elizabeth and Moses if we lost Claire? After I sent her to her room for breaking the stein, she ran into the storm to spite me. She has a good mind. After her indenture, I imagine her as a teacher of Negro children. She has a gift for reading. She shattered my mother's Hessen beer stein because she tried to reach a book on your library shelf."

"Not even our sons love the beasts like Claire does. It's that love plunged her into the creek. She wouldn't let the little goat go even though I told her to," Raymond said.

"Aye, Raymond, she followed her own will rather than her master's. I fear she's on the road to ruin. I dread she'll bring young Lawrence with her."

"Claire's on a rough road, Anna, whether it leads to ruin or glory, who's to say? I've learned to listen closely when she comes up with a better way to organize the harvest or to house the chickens to salvage more eggs. I intend to give her the kid she saved, once this infernal storm passes, and she's back on her feet."

"That's the perfect solution. There's no better way to understand rules and responsibility than ownership. You're a good man, Raymond. Not everyone is as willing to tolerate her waggery."

"I remember a young German barmaid who tended to waggery herself." He touched Anna's shoulder. "Are you to stay the night with her?"

"Who better to keep an eye on the rascal?" Anna smiled. "Barmaid! I was the owner's daughter, you may recall."

Miss Anna's hand on Claire's forehead smelled of rose water. Claire fell asleep with taste of the Wissahickon on her tongue.

CHAPTER FOURTEEN

GERMANTOWN MAY 1822

G ermantown Market noise clanged in Claire's ears. She hurried to display pots of soft goat cheese on a long table. To her right, Mr. Raymond and Lawrence hung hams, sheep legs, and pigs heads on racks behind the Wissahickon Farm meat stand. In the animal pens behind them, Duff cleaned piglets and brushed Claire's three male goats.

After September's gale, Mr. Raymond gave Claire the black baby doe, and loaned her four does of breeding age. He and she signed an agreement that gave Claire all kids the does produced to start her own herd. She paid Mr. Raymond half of her earnings from the loaner goats and their kids. Once her herd was established, she'd pay their full expenses. She was thrilled. She kept her accounts in the leather journal Mr. Raymond gave her.

"Managing a business means paying your bills before you count your your receipts," he told her.

Today, Claire hoped to sell the three bucklings from the loaner does' litters. If they sold, she'd first pay Mr. Raymond, then send money to her parents.

Miss Anna, Molly, and Claire had worked together to turn goat milk into cheese and cow's milk into butter. They'd divide the money earned from those sales. Miss Anna sent pretzels, and Molly sent jars of pepper jelly. This was Claire's first time working the table alone, and she intended to keep good records of sales and earnings.

"Watch it, Lad, you'll tip over and take the hams with you," Mr. Raymond called.

Lawrence teetered on a step stool as he tied a huge ham to the rack. Claire rushed to steady the stool while Lawrence tethered the ham. Although the morning remained chilly, sweat beaded on his forehead. When he reached into the crate for a sheep's leg, Claire touched his shoulder.

"I need to set out Molly's jellies and your mother's pretzels. Miss Anna told me her pretzels sold out before noon at the last market." Her voice was breathy with excitement.

She stopped for a moment at the animal pen. "The buckies look grand, Duff. We'll have a day of it."

"Indeed, they do. I'm about to take a walk-around afore we're overrun. The creatures will manage on their own for a bit," he said.

In the market's meat and dairy section, live chickens scratched in cages, calves cried, pigs squealed, and lambs snuffled. Soon after a farmer two stalls down chopped off a chicken's head and hung the bird to drain, the smells of blood and guts drifted by. The rich aroma of boiling coffee made Claire want a cup.

After she set out her wares, she retrieved the accounting journal and cash box from under the table. As she organized coins, she felt eyes on her. A small boy with yellow skin and hazel eyes stared at her. He looked like a miniature Felix, with parents of different races.

Claire smiled. "What can I offer you?"

The boy nodded towards the pretzels.

"That will be one penny."

Well-dressed women with baskets over their arms milled around the stalls, squeezing fruit, running their fingers over quilts, or pointing to cuts of meat, while gentlemen in dark coats sniffed jugs of rum and bottles of wine. A woman stopped to inspect a jar of pepper jelly.

"Do you have a penny?" Claire asked the silent boy.

The child stared with hungry eyes. Claire chose a small pretzel, handed it to him, and said, "Go on with you now." She recorded the sale and would pay Miss Anna's penny from her own earnings.

Duff's voice carried from the animal pen. "This laddie's braw and healthy. He'll make a strong stud."

Claire smiled as she turned her attention to the woman at her table. "You'll like that jelly, Miss."

The woman glared at Claire from hard dark eyes. "Is it your practice to give away goods?"

Claire hesitated, not sure what the woman meant. Then, she realized —
the little boy.

"Oh no, Miss, but the poor child be hungry. I know to pay a penny to
make it good. Indeed I do."

On market days, Claire spoke to white customers in the manner Mama
called, *easy talk*. Otherwise, many whites looked at her suspiciously, and
Claire feared they'd think her uppity. She slipped into easy talk without
even trying. She cleared her throat and nodded to the jelly jar.

"Now you can't go wrong with that pepper jelly, Miss. Only a half-
dime and the jar go with it. Or you might like our goat cheese, and I got a
tub full of fresh Wissahickon Farm butter, ten cent a pound if you brought
a jug to fill, fifteen if you ain't."

The woman narrowed her eyes but handed Claire her butter jug,
dropped the pepper jelly into her basket, and counted coins from her
purse. Claire ladled butter into the jug, smoothed the top with a knife, and
clipped on the lid. She dropped the coins into the cash box. After the
woman walked away, Claire let out a breath she didn't realize she'd been
holding. She marked the sale in the journal.

In a few minutes the woman returned, and Claire's heart raced. But the
woman took five pretzels from the basket and gave Claire another half-
dime.

"My husband insists I buy these before you run out."

By noon, Claire sold every pretzel, the jellies, relishes, and pots of goat
cheese. An inch or so of butter glistened in the bottom of the tub, unlikely
to sell. The farm's livestock sold quickly too.

Each time Duff led a buyer to Mr. Raymond to negotiate the price and
method of payment, Claire kept her eyes on the transaction. Since Mr.
Raymond trusted only silver and gold, she was surprised when he
accepted the new paper money from a man he knew. Then he sold two
sheep to a city man for a half-barrel of rum, a Spanish hunting knife, and a
long-bore pistol.

Each of Claire's goats sold for three dollars, an amount which astonished her no matter how many times she whispered the number to herself.
This morning she felt a little sad to bring her goats to market, but now she
was overjoyed. She traced the numbers on the table. From nine dollars,
she'd pay Mr. Raymond five, send three to Daddy and Mama, and tuck
one dollar in the top drawer of her bureau. She ran her finger down the

goat cheese column in the journal. Her share amounted to ninety cents – eighty-nine after she paid a penny for the little boy's pretzel. She counted the money in the cash box and compared it with her journal entries.

When she handed the cash box to Mr. Raymond, her mind raced with the amount of money she earned.

"Mr. Raymond," Claire said, voice proud, "the money in the box matches the journal. I sold all but the last few scoops of butter. Duff helped me take down the table."

Claire waited while Mr. Raymond glanced at two remaining hams and a leg of lamb. A brick of Miss Anna's scrapple was the only other meat left for sale. Lawrence and Duff, smelling like dung, dragged a wood crate from the livestock pen to the scavenger's corner outside.

"We had a good day, all of us," Mr. Raymond said. "I'll keep the stall open a bit longer. You run along, Claire, and have a look around." He handed her some coins. "Buy yourself a sweet, and candies for Miss Anna and Molly. But don't dawdle. We'll head home in an hour."

Before she left to visit other stalls, Lawrence brushed against her. His apron was streaked with blood and grease. Pieces of straw stuck in his hair.

"Shall I buy you a sweet, too?" she asked.

"I'll find you after I finish loading our stuff."

As she headed off to explore, Claire looked for Duff, but the boy wasn't in sight. The smell of turtle stew drew her to a black woman who stirred two heavy pots that teetered on a small, cast iron stove.

"Pepper pot, nice and hot," the woman chanted. "Fresh turtle stew, waiting for you."

Embers glowed orange in the stove's chamber. The smell of salty meat, potatoes, and carrots made Claire's mouth water. At the sound of Claire's toe tapping, the woman whipped around.

"You want to buy?"

When she saw Claire, she stared, pursing her lips as crease lines deepened across her forehead.

"You Moses' child?"

"Yes, I'm Claire." She felt pleased to be recognized. "I came with Farmer Williams from Wissahickon Farm. That turtle stew smells good. How much for a bowl?"

The woman returned to the pots and filled a chipped earthenware cup.

"God bless you, Child. Moses' girl welcome to my stew. I 'bout ready to close shop and get Mrs. Deckle's supper started come what may. Try this."

Claire slurped the last drops of the thick buttery stew, and licked her lips. From the corner of her eye, she noticed the small boy she gave the pretzel to. He had a furtive, animal look as he skittered from stall to stall. He snatched discarded bits of food from the ground and tucked them in his shirt. Claire shook her head. She returned the empty cup and thanked the pepper pot woman. She searched the stalls for the yellow boy to no avail. A sugary smell drew her to the confectioner's stall.

Claire waited while white patrons pushed ahead to examine the candies and small cakes on display. She jingled the coins in her small purse and decided what to buy. After two white women and a white man stepped away with their sweets, she caught the eye of the vendor, a ruddy-faced fellow with wispy hair and close-set eyes. He folded his arms across his chest and glared. She almost turned away, but smiled and spoke in the easy talk.

"Mr. Raymond Williams from Wissahickon Farm send me to buy sweets for his wife. Mr. Raymond say he don't dare go back without candy from the confectionery man."

The vendor unfolded his arms and looked at Claire with interest.

"Well, then," he puffed, "many ladies are partial to my marzipan balls."

He placed a tray of almond-colored shapes sprinkled with white sugar on the table.

"I ain't never seen no candy look like that before. Mr. Williams want me to taste them afore I spend his good money." She jingled the coins.

The man huffed but obliged Claire by dropping a small piece in her hand. It was soft on her tongue, sweet, a bit gritty, with a taste like rich cream over almonds.

"Miss Anna surely like these," Claire said. "I take a measure of those martzy balls and a good size bag of lemon suckets, and I know Mr. Raymond be happy to have some horehound sweets."

She liked the lingering flavor of the marzipan. She wished she could kiss Lawrence and share the taste. The man scooped candy onto his scale, placed the marzipan balls in a white box he tied with a string, and slid the lemon suckets and horehound candies into small brown bags.

Claire thought Lawrence and Duff must have packed the wagons by now and worried she was taking too long. When the confectionery man leaned over to total the bill, the little yellow boy brushed against Claire. Quicker than lightning, the boy's hand shot out and grabbed a handful of marzipan candies off the tray. The vendor looked up as Claire gasped and put her hand to her throat. The boy disappeared in the crowd.

"You're in cahoots with that thief!" the candy man hollered, face contorted with rage. "Those are my most costly confections, and you distracted me so a street nigger could steal my best goods! Constable, Constable!"

Claire shook her head, confused and frightened.

"No," she began, "I would never . . ."

The confectioner yanked her arm, and smashed her nose on the display table. Stunned and hurt, she took a moment to push herself up. Blood trickled from her nose.

White people surrounded her and took up the call, "Constable, Constable!"

Claire clutched the money purse to her chest. She couldn't breathe. Behind the vendor, she spied the little boy, his eyes wide and sorrowful. *Get my people*, she mouthed. A look of understanding passed over the boy's face, and he ran toward Mr. Raymond's stall. Fear and shock turned to anger. Claire wiped her nose with her apron, squared her shoulders, and faced the confectioner. No more easy talk for this mean man.

"Sir, I don't know that boy. I was as unawares as you when he snuck past. Mr. Raymond gave me more than enough money to buy his candy. You wrongly accuse me."

Claire held her head high and met the man's eyes. The sugary candy smell and the coppery taste of blood trickling down her throat nauseated her.

"Don't look at me that way," the man sneered.

"Let me through."

Lawrence's voice drew murmurs from the crowd. As soon as he reached the stand, he put a hand on Claire's elbow. When he noticed her bloody nose, he handed her a dingy handkerchief, and she pressed it under her nose.

Hands in fists, Lawrence stepped toward the confectioner. A constable rushed to the stall.

"What's the trouble here?"

"The girl helped a nigger boy steal my most expensive candy."

Lawrence spoke to the constable. "This girl is no thief. My father trusts her with our livestock, our crops, and our money. Ask the confectioner why she's bleeding."

The confectioner huffed and straightened his apron.

"Where is this nigger boy?" the constable asked. "Who can describe him?"

Still upset but beginning to calm, Claire thought about the boy, his fear, his hunger, his help getting Lawrence.

"I didn't get a good look at him," the confectioner said. "By the time I realized he robbed me, he was running away."

"The little boy's white," Claire said.

Lawrence stared at her.

Someone said, "I saw a little white boy run out to the street."

"What of my marzipan? Someone must pay for the stolen candy," the flushed confectioner demanded.

The constable looked from the confectioner to Lawrence to Claire. People drifted away. Mr. Raymond, breathless, reached the stall. His expression concerned, he addressed Claire.

"Are you hurt?"

"Not much, Mr. Raymond. The candy man accused me of helping a little boy steal his candy, but Lawrence told the constable I don't steal."

Claire's heartbeat slowed. With Mr. Raymond and Lawrence beside her, she felt safe.

"I expect you to apologize to Miss Penniman," Mr. Raymond told the confectioner.

"There's no need for me," the constable said, and hurried away.

The confectioner harrumphed. He studied his journal. "Sorry your girl bumped her nose," he muttered. He handed the box and bags to Lawrence but addressed Mr. Raymond. "It's one dollar for the candy. It seems the loss from the theft is on me."

Mr. Raymond handed the man two silver dollars.

"Do not be quick to accuse, Sir," he said. "It harms the innocent and labels you a lout. Be assured, in the future you will have no trade from us."

～

In the bed of one of Wissahickon Farm's Conestoga wagons, the yellow boy waited with Duff. Mr. Raymond approached the child.

"You caused trouble for our Claire, my lad. What do you have to say for yourself?"

"Mammy don't have no food, Mister," the little boy muttered. He fidgeted and cast his eyes down.

"And what of your father?"

"Gone to sea."

"Very well. Duff and I will carry you home. Perhaps your mammy would be willing to take the small ham leg and scrapple we didn't sell so we don't have to bring it back to the farm. And there's a bit of butter in the barrel I'd be happy to unload."

Tears welled in Claire's eyes. Mr. Raymond's compassion almost made up for the awful candy man's accusations and rough handling.

The boy slid down from the wagon and approached Claire. "Didn't want no trouble for you."

"Don't be stealing from white people. When your mammy needs help, you ask around until you find Moses Penniman. Tell him, Claire sent you. Can you remember that?"

"Un hunh," the boy whispered.

"That's all right then," she said.

"Take Claire home," Mr. Raymond told Lawrence. "Duff and I will be along soon."

As she climbed onto the wagon bench alongside Lawrence, Claire sighed. She touched her nose. The bleeding stopped. Lawrence's hand, warm and firm, took Claire's.

"You've a bruised cheek and fat lip to explain to my mother."

Tears spilled from her eyes. "I was afraid the constable would take me away."

"I'd never let that happen."

After they passed the shops and houses, Lawrence pulled over. He wrapped his arms around Claire and held her.

"I promise to keep you safe," he said.

Claire left the confectioner's bitterness behind and surrendered to the sweetness of Lawrence's lips.

CHAPTER FIFTEEN

WISSAHICKON FARM AUGUST 1822

C laire woke to the sound of bleating goats. After she straightened the quilt Granny made, now worn soft, she reached for the water cup on the pine table. She rubbed her teeth and tongue with a rag, rinsed her mouth, and spit outside. Then she tucked her nightgown under the pillow, pulled a wool shirt over her undervest, and stepped into Lawrence's hand-me-down corduroy britches.

She took the path to the cesspit to dump her pot. Trees and brush surrounded the pit, while a log barrier hindered animal access. The stench, thick and carnal, was suppressed by the weekly scattering of ashes and lime, as well as the mock-orange bushes planted along the perimeter. A snapping branch startled her. Her black goat, Queen, leapt over the stacked-logs barrier into the cesspit area.

Claire yelled and waved until the doe jumped back over the barrier and raced toward the pasture where other goats grazed. A breeze carried the scent of cut hay.

~

Pink and yellow colored the eastern sky. The sun rose in golden splendor. At the goat pasture, Claire clapped her hands. Two little bucks, born in June, bounded to her. She hid barley treats behind her back. When the black kid settled, she fed him a treat and examined his skull. The other buckling, black and white with a mottled trunk, butted her legs.

"Hold on. You're next."

Mr. Raymond taught Claire to disbud her goats – remove the horn buds when the kids were days old. Though it was a hateful job, bucks were more valuable as breeding stock when they didn't endanger other goats with their horns. On these newest kids, Claire had wielded the disbudding tool while Samuel held their heads steady. She'd heated the iron to red-hot, then pressed the tip to the horn buds – *for ten seconds, no longer*. Now, with the burn scabs peeled off, only copper-colored scars remained.

"Aren't you both grand?"

The breakfast bell gonged. Claire released the little bucks and hurried to the kitchen door. Inside, Samuel motioned for her to sit between him and Duff. The Williams family sat together at the head of the table. Reuben would soon return to Boston where he practiced medicine, and Lawrence planned to enter the University of Pennsylvania for the fall term. Claire smiled at the boys. Something was missing when they were away.

After she cut thick pieces of buttered rye bread in squares and dropped them in a bowl of warm milk, she dripped a spoonful of molasses over them. When she raised her head to hear Mr. Raymond's announcements, milk coated her upper lip. Samuel handed her a napkin.

"Today, Miss Anna, Lawrence, and Claire will plant the fall vegetable garden – peas and potatoes, rhubarb and radishes, carrots and cabbage, onions and beets. Hamish, Samuel, and Duff will tend the horses. Reuben and I will join the farm hands harvesting the oats. Are we ready, boys? Claire?"

Claire finished a hard-boiled egg before heading outside. She slid a flower-print seed bag over her shoulder and followed Miss Anna to the nearby vegetable garden to seed the onion rows.

Lawrence worked on the row beside her, his feet touching hers as they knelt in damp soil and drilled one-inch holes with their fingers before dropping in the seeds. Below his felt hat, Lawrence's blond hair fluttered. The soil exuded a strong rich scent. A drop of sweat trickled down Claire's cheek, leaving its salty taste on her lips.

"After lessons, let's take a walk and swim in the creek," Lawrence whispered.

Claire moved a knee-length down her row. "I have to muck the stables and tend the goats. There isn't time."

"I'll muck the stables while you take care of the goats. We'll have time enough. On Monday, I saw a golden eagle. I want to find its nest. . . Don't come if you're scared to climb the ridge."

"I climb the rocks and ridges as well as my goats."

"Today is my last chance to find the nest before I leave for the university. . . And to be with you."

As the sun burned red, the temperature rose. Claire wiped her brow, tightened her green bandana, and pulled off her wool shirt to work in her undervest. A walk with Lawrence would be a welcome respite. As she thought of his hand in hers, she felt his eyes and turned to see his grin.

"You look like a boy but for those brown duckies peeking from your vest," he whispered.

Claire flinched like she'd been slapped. How could he be sweet one minute and cruel the next? She scooped up a handful of black soil.

"Lawrence."

He turned. She smeared his face, and dumped the rest on his hat.

"I'd piss on you if I were a boy," she said.

"What's going on in the onions?" Miss Anna called.

"Nothing," Lawrence called back.

He kicked at Claire's feet, but she hopped aside and spattered dirt in his eyes. She raced away.

"Going to the barn for a trowel," she called over her shoulder.

When she reached the backyard, she ran smack into Molly, who dropped the sheet she was hanging. Her red hair gleamed orange in the sunlight.

"Mind where you're going, Lass. Now the sheet needs washing again."

"I'm sorry, I'm sorry," Claire choked through tears.

"It's not the first nor last time my sheets were spoiled before they dried. Stop blubbering." Molly stared at Claire. "Go wash up and sit on the step. I don't want you tramping dirt into my clean kitchen. I'll bring us cups of tea."

Claire dipped her bandana in the wash basin, wiped her face, neck, and arms, then tied the damp bandana on her head. She glanced down. The vest didn't cover them. They were growing, and nothing would stop them, like nothing would stop the blood that came with each new moon.

Molly handed Claire a cup of tea in the fine china. "Tea tastes better in the good dishes. My mam often said, 'Nothing looks as bad from the far side of a cuppa tae.' Isn't it a blessing we have as much tea as we want, and sugar as well? Now, my girl, what brings you to tears?"

"Lawrence said my brown duckies peek out of my vest. I hate him."

Molly put her arm around Claire's shoulders. "Those brown duckies mean you'll soon be a woman, my girl, but Lawrence is cheeky to say so."

The tea was steaming hot, brown-sugar sweet, with a mint leaf floating on top.

"Your mam was right," Claire said, "about the cuppa."

"Sure and I miss the old girl. With Da gone, and herself and our wee brother coughing blood, Mam begged a ship's captain to take Bridget and me to America. I was but nine-years-old. On the voyage, an old fella took a fancy to Bridget and promised jobs for us both. But when the ship landed, for the life of me, I couldn't find Bridget or her old fella. Glory to God, Miss Anna saved me. Yet I still wonder every day what happened to Bridget."

"Do you wonder what happened to your mam and brother?"

"For years, Miss Anna gave me coins to tuck into letters I sent every few months to Mam at her parish church. She never wrote back. Finally, after five years I received a letter from the priest. He thanked me for all my donations in memory of Moira and Tomas Sullivan, and thought surely, I'd want to honor my mother and brother with a stone marker for their graves."

"You didn't know they died? What a terrible way to find out. What did you do?"

"I gave Miss Anna the letter, and she sent money for the marker. Then, she and Mr. Raymond drove me all the way to St. Mary's Church in the city. They sat on either side of me while Bishop Egan celebrated a funeral mass for my mother and brother." Molly patted Claire's knee. "This is my family now."

Claire trembled as she sipped the last drops.

"Let me put back the cups before they get cracked. . . I sometimes wear Reuben's castaway shirt to clean the oven. It will do fine for you and your duckies. Wait here. Won't take but a snap to find it."

The apricot-colored shirt was soft with wear, the patches hardly noticeable. When Claire slipped it over her head, the cloth smelled like burned pumpkin pie.

"It's time I make new blouses to keep those duckies in the pond, yeah? Because, my darling, they are here to stay. Go back to the garden before Miss Anna comes looking."

Much comforted, Claire ran to the privy houses at the far end of the backyard, on rocky land dotted with scrubby bushes. The family privy was whitewashed with a half-moon carved in the door. Next to that sat the one for Molly, her, and other women who worked on or visited the farm. The workmen's privy was larger, with four seats. About fifty yards away, surrounded by brush, the farm cesspit had been cut into limestone bedrock.

As she exited the dim privy, the sky enveloped her like a blue blanket. A muffled sound came from the cesspit area. Claire cocked her head – birds perhaps, or an opossum searching for termites beneath the rotting logs. She stepped toward the garden, resigned to work alongside Lawrence, but she wouldn't speak to him, not a word. Another sound from the cesspit — a different pitch, like a scream from a frightened child. Not again!

"Queen!"

Claire raced to the cesspit with Reuben's shirt fluttering like a sail.

The black goat thrashed in the pit's tarry goo, her bleats strangled. Claire tied her bandana over her mouth and nose. She darted from tree to bush, searching for a sturdy branch, anything Queen might get her hooves on. Nothing was firm enough.

She emerged from the spiny thistle and stinging nettles in sight of the vegetable garden, and cupped her hands around her mouth.

"Help! Help me!"

"Claire? Where are you?" Lawrence's voice broke through her frenzy.

"The pit! Queen's in the pit."

She waved until Lawrence saw her, then dashed back and crawled to the pit's edge, stretching her arms for Queen. Lawrence burst through the trees.

"Queen's sinking. She'll die!" Claire cried.

Lawrence met Claire's dark eyes with his clear green ones. "Find Papa and Reuben. I'll stay with Queen."

Claire raced from the pit, but at the sound of Lawrence's grunt, sprinted back. Now Lawrence, too, was in the sucking slime, struggling with Queen, covered in muck, and sinking.

"Lawrence! No!"

"Get my father!"

Claire gagged as she raced to the corn field where Mr. Raymond and Reuben were working.

"Lawrence is in the pit! Help! Hurry!"

As soon as Claire saw them coming, she dashed back. Reuben, running like a man on fire, passed her, and leapt over the pit barriers.

"Hold on, Lawrence, I'm here," he shouted.

"Help me, Reuben. I'm sinking."

Claire helped Reuben wrench a log from the barrier. He rolled it to the pit and shoved it toward Lawrence.

"Grab the log. Get it," Reuben shouted.

Lawrence, gagging, tried by failed to reach it. The goat flailed its head. Claire raced along the edge of the pit, whimpering, until Mr. Raymond, Samuel, and Duff crashed through the brush.

"Tie the rope around that tree, Samuel," Mr. Raymond ordered. He turned to Lawrence. "Are you with me, Son?"

"I'm sinking, Papa."

Samuel made a bowline knot to secure the rope to the tree, then made a sliding hitch loop on the other end. Duff pitched the rope to Lawrence. It fell short.

"Again, again," Lawrence cried.

Duff hauled in the rope and threw it. This time, it struck Lawrence's head, then dropped beside him on top of the slime. The boy grabbed the rope. Claire gasped when he jiggled the loop over Queen's head and front legs.

"Don't be a fool, Son. Save yourself," Mr. Raymond yelled.

"Bring her in," Lawrence shouted. "Bring her in."

Mr. Raymond and Reuben pulled the rope hand-over-hand. Samuel pulled from the tree. Duff and Claire knelt at the pit.

Up to his chest in muck, Lawrence shoved Queen's rump and took a hoof to the eye. As soon as the goat's hooves clawed the edge of the pit, Claire and Duff grabbed her legs and dragged her out. After Samuel worked the rope off Queen, Claire smacked her rump. The goat galloped back to the pasture.

Claire ripped the rope from Samuel's hands, and flung it to Lawrence. He caught it.

"Hold on, Son." Mr. Raymond's voice quivered.

After Lawrence got the rope under his arms, Samuel stepped behind Mr. Raymond, planted his feet, and wrapped the rope around his wrists. Reuben, Duff, and Claire lined up next. They heaved. Lawrence moved only a few inches.

The veins in Mr. Raymond's neck bulged like blue ropes. Sweat spilled down Samuel's face. Reuben grunted. Duff panted. Claire's hands bled. The stench made her gag. Lawrence strained to keep his face above the muck. The men heaved and heaved. Claire sobbed with exhaustion, fearful they'd never get him out.

Footsteps pounded the ground and Miss Anna burst through the brush.

"Lawrence!"

Her cry pierced the air like the screech of a bald eagle. She pushed in front of Claire and grabbed the rope.

"One, two, three, heave," Mr. Raymond yelled.

They pulled. The pit belched. Lawrence slid close to the edge. Raymond dropped the rope and dragged Lawrence out of the mire. Reuben picked up his brother and raced to the farmhouse, with Miss Anna and Mr. Raymond running after them. Claire stared wide-eyed.

"It's my fault. I called him to help with Queen."

"You push him in the pit?" Samuel asked.

"No, I never would."

"Lawrence knows better," Duff said. "It's not your fault."

"Come on, Duff, we wash off in the creek. They call us if they need us. You coming, Claire?" Samuel asked.

"I need to be with Lawrence," she said.

"Stay away, Claire. Let the family tend Lawrence."

After Samuel and Duff headed for the creek, Claire, trembling and miserable, stayed out of sight but crept close enough to watch.

Mr. Raymond held Lawrence's head while Reuben doused him with water. When Anna cleaned scum from his eyes, nose, and mouth, Lawrence gagged. Reuben flipped him on his side and pressed his stomach. Foul brown liquid gushed out. Reuben pressed his ear to his chest.

"He's breathing. I'll get my bag," Reuben said.

Anna stripped off Lawrence's clothes, and Raymond washed the terrible slime off his trunk, legs, and groin. Reuben returned, and held a wooden stethoscope against Lawrence's chest.

"His heartbeat's strong. Let's get him to bed. Bring a bucket."

By the time Molly found Claire weeping behind the quarters, the sun hung like a red ball in the western sky. The pit stench was pervasive. Molly took Claire's hand.

"Lawrence is resting. He finally kept down a cup of tea and rum. Mr. Raymond, Miss Anna, and Reuben take turns keeping watch. Lawrence asked to see you, but Miss Anna says it's no time for visitors."

"Will he live?" Claire's heart banged in her chest.

Molly's hazel eyes crinkled. "Miss Anna pounded the boy's back hard enough to ensure his lungs are clear.'

Claire got to her feet. "The goats need milking. I'm selling Queen to the butcher. She's been trouble since she was a kid drowning in the Wissahickon."

"Duff gave Queen a good washing, and milked the does. He put the herd in the paddock for the night. With the smell on you, your own mother would ban you from her house. Come, my heart, Samuel filled the wash basin with fresh water, and I borrowed a bar of lilac soap. Don't worry, the family's inside for the evening. I'll help you wash and change into clean clothes. Afterwards, I'll bring your supper to the quarters. Best you stay out of sight. Lawrence will be better tomorrow, and Miss Anna will be herself again."

Claire hoped Miss Anna would be herself again, but Claire would never be the same. She cried herself to sleep.

CHAPTER SIXTEEN

WISSAHICKON FARM OCTOBER 1822

Claire and Lawrence hobbled to the Wissahickon and sat on partly submerged rocks to let water run over their throbbing legs. The final harvest of pears, apples, pumpkins, and a bumper crop of squash required extra efforts. Now that the fruit and vegetables were boxed and ready for sale, Claire longed to visit home. Yet, despite Miss Anna's animosity since Lawrence went in the pit, she fretted about being away from the farm.

Here, on this land, even when Lawrence was at school, Claire felt his spirit with each breath. Sometimes, her love was so fierce it scared her. She felt like she'd been formed from the rough stones of the Wissahickon, and Lawrence was the mortar that held her together. Yet, his childish refusal to acknowledge the insurmountable obstacle of race infuriated her. How long could their love endure?

Lawrence leaned against her, and her arm tingled from his warmth. When her feet grew numb, she splashed out of the water and sat on the bank. Across the creek, a flash of gold behind a mountain laurel caught her eye – a warbler. The bird cocked its head to stare at Claire from yellow-ringed black eyes. Its slate-blue wings framed its bright chest. Its staccato chirps sounded like a Ring Shout —

By myself, I got to go, you got to run, I got to run, you got to run, oh my Lordy, well, well, well, my Lordy.

Claire bobbed her head to the beat of the silent song. Lawrence watched with a confused grin. He sloshed to her side and took her hand. The sun's rays spread across the western horizon in a ribbon of pink. With a long blade of grass, Claire stroked a turtle sitting on a rock and swished away a bug. Lawrence sat quietly, skipping stones. He pointed to a planet, visible in the waning daylight.

"Venus, the goddess of love."

Claire wondered if the planet shone so bright in Germantown. From down the creek an owl hooted. She inhaled the scent of wet dirt and leaves.

"Tomorrow I return to the university," he said.

"And the day after tomorrow, Samuel and I get to visit home. Duff will be left to care for the horses. Hamish's wound is healing, but he's in no shape for hard work."

"Don't talk about Duff."

Lawrence lay his head on Claire's lap. She ran her fingers through his hair. When did their friendship turn to love and desire?

Claire enjoyed working with Duff. He made her laugh. She liked Felix too, with his elegant manners and musical voice. But she didn't long to press her lips against theirs or feel their caresses. Late at night, she never imagined letting her hand linger below their waists until they arched with pleasure. It was Lawrence she dreamed of, Lawrence whose parents held her indenture, Lawrence whose skin was white.

As if he read her thoughts, he got to his feet, took her hands, and pulled her into his arms. He held her so close she felt his heart beat. He touched her cheek and lifted her chin. He kissed her eyes, nose, throat. When he pressed his mouth to hers, Claire's stomach tightened. He unbuttoned his shirt and dropped it to the ground. His bare flesh felt smooth and warm.

She glanced across the fields to make certain they were alone. When he kissed her again, her breath came faster, and she wanted to give in, to share this moment without worry or regret. But though Lawrence lived in her heart, Miss Anna lived in her mind. Love between the races was forbidden. Doomed.

"Stop." Claire broke away from his embrace. "We have no future. You'll find some wealthy white girl your parents approve of. I'll return to Germantown and live among my people. Wissahickon Farm is the only place in the world where we can be together, but even here, we have to hide our love."

Lawrence kissed her again, long and lingering, and she felt his urgency. "There is a future for us, and I will find it. We'll find it together."

Claire gazed at him, with his boyish convictions and earnest green eyes. Her heart ached for what could never be.

CHAPTER SEVENTEEN

GERMANTOWN OCTOBER 1822

At last home in her childhood bed, Claire closed her eyes and huddled under her quilt, breathing the sweet scent of lavender. A smoky tallow smell rose from the snuffed candle on her night stand. Mama's hand-me-down night dress, soft with wear, felt smooth against her skin. The sounds of quiet conversation drifted up the stairs – the words indistinguishable, but the soft cadence of her parents' voices fed her longing for the time when she could spend every day with her family. Yet, she couldn't imagine life without Wissahickon Farm, without Lawrence.

Sounds from outside – scuffling feet and harsh whispers – startled her. She sat bolt upright, heart racing. In the next room, Samuel's feet hit the floor and stomped down the stairs. Her parents' voices took on shrill but muted tones. The back door opened and shut.

Her heart thumped in wild beats. She scanned the room for a hiding place. Robbers? Slave catchers?

Soft, deliberate footsteps mounted the staircase. She shimmied under the quilt, trying to sink into the mattress, fearful that her soft bosom and widening hips made her a target for despicable men. The door opened. Candle light cast a flickering shadow on the wall. She held her breath as the floorboards creaked.

"Claire," a familiar voice whispered. "It's Felix."

Like a cat, she sprang from her bed and hugged him. With her head pressed to his chest, she listened to his heart and her fear beat away.

"Claire, there are visitors. Night visitors. There is great danger in helping them. Do you understand?"

This was the first time she was home when night visitors came. Helping slaves to freedom was the family business.

"I'm not afraid."

In darkness, Claire followed Felix down the steps to the hushed, busy kitchen. As her eyes adjusted, she saw Mama preparing food and Granny choosing clothing from a wicker basket. Mama nodded to the kitchen door. Claire and Felix stepped outside.

The moon and stars illuminated the backyard. Near the shed, she made out her father's figure. At Claire's approach, he coughed.

"It's me, Daddy."

"Don't creep up on me," Moses said. "We got visitors. They need our help."

Five people huddled in the shed, their smell like boiled vinegar and rotten eggs. In the moonlight, Claire saw three young men who seemed near Lawrence's age, sixteen, and a leader who might be twenty. Behind him a child squatted, boy or girl, she couldn't tell. But when the child's eyes met hers, Claire beheld a frightened little girl, dark as night, with big teeth and puffy eyes.

"I'll take care of the child," she said.

The girl, no more than eight, hung back until the man Claire took to be leader pushed her forward.

"You go on now. These peoples help us. Don't be scared."

Claire led the child to the wash basin outside the kitchen. She helped the girl undress and set her on a step. It was difficult to see, but she cleaned the child's skin with a washrag and rough soap. When she stooped to wash the girl's feet, the child yanked them back and whispered, "They's sore." Claire gently patted her feet, wrapped her in a towel, and carried her inside.

Elizabeth helped the anxious child into a blue-striped cotton dress and rolled up the sleeves so her hands poked through. Granny sat the girl on her lap while Elizabeth, with a few quick stitches, hemmed the dress to fit. The child's hair stuck out in irregular twists with bits of leaves and twigs still intertwined.

"What your name, Child?" Granny asked.

"They calls me Lammy. But afore they send my Mammy away, she say, 'Your name, Mary Baker. That the name I give you.' I ain't gone be Lammy Cleveland no more. My true name be Mary Baker."

The little girl raised her face and sucked her bottom lip. The sound of hushed voices drifted into the kitchen. Granny picked debris from Mary's hair and sighed.

"Mary, you're safe with us." Elizabeth kissed her forehead.

"Thank you, Ma'am. It be a powerful frightening journey."

Claire crept up the stairs and rummaged under her bed. Yellow wool socks Molly knit were stuffed inside her shoes. When Claire returned to the kitchen, Granny was tying her favorite bandana around Mary's hair. The child leaned against Granny while Claire worked the socks onto her little feet. At the buffet, Elizabeth placed crackers and bacon on a tray while Felix hovered nearby. When Elizabeth finished, Felix carried the tray outside.

On the front porch, Claire gazed at the sky. The moon was full. There was Venus. There was Mercury and the North Star. As Claire tiptoed around the house to the backyard, a dog barked. The runaways, washed and dressed in fresh clothes, squatted outside the shed, savoring every cracker crumb. Their slave clothes soaked in a barrel of water and lye soap. Claire doubted those clothes could be saved, but Mama and Granny were skilled seamstresses. They salvaged what they could to fabricate new dresses, shirts, and britches for the next visitors.

Claire studied the runaways. She tried to understand their courage and desperation with nothing more than a dream of freedom to urge them north despite the horror waiting if they were captured. She caught the eye of the leader and smiled. Felix appeared at her side.

"Our visitors arrived as Livy, Orion, Phoenix, Hercules, and Lammy. They will live in freedom as Louis, Oliver, Felix, Harry, and Mary."

"Good names, especially Felix," Claire said.

"We need a last name," Harry said.

"Newman," she said. "You're new men, no longer slaves."

"We Newman brothers now," Harry said. "What we do with baby Mary? Traveling be hard on her."

Without thought, Claire blurted, "We'll keep her."

"We'll keep her," Moses said. "Boys, you got to move on this night. Samuel and Felix carry you to the next stop."

Moses led the young men to the kitchen door, where Elizabeth gave them sacks with crackers, hard cheese, apples, flint stones, and knit socks. Mary Baker limped outside and ran to Harry, who knelt to embrace her.

"You safe here, Baby. You brave, never cry once. Your mammy be proud you free. You rest now. We moving on."

Mary clung to Harry. The others touched her cheek and told her good-bye. Finally, Harry carried her inside, kissed her hands, and left her in Granny's arms.

The runaways crammed into the delivery cart. After Moses covered them with blankets, Felix and Samuel drove out of the yard, headed for the docks and a ship to Canada.

Claire carried Mary to the settee in the front room. Elizabeth and Granny sat beside the little girl, whose cheeks glistened with tears.

"Mary, from now to forever, we are your kin. I'm your Aunt Elizabeth. You're my sister's child, come from Lancaster after your mama died to live with Uncle Moses, Granny, and me. Claire's your cousin. Understand?"

The child nodded and yawned.

"Mary best sleep by me tonight," Granny said.

∼

Claire reeled with exhaustion. In her bed, she ran her fingers across her brow, over her cheeks, and through her hair. Her hair was thick and black — Molly called it wooly. She thought about Molly's curly red hair, hazel eyes, and white skin. Both Molly and she entered Wissahickon Farm as indentured servants, but they were not the same.

When Molly came to the city, she didn't think about her white skin. She was a simply an unremarkable serving person going about her business. Claire always thought about being black. Wherever she went – the farm, home for a visit, in a church filled with black worshippers – Claire wasn't just Claire. She was an African, a Negro. Tonight, she helped her family guide Negro runaways to freedom, and felt proud. But sometimes, she thought, she'd like to be unremarkable.

As she fell asleep, Claire prayed the runaways would find safe-haven in Nova Scotia where they could live in freedom and be unremarkable.

∼

Two days later, Mary waited for Granny outside the privy, then followed her to the garden.

"Granny found herself a helper," Moses told Claire.

In the garden, Mary knelt next to Granny. They filled a flannel vegetable bag with fall beans and orange carrots. Chickens pecked for seed outside the coop. On her way to collect the eggs, Claire swung a wicker basket. Mary hurried towards her and put out her hand for the basket.

"Cookie like me get they eggs 'cause I ain't break 'em."

"Thank you, Mary."

"Mammy say work hard, don't make trouble, know your place." Mary stared at Claire from wide dark eyes.

"Claire might should listen to your mammy's advice," Moses said. "Let's see how many eggs you get without breaking any."

After Moses checked the cistern water level, he filled a pitcher for coffee. Claire splashed her face from the wash bucket.

"It's so sad. They sold Mary's mother, and she's no more than eight-years-old. Those boys were brave to bring her along when they ran to freedom. She must be confused and frightened. She's trying so hard to help."

Moses put his arm around Claire's shoulders as they walked to the kitchen. "You and Samuel are indentured, but we signed a contract, and you have rights. Nobody owns you. The Continental Congress signed the Declaration of Independence right here in Philadelphia." He cleared his throat and, to Claire's surprise, quoted the Declaration of Independence almost exactly —

> We hold these truths to be self-evident, that all men are created equal, endowed by the Creator with rights to Life, Liberty and the pursuit of Happiness.

"It don't say, all white men, it says, *all men*."

Moses and Claire stepped into the kitchen. Moses pried the lid off the tin coffee pot Mrs. Shipman gave Elizabeth years ago. Although it was dented here and there, it was lovely, with birds and flowers engraved on the body of the pot. He spooned ground coffee into the pot, poured in boiling water, and set it aside to steep. Felix insisted on this method after Moses served him boiled coffee.

"Do not boil the beans, or the coffee becomes bitter. Steeped coffee is a pleasure to drink," Felix said then.

While he and Elizabeth preferred tea, Felix suggested coffee as an antidote to Moses' sick headaches, and it helped. The good Lord knew he needed whatever relief he could get.

Claire wiped the table, then sat across from him. Steam rose from their cups. Moses sipped coffee and sighed. After Samuel and Felix drove the runaways to the docks, another crippling headache hit him like a brick. It seemed the older he got – and the more runaways who needed help — the more frequent the headaches. For days after a sick headache receded, he sensed the pain hiding, waiting until his guard was down to slam his head against a wall and make him vomit. He stirred molasses into his coffee and savored the taste.

"Where's Mama?" Claire asked.

"Dropping off Miss Drinker's laundry. When she gets home, she plans to make new clothes for Mary, and change up her looks."

"Mary looks fine the way she is." Claire set down her cup and raised her eyebrow. "Oh, you mean. . . "

Moses nodded. "Where your brother get to?"

Samuel was nowhere to be found, but the stable was mucked, clean sawdust covered the floor, and fresh hay filled the feeder. The boy's growing into a good man, Moses thought. In fourteen months he'd finish his indenture, and come home to find a job, maybe take on Moses' delivery business.

Whenever Samuel was home, he ran off with Felix. Young men had to have their rowdy times, Moses knew, and Felix always had money. The young Haitian opened his own barber shop some time ago. Each time Samuel came home, Felix got him slicked up with a fancy haircut and shave. Felix took good care of Moses too. And as soon as Felix learned about the family business, he jumped in to help.

It was Felix who told Moses to bring Claire into the business, especially since Samuel found it hard to disappear from the stables for hours at a time. Samuel said Claire's chores left her more free time to hike to Mystics cave and the runaways hiding there. His girl was stubborn and headstrong but hardworking, practical, and kind in her heart. But Moses feared for her and her crazy ideas. Even decent white folks didn't tolerate uppity Africans. He doubted Claire understood the difference between whites being friendly with blacks and being friends. He sighed and turned to his daughter.

"What you think about our visitors, Claire?"

"Mary said their journey was powerful frightening."

"They made their way north through creeks, and swamps, and forests, more than a hundred miles, running at night, hiding all day, praying they don't get caught."

"If I was a slave, I'd run so fast they'd never find me."

"I expect you would. You know we break the law when we hide runaways, give them food and clothes, and help them on their way?"

Claire nodded.

"Every time we help, we put our family in danger, but the runaways our people too, and we take care of our own."

"I took care of Mary, poor little girl."

"You surely did. The other night when the visitors came, Felix told me, Claire is ready to learn the business. But it's up to you. You ready?"

Claire jiggled. She snapped her fingers like she was singing at church. Oh, Lord, Moses thought, what's this gonna be?

"I'm ready."

Claire's shoulders moved to and fro. Moses envisioned her dancing with that determined look, eyes upraised and sweat pouring down her face, in a faraway place beyond his reach. He took her hands in his.

"This for real. It's dangerous and not for children."

"I'm not a child."

"Then you got to learn the special delivery business. We pick up packages. Men and boys be cotton. Women and girls be lace. Babies be buttons. When a shipment comes in, Granny and Mama wrap the packages with different clothes, because runaway notices tell the clothes the people be wearing and what they look like. Felix ties ribbons on the wrapping. He changes their hair — shaves it or braids it or smooths it with grease. Maybe he shave off one eyebrow or cut lines through to look like scars. He gives them hats – might be a sailor's cap, a top hat, a bonnet, a turban. Some packages get a change of address – men change to women and women to men. Remember – packages, wrapping, ribbons, change of address. Then we ship the packages. Some go to Canada, some to Boston, some to farms out west, some sail to England or France, and some be delivered to families in the city, like the small piece of lace we kept. The packages of cotton delivered the other night been sent to Nova Scotia."

"Packages, cotton, lace and buttons, ribbons and wrapping, change of address," Claire said. "I'm ready."

CHAPTER EIGHTEEN

GERMANTOWN OCTOBER 1822

At dawn the following day, Moses led Claire, Samuel, and Felix to Old Caesar's cabin. A barking fur missile launched at them as they skittered down the path. When Claire knelt to greet the muscular dog, Pretty Boy shook all over and licked her face.

"Who there, Pretty Boy?" Old Caesar called.

"It's Claire, come to visit."

Overhead, the sharp caws of crows drowned out the delicate chirping of lesser birds. Claire followed the scent of catfish and corn cakes to an outdoor grill where Caesar scraped a fork on a pan. He seemed smaller than last time she saw him. His eyes were cloudy, as if draped with spider webs. When he reached for Claire, she felt every bone in his delicate hands.

"My goodness, where my little child go? Who this young lady come visit me? What you think of that little pup? He gone same place that little girl go. Pretty Boy bigger than me now. I just do as he say, feed him what he want, and we get along fine. Sometime he bring me a rabbit to cook, and he share it with me, very mannerly."

"Pretty Boy's a herding dog, and you his herd," Moses called as he and the boys joined them.

Moses sat on a rock by the creek and rubbed Pretty Boy's ears. Samuel stowed a sack with tins of corn meal, coffee, tea, and sugar in Old Caesar's cabin.

"We bringing Claire into the business, Caesar. While the boys show Claire the way, I'm going to hook some catfish for supper."

"We all in this business, Child, from the moment we born," Caesar told Claire.

Samuel, Felix, and Claire walked eastward along the creek. The gurgling water smelled mossy as it spilled over little waterfalls and splashed the rock-laced bottom. Their feet left impressions on the bank's soft sandy soil. At the base of a hickory tree, a glint caught Claire's eye. She stopped to clear away dead leaves and debris. There, in a pocket of moss, she discovered twelve flat stones, each pointed on one end and notched on the other. She cradled the stones before spilling them into Samuel's hands.

Samuel held up each one – cold yet full of life. He shifted his pack, stuffed with lunch and a quilt Granny made, to his other shoulder.

"Indian arrowheads. Been hiding a long time."

In speckled light that filtered through the trees, Felix examined them. "Perhaps the Indian will return. We should leave them."

"Indians long gone – all but a few old chiefs and squaws who wander onto the farm looking for food," Samuel said. "But we should leave them."

As Claire returned the arrowheads to the earth and covered them with moss, she bore witness to the Indians who roamed the rocky land along the Wissahickon.

Samuel hopped onto a huge boulder that jutted over the creek, and gave Claire a hand to help her up. In the shade of uncountable pine trees, the granite felt cool. Dapples of sunlight danced across its surface. Felix lay stomach down and dangled his fingers toward the creek.

"Claire, drop your arm. You feel a crack?"

"It's craggy, but I don't feel a crack."

Felix moved her hand to a fissure a foot above the water. She leaned farther and inhaled the dank smell of wet leaves and mud.

"There it is!"

Samuel tugged off his boots, rolled up his trousers, and slipped into the creek. Claire and Felix did likewise. Bottom rocks jabbed her tough soles, and her legs ached from the frigid water. Despite the cold water and chilly air, Samuel splashed his arms and face like he was bathing.

"Come to the boulder, hop in, and act like you washing up." Samuel dipped down, with his fingers grazing the fissure for balance. "Check the crack for a note."

Claire stared at the crack and furrowed her brow. "I thought peddlers carried the news to Samuel — two or three stop at the farm every week."

"Only African peddlers bring news," Samuel said. "I check here my own self whenever Hamish let me go fishing."

"Runaways come when they come. They're frightened, hungry, and confused. We can't leave them alone too long, or they may put themselves and us in danger," Felix said.

On the bank, while they pulled on their shoes, Samuel said, "Make sure nobody see you. Don't leave a trace."

Felix led the way through the trees and shrubs. His words the night he freed Pretty Boy ran through Claire's mind — 'No fear.' Now she silently chanted them.

They clambered over exposed roots and trod on soft cushions of moss among the leaves, sticks, and stones of the forest floor until they reached a steep path.

"We follow this to Mystics Cave where the travelers hide and wait," Felix said.

As they moved single file up the narrow path, Claire asked, "Why is it called Mystics Cave?"

Samuel moved to her side and told the story Granny told him.

"Back in olden times, a German mystical man named Johann Kelpius brought his followers up the ridge to the cave to wait for the end time. But the end time never came, the mystic died, and they all moved on. Sometime after that, Billy Penn freed Jack Penniman, and he built our house in Germantown. He heard talk about Mystics Cave and searched the ridge until he find it. Jack liked to go to the cave to think. One day, he come across two runaways lost in the woods. He left them in the cave until dark, then bring them to the house. He kept them hid until he find a captain willing to give them passage to Canada. Been our family business ever since."

"It's a good story." Claire stopped and tilted her head. A different sound cut through the trickling water, chirping birds, and rustling leaves. "Men and machines."

"We are not far from Ridge Road," Felix said. "The noise of road work carries like echoes. No fear. There are only forests paths where we are going. . . At the barber shop, an old man told me of a battle in your War for Independence fought along the Wissahickon."

"Yes, indeed. Hamish told me he tended Old Nelson, George Washing-ton's horse, when the Continental Army come through Wissahickon Farm," Samuel said. "George Washington fought the Brits on Germantown Road. Mr. Chew's house — Cliveden — got bullet holes in the walls to show for it. Our daddy only a child, but remember the day a Redcoat stagger into the front yard all bloody. While Granny stitch up the man's head, Daddy drag away his musket so he can't shoot them dead. That man, Peter Johnson, tell Granny he never go to war again. He pay Granny silver coins for new britches and a shirt, and tell her to burn his red coat to ashes. In dark of night, the man walk away. Seven years later, Peter Johnson come to visit Granny. He give her a fine milk cow, and stay for tea."

A narrow spring trickled alongside the path. As they moved higher, broad-leaved ferns clutched their legs, then sprang back into place. Claire felt they entered an ancient world. Samuel moved off the path to a small clearing. Only after he pushed aside a curtain of ivy did Claire see the cave it covered.

The cave entrance was granite, fashioned like a doorway. Samuel rummaged through his pack for a candle and tinderbox. After he caught a spark on a piece of charred linen, he lit the candle and led them inside.

The cave smelled of earth, decay, and frightened men. The candle cast a shimmering glow across a dank room the size of a horse stall, about eight feet wide by ten feet long. A tall man would have to stoop inside. The floor was dirt and crushed rock.

"Packages arrive here. A year ago, Caesar's legs got too stiff to climb, and I took over storing packages," Felix said. "But one person can't do it alone. Samuel comes when he can get away, but we need your help, Claire. After runaways arrive in Germantown, I help your mother and Granny wrap packages from top to bottom. Your father organizes transportation to safe havens."

"We stash a blanket, candles, tinder box, a tin of crackers if we got it, in the corner for the next package," Samuel said.

Sparse sunlight filtered through the trees. Brush rustled nearby, and Claire cringed.

"A squirrel or chipmunk, not a bear," Felix said. "Samuel and I like to visit the lovely meadow on the ridge top when we're out this way. We can rest there and enjoy the meal your mother packed."

The rocky climb to the ridge top proved strenuous. Claire's breaths came heavy and her heart pounded. Samuel reached the top, lay on his stomach, and reached down to pull her up. Felix scrambled up behind her.

Trees surrounded the beautiful green meadow. A clear stream fed a slender waterfall that spilled into the Wissahickon. Felix was right. This was a lovely secret place.

"I need to piss," Samuel said, "then we eat."

Felix touched Claire's arm. "Will you be fine for a few moments if I, too, pass water?"

"Only if you promise there's no bears."

On the far side of the meadow, a tulip poplar grew along the stream. Claire glanced toward the trees where Samuel and Felix disappeared. Billowy clouds drifted across the sun. A cardinal fluttered off a branch with a shrill whistle and a flick of red, and flew across the meadow to an oak tree. A flock of wrens crossed the azure sky.

She lay on soft grass and shut her eyes. The sound of a horse grazing reverberated through the ground. For a moment, Claire thought she was back on the farm. Then heavy footsteps muffled the horse sounds. As she pushed herself up, her upper arm erupted in pain. She was yanked to her feet.

"Gotcha, Tar Baby!"

The coarse and raspy southern voice, vaguely familiar, terrified her. She wiggled to get free, but the tall lean man squeezed tighter. Grease coated his hands, clothes, and the bandana around his neck. Under a crusty mustache, his black teeth were bared like a mad dog's. His breath smelled like dead rats. Claire kicked his shin.

He punched the side of her head, threw her down, and straddled her, his knees pinning her arms, and his crotch in her face. Tobacco drool dripped from his mouth. He leaned forward so his forehead touched Claire's. She recognized him – the slave catcher who burned Pretty Boy. The man snickered.

"Looks like I found coffee for my cream."

He unlatched his belt and pulled out his rod. When he flopped it against Claire's chin, he leaned back. The pressure from his knees lightened.

Claire shoved him and flipped herself over. She clawed the ground to shimmy away. The man jumped on her back.

"I'll cream you anyway you like," he growled.

He dug his fingernails under the waist of her britches and tugged. She kicked backwards, her heels jamming the small of his back. He grunted, grabbed a fistful of her hair, forced her head to the side, and stuck his tongue in her mouth. She bit down, hard, and tasted blood and dirt. The man made a horrible gasping sound, and slapped her. She spit out the gristly chunk of tongue.

From across the meadow, Samuel's voice rang out, "Get off her or I kill you."

The man rolled to his feet and kicked Claire's ribs. He turned to watch Samuel approach, and snorted. Claire squirmed away like a snake, filling her hands with dirt and debris. She spit to purge the man's vile taste. She thought she'd moved beyond his reach, but he kicked her legs.

"You going nowhere, Nigger." His words sounded like his mouth was full of water.

She rolled to her back and tucked her knees to her chest. When the man swatted her legs, she flung both fistfuls of dirt in his face. He gave an angry, strangled cry, and wiped his eyes. Claire scooted backwards. Then, Samuel was there, swinging a thick branch. The man grunted and stumbled when the branch cracked his back.

"Run," Samuel yelled, "Run!"

Claire got to her feet. The slaver righted himself. He drew his pistol, cocked it, and aimed at Samuel.

Claire screamed, "Leave us alone!"

A black beast burst from the trees and raced towards them. Pretty Boy! The dog leapt. The man fired. Pretty Boy seemed suspended, then dropped, whimpering. Acrid smoke smell filled the air.

Claire rushed to Pretty Boy. Blood trickled from a shallow wound on his side. The dog got to his feet. The man reloaded, brandished the gun, and cocked the hammer. As he raised his arm to shoot Pretty Boy again, Samuel hurled a rock that struck the man's back with a dull thunk. With a ghastly smirk, the slaver turned to Samuel.

Claire dashed at the man. Hands locked, she chopped his arm until he dropped the gun. Samuel dove for it, but the man kicked him, and the gun skipped towards her. The man grabbed Samuel, who struggled to escape.

Pretty Boy snarled, charged, and sank his teeth in the slave catcher's leg, then yelped when the man landed a blow on his jaw.

Blood streaming from his nose, Samuel inched toward the ridge.

"Stop!" With both hands, Claire pointed the man's heavy pistol at him. Pretty Boy growled.

"Give me my gun, Nigger, or I'll see you hanged."

The slaver's brown horse galloped across the meadow with Felix in the saddle.

"You have no right to attack these people, *Monsieur*."

The man pulled a wood-handled knife from his boot and tapped the blade on his palm. Breathing heavily, he stared at Felix. Claire's arms ached from the gun's weight, but she held it steady.

"Luther Cleveland down Dorchester County hired me to bring back his runaway slaves." His words were garbled. Blood darkened his bearded chin. "This here's two of them. Girl and boy, right ages. Law says you got to help me get them back to their rightful owner."

"These are no runaways."

Sunlight glinted off Felix's yellow hair. He kept the horse beyond the man's reach. Claire, eyes on the slave catcher, joined Felix. Near the ridge, Samuel got to his feet.

"Me and my brother are free born. We work for Raymond Williams at Wissahickon Farm," Claire said.

"Pack up. Move on. You have no business here," Felix said.

"Your niggers need whipping." The man glared at Felix, and brushed himself off. Black blood caked the side of his mouth. "I know when I been licked. Give me my pistol, Tar Baby, then I'll go."

"You'll go without your gun." Felix said.

The man stepped toward Samuel. Pretty Boy growled, but stayed at Claire's side. Samuel moved aside to let the slave catcher pass, but the man spun and lunged, slashing Samuel's face. Blood spurted. Samuel dropped to his knees, pressing a hand to his cheek. Blood oozed between his fingers. The man raised the knife again.

"Leave that boy or I'll send your horse over the ridge to kingdom come, *Monsieur*," Felix yelled.

The horse pawed the ground and turned in a circle.

"Leave him or I'll shoot you dead," Claire shouted.

The man snorted. "No nigger girl know how to shoot. Give it here."

Pretty Boy growled from deep in his throat. As Lawrence taught her, Claire aimed the gun with both hands, locked her eyes on the target, cocked the hammer, and pulled the trigger. At the shot, the gun flew out of her hands, but the bullet caught the man's shoulder. He grunted and looked shocked, then angry.

"I'll kill you niggers," he slurred and lunged at Claire.

She turned to retrieve the gun. Before she reached it, the slaver caught the back of her shirt, swung her around, and slammed his fist in her ear. She stumbled and fell.

Felix slid out of the saddle. "Take the horse and go."

The man picked up his gun and raised a hand to pistol whip Claire.

Samuel charged. He rammed his foot into the slave catcher's knee. The man crumpled to the ground.

Pretty Boy snarled and attacked. Man and dog rolled toward the ridge, a blur of black and brown. The dog clamped his teeth on the man's throat, and blood sprayed like beet juice from a press. The slaver hammered the gun on Pretty Boy's head until the dog released him. Dark blood spurted from the slave catcher's neck. He glared at Samuel with red-rimmed eyes and aimed his gun.

Felix kicked the gun out of the slaver's hand, then kicked him to the edge of the ridge. The man's eyes widened and glazed. His throat gurgled. Pretty Boy barked. The slaver's legs jerked. His back arched the instant before he slid off the edge and disappeared.

Thumps and breaking branches sounded like a boulder rolling down the rocky slope. Claire, Samuel, and Felix stared down on the rocks and trees. Pretty Boy panted.

"There's broken branches, but I can't see the man." Samuel sounded like a drunk. Teeth showed through his cheek.

"He's covered by brush." Claire shuddered. Every part of her ached. She heaved at the taste of the man's foul tongue.

"Do we see if he's alive?" Felix's face was flushed and his eyes were wild.

"He's dead," Claire said.

"We must remove all trace of him. What will we do with the horse?" Felix asked.

"Daddy can use it in the business," Claire said.

"No." Samuel's face was ashen. "Tie his things to the saddle, and let the horse go."

Claire's face and hands were battered and bruised, and blood trickled from her nose. A lump the size of a goose egg bulged from her forehead, and one eye was swollen shut. Her ear throbbed. Her ribs ached. But she was whole, and she was free.

Samuel attempted a few steps, and collapsed.

"Easy," Felix said, his voice soft.

He and Claire put Samuel's arms over their shoulders and dragged him to the tulip poplar by the spring. While Claire washed her face and hands, Felix poured water over her brother's wounds. Samuel's face was swollen. Each time he tried to speak, blood oozed through the slash in his cheek. Felix removed his shirt and tore the fabric into strips. Then, as gently as if Samuel were an injured child, Felix wrapped his face.

While Pretty Boy lapped water from the spring, Claire rinsed blood off his fur. She felt furious and frightened, proud and worried. What would they tell Mama?

~

On the walk to Old Caesar's cabin, Claire's ear throbbed with pain. She longed for the safety of Wissahickon Farm. Her heart beat so loud, she was sure Felix and Samuel could hear it.

When she returned to Wissahickon Farm, everything would be fine. She'd brush the horses, milk the goats, and be so good Miss Anna wouldn't ever be angry. The man's filthy face, his smell of decay, and the taste of his tongue – like pickled okra – made her retch. Even his voice was vile. 'I been hired by Luther Cleveland to find his runaways.' Cleveland. Lammy Cleveland. He was after the child and the boys she came with. She wondered whether other slave catchers were searching for them. Claire was glad the man was dead. She wiped her mouth.

"That man thought I was Lammy! How can we keep that child safe?"

"There is no Lammy. There is only Mary Baker, your cousin come from Lancaster after her mother died," Felix said.

"Poor orphan girl," Samuel whispered.

Claire ran her hands over Pretty Boy's trunk, and the dog licked her neck. "Pretty Boy's not bleeding much. The bullet must have grazed him. Caesar's going to be mighty upset his dog got shot."

Overhead, birds chirped. Twigs snapped under foot. Claire stumbled and fell. She opened her eyes to Samuel's swollen face and Felix's almost-white one.

"I'm scared a slaver will take me away," she said.

Felix pulled her to her feet and showed her the slave catcher's gun in his belt.

"No fear. We are in this business whether we choose the business or the business chooses us. That slave catcher will take no one away ever again."

~

A rapping hammer alerted them to the proximity of Old Caesar's cabin. They shared glances as they approached. Moses knelt on the roof with nails in his mouth and a hammer in his hand, replacing shingles. On the ground, Old Caesar pointed to where the roof leaked.

"What took so long?" Moses swung his legs over the side and dropped to the ground.

"Business," Samuel said, voice husky.

"Business," Felix said.

"Business," Claire said.

When Moses came close, his eyes widened. He touched Samuel's face. "Son, you hurt. Claire, you too? Felix?"

"I have no injuries. Samuel fought the slaver to save Claire, and she fought to save him. I merely distracted the man."

"Slave catcher?" Moses looked sick. "You have a run-in with a slave catcher?"

Pretty Boy limped to Old Caesar and whined.

"Pretty Boy fought, too," Claire said. "It was the same slaver who came after Caesar. Daddy, the man was hunting Mary and the boys. He shot Pretty Boy, and I shot him. He tried to hurt me, but Samuel fought him off. He cut Samuel's face, and Pretty Boy bit him. Then, Felix sent him over the ridge."

"He's dead, Moses, of this I'm certain," Felix said. "We tied his pack to his horse and set it free. Then we brushed the ground to cover the blood and hide our tracks. No one will know a fight took place there. No one will find his body under brush in the ravine."

Moses trembled as he inspected Samuel's face and Claire's bruises.

"What your mother say, she sees her children broke and bloody? This is bad business."

"This business too dangerous for a young girl," Old Caesar said. He took Claire's hand.

"Caesar's right," Moses said.

Pretty Boy put his snout in Claire's lap. She stroked the dog, her hands curled like an old woman's.

"I'm in the business, Daddy," she said. "But that slave catcher lost his job."

Felix ran to the alley for a cart to carry Samuel home. Soon, Elizabeth dashed down the path with her skirt in her hands. Tears spilled from her eyes as she examined Claire's wounds, then Samuel's. He flinched when she touched his cheek.

"We shouldn't never left Claire on her own, not for a minute," he said.

"Samuel, you saved me."

"Oh Samuel, my brave boy." Elizabeth looked from Samuel to Felix to

Claire and Moses. "Nothing like this happened before. What will we do, Moses?"

"We do what we we have to do, Elizabeth. Next time we do it better. We watch our steps. We check our tracks. No one goes up that meadow again."

Felix stared at the ground, then took Samuel's arm, and helped him into the cart.

"When will it end?" Elizabeth asked.

CHAPTER NINETEEN

WISSAHICKON FARM NOVEMBER 1823

C laire feared she was being followed. She crossed the sheep pasture, climbed the fence, and ran to the bank of the Wissahickon Creek. With each step, a heavy sack slapped her back. She shifted the sack, looked over her shoulder, then sprinted past the farm's border to the old Indian path into the woods and rocky ridges.

The closer Claire got to the huge boulder over the creek, the more she worried. Last week, three men on horses questioned Miss Anna about a runaway slave family. When the slavers spied Claire walking from the stables, a thickset man on a dun horse raised his rifle and shouted, "There's one of them."

"The girl is no more runaway than I am," she heard Miss Anna say. "Be on your way, and do not so much as glance at the workers on this farm, or by my immortal soul, I will shoot the lot of you."

Claire had hurried back to the stables and hid in a stall until Hamish assured her Mr. Raymond and Miss Anna drove the slavers away from Wissahickon Farm.

Even now she trembled, convinced those men were partners of the dead slaver. She imagined they found his horse, and then his body. Somehow, they learned the man died at her hands, Samuel's, and Felix's. They were coming for her, to drag her south and sell her to the highest bidder.

The slaver's face, blood spurting from his throat, leered at Claire in her dreams. All year, in the middle of the night she woke screaming, the taste of his tongue in her mouth. The scars on her knuckles reminded her of the scars on her soul. But she, Samuel, and Felix pledged, no fear. She wouldn't give in to it now. This was her family's business.

Overhead, birds and squirrels rustled the leaves. From the distance came the rumble of road men – sledgehammers on rocks, axes splintering trees, and the sharp cry, *Look ho*. Philadelphia grew like the trumpet-creeper vine they cut back all summer before it choked off the berry bushes that gave them fruit for jelly.

Supper table talk was of steam engines replacing horses to pull wagons over roads laid with iron rails — the land version of Robert Fulton's noisy and smoky steamboats that traveled the Delaware River.

Fragrant pine mingled with a sodden mossy scent around the huge boulder. Claire's heart raced like Star of Night's after a hard run. She pulled herself onto the cool, smooth granite surface, slid off the sack, and let her breathing slow. Sunlight dappled her face. She shut her eyes and drifted to sleep, but woke with a start at a blue jay's *aack, aack, aack*. She couldn't delay, couldn't miss afternoon chores.

Like Samuel showed her, Claire slid into the creek. She cupped a hand to drink, tasting rock, decaying leaves, catfish, and pine. An edge of paper poked from the crevice. She looked left and right, up and across, then yelped, splashed, and flailed. Her hand brushed the crevice and secured the note.

She stumbled up the bank, shivering, took a deep breath, and jogged to the path to the ridge, still worried she'd been followed. After the run-in with the slave catcher last year, Elizabeth said she didn't want Claire involved with this part of the business. But yesterday, when the Negro peddler drove his cart to the farm, he whistled the tune that meant check on a delivery.

As I was a traveling the North Country, a pretty little buy-a-broom I did see. She was right, I was tight, everyone has their way. . .

Samuel had accompanied Mr. Raymond on a trip to Lancaster to buy a horse. This was her business.

Claire scanned the woods before she read the tiny note — *cotton, lace, button* — then she swallowed it. Nearby rustling startled her. She held her breath until she spotted a red doe chewing the mitten-shaped leaves of a sassafras tree, giving off a lemony scent. Claire clapped and the deer dashed away. She put sassafras leaves in her sack. Went out to get some sassafras, she'd tell Miss Anna if she asked. She must get to the cave and get back to the farm.

Ferns swayed along the path to Mystics Cave. Tall pines blocked the sun. A ghostly butternut tree gave her pause. She thought again of the meadow. She felt the slave catcher's weight on her body, saw his leering bloody face, and his look of hatred before he tumbled over the ridge. Even after all these months, she expected him to rise up and grab her.

Her stomach rumbled. In her haste to do this job before anyone missed her, she'd toyed with her food at the midday meal. Hickory nuts spattered the ground. Claire chose a firm, green ball the size of her fist and peeled off the husk. She set the shell on a rock and pounded it with a stone until it cracked open. Despite its bitter taste, she swallowed the nutmeat.

The cave was hard to find, but Claire remembered the landmarks Samuel and Felix showed her – a gouge in craggy granite, a notch in an oak tree's trunk, glinting mica marking a trail only trained eyes could follow.

Once she hiked up to the clearing outside the cave, she picked up three small stones, and hurled them at the entrance. She waited a moment than sang the safe song —

Oh, what is longer than the way?
Oh, what is deeper than the sea?
Oh, what is louder than the horn?
Oh, what is sharper than a thorn?

She heard a rustle and a woman's voice.

Oh, love is longer than the way,
and hell is deeper than the sea,
thunder's louder than the horn,
and hunger's sharper than a thorn.

Claire pushed aside the ivy curtain and entered the damp cave. Sunlight streaming through the trees cast streaks of light on the floor. Her eyes took a moment to adjust.

A few feet inside, a man sat with his back pressed against well-hewn rocks. His dark face glistened like it was polished with bear grease. His eyes glared red and dangerous. He held a thick branch across his lap. The woman crouched at his side, her arms around a baby tied to her chest with a shawl the color of mud. The cave was cool even on the hottest summer day. Now, November, it was cold and dank.

"I brought food and supplies. Tonight or tomorrow night, someone will come to lead you to a safe house where you can rest in peace."

The woman stared while Claire unloaded the sack. She gave the woman a jar of fresh goat milk for the baby. Then, she unfolded a horse blanket, and set biscuits, goat cheese, dried venison strips, dried plums, and apples on it. She dug deeper for a candle stub, a flint starter, and a chunk of soap from her personal store.

"Wait until the sun goes down to get water from the spring. Don't go down the path. Stay here. Hold fast. Someone will come." Claire turned to go.

"Wait," the man's deep voice rumbled. "I hear men. Slave catchers?"

"Road men. You can't trust them." Claire hesitated then continued. "Slave catchers travel on nearby roads, but they don't know about this cave. Stay inside and stay quiet."

"You talk white. All colored talk white up north?"

"Some do. Some don't. I work on a white farm, where I learned to read and write, and talk white."

Without a word, the woman handed the baby to Claire and knelt to organize the food. Claire cradled the infant.

"What's his name?"

"We calls him Bo," the woman said. "What they calls you?"

"My name is Claire Penniman. My family's been helping black folks to freedom for a hundred years."

The man looked at her solemnly. "My slave name Moody, but I never be a slave no more. This cave swallow us like the whale swallow Jonah. And here I stand tall and free like the chestnut trees in this forest. My free name be Jonah Chestnut."

The woman spoke then. "My slave name Tiny. When Moody – Jonah – tell me he running, I think 'bout Ruth in the bible and I say, *Do not tell me to leave you or turn back from following you. Wherever you go, I go.* Ruth be my free name. Now we need a freedom name for little Bo."

Claire looked at the red-brown woman, hair dusty and tangled, then gazed at the baby, a child who, she prayed, would live forever in freedom.

"James Forten is the richest Negro in Philadelphia. He's a fine man who helps his people. You should name Bo, James Forten Chestnut."

"You free, James," Ruth told the child.

"Jonah, Ruth, and James Chestnut," Jonah said. "Free."

CHAPTER TWENTY

Claire, exhilarated, left the Chestnut family and clambered down the ridge, eager to get back to the farm. She fully understood her father's insistence that they help their own. She'd always sympathized with the exhausted runaway slaves who straggled into Philadelphia half-dead, but now she realized that Jonah, Ruth, and James weren't just poor runaway slaves, they were family.

Star of Night was black and the best horse on the farm, winning more races than the dapple-grey, Hercules, or the chestnut gelding, Mercury. Her goats ranged in color from white to sable, some piebald and mottled, yet color didn't influence milk yield. Molly, with pale skin and red hair, was a fine cook and excellent seamstress, but less skilled than Claire's mother, Elizabeth, dark of skin and coarse of hair. Wasn't Samuel a better man with the horses than Lawrence, son to the farm?

Her father's great-great grandfather, Jack, freed from slavery by William Penn, built his family a house finer than many white folks lived in. Jonah and Ruth traveled with an infant through treacherous country to raise their child in freedom. They were a family, no different from her own, or from the Williams. Claire read, wrote, and ciphered as well as anyone on the farm — except Mr. Raymond and Miss Anna. Why did slave catchers presume she was a runaway? Why did anyone assume anything about her? Claire's exhilaration turned to anger. Why shouldn't she own land as expansive and rich as Wissahickon Farm? She would someday. She would live as she pleased — but she needed a gun for protection, and to get one, she needed . . . Lawrence.

Claire leapt off a ledge six feet above the path and ran toward the farm, thoughts filled with the business and the end of her indenture next summer.

"Who's chasing you?"

Claire gasped and tripped. She recognized the voice.

"Lawrence! You followed me?"

Her voice was high-pitched and tight. Every muscle tensed. Did he see her go into the cave? Would he report the Chestnut family to slave catchers?

"I didn't follow you, I came looking for you. I supposed you took a walk along the Wissahickon, and here you are."

"Why? Did you think I ran away? I came to get sassafras leaves for Molly. I haven't been gone long. I'm on my way back to milk the goats and do my chores."

She hated her shaking hands, and she hated Lawrence for following her. Cicadas' buzzing filled the air. Claire felt they burrowed into her brain.

Lawrence approached. He tripped on a root. Something glinted. He righted himself and pointed his pistol at her. Claire braced herself. This is how I die, she thought. Lawrence found the slave catcher's body. He knows what we did. No matter our kisses, he's white and I'm black. Now he would kill her.

"I'm going back to the university tomorrow. I came looking for you so we could be together. Do you have time to practice shooting before your chores?"

Lawrence's translucent green eyes stunned her in their innocence. His voice was sweet and hopeful. Why did she think he'd hurt her?

He offered her the gun's grip. Claire marveled that as soon as she wished for a gun, Lawrence appeared with his.

"I should get back," she said, but ran her fingers over the cold steel barrel.

Opportunities for Claire to practice were rare. Miss Anna would never think it appropriate for a Negro to wield a firearm. Lawrence handed her the powder flask, the push rod, and a lead ball. She loaded the gun as he taught her, and inhaled the sulfurous smell.

Lawrence gathered six hickory nuts and set them on the trunk of a fallen tree. "Try to hit these."

She cocked the pistol and pulled the trigger. A skittering whine followed the blast, and a green hickory nut shattered. Her heart leapt. She felt powerful. She reloaded, shot again, and another hickory nut burst into pieces.

Lawrence's face glowed. "You're as good a shot as I am. I'm ready for a bigger handgun. In fact, Mr. Deringer has a new model I plan to buy while I'm in the city."

"Oh?" Claire returned the hot pistol.

"I thought you might want this one," Lawrence said. "If you keep it secret."

The buzzing cicadas returned to her brain. She wondered if the family in the cave heard the gunfire, if it frightened them.

"You would give a gun to a Negro?"

"I'm not giving a gun to a Negro. I'm giving it to you."

Lawrence moved closer. His clothes smelled like grass. He pressed his hands against her cheeks. She leaned into him, ran her tongue over his lips. Lawrence wasn't like other whites. He never talked down to her. He helped with her work and defended her to his mother. He risked his life to save her goat. He brought her a book when he came home from the university — *Poems on Various Subjects, Religious and Moral*, by Phillis Wheatley, an African woman, once enslaved and later emancipated by her owners. Claire had memorized her favorite poem.

> *O Thou bright jewel in my aim I strive*
> *To comprehend thee. Thine own words declare*
> *Wisdom is higher than a fool can reach.*
> *I cease to wonder, and no more attempt*
> *Thine height t' explore, or fathom thy profound.*
> *But, O my soul, sink not into despair,*
> *Virtue is near thee, and with gentle hand*
> *Would now embrace thee, hovers o'er thine head.*
> *Fain would the heaven-born soul with her converse,*
> *Then seek, then court her for her promised bliss.*

Claire allowed Lawrence's gentle hand to guide her to a bed of pine needles, and embrace her. He slipped off her blouse, ran his tongue from her stomach to her breasts, and kissed each one. She held herself still. They never went this far before. She wanted him to linger, wanted him to stop. Did he think he could have his way with her because she was black and a servant on his farm?

As if he could read her thoughts, he whispered, "I think about you all the time. I dream about you. Do you dream about me?"

Claire's dreams of Lawrence were of Wissahickon Farm. She felt his desire against her thigh. If only, she thought. But when he tugged her britches, she pushed him away. The memory of the slave catcher, the weight of his body, the scrape of his fingers against her skin flooded her mind. Passion turned to fear. She squirmed out from under him. Her face and neck burned. Her lips stung.

Lawrence, panting, rolled onto his back. He took her hands and moved them to his groin. She felt awkward with Lawrence so exposed. She loved kisses stolen behind the stables when the sun was a red streak on the horizon, but this? She moved her fingers to his belly and traced circles until he rolled away. He sat up and adjusted his clothing. His wide green eyes glistened. Goosebumps rose on his arms in the cool November air.

"I thought you loved me."

"I'm afraid to love you, Lawrence. I dream of us being together forever, living on the farm, and having a family. But in truth, that dream's a nightmare. Next year, I'll complete my indenture and return to Germantown to work with my mother sewing clothing for the likes of you. You'll become a doctor or a solicitor, meet a daughter of Philadelphia society, and forget you once loved an African servant."

Lawrence took her face in his hands and kissed her. "I dream only about you, about this, every night. I never dream of other girls. We will be together. I can't live if we're not."

While Lawrence picked twigs and brush from her hair, Claire brushed off pine needles and leaves.

"I must get back. Wait a bit before you follow," she said.

The sun flared red, a giant ball sinking in the western sky. Sheep lolled on the hill and the sound of working men drifted from the fields. Claire removed all expression from her face, threw her sack over the farm fence, and climbed over. Smells of animals, fresh cut grain, and the muddy creek mingled with the memory of crushed pine needles and Lawrence's musk.

Someday, I'll own horses, cows, sheep, goats, and my own land. Claire felt the small pistol tucked in her waistband and knew Lawrence would give her whatever she wanted.

CHAPTER TWENTY-ONE

Much of December had been unseasonably warm, but now, as Christmas approached, a strong northeast wind brought frigid weather and snow. In her bed in the quarters, Claire, roused by Duff's excited voice, sat up. She stepped onto the stoop, and inhaled the cold air.

At the farmhouse's kitchen door, Duff stamped snow off his boots and shouted, "Star is foaling, Mr. Raymond. She's having trouble."

"What's wrong?" Claire called.

Duff blew onto his fisted hands. "Samuel says Star of Night's too tight to birth."

As he stepped outside, Mr. Raymond swung on his jacket.

"I expected the birth tonight, what with the waxing of her teats. Trouble, you said, Duff?"

Claire pulled on wool pants, a calico shirt, a green bandanna, Lawrence's old work boots, and slid her arms into a corduroy jacket. She followed Duff and Mr. Raymond to the stables. Lawrence joined them. They crunched over icy ground.

On the slick surface of the stone bridge, Claire's feet slid from under her. Lawrence took her hand to help her up, and they continued hand-in-hand through lightly falling snow until the whitewashed stable loomed like a ghostly abode. Neither spoke.

Inside the stable, Mr. Raymond joined Hamish. Horses snorted and banged stall walls. The acrid smell of piss told Claire the horses were nervous. In the birthing stall, Star of Night whinnied and dropped to the ground, eyes wide with distress. Samuel whispered to her. Sweat trickled down his broad face. Duff crouched in the corner, eyes fixed on Samuel.

Shoulders touching, Claire and Lawrence watched from behind the wall. Each time the mare grunted, Claire's stomach tightened and tears welled in her eyes. She glanced at Lawrence and remembered the night he spoke his first words, then led her to the stables to watch Star's birth. Now Star of Night's time had come. The mare made desperate noises each time she strained, and Claire choked with fear. Please God, let Star have her baby.

"There now, Star, you be fine." Samuel's voice was so soft it surprised Claire. "You know Samuel here to help you."

"She started the groaning and up and down two hours ago," Duff said.

"I don't like the look of her," Mr. Raymond said.

"She's in Samuel's good hands," Hamish said.

Star lay on the straw, panting. Samuel wrapped her tail with a cloth, and it flopped miserably. Finally, the mare strained and a white sheath protruded, then ruptured. The foal's forelimbs presented.

"That good. We got the legs, now push out the head. Your baby coming," Samuel said.

Star's every sound resonated in Claire's chest. Duff's expression was stoic if squeamish as he watched Samuel work. Lawrence took her hand, and her muscles relaxed. Then, with a great heave and grunt, a baby horse slipped out, sprawled in straw that stuck to its coat.

"A filly," Samuel said.

The filly was dark and wet. Wide-eyed, Samuel stared at Hamish and Mr. Raymond. The newborn didn't move. Star of Night rolled to her feet, chest rising and falling. She nudged the filly, licked it.

"Ain't breathing," Samuel called.

The way the filly lay — head flat and forelegs splayed — reminded Claire of a boy she'd seen fishing along the Wissahickon with his father. The child fell into the creek and hit his head on a rock. When his father pulled him out, the boy's mouth and nose looked like the filly's, clogged with mud and blood. His head wobbled in his father's arms. The father wiped away the muck, then turned the boy on his side and pressed his stomach until creek water gushed from his mouth. When the boy still didn't breathe, Claire watched with awe as the father put his mouth on the boy's lips and blew. Finally, the boy coughed and sputtered, and breathed on his own.

Claire pushed past Lawrence, took off her bandana and wiped away the gunk on the foal's mouth and nostrils. She covered one nostril with her hand, then blew into the other. Air escaped with a hush. She blew again, waited, blew again, harder. The baby horse sneezed, splattering Claire's face and arms. She and Samuel locked eyes.

Star of Night nudged Claire to move away, then sniffed and blew on the foal. As Samuel and she left the stall, Mr. Raymond, Hamish, and Duff stared with shock, but Lawrence gazed at her with respect, pride, and something else — love.

"Missy, well done, well done indeed," Mr. Raymond said. "Reuben spoke of the inspiration of drowning victims, but never, my girl, could I have imagined inspiration from a human to an animal. I would not believe it possible if I hadn't observed it."

Still jittery, Claire wiped her face and mouth with her sleeve. Mr. Raymond gave her his handkerchief.

"I intend to name this filly, Inspiration, and I'll note on the delivery record, *Saved at birth through the inspiration of Claire Penniman, December 20, 1823*. . . Lawrence, make sure Claire returns safely to the quarters. No need to report for work before noon tomorrow, Missy."

On the stone bridge, Claire and Lawrence watched a thin band of gold spread over the eastern fields. The rising sun struggled to illuminate the wintry sky. She filled her lungs with Lawrence's essence. Below them, the waters of the Wissahickon flowed dark and relentless, like the blood that ran through their veins. They crossed the bridge, headed away from the farmhouse and quarters. Instead, they walked among the orchard's dormant trees, all but forgotten in the cold, fruitless months.

It was Claire who led them to the far end of the orchard, pulled Lawrence close, and pressed her lips to his. In the chilly dawn, she felt powerful and reckless, as impulsive as when she breathed life into the baby horse. She wanted recognition, she wanted life, she wanted Lawrence. No longer would she deny her longing or her love. When their bodies joined, she clung to him and dreamed of liberty, power, and land along the Wissahickon Creek.

Neither spoke. Lawrence stayed behind when Claire trudged across the field and slipped into her room. Inside, she drew a breath, held it, expelled it. Such a simple act – inspiration – yet the difference between life and death.

How would she breathe when she no longer shared Wissahickon Farm's life-giving air with Lawrence?

CHAPTER TWENTY-TWO

WISSAHICKON FARM JANUARY 1824

S amuel strode across the bridge, in fog so thick he couldn't discern the farmhouse or barns. He held out his arms, and his hands vanished in the mist. A verse that touched him last time he attended Mother Bethel Church in Germantown ran through his mind.

Ye know not what shall be on the morrow. For what is your life? It is even a mist, that appears for a little time and then vanishes.

Samuel knew not what his tomorrow, or day after, or many days after would be, but his life on Wissahickon Farm was vanishing in the mist. Yesterday, he completed the term of his indenture. Today, he would leave the farm for life as a twenty-one-year-old black man in Philadelphia.

Outside the kitchen, Mr. Raymond, Miss Anna, Claire, Molly, and Hamish waited, looming ghostlike in the January fog. Since his injury more than two years ago, Hamish never fully resumed his duties, and Samuel worried his leaving would set the old man back. Yet, Duff proved to have a strong back and a way with the horses. Thank goodness for that, because Claire's indenture would end in August. Mr. Raymond had asked Samuel to return to Wissahickon Farm for paid work from time-to-time, and he'd agreed.

"There's the lad." Hamish hobbled to Samuel's side. "After dinner you'll be on your way to Germantown with a full stomach. Molly made a hotchpotch with the lamb what broke its leg."

Samuel averted his eyes from Hamish's tears. Instead, he took Hamish's arm. Together they climbed the stairs and stepped inside.

The dinner table was set with the good blue-and-white chinaware plates. After Mr. Raymond lit the oil lamps, Miss Anna dropped chunks of rye bread into bowls of steaming stew.

Samuel lowered his eyes and joined his hands while Mr. Raymond prayed.

> *Ye shall serve the Lord, your God, and he shall bless thy bread and water;*
> *and I will take sickness away from the midst of thee.*

"I pray for the day the sickness in my leg is taken away, what with the loss of Samuel," Hamish said.

Samuel scooped savory chunks of lamb into his mouth, and wiped his mouth with his sleeve.

"Your mother will wonder what sort of manners you learned with us, Samuel," Miss Anna said. "I have something to help preserve your sleeves when you return to Germantown."

She reached into the sewing bag at her feet, and presented two white cotton handkerchiefs embroidered with the initials *S P* to Samuel.

"Thank you, Miss Anna. I never have my initials on anything afore."

Molly and Claire cleared the dinner plates. Mr. Raymond tapped his pipe. Hamish folded his napkin, placed it on the table, and sat back.

"I remember well the day Mr. Raymond returned from Germantown with a wee black laddie tucked in a corner of the wagon, whose big brown eyes peered from under a patchwork quilt covered with stars," Hamish said, "and delivered the same to me."

"It's well you've done with him, Hamish," Mr. Raymond said. "Samuel's grown into a fine hardworking young man, impossible to replace."

The tea cup rattled when Hamish set it down. For a month after the accident, Hamish stayed in Molly's room. Later, when he could walk with a cane, he moved to the servants' quarters, and slept there still. Each day he rode a cart to the stables to oversee Samuel and Duff's work. Although the injury aged Hamish, under Molly's care his appearance improved. Now freshly shaven, his wiry hair cut short and pomaded, his clothing patched and pressed, Hamish looked go-to-town tidy. He'd added half a stone to his scraggy frame. This morning he'd announced he was returning to his cottage behind the stables. There, Samuel felt certain, Hamish would revert to his former habits.

"Samuel," Hamish said, "you came to me in 1809 during a time of sadness. Three months before you arrived, Maude, my dear second wife, died along with the baby she carried. You, of course, knew nothing of those losses. You followed me like a little soldier and gave me no time to mourn. After a few months, just a lad of six years, you mucked the stalls, curried the horses, and led them to pasture. The horses came to know and love you, and soon enough, so did I. I'll miss you sorely, Lad." He raised his tea cup.

With eyes downcast, Samuel brushed table crumbs into his palm and cleared his throat. "The road to Germantown ain't so long I won't be back. What I know about horses, I learn from you, Hamish."

"The road to Germantown is not so long," Miss Anna corrected.

"No, it ain't," Claire said and grinned.

Mr. Raymond leaned forward, pipe clasped between his teeth. "I don't know that it was Miss Anna's intention to fill our bowls with reminiscence, Samuel, but since Hamish has offered his memories, I will contribute my fondest recollection. Like Hamish's, mine is filled with joy, although tinged with sorrow at your leaving." He sighed. "You'd been with us only six months when we traveled to the City Tavern with a delivery. It was your first trip off the farm for business. We took you along as a companion to Lawrence and, Lord knows, it was a blessed decision."

Samuel smiled. "I remember."

Miss Anna pursed her lips. "Though for months, not one of you had the courage to tell me the whole story."

"What happened?" Claire asked.

"Lawrence got lost," Samuel said, and accepted a piece of cherry pie from Molly.

"After we made the delivery and enjoyed a meal, we headed to the wharf to join the crowd gathered to welcome the arrival of *The Phoenix* from New York City, the first steamboat to travel the ocean," Mr. Raymond said. "When boys on a fish stall roof shouted, 'Here she comes!' I took Lawrence by the hand and moved closer so he could see. Samuel stayed at the wagon with Hamish. But the crowd surged forward, and Lawrence's hand slipped from mine. I reached for him, but he was gone."

Hamish cleared his throat. "As for me, I was strapping feed bags on the horses and keeping them calm when Samuel leapt from the wagon and took off running. I thought the lad caught a glimpse of the ship and wanted a better look."

"I never felt such a fright as when I lost my mute little son." Mr. Raymond shook his head. "The crowd was good-natured, but I feared Lawrence would fall off the dock and drown. But you found him, Samuel."

"I see you searching, and shouting. Afore I jump off the wagon, I spy a tiny white head bobbing in-and-out of peoples, and I ran for him."

"How did you get to him?" Miss Anna asked.

"Nobody pay me mind when I squeeze through their legs. Lawrence hair shine like a candle in a cave. I get close and call his name. Then he see me. I reach for him, and he reach for me. A man get between us but I poke his knee and he step aside. Then I grab Lawrence and don't let go."

"I was beseeching a constable's help when our sturdy little Samuel emerged from the crowd with Lawrence in his arms." Mr. Raymond dabbed his eyes with a napkin.

"He didn't weigh nothing."

"Samuel set Lawrence at my feet, as if he'd collected Lawrence from the backyard."

Miss Anna had a wry but affectionate expression, then shook her head. "And the lot of you said nothing about it."

"We thought to spare you upset, Anna." Mr. Raymond sucked his pipe and puffed a smoke ring.

At the wash tub, Molly rinsed the last dish. Fog pressed grey against the window, leaving drops that trickled down the glass like tears. After she dried her hands, she took a seat at the table. Her eyes brimmed.

"And don't I have my own special memory? The day after the great gale, when our Claire near killed herself to save the young goat, the entire farm was in an uproar. The weather vane lay crooked in the earth, roof slates littered the yard, and the beasts were as frazzled as ourselves."

"It took until spring to set the farm in order," Mr. Raymond said.

He moved to the fireplace, poked the ashes, and added logs from the crooked apple tree felled last summer. Glowing embers spewed up and floated haphazardly, like sparrows before a storm.

"Aye, and the mess that covered the yard was more than I could bear," Molly said. "The clothesline blew down, the wash basin was gone, the fence was bent and broken, the privies had tipped over, and so much hay scattered about, the yard looked like the inside of the barn. Tears filled my eyes to think of the work facing me."

After Samuel refilled Hamish's cup, he helped Claire put the dishes away. When they returned to the table Molly continued.

"So the next morning, worried as I was about Claire, I shuffled into the kitchen, taking fierce hard the thought of lugging a heavy bucket from the well. God and Mary bless me, I stepped outside to a miracle. The yard appeared like a dream. Across the way, the privies sat upright. The cistern glistened with fresh water, the yard was raked clean. And don't you know? Samuel was stringing a clothesline from the house to the oak that survived the storm. When I called to thank him, Samuel's words were, 'Don't worry none, Molly, I'll fix the picket fence after I tend the horses.' The lad spent the entire night putting the yard to rights yet promised to return for more work before day's end. As me da used to say, 'A handful of skill is worth more than a bagful of gold.' Well, you have skill, Samuel, and are worth many bagfuls of gold."

"Weren't nothing. Anybody do the same."

"That wasn't anything," Miss Anna said. "But that was something, indeed. As Proverbs says —

Whoever tends a fig tree will eat its fruit and he who guards his master will be honored.

"As you make your way in the world, Samuel, know that we have been honored by your service."

"Well said, Anna." Mr. Raymond rose. "The sky is clearing and it's nigh time you to return to your family. If I may join Anna in quoting the Holy Book, let me repeat to you what the Lord said to Samuel.

The Lord does not look at the things man looks at. Man looks at the outward appearance, but the Lord looks at the heart.

"Samuel, you showed us your heart every day, and we thank you. Come now, the wagon is packed, your payment is secure in this wallet, and the horses are shod and ready."

Amidst the hustle and bustle of goodbyes, Samuel wiped away a tear.

"Mr. Raymond, you always treat me fine. Hamish, you took care of me and teach me everything I need to know." He turned to Miss Anna. "Miss Anna, even though I'm a sorry student, I can read, and write, and cipher thanks to you. I'll try to keep away from *ain't*. Give Lawrence and Reuben my regards. Molly, I sure will miss your custard pie."

~

With a sinking stomach, Claire watched the wagon roll across the bridge over the Wissahickon Creek and vanish. She put her hand on her waist and sighed. What will I do without my brother? Who will understand? Even thoughts of Lawrence didn't ease her gloom, or the sense that, for the first time in her life, she was truly alone.

CHAPTER TWENTY-THREE

WISSAHICKON FARM JULY 1824

L ittle more than a week remained in July. Work on the farm had slowed. The air hung heavy. Claire woke with sweat on her brow, an upset stomach, and heart beating wildly. At the thought of rising, heartburn surged bitter in her throat. Outside, sounds of stamping horses and bustling people roused her out of bed. She rubbed her stomach, then pulled on the green dress her mother made – the one with the scooped neck, empire waist, and short sleeves. For the ride to Germantown, the dress suited her perfectly. The high waist kept attention off her middle.

She prayed no one would learn her secret in the few weeks remaining in her indenture. But even bibbed work pants pressed tight against her body. She stepped into the heat and looked for Lawrence. She must tell him today. What would they do?

Miss Anna caught sight of her and waved. "Claire, there you are. Get a move on, or you'll not reach your parents by supper time. Do you have the list for the shops? Lye soap, molasses, coffee, sugar, cinnamon, and chocolate. Please buy pins, needles, calico, and worsted from your mother, and a bolt of silk if she has it. Don't forget to commission her to sew a mattress for Hamish! His must be a hundred years old." Strands of yellow hair fluttered from Miss Anna's bonnet. Her cheeks flamed in bright circles. "Oh, and the apothecary – we need three bottles of laudanum."

Mr. Raymond called, "Missy, order a barrel of rum and on the morning you return, procure a bucket of fresh oysters. Anna, did you give the lass your list?"

Claire's fingers tingled. Lawrence approached the wagon with his leather book bag slung over one shoulder and a carpetbag in his hand. He stowed them and waited by the horses, rubbing their necks. Miss Anna took two steps toward the house, stopped, took three steps to the wagon, peered in, then hurried off. She and Molly returned, both laden with small wrapped items to deliver to this house or that in the city. Claire found herself drawn into the anxious dance. She remembered she tucked Miss Anna's list in the belt under her chest, retrieved it, and waved it in the air.

Mr. Raymond rearranged the bags Lawrence stowed. "Anna, don't get yourself in a tizzy. It's not as though they're traveling to New York. My word, Woman, you'll have the entire lot of men and beasts so excited they won't be able to work. It's curdled milk we'll be tugging tonight."

"After you drop Claire with her parents, Lawrence, you'll deliver the hams and apples to the City Tavern? I promised Otto Baumann these bags of seeds for his farm near the university," Miss Anna called.

Lawrence rolled his eyes. "Yes, Mutti, I'll deliver the hams, apples, and seeds, then I'll stable the horses, and walk to the university. Everything will be fine."

As Duff helped load the wagon, he brushed against Claire. He looks sad, she thought, with his owl eyes and stern mouth. Since Hamish returned to his cottage, the old man struggled to regain his strength, leaving Duff with almost all responsibility for the horses, though Claire helped whenever she could. She felt she was abandoning him, but she ached to see her mother. She needed her mother.

As Mr. Raymond and Duff tied barrels to the sides and arranged boxes in the wagon bed, Hamish rode Star of Night from the stables. Claire reached for Star's reins and rubbed the horse's neck.

"Hamish, you made a fine seat and awning for the wagon," Claire said.

During the long winter, Hamish transformed the wagon's bench seat into a small cab, adding back support and an overhead cover. Behind the front bench, Hamish attached a dickey seat for servants and Negroes. Jostling had caused many a bruised rump on rides to the city. After Hamish finished, Molly made seat cushions covered with canvas.

"We'll be on our way." Lawrence swung up onto the bench.

Claire retied her green bonnet, the same block-print cotton as the dress. Elizabeth's half-boots pinched her toes – Claire was unused to the pressure of shoes. When she wore boots in cold weather, they were hand-me-downs from Lawrence, wider than these go-to-town shoes and soft from wear. Claire eyed the dickey seat.

"Where shall I sit?"

"Sit with me."

Lawrence looked the dandy in his top hat, high-collared white blouse, and buff-colored britches tucked into riding boots.

"We're off," he said and shook the reins.

The wagon jerked forward.

"Don't forget the *Chronicle!*" Mr. Raymond called.

As the wagon rattled past, Duff raised his hand in a half-wave. Duff's tartan had torn yet again, and Claire packed the pieces in her small carpet-bag, hoping her mother could form the pieces into patches for a quilt. Otherwise, the boy's precious tartan would deteriorate until not a strand of his home remained. She tucked her hands under her shawl. *How will I tell Lawrence? And my family?*

As the horses clopped down the gravel drive, thick white clouds floated like puffs of lamb wool. When the wagon emerged from the tunnel of trees and pulled onto Germantown Road, heat rose from the ground and burned from the sky. Claire feared she might swoon. She held onto the bench with both hands. From the distance, the thunder of sledge hammers crushing rock reverberated like the angry growl of a mother bear protecting her young.

The wagon jostled Claire against Lawrence. A carriage passed them at a speedy clip. Inside, two gentlemen gestured toward Lawrence and Claire. The negro coachman caught Claire's eye and shook his head as if to warn her – *Don't make trouble.*

"Lawrence, I must move to the back. No sense bringing stares and jeers upon us. Will you slow for a moment?"

"Stay where you are. I don't care what they think. Sit closer." His eyes were glazed and his cheeks were flushed. "If anyone questions me, I'll say I have an aching head, and my mother insists you ride close to comfort me."

Heat pulsed from his body in waves. Sweat stained his shirt. At seventeen, Lawrence was hardly more than a boy. Though Claire had yearned to share her anguish with him as soon as she knew, she hesitated the first few times they were alone. Then, whenever she gathered her courage, Miss Anna, or Hamish, or Molly appeared as if by black magic, and she swallowed the words like gall. The wagon rocked. Claire grew nauseated. She took long slow breaths to quell the upset, but it wasn't enough.

"Stop! Stop, please."

While she leaned over the side retching, Lawrence stared with alarm. He directed the horses to the abandoned DeWees paper mill along the Wissahickon. Claire let him help her down. She took two steps toward the creek before she spewed the contents of her breakfast in a bush. Lawrence led her to a stone bench in what was once the yard of the DeWees family home.

"Did the sausage disagree with you? Shall we return to the farm?"

He put his arm around her shoulders and pulled her close. Claire sobbed. Once spoken, it would be true. She couldn't bear it. Mallard ducks bobbed and quacked in the creek, oblivious to the human presence. A warm breeze sent maple leaves the size of dinner plates tumbling along the bank. With a deep breath, Claire whispered the awful secret.

"I must tell you something, but I'm afraid. My monthly, I haven't had it since . . . Inspiration's birth."

Lawrence's Adam's apple rose and fell. "It doesn't happen the first time, and we haven't ever again."

"My stomach is upset and swollen. Your baby moves in my womb."

He jerked away as if it burned, then rose and walked to the creek bank. Claire felt lost as she joined him.

"There are doctors, midwives, who handle these things," Lawrence said, staring at the water. "I'll make inquiries at the university. If you were white, we could marry."

Claire collapsed. Never, never would Claire allow anyone to hazard her womb. She knew the aftermath was fever-illness . . . often death. She wouldn't deny this child to spare Lawrence humiliation or herself disgrace. How foolish to believe his assertions of love, to hope they had a future together, to imagine their relationship surpassed the boundaries of race? She hated herself and she hated him. She was alone.

Lawrence crept close, sat next to her, and took her hand. "I don't know what to do."

Below cloud mountains, a band of geese flew in a wide V. The lead goose swooped off, settled at the back, and another took the lead. Claire wanted to swoop back and let Lawrence lead. She didn't have the strength, nor did he.

"When will the baby come?" he asked.

"The end of September — soon after my indenture ends. But there's no hiding this." She stretched her dress across her waist. "I can't return to the farm."

"There's time to decide what to do," Lawrence said.

Time? There was no time. What did she want him to say? Had she hoped for marriage, like the white Englishman William Purvis and his colored wife, Harriet? Their son, Robert Purvis, denied his white complexion to live as a Negro, yet was respected by whites as well as blacks. She'd hoped Lawrence's love would give him courage to . . . what?

She knew he'd be shocked – wasn't she? She'd been terrified to tell him. Why had she imagined Miss Anna's and Mr. Raymond's love for Lawrence was strong enough to recognize a negro grandchild? What would her parents say? Her pathetic dreams became the nightmare of reality.

"Are you well enough for the road?" Lawrence took her hand and helped her up.

They returned to the wagon. For the first time, the trip home held no joy. Lawrence announced every bird, deer, and man they passed, foolishly trying to make the trip seem normal. The horses' hooves clopped a pleasant rhythm on the cobblestone road.

"I'll talk to my father," he said.

"Your father's a kind man, but what of your mother? She'll want me far away from you." Fear and heartsickness overwhelmed her. "Lawrence, we have no future except pain and punishment."

"I'll write to Reuben. He'll know what to do."

He sounded again like the Lawrence she knew – who assumed problems would resolve themselves, who lived in the moment without considering the consequences, who threw himself into a cesspit to save her goat. When she looked at him, she saw a child's face. She shuddered.

"It will be too late by the time we hear from Reuben. Slow down, I'll sit in the dickey seat."

Each turn of the wheels brought Claire closer to her mother and grandmother and, despite her fears, she felt lighter. Finally, she'd be with women she loved.

CHAPTER TWENTY-FOUR

GERMANTOWN JULY 1824

Germantown Road bustled with commerce. The pavement was smoother here and the stone houses closer together, many scarred by bullet holes from the Battle for Germantown fifty years ago. Claire gazed at Samuel Johnson's stone house. The Johnsons, Quakers, supported the business, storing packages and preparing them for their final destinations. In a dormer window in the attic, a shadow appeared, then disappeared.

Claire averted her eyes. Cliveden, the Chew Family mansion, was half a mile down the road. She thought it ironic that the Johnsons protected runaways, while the Chew family owned slaves they moved from Pennsylvania to their farm in Delaware to avoid the 1780 abolition law. Claire stared again at the Johnson house. Would she and her child become shadows in an attic, peering at the street, waiting for strangers to collect lace and a button to deliver to a place far away?

The road became crowded with carts and people. Young boys leapt from stoops to scoop horse droppings for a penny. A little ginger lad chased after the wagon with a bucket and trowel. He smiled up at Claire a moment before he slipped in dung and caught his eyebrow with the trowel.

"Stop!" Claire said. "The little one's hurt. Pull over."

Lawrence sidled the horses to the edge of the street. He looped the reins on a hitching post then helped Claire jump down. A beefy man with a ruddy face, fierce red eyebrows, and the sound of Ireland in his voice, picked up the boy by the braces of his corduroy britches.

"Ah, don't bloody your blouse, Donal, your mam'll box my ears for letting you get hurt," the man said.

"Bring the child to the bench, there," Claire said.

"Who might ye be, a colored girl, to tell me where to put my boy?"

The man's halo of rusty hair fluttered in the breeze. He glared at Claire but complied. Lawrence, too, made his way to the bench. A Quaker woman, grey hair edging from her bonnet, dragged a splashing bucket of water and rags from the Johnson house, and set it beside Claire. The water was clear and the rags were clean.

Claire chose a red calico rag, squeezed out excess water, and wiped blood from the child's eye and eyebrow. Lawrence placed his hand under the boy's head, took another rag, and cleaned blood from his cheek and nose.

"How old is he?" Lawrence asked the father.

"Donal is nine-years-old," the man said. "Sir, does your girl know the tending to wounds?"

Claire dipped the bloody rag in the bucket, clenched her fists, and wrung it out.

"Hold this against your eyebrow," she told Donal.

"Of course she does," Lawrence said. "She's a Penniman, born free for a hundred years. And you, Sir, your name?"

"Seamus Reilly, but known as Reds Reilly to all."

"Are you fine, Donal?" Claire asked. The boy nodded. "Are you strong and brave?" He nodded again. "Have you watched your mama sew your stockings?" He nodded. "I will sew your wound the very same way. You'll have a fine crease in your eyebrow to remember this day all your life." She turned to the Quaker woman. "Is there a place away from the flies for the boy?"

"Ye can tend him in my parlor." Mrs. Johnson asked Reds Reilly, "Have ye something to wrap the boy in? His clothes are covered in blood and dung."

"Nay," Reds said. "We wear what we have."

"We shall make do. I have needles and thread, Miss Penniman, to close the wound. I know your mother and father, and I know Farmer Williams' family. Aren't ye the youngest boy?"

~

Twenty minutes later, Reds Reilly emerged with Donal in his arms. The boy's eye was swollen, and a track of eight black stitches ran through his eyebrow. He wore a girl's blue dress. His clean wet clothes hung from his father's belt. He sucked a piece of molasses brittle.

"We be grateful for your help," Reds told Lawrence.

"Miss Penniman deserves the thanks," Lawrence said.

Donal took Claire's hand, brought it to his face, and rubbed it against his cheek. He smiled and yawned.

"I was brave," he said.

Lawrence gave him three pennies. "You were most certainly brave."

Though the afternoon breeze blew hot, Claire shivered. Still, as the wagon jostled toward her home she felt better. Lawrence had not allowed Reds Reilly to belittle her. Mrs. Johnson and the child, Donal, treated her with kindness and respect. She allowed herself to hope.

Baby James Forten Chestnut toddled across the kitchen to the table where Moses drank coffee, thick with cream. Moses lifted the little boy to his lap. When the child reached for the coffee cup, Moses pushed it away but dipped in his finger and let James suck the drops.

"Don't give that child coffee, Moses Penniman," Elizabeth warned from across the room, where she and Ruth, the runaway from Mystic's Cave, stirred onions, celery, potatoes, spices, and peppercorns in a huge pot.

Moses' mouth watered. Outside on the grill, honeycomb tripe simmered in butter on a cast-iron pan. The gamy smell hung heavy in the air and announced to the neighborhood that pepper pot soup soon would be ready for sale. At the sound of wagon wheels crunching over gravel, Moses walked outside with James on his hip and watched while Lawrence brought the wagon to a stop. After Claire hopped down, she stared at Moses and the toddler.

"You don't recognize James? He's growing like a weed. Ruth's in the kitchen with your mama," Moses said. He hugged Claire with his free arm. "Thank you for bringing our Claire home, Mr. Lawrence. Before you go, let me water and feed your horses." He handed James to Claire.

"The mares will enjoy the rest while I unpack the packages my parents sent."

On a hollow branch above the privy, a woodpecker drummed relentlessly. After Moses unhitched the horses and led them to the water trough,

Claire and Lawrence stared at the squirming toddler. Lawrence held out his hands for James, but the child drove his face into Claire's shoulder. The kitchen door opened and Elizabeth hurried out.

"Claire, I'm so happy to see you. . . and you, Mr. Lawrence. Shall I bring you a glass of lemonade?"

"I'd be grateful for a drink, but then I must be on my way. I have deliveries to make, and I'd like to get settled in my room. Classes start tomorrow."

After Elizabeth returned with the lemonade, she and Claire distracted James while Lawrence stacked brown-paper-wrapped packages of bacon, tongue, a leg of lamb, and pigs' feet on the kitchen steps next to jars of pickled beets, pepper hash, and rennet.

"These are wonderful additions to our larder. Give our thanks to your parents, Mr. Lawrence." Elizabeth turned to Claire. "Let me take James."

Claire waited outside while Lawrence re-hitched the horses. When he swung himself onto the wagon bench and took the reins, she sighed. There was so much to say, yet with her mother lingering inside the kitchen door and her father a few feet away, she must not. She stared at Lawrence, willing him to know how much she needed him.

"Farewell," came from her heart and her lips.

"I'll come back for you." Lawrence's eyes held Claire's an instant before he turned to Moses and said, "Claire stitched up a young boy's bloody brow at Mrs. Johnson's house. Elizabeth taught her well."

As Lawrence steered the wagon down the alley, Claire stayed on the steps, watching. Before he turned onto the road, he looked back and waved.

～

When Claire slipped inside the kitchen door, Ruth was wiping her forehead with a rag.

"Well, here come Sister Claire. Hope you got an appetite for my pepper pot. Your mama talking 'bout how you soon be home for good and help her start a dressmaking business down the road."

"Mama's last letter said people line up for your pepper pot soup, and Jonah gets day work at the sail-making factory."

"Yes, indeed. We tucking away our money so's we can let Old Caesar live in peace. That cabin be mighty tight since we moved in with him."

Under the table, Baby James ran his fingers through flour Elizabeth sprinkled there. Flour streaked his hair and face like Indian war paint.

Claire picked him up. She smelled his milky neck and rubbed her cheek against his soft skin, but the squirmy toddler slid down and walked like a drunk to his mother. Claire held her hand against her waist, feeling the bulge and hoping no one noticed.

When Moses came back inside, he handed Elizabeth a platter of cooked tripe. "Mr. Raymond and Miss Anna be mighty generous. Most all the shelves in the food cellar are filled."

Moses grabbed Baby James and bounced him on his knee. In a deep voice, he sang,

> Ride a cock-horse, to Banbury Cross, to see what Jamie can buy; a penny white loaf, a penny white cake, and a two-penny apple pie.

"What are the goings-on at Wissahickon Farm, Claire?" Elizabeth asked over her shoulder.

She and Ruth chopped the tripe and dropped the pieces in the pot. Claire paused for a moment before answering.

"Reuben's letter came last week. He performed a trephination on a man who fell from a horse and lost consciousness. After Reuben drilled a hole in the man's skull, a large blood clot seeped out. The man made a full recovery."

"What you say Reuben did?" Moses asked.

"Trephination. He bored a hole in a man's head."

"Lordy, young Reuben must have a hole in his head to go after a man like that."

"The man lived, Daddy. Reuben saved his life."

"Lord, I can't see that turn out good," Moses said.

"How are Anna and Raymond?" Elizabeth asked.

"Miss Anna sorely misses Reuben. His wife had a baby girl in the spring and Miss Anna has yet to see her. She says all she has left is Lawrence." Claire sighed and gazed at the ceiling. She took a deep breath. "Mr. Raymond says it's hard to manage the farm with Reuben gone to Boston, Lawrence at the university, Samuel's indenture completed, mine soon to be, and Hamish not fully recovered."

Ruth stopped stirring and stood with her wooden spoon in the air. Sweat ran down her face, and she wiped it away with her apron.

"They lookin' for help?" Ruth asked. "Need a hardworking man, good for field work and tending animals, and a woman who do most everything?"

Moses raised his eyebrows. "No slaver come after you and Jonah at Wissahickon Farm. What you think, Claire?"

Claire didn't know what she thought about anything anymore. The heavy smell of the pepper pot and the heat in the kitchen after her long ride made her woozy and nauseated. She struggled to pay attention, but her heart raced and she felt faint. She took a deep breath and rested her chin in her hands.

"Mr. Raymond's looking for help."

"I can cook, wash, sew, and clean the privy and chicken coop," Ruth said. "James, he a good boy, soon two-year-old. He won't cause no trouble to no one never."

The sweat on her cinnamon face shone, and she seemed taller. Perhaps this was a way to fill the gap when she failed to return to the farm.

"When Lawrence returns, I'll ask him."

"Miss Anna and Mr. Raymond would look long and hard to find better workers than Ruth and Jonah," Elizabeth said.

"Sure enough," Moses said. He bounced little James on his knee. "Sure enough. How you doing, Claire?"

Claire felt his eyes bore through her like a drill – a trephination.

"I want to see Granny."

"Young Mary has her in the wheelchair, walking along Germantown Road. Granny sure does enjoy the outside, but I worry about this heat. Mary is growing up fine, and I've been teaching her to read. I expect she'll soon wheel Granny back for tea." Elizabeth studied Claire. "You look peaked."

Claire pushed away from the table, stood, and fainted. When she opened her eyes, Daddy, Mama, and Ruth looked down at her. Baby James patted her face.

"Moses, help Ruth with the pepper pot. I'm taking Claire upstairs," Elizabeth said.

With her mother's hand on her back, Claire climbed the oak stairs, each creaky step a comfort. At the top, she saw her room filled with baskets of clothing to mend. A bible sat on the little side table. A blue quilt with shoo-fly patches lay across the small bed.

"We decided to let Mary sleep here when you're away," Elizabeth said, her voice apologetic, "but she'll sleep with Granny since you're home."

Claire felt numb, as if she'd given it up, all of it – Granny, her home, her bed, her job, the horses, her goats, Molly, Hamish, Duff – for what? She lay on the childhood bed where her mother had comforted her when she was sick, frightened, or lonely. She wanted to stay here forever.

"Tell me," Elizabeth said, her fingers touching Claire's face, her brown eyes rich with sorrow and concern.

Claire choked. Her eyes filled. Her mother smelled of soup and bread, tripe and onions – a strong, earthy smell. Her mother. She needed her mother.

"It's Lawrence," Claire whispered.

Elizabeth nodded. Claire couldn't find words. She wanted her mother to hear the silent scream of her heart. With a sob, she pulled her dress tight across her stomach. Elizabeth recoiled, took her hand from Claire's face, and rested it against her own throat.

"Who knows?"

"No one. You. Lawrence. No one else."

"When did it happen?"

"Christmas." Claire paused and thought. "Two or three days before. When Samuel helped Star of Night birth Inspiration."

Elizabeth counted her fingers. "September. You hardly show. I carried my babies tight, too. But why, Claire, how could you let this happen?"

"Since my first day on the farm, Lawrence has been my best friend. I know it's wrong, but I love him, and he loves me. After Inspiration was born, we left the stable at dawn. It was cold. I wanted his warmth. I wanted to be his first, so he never forgets me. I never thought this would happen."

"Claire, how could you? He's white and the son of your indenture holder. Your best friend does not force you or trick you with promises he can't keep."

How could Claire explain her longing for Lawrence? When he was away, she saw his reflection in the waters of the Wissahickon. Without him nearby, she felt nervous and upset, like she forgot something important. How could her mother understand when she didn't? Did she give herself to him from fear he'd find a sweet, fair-haired daughter of his parents' wealthy friends to love? She only knew that when they were together, she felt whole.

"Lawrence never acts like I'm stupid or ugly. He treats me like I'm me, Claire, a human being. He loves me. Sometimes I think he forgets I'm African."

"When I was a child, Anna was good to me. She taught me to read and write. She and Raymond took you and Samuel to their farm and treated you fairly. But Anna never forgets we are Africans. No white man or woman ever does, Claire, believe me." Elizabeth stared out the window. "Thank goodness you've nearly completed your indenture. You're eighteen. We'll find you a husband."

"What about Lawrence? Perhaps he'll marry me."

"What you say?"

Moses voice came from the top of the stairs. When he appeared in the doorway, Elizabeth frowned, and shook her head.

"I want to know what Claire say."

With the whites of his eyes shining, Moses' looked like Lightning Strike when he sensed a threat.

"I love Lawrence. I want to marry him."

Claire caught her breath and narrowed her eyes, sad, angry, and confused.

"I know what that boy want and it ain't marriage. Did he have his way with you? Did he make like he'd marry you to get what he want? You that stupid to believe him?"

Elizabeth looked at Moses with exasperation, and Claire looked at him with fear. Then Claire swung her legs over the side of the bed and stood.

"This is his baby, Daddy. So you can yell, and carry on, and tell the whole neighborhood, but if Lawrence doesn't marry me, what will I do?" She squared her shoulders – defiant, but desperate.

The quiet voices of Ruth, Granny, and Mary rose up the staircase. Moses stared at the ceiling shaking his head until Elizabeth took his arm.

"No one is happy about this, but Claire needs our help." She turned to her daughter. "But Claire, the boy's parents will never allow him to marry you. Don't make yourself sick with false hope."

Claire looked at her waist and thought about the wagon ride. Lawrence agreed to nothing. He wanted time – time to think this through, time to seek advice, time to consider his options. There was no time. Lawrence was a boy, not ready to father a mulatto child, not ready to marry a young Negro woman, not ready to defy his parents. Claire's needs and the needs of this poor baby meant nothing to him. How foolish to believe she was more than a servant. Lawrence wanted time, yes, to disentangle himself from their ill-considered intimacy. Bitter heartburn rose to her throat, and her stomach lurched. She vomited.

After her mother helped her out of her fouled clothing, cleaned her, and settled her under the quilt, Claire felt like a baby herself. Hours later, she woke to the grey evening. The ache of hunger competed with the ache in her heart. The smell of bread and soup made her mouth water. She pulled on the fresh dress her mother left draped over a chair, and cringed at the tight fit.

When she crept into the kitchen, Elizabeth gave her a sad look, but Moses focused on baby James at his feet. Ruth, though, smiled.

"Sit down, Sister. See if this ain't the best pepper pot you ever eat," Ruth said.

With heart racing and face flushed, Claire crumbled a biscuit into the spicy soup and sipped from a spoon. Ruth filled the silence with chatter and song.

> When the Lord get ready, you got to move. When the Lord get ready, you got to move. You may be high, you may be low. When the Lord get ready, you got to move.

Claire felt like a child who pitched pennies in the creek and arrived at the grocery store without a cent to buy the family's bread. No matter how hard she searched the creek bottom, the pennies were gone. She couldn't make this go away, she couldn't find what she'd lost. Still, the soup warmed her.

With her left arm curled crooked against her body, Granny sat on the porch in a wicker rolling chair. The chair had two wide wheels on the front and a smaller wheel below the handles in the back. Her feet, too short to reach the footrest, dangled against the leg boards. Spectacles balanced on the bridge of her nose. She was wrapped in a flying-geese patchwork quilt.

Years ago, Granny told Claire this pattern of triangles signaled runaways to follow the geese when they flew north in the spring. Claire thought of the five geese she watched on her ride home, how they formed a perfect *V*, just as the quilt depicted. They swooped through the sky and disappeared in thin straight lines swallowed by clouds. Claire wished she could disappear.

Granny motioned for Claire to move a chair so they faced each other. Last February, a sudden strike of apoplexy left Granny's left side paralyzed. Her mind remained sharp, except she sometimes forgot she couldn't walk and spilled out of bed. After the stroke, young Mary proved kind, competent, and a blessing for Granny. Claire scolded herself for being jealous.

"Well," Granny said, her voice deep and slow. "Tell me, Child, 'bout the trouble."

Claire took a breath, but when she opened her mouth, she sobbed. With tears streaming down her face, she blurted, "I'm carrying Lawrence's child. I don't know how it happened. I love him."

Granny sucked her lower lip and looked into Claire's eyes. "I think you know how it happen, Claire. You ain't the first black girl get in trouble with a white boy. This baby not the first born of mixed blood. My mama have mixed blood. Felix have mixed blood. What Mr. Raymond and Miss Anna say to all this upset?"

"They don't know. Do you suppose Miss Anna and Mr. Raymond will allow Lawrence to marry me, and let us live on the farm?" Claire clenched her fists.

Granny drummed a beat with her good hand. "No, Child, indeed I don't."

CHAPTER TWENTY-FIVE

GERMANTOWN AUGUST 1824

A week passed. Some days, as she scrubbed white men's shirts against the washboard and hung them to dry, Claire envisioned the rest of her life like this – washing and sewing, raising her child in Germantown — as if her years on Wissahickon Farm were a dream. Other days, while she kneaded bread or darned socks, anxiety and fear strangled her. Mr. Raymond and Miss Anna expected her back in a few days. Daddy avoided her. Mama play-acted cheerful.

Only Granny looked her in the eyes. "That baby ain't going away. You think you ever see Mr. Lawrence again?"

Claire responded with a shrug.

Sunday, Claire stayed home while her family went to the church meeting. She walked down the path to Old Caesar's shack. She peeked in the tiny window and when she saw he wasn't home, pushed open the door and went inside. Despite the August heat, the cabin was cool, shaded from the sun by enormous trees. In the far corner, a mattress lay on the floor, covered by a quilt with a large center block in the shape of a sailboat. Claire remembered the day Granny finished and said, 'The way to freedom be across the water.'

Old Caesar kept his home neat. Behind the door, Ruth and Jonah's clothes filled a large wicker basket. A small table and two chairs sat in the center of the room. Shelves lined one wall from floor to ceiling and held Caesar's few belongings. Pretty's Boy's blanket lay at the foot of the mattress.

Claire went outside and called, "Caesar, Pretty Boy!"

Her words died in the rustling leaves and trickling creek water. The Wissahickon ran so low it was little more than mud, little more than a promise.

Lawrence promised to come back for her, but Claire no longer believed in promises.

The following morning, Claire woke to voices. She rolled out of bed, dressed, then crept downstairs.

"The boy is no more at fault than Claire. He didn't force her," Elizabeth said.

"Sure he force her, same as white men force our women since we land on these shores," Samuel said.

Claire found her family on the porch. When she stepped outside, Samuel glared at her. He smelled of horses and leather.

"When I find that boy, I'mma drown him in the creek until his googly eyes pop out!" Samuel said.

"No, Samuel," Claire said. "I love him."

"What will you do, Claire?" Felix's voice was quiet and urgent. He stepped in front of Samuel, as if to protect her.

"If I was white, Lawrence would marry me."

"I will marry you." Felix leaned against the porch railing. "Look at me. The white man who took my mother had yellow hair and blue eyes. Who could say I'm not your baby's father?"

"I could." Lawrence appeared from the side of the house and bounded up the steps to the porch, his face red, a tremor in his voice. "I say it. I'm the baby's father. I will marry Claire."

Claire's head swam. Lawrence came back. After more than a week, she'd lost all hope. Did he say he'll marry me? The tension made her woozy. She felt her mother's hand on her shoulder.

Fist raised, Samuel stepped toward Lawrence. "Boy, get out my house."

"Samuel, you know this boy all your life. He's young and foolish but Claire swear he never force her. You can't fix nothing with fists," Moses said.

From her wheeled chair, Granny said, "Samuel, you go on. Let this young man have his say."

Felix took Samuel's arm and drew him toward the alley. Even after they'd gone from sight, Claire heard Samuel's voice. "You can't trust them."

Ruth's song echoed from the kitchen.

Steal away, steal away! Steal away to Jesus! Steal away, steal away home!
   I ain't got long to stay here!

"Mama, let me take you inside," Moses said.

Before he pushed Granny's wheeled chair through the front door, Granny spoke to Claire and Lawrence.

"Ain't nothing in life but trouble. You getting your share early."

A few minutes later, Moses returned. He sat with Elizabeth on the glider. The dull thump of horse hooves, the crunch of wheels on gravel, and indistinct voices drifted from Germantown Road. Lawrence, clothes bedraggled and hair sticking out at odd angles, stood awkwardly by a pillar. Claire wrung her hands and tapped her foot. Finally, Elizabeth broke the silence.

"Please, Mr. Lawrence, make yourself comfortable."

She gestured toward the bench across from the glider. Claire glanced from her father to her mother to Lawrence and wanted to disappear. Lawrence slithered onto the bench. Elbows on knees, he leaned forward and took a breath.

"Each day this week I walked around the city. I watched black men and women step back to allow whites to pass. One rough fellow went out of his way to kick an old Negro man's cane and send him sprawling. When I helped the old man up, the bad bargain spat and said, 'Mind your business, let the nigger crawl.' If someone tried such a prank on the farm, my father would send him on his way." Lawrence stared at his hands. "I watched university classmates drink too much and make ribald comments to women, black and white, though their words to Negro women were without restraint."

His knees jittered and his right eye twitched. He glanced at Claire and began again.

"Whenever I witnessed such actions before, I considered them ignorant but of little concern to me. Now, I realize Claire and our child will confront such loutish behavior on Philadelphia streets, and I cannot bear it. When I tell my parents of the child, I'll tell them I intend to marry Claire, and beg them to allow us to make our lives on the farm."

"Mr. Lawrence, you too young to take this on," Moses said. "It's best you put this behind you and let us take care of our own."

Lawrence looked up and met Moses' eyes.

"I will take care of my own."

CHAPTER TWENTY-SIX

Lawrence drove the wagon up the gravel path to Wissahickon farm. A sturdy black man, Jonah, swayed on the Dickie seat behind him. The barrels of rum, beer, flour, coffee, tea, and sugar emitted a pleasant scent each time the wagon jostled. Lawrence touched the wicker basket beside him, filled with six oranges. He let his mind wander.

This morning, he stopped at the Penniman's house to call on Claire. Samuel's friend, Felix, opened the door and told him she was indisposed. The Haitian mulatto gave him the basket of oranges. When Lawrence turned to go, the man called, 'No fear.' It seemed a peculiar good-bye.

Then, as he prepared to drive away, Moses introduced Jonah Chestnut, and requested he bring Jonah to the farm to speak to his father about work. Lawrence dared not refuse.

As he steered to the back of the house, Lawrence saw his mother and Molly in the vegetable garden picking eggplant, cucumbers, lima beans, and squash – work Claire normally helped with. His mother turned, brushed herself off, and met him when he swung from the wagon.

"I didn't expect you for another week, when Claire returns. What of your classes?"

When Anna noticed the large black man, she wiped sweat from her brow and studied him. The man doffed his cap, but kept his eyes on the ground.

"Mutti, this is Jonah Chestnut. I decided to bring Jonah to meet you and Papa. When I mentioned the farm was short-handed, Moses said there's no harder worker."

In the garden, Molly stood with one hand on her hip and the other shielding her eyes. Something about her expression made Lawrence wonder if she suspected Claire's condition.

"Your father's in the far field showing the day hands the reaping contraption Reuben built last time he was home. No one can figure out how it works." Anna turned to Jonah. "You're welcome to wait outside until Mr. Raymond returns. Dinner was served an hour ago, but Molly will fix you a plate."

"Thank you, Ma'am," Jonah said, head down and hat in hands. "If you don't mind, I walk to the field right off. I be obliged for a sip of water."

Jonah wore work clothes – corduroy britches, a thin cotton shirt, and a canvas vest. His feet were bare and his large hands were scarred and work-hardened. After he accepted a drink and biscuit, he pulled on his soft-brimmed sailor hat. Lawrence pointed the far field and Jonah marched off.

Lawrence reached into the wagon and handed his mother the basket from Felix. When she pulled back the cloth, her eyes grew large.

"We haven't had oranges since Christmas. Six fine ones. You're a good boy, Lawrence, what a treat."

"Claire's family sent them."

"It must have cost them dearly. How generous."

She placed the basket in shade under the back steps and returned to the garden while Lawrence unloaded the supplies. After the barrels and bags were stored in the cellar, he drove the wagon across the stone bridge to the stables.

He found Duff cleaning tack. Without a word, Duff unhitched the horses. While Lawrence tended one horse, Duff took care of the other. They wiped down the mares, brushed road dust off their legs, and picked their hooves. Lawrence silently observed Duff, thinking Duff's life would go on as always, while his would never be the same. He wished Reuben were here to tell him what to do.

"Are you needing something?" Duff asked when he caught Lawrence staring.

The boy has a sullen look, Lawrence thought. He shook his head, and walked to the Wissahickon, not ready to face his mother. His bout of courage had vanished. A cloud passed over the sun and the air smelled of rain. Lawrence dug his fingers in the muddy bank to search for smooth, flat stones. Each time he found one, he piled it by his side. A shadow flitted under the water, hardly discernible in the leaf-covered murk of the low-running creek. Lawrence pitched a rock, and the catfish slithered downstream toward Germantown, toward Claire.

He skipped a stone three times over the surface. Footsteps padded toward him through the soft pasture. Duff sat beside him, picked up a stone, and pitched it in the creek. It sank.

"Hold it like this." Lawrence held a flat stone between his thumb and forefinger, flicked his wrist, and let it fly.

After a few attempts, Duff's stones hopped once or twice. They depleted the pile and dug up more stones, comparing which shape skipped the most times, or traveled the farthest.

"Claire hasn't been herself," Duff said.

"She's not feeling well."

"She's not been sick a day since I came to the farm. Has she come down with something?"

"Yes. It's good she's with her mother. . . I don't think she's coming back."

Duff's eyes grew dark. "Without goodbye?"

A red flush rose from Lawrence's throat. He swallowed.

"She completed her indenture except for a week or so, and my father will forgive that time. . . We're no longer children. Our lives are changing. The farm's hard to manage, and my parents are growing old. Reuben's life is in Boston, and I'm at the University. Hamish is old and half lame. I wonder what will become of Wissahickon Farm."

Duff furrowed his brow. "Mr. Raymond told Hamish to write his son in Ohio and ask him to come home. Young Hamish has an Indian wife and child, and may not be eager to return."

"Claire's father sent an African man with me to speak to my father about work. I hope Papa likes him. Molly's a great help. She's stayed on long after her indenture ended." Lawrence looked at Duff. "You're good with the horses, and carry a heavy load. I'm glad you found your way here. You're helping Wissahickon Farm live on."

The sky darkened and thunder roared. Rain drops pounded the ground like bullets. Lightning flashed across the sky. Lawrence and Duff raced across the meadow, slipping in mud. When Duff crossed the stone bridge to the stables, Lawrence wished he could trade places with him. He slogged up the hill to the farm house.

Farm hands moved from the fields to the quarters like horses on stampede. Lawrence leapt to the front porch and hugged a pillar, grateful the rain drops hid his tears while he summoned the courage to face his parents. The front door opened.

"Take off your shoes and come in from the rain," Molly ordered.

In the kitchen, Molly hung sodden shirts by the stove, and handed out towels. At twenty-six, she'd lost her baby fat, she liked to say. Her unruly red hair escaped ribbons and bonnets. Her hazel eyes missed nothing. She should find a husband, Lawrence thought. He noticed Jonah Chestnut hovering in the kitchen door, gripping his hat.

Raymond took a seat. Jonah glanced at Molly, then crossed the kitchen. He dropped to a knee, gently tugged off Raymond's boots, and set them near the stove. Then he backed to the door frame.

"A kind gesture, Jonah. The older I get, the harder it is to bend for my boots. Moses sent us a good worker, Lawrence. Welcome to Wissahickon Farm, Jonah."

"And his wife and child too?" Lawrence asked.

Jonah looked stricken. "I ain't had time to tell you 'bout them, Mr. Raymond. My wife, Ruth, she work hard. Cleaning, cooking, sewing – she do most everything. My James, he just start walking. A good boy, no trouble. We ain't need much."

"At present, I can afford wages for you alone, Jonah, but if your wife will work for food and shelter, your family may live in the quarters with you. After a time, depending on the prices we get at market, we'll discuss bringing on your wife for pay. Did you say her name is Ruth?"

"Ruth, yes Sir. Thank you, Mr. Raymond. That's more than fair." Jonah smiled a broad, broken-toothed smile.

"Molly will give you a room in the quarters, and you can stay there tonight. In the morning, take the small wagon to collect your family and your things. You can bring Claire back too."

"Yes, Sir," Jonah said. "Won't take no time at all."

After Molly and Jonah departed for the quarters, Lawrence caught his breath and spoke.

"Claire's ill, Papa. She won't return."

Raymond sucked his pipe. The sweet smoky smell hung in the air. Anna entered with the basket of oranges. As she took out each orange, she held it to her nose then placed it in the center of the table, six of them forming a cross. The kitchen door opened and Molly returned.

"Wasn't it kind of Elizabeth to send me oranges? Molly, you must have one, and we'll save one for Hamish"

"And Duff," Lawrence said.

Anna turned to him with surprise, but nodded. She passed oranges to Raymond, Lawrence, and Molly, then took one for herself.

"Save the skins," Anna said. "We'll dry them and crush them for flavoring."

As Molly inspected her orange, she seemed circumspect, almost fearful. With a small knife, she pierced the skin and licked the juice. She closed her eyes. Then slowly, deliberately, she peeled off the skin in patches. Finally, she licked her fingers, picked out the seeds, and bit into the pulpy ball.

"You'll never be done at that speed," Anna said.

Lawrence felt relieved his mother seemed so jolly. He approached his orange mechanically, as if it were a chore rather than a delight. They were so expensive he wondered how Felix acquired them. Did he skulk along the docks at night, stealing oranges, rum, guns, and whatever else he wanted? He felt a pang of guilt and jealousy. Would Claire truly consider marrying Felix? Would Felix dare claim the child as his own? He piled his peels and seeds next to his father's and popped the last bit of orange in his mouth.

"The man Moses sent, Jonah, is not afraid of work," Raymond said. "Thank goodness, he figured out how to get the reaping contraption hooked up to the horses. If it cuts the grain as well as it did today, the reaping will go much faster than with sickle and scythe. The weather put us off a day or two, but I'm confident with Jonah we'll get back on schedule. If Ruth works as hard as her husband, some burden will be lifted from you, Molly."

Anna sighed. "There's plenty to be done, more than ever with the boys so rarely here. I always thought Reuben would practice medicine in Philadelphia. Ah, well, Lawrence, we have you. After you complete your studies, you'll return to the farm and your legacy."

"Jonah and Ruth have a little boy named James," Lawrence said. "You can teach him to read and write, Mutti, like you taught us."

"When were you to tell me of the child?" Anna asked Raymond.

Raymond laughed. "It will be good to have a child on the farm again. Now, Lawrence, tell me what's ailing Claire."

Lawrence blanched. He wasn't ready for this, but the time had come. Since the farm was short of hands, perhaps Papa and Mutti would be glad to have Claire and him live here, forever. They would work hard every day. Whatever his parents wanted, they would do. The driving rain subsided.

Molly gathered the peels and seeds. She glanced at Lawrence before she disappeared in her room. The smell of shoes drying by the stove hung heavy in the air, and Lawrence's heart hung heavy in his chest.

"I have something to tell you."

Anna's smile faded to concern. She looks old, Lawrence thought, her once bright blonde hair a sallow yellow-grey, and her full face beginning to sag. Even her eyes, once as blue as the summer sky, seemed now like winter.

"Have your say, then," Raymond said, leaning back and relighting his pipe.

"Claire is ailing because of me."

"How can that be?" Anna asked.

"She carries my child." Lawrence choked, unable to form better words. "I'll marry her. We can live on the farm, away from troubles in the city. It's what you want, Mutti. I'll stay on the farm . . . with Claire." His eyelid ticked and his heart beat to burst.

Anna's face grew scarlet. She struggled to breathe. "Not your child," she said, voice cold. "Lawrence, don't you see? She's gotten in trouble and decided you're the solution to her problem. She takes what she wants, and she wants the life we gave her. Don't fall for her lies."

"Claire doesn't lie! It is my child. I love her. My first and last thoughts each day are of Claire. When we're apart, I feel empty. I cherish every moment with her. I do everything I can think of to make her love me. And she does love me. . . We never expected this. It was only one time. But it happened, and I don't know what to do. I hoped . . . I thought we could raise our child together on the farm, in peace." He fought back tears, but they welled in his eyes and trickled down his face.

"You're a boy, Lawrence, not yet eighteen," Raymond said. "It's not possible to marry Claire."

"It is possible. The English cotton merchant, William Purvis, is married to a black woman. Claire's mother knows his wife, Harriet, and their three sons."

"Don't be ridiculous, trying to convince us with your schoolboy nonsense." Anna's voice was shrill. "Do Moses and Elizabeth support this marriage?"

Lawrence stared at the floor. "They say I'm too young."

Raymond rested his elbows on the table. "Moses and Elizabeth show good sense. Anna, we must send him to Boston. Reuben will see to his placement at Harvard. Claire completed the terms of her indenture, and I'll pay her freedom dues. I'll speak to Moses. After birth, if the baby appears to be yours, I'll fund an account for the child's future. But if the baby's clearly African, we have no obligation. Lawrence, your behavior is unacceptable. I'll write to Reuben tonight."

"She ruined us," Anna said. "She tarnished Lawrence's good name, and forces us to send him away. Samuel never caused trouble, but a bad seed will choke the finest fruit. How could Elizabeth's child cause such misery?"

Lawrence wished he could put this behind him, move to Boston with his brother and start fresh – away from his mother's anger and his father's anguish. But they were wrong. He begged Claire to love him as much as he loved her. He sought her out, brought her gifts, longed for her embrace. He dreamt of their love. In the weeks since Inspiration's birth, Claire's refusal to make love frustrated and hurt him. Rage pulsed through his veins. He pounded the table.

"I won't go to Boston! I'll stay with Claire and my child."

"Then you're not my son. God cursed me with your birth," Anna shouted before she stormed away.

"Anna!" Raymond turned to Lawrence. "You must go to Boston, Son, it's the only answer. In time, memory of your childish indiscretion will fade away. Claire has family and friends. No matter the father, the child will be well cared for. And you, with your brother's guidance, will become the man you're meant to be. It's the manner we choose to deal with our worst mistakes that shows our true colors. I believe yours are bright."

Early the next morning, Lawrence packed clothes and his pistol in a canvas bag. He crept down the stairs and found his father waiting. He wished he'd climbed out a window.

"You packed your bags, Lawrence. For Boston?"

"No. I'm going to Germantown to be with Claire."

Raymond frowned. "They'll not want you there."

"I'm not wanted here."

"Of course you're wanted here, but you dealt a terrible blow to your mother and me. We tried always to treat people fairly, no matter their color. But work is one thing and mixing the races is another. What you think is love is a young man's lust and folly."

"I'll be gone, then."

"Take this." Raymond handed him a money pouch. "Go to Boston."

"Thank you, Papa. I never meant to hurt you or Mutti, and neither did Claire. Mutti judges Claire harshly, but I can't fathom life without her."

As Lawrence left the kitchen, his father's tobacco smell followed him. Before he climbed onto the wagon to return to Germantown with Jonah, he heard footsteps — Molly's.

"Lawrence, it's a sorrowful thing happened, but who bears blame for love? Last night I collected Claire's things." Molly handed him a stuffed pillowcase. "Tell Claire I love her like a sister. Ask her to remember me."

"She won't forget you." Lawrence paused. "Tell Hamish and Duff I'm sorry."

"I best get to work," Molly said. "Take care of Claire and the child and yourself."

Jonah shook the reins and the wagon jerked forward. Lawrence turned for a last look at his home. In an upstairs window, a silhouette rippled behind a curtain, then disappeared.

CHAPTER TWENTY-SEVEN

On the front porch with Granny who was sound asleep, Claire rocked as she stitched binding on Duff's quilt. Elizabeth helped Claire weave green and blue yarn through the tartan's remnants to fashion new patches. Now those patches made a quilt, and Duff's pieces of home would stand the test of time.

The baby's heel skimmed under Claire's waist. Tears welled in her eyes. What would she do? Her father urged her to accept Felix's offer. At twenty-one, Felix was smart and settled, capable of raising a family. He owned a building on Germantown Road with his barbershop on street level, and his living space on the second floor. With Samuel's help, he built four rooms on the third floor for lodgers. Samuel rented a large corner room, with windows on two walls.

Felix was white enough to be the baby's father. He'd always been kind to Claire, and was devoted to her family, especially Samuel. She didn't understand Samuel's fury at Felix's offer to marry her. Did he think Felix was too good for her? That she was a fallen woman who didn't deserve a good man? Did Samuel loathe her?

The quilt slipped from her hands. *Tar Baby*— the slave catcher's taunt — circled her brain. She smelled the man's foul breath, felt his filthy hand at her britches. Then Samuel burst from the woods with a frightened look and a stout branch. Samuel loved her, almost died to save her honor. Did he think Lawrence no better than the slaver? He once cared for Lawrence. Why did he hate him now?

Mary stepped onto the porch, wiping her hands in her apron. Granny slumped in the wheelchair, mouth open, sleep whistling from her throat.

"Granny sleeps all day and lies awake all night," Mary said. At the sound of horse hooves, she leaned over the railing and stared down the alley. "Here come Jonah with the white boy. Why you get yourself in trouble with him? He so scrawny seem you could push him away did you want to."

"I didn't want to."

Claire rocked, measuring her breath and feeling the baby's pressure. Mary roused Granny, and they moved inside.

Jonah pulled up the wagon and Lawrence, pale and thin, with dark circles under his eyes, hopped down.

"Molly sent your things." He dropped the pillowcase at Claire's feet and tapped his bag. "My clothes and pistol."

Claire smelled the farm – horses, goats, barley, rye, and the odor of whale oil lamps. Lawrence looked like a child, and she pitied him. For all his fancy talk of marrying, in truth, he was not yet a man. Her heart broke at his sorrowful expression.

"My parents say I must go to Boston and study at Harvard."

"There's more. I see it in your eyes."

"Mutti says the baby can't be mine."

Claire's head snapped back as if Miss Anna slapped her. "Do they think Duff lay with me?"

"They think it's a man of your race."

"Because I'm not good enough for a white man?"

"I don't know what they think. They say I'm too young, like your father says. Mutti says I'm not her son. Papa says go to Boston. He gave me this money pouch."

Jonah climbed the porch steps and cleared his throat. "Once Ruth come back with James, we take the horse and wagon back to Wissahickon Farm. You want me drive you out afore we go, Mr. Lawrence?"

"I have no place to go."

Lawrence sat on a step. Claire rocked and bit her nails.

As noon approached, the wind carried the scent of rain. Moses and Samuel returned from deliveries and drove the cart around back to the shed. Claire heard Moses tell Samuel to unhitch and water the horse. The front door squeaked open. Moses stepped onto the porch, tapping his pipe on his pants. He sat on the steps with Lawrence, lit his pipe, and puffed smoke rings in the air.

When Elizabeth appeared down the alley lugging a basket of clothes to launder and mend, Lawrence hurried to take the basket from her arms.

"What his Daddy say?" Moses asked.

"That he's too young and must join Reuben in Boston. Miss Anna said the baby's not his."

Moses picked a piece of tobacco off his tongue. "That's fear talking. She scared what people say if her boy admit to a Negro child. He going to Boston?"

"I don't know. He has no place to go until he figures out what to do. Can he stay here, Daddy?"

"Might look unusual to our neighbors, but I suppose he can stay a bit. Claire, the boy got to find his way, and it ain't in my house."

"Jonah and Ruth got work on the farm," Claire said.

"I saw the wagon, and figured as much. Safer for them there."

Ruth stepped out of the line of trees that separated the white homes and businesses on Germantown Road from the Negro houses in the alley. She swung the empty pot in one hand and balanced James on her hip with the other.

The toddler chanted, "Pepper pot, smoking hot, pepper pot, smoking hot."

When Jonah heard James, he raced to join them. He took his son in his arms.

"We got us a job on Wissahickon Farm," he said, voice deep and joyous.

As the Chestnut family approached the Pennimans, Jonah told Ruth, "Mr. Raymond say he pay me same the other workers, three-fifty a week, and a room. He say you can work for food and lodging. If you work hard and they need you, they pay you too.

"Three-fifty a week? And food? And a room for you, me, and James? You hear right?"

"That right, Mr. Lawrence?" Jonah asked.

Lawrence nodded. "They'll pay you fair for good work."

"Mr. Raymond give me his horse and wagon to carry you and James to the farm. What you think 'bout that? He trust me with his horse. Girl, we moving on." Jonah spoke the last words like a preacher urging the congregation to come to Jesus.

Claire smiled to see the happy couple gathering their belongings, saying their goodbyes, and tending their little boy — all she wanted for

herself, her child, and . . . husband. She gazed at Lawrence, eyes downcast
as he helped Jonah load the wagon. How could Mr. Raymond and Miss
Anna welcome Jonah and Ruth to the farm but banish Lawrence and reject
her and their baby?

James fussed, and Lawrence took the child from Ruth. He held the dark
boy on his lap, facing him. The child took a lock of Lawrence's hair, rubbed
it against his face and purred like a cat. Lawrence touched the boy's tight
curls, pulled one, and let it spring back. When drool spilled onto his shirt,
he wiped James' mouth with his sleeve.

"Let me take him." Elizabeth swooped up the toddler. "Are you
hungry, Little Man? Won't we miss him, Moses?" She felt the toddler's
bottom. "A dry nappie will ease your trip, James, and a bowl of milk toast
may put you to sleep."

Lawrence shimmied to Claire's feet. "James' hair is soft. I thought it
would be stiffer. I wonder what our baby will look like."

Claire stroked Lawrence's hair. She imagined how fine life would be if
Mr. Raymond and Miss Anna let them live on the farm – a happy family
living and working away from trouble. Then, she visualized their existence
on the outskirts of society where they'd be despised for their mulatto
child. Perhaps they could live with her parents. Lawrence could find a job
as a bank clerk or journalist. Surely someone would hire him without
regard to his black wife and baby.

"What will we do, Lawrence?"

"After Jonah, Ruth, and James are off, we should marry. When we're
tied together, no man can tear us asunder. This is our child, and I love you.
Will you marry me?"

Claire put her hands on his shoulders and rubbed his neck, disbe-
lieving but hopeful. Her heart raced but she calmed her breathing. She
rolled the quilt.

"Yes, but we can't tell anyone. Let me send Duff's quilt with Ruth."

She crossed through the house and out the kitchen door. In the back
yard, Ruth packed her family's things in a wicker basket.

"Will you give this to Duff, the Scottish boy at the stables?"

"I surely will."

Ruth put her hands on Claire's shoulders and looked in her eyes. Then
she pulled her close and hugged her.

"You be all right, Claire. You strong, you brave. Your child be the
same."

Somehow, Claire believed her.

CHAPTER TWENTY-EIGHT

Claire stepped back as Lawrence knocked on the door of St. Michael's Lutheran Church. A soft young man, fair hair parted in the middle, wearing a black shirt and trousers, opened the vestibule door. The scent of incense escaped.

"Is Reverend Keller in, please?" Lawrence asked.

"He's gone to Baltimore to visit his family," the man answered. "I'm tending to parish needs in his absence. I'm Reverend Whitmore, from Lancaster."

Lawrence peered into the church. "Can you marry couples?"

"Most certainly, I can." Reverend Whitmore sounded insulted.

"Then we're here to be married."

The reverend stood a bit taller. "Come in. . . Where's the bride?"

Claire cowered behind Lawrence, who took her hand and brought her forward. The reverend blushed, and sputtered, and shooed them away.

"I cannot marry you. It's not proper. In any case, you're a boy, too young to wed. Run along."

"I assure you, Reverend, we're of an age to marry. I'm seventeen years old, and Claire is eighteen."

"I'm sorry, Young Man, Reverend Keller gave me no authority to marry a man and woman of different races. I'm afraid you'll have to wait until he returns next month."

The reverend glanced at Claire, then averted his eyes.

Doubt and fear collided in Claire's brain. She tugged Lawrence's sleeve. This was not to be. How foolish to believe. And yet, it was a relief to have tried and failed. But Lawrence would not be dissuaded.

"My father, Raymond Williams, has been a member of this congregation his entire life. Reverend Keller regularly visits our farm and enjoys my mother's meals. When the great gale damaged the church roof a few years ago, my father, brother, and I cut and placed the slate shingles now protecting the vestibule. It will be a sad day when Reverend Keller learns you refused the request of one of his most loyal parishioners."

The minister tugged his collar and stared at his hands.

"I'll write to Reverend Keller today and seek his counsel. Come back in two weeks."

"My father and mother will be in a terrible state when we return unmarried, given Claire's delicate condition. Let's go, Claire. My family will find a church more worthy of our donations."

"Delicate condition?" Reverend Whitmore cleared his throat. "You, Miss, what do you say?"

"I wish to marry the father of the child I carry, Reverend, and make a family for the three of us."

"This is irregular," the reverend said. "But your father sanctions this union?"

"Due to the circumstances, my father directed me to make a generous offering of three dollars. Of course, the extra dollars are for you, in appreciation for your understanding, Reverend."

Brows furrowed, Claire listened to Lawrence with surprise and admiration. This wasn't a boy, but a man. Still, her heart raced. But Reverend Whitmore put out his hand, and Lawrence dropped three silver dollars in it.

With the coins in his fist, the reverend left them in a small chapel, then returned with a worn book and nervous look, sweat shining on his forehead.

"State your names," he said, and then, "Wilt thou, Lawrence, have this woman, Claire, to be thy wedded wife, to live together after God's ordinance in the holy estate of matrimony? Wilt thou love her, comfort her, honor, and keep her as long as you both shall live?"

"I will." Lawrence's voice echoed, strong and confident.

"And wilt thou, Claire, have this man, Lawrence, to be thy wedded husband, to live together after God's ordinance in the holy estate of matrimony as long as you both shall live?"

Claire hesitated. I can't do this, she thought. What will Daddy say? Where will we live? This is a terrible mistake. Her heart beat to the rhythm of the ring shout Ruth sang as she gathered her family's belongings for the move to Wissahickon Farm.

> *Hold my baby, hold my baby, hold my baby, hold my baby. What the matter, what the matter, what the matter, what the matter? He got the fever, got the fever, got the fever, got the fever. Rock my baby, rock my baby, rock my baby, rock my baby.*

Lawrence declared for her and now waited, proud and expectant, for Claire to declare for him. For him and their baby. She ran her hands across her middle.

"I will," she whispered.

Reverend Whitmore wiped his forehead. "Then, with the power vested in me, I pronounce you husband and wife. Wait here while I fill out the marriage certificate."

They sat, husband and wife, in the front pew of the private chapel reserved for rich church members. Lawrence's damp hand grazed Claire's. She brought it to her lips. His sigh filled the church. She giggled, and he laughed. When the chapel door opened, they assumed serious expressions. The ink was still wet on the marriage certificate.

"Give my regards to your father," Reverend Whitmore said as he ushered them to the side door.

Limp with relief and exhaustion, Claire walked a step behind Lawrence along the cobble road, danger escalating as the ink dried on the paper Lawrence clutched. It was done. She should be happy but felt feverish. The shops along Germantown Road blurred. When an approaching woman eyed Lawrence then her, Claire's hands trembled.

"Claire?" Felix stood in the barber shop door. "Claire, Mr. Lawrence, come in, have a cup of tea."

At the sight of Felix, Claire's upset evaporated. Her eyes cleared, and her heart quieted. She and Lawrence, both shy, stepped inside.

Felix's shop was small but bright. Along one wall, shaving mugs, brushes, straight razors, combs, and scissors filled a shelf. Another shelf held glass bottles and tins of powdered soap. Near the barber chair, two washbasins sat on a cabinet. Round mirrors hung directly across from each other. Chairs lined one wall alongside baskets filled with newspapers and pamphlets.

In the corner, Felix stoked a small stove and spooned dry leaves into a pot. After the water boiled, he bustled with competence as he poured tea into delicate china cups. He served them, then stepped back and considered Lawrence like an artist choosing the angle for a sketch.

"Mr. Lawrence, I'd like to cut your hair. It seems unkempt, does it not, Claire?"

"It does. He could use a bit of spiffery."

Felix led Lawrence to a chair, then ran his fingers through Lawrence's hair.

"So straight. Will you allow me to cut it short, in the new style? I believe it will suit you better."

Lawrence glanced at Claire, eyebrows raised in a questioning look. She nodded. He relaxed.

Felix combed and clipped, considered the results, and resumed clipping. He spoke while he worked.

"Samuel spoke of your dilemma, Mr. Lawrence. And here you are with Claire. What will you do?"

Lawrence stuttered. Claire got to her feet.

"Not an hour ago we were married at St. Michael's Church. We're husband and wife."

Lawrence flinched. Felix nicked his ear.

"We agreed to keep it secret," Lawrence said.

Felix eased Lawrence back, and gazed at Claire with sad eyes.

"Your secret is safe."

"Now, no one can keep us apart," Lawrence said.

Felix left Lawrence's hair long on top, but tapered at the back and around his ears. He rubbed in pomade, and parted it in the middle. Next, he soaped Lawrence's chin and cheeks, and shaved him with a straight razor, though Lawrence had little facial hair. He toweled off Lawrence's face.

"*Voila.*"

"You look quite the man, Lawrence," Claire said.

Lawrence stared at himself in the mirror, turning this way and that. As he slid out of the chair, Felix crossed the shop, shut the door, and turned the sign to *Closed*.

"Stay a moment, sit. I have a gift for the married man." Felix disappeared into a back room and returned with a low-crowned felt hat. "This is a new style I've been working on, more sensible than a tipsy top hat." He set it on Lawrence's head. "A perfect fit."

Felix added hot water to the tea pot, swished it, then refilled their cups. He pulled up a chair so they faced each other.

"Tomorrow, a shipment leaves for Canada. Shall I add two packages to the cargo?"

"My brother lives in Boston." Lawrence took Claire's hands. "We may go there."

Claire's eyes widened. "Your father wants you to go to Boston to separate us. How is Boston better than Philadelphia for a white man married to a black woman?"

Felix rose and returned with oranges. "I often think about returning to Haiti. Since the revolution, Haiti is an independent country ruled by blacks and colored. The President, Jean Pierre Boyer, is offering free passage to American blacks who move to Haiti to live in freedom." He juggled the oranges before he gave them to Claire and Lawrence. "My uncle, Henri Renaud, bought an abandoned plantation near Jacmel on Haiti's southern coast. He sends me oranges, lemons, and coffee every few months, and begs me to return. He's desperate for help with his land. Yet I find I cannot leave Philadelphia, my shop, or your family."

"Some Negroes from Mother Bethel traveled to Haiti, but returned in less than a year," Claire said. "They told Daddy they struggled with the language, and the work was too hard for bad pay."

"It is true. Since the revolution, Haiti's sugar cane production and exports have languished for lack of knowledge and organization, and I will add, bias in European markets. The black immigrants who returned to Philadelphia did not anticipate the desperate condition of Haiti's economy, or the difficult adjustment to the mishmash of races and cultures. But Jacmel is a world unto itself. It's beautiful and spacious, unlike crowded Port-au-Prince. My uncle's land is rich with potential, but he is no farmer. With your knowledge and experience, Jacmel may prove the place where your marriage can flourish — along with my uncle's orchards."

Lawrence looked interested but puzzled. "I read newspaper accounts of Prince Saunders' efforts to recruit American blacks to Haiti. But I'm white. Claire would be welcome, but I wouldn't."

"True, you are white. So am I, no? My hair is yellow like yours. My eyes are blue while yours are green. Our skin is not so different in tone. President Boyer's father was a white Frenchman, and he was educated in France. He offers asylum to American descendants of Africans. So, Lawrence, when you apply to the Haitian Emigration Society, declare you have African blood and skills – farming, orchardry, and animal husbandry. Such skills are more important than your white face."

Claire, stunned, looked from Felix to Lawrence. She waited for Lawrence to scoff at Felix's proposal. No white man would claim African blood. The baby kicked. She grunted. Lawrence took her hand, but averted his eyes. Felix busied himself arranging tools and hanging towels.

"James Forten himself told me the *Charlotte Corday* sails for Haiti in ten days," Felix said.

"Your uncle would give us work and a place to live? We wouldn't be on our own?" Lawrence asked.

"Of that, *Monsieur*, I am certain."

"Does you uncle keep goats and horses?" Claire asked.

"I do not know whether he has a horse, but he has goats, and chickens, and oranges, and coffee."

Lawrence put his hands on Claire's cheeks. "Shall we go?"

Claire nodded. Lawrence turned to Felix.

"My wife is black. My child is black. And I will declare I am black. We'll make application to emigrate to Haiti today."

"I will write to my uncle immediately and post it on the ship leaving for Haiti tomorrow morning."

Eight days later, when the Penniman family sat down to supper, Mary Baker dropped a steaming potato on each plate, and passed a bowl of sour cabbage. After she sat, she mashed butter into Granny's potato, and helped her eat. Moses popped a piece of potato in his mouth, then waved a hand.

"Hot, hot." He sat back and pointed his fork. "Mr. Lawrence, it's time you go home and make it right with your parents. You made a mistake, but you're still a boy. You need to go on with your life without this burden. We ain't happy about Claire's condition, but we take care of our own."

"I'll find other accommodations tomorrow. Thank you for allowing me to stay here. I know I'm young, but I'll find a way to be a father to my child."

"We're sorry Claire's indenture ended like this, but her time at Wissahickon Farm was all but up," Elizabeth said. "I know your heart's in the right place, Mr. Lawrence, but Moses is right. Go back to the farm and reconcile with your family. Don't worry about Claire. With her help, I can open a dressmaking shop. Felix told me about a building for lease on Germantown Road."

Claire rushed from the table to the backyard, and vomited. Elizabeth followed and touched her shoulder.

"I know you think you love Lawrence, but he's a boy, too young to take on a wife and child, no matter their race. Mr. Raymond and Miss Anna have been good to us since I was a child. Lawrence must make amends with his parents. I sent you away too young, I see that now. It seemed safer out of the city, away from rowdy men and the yellow fever. We knew you'd have good food and shelter at Wissahickon Farm, and learn to read and write. I hope you'll forgive me. We wanted the best for you and Samuel."

"Even though I missed you every day, I loved the farm, the fields, the goats, the horses, and Lawrence. We never thought loving each other would ruin everything."

"I'm happy you're finally home, and Daddy is too, but it's hard for him. Now, you can start a new life. We'll have plenty of business when we open the shop. Felix will be a good husband. He earns his way, and information he learns from his white customers helps the family business. He's a kind man, Claire."

"Mama, you don't understand."

Claire rested her head on her mother's shoulder. She couldn't tell her she married Lawrence. She couldn't tell her they planned to travel to Haiti like vagabonds. How could she explain her fear of the stares and jeers her half-white baby would encounter on city streets? She had to protect this baby from feeling tainted, dirty, stupid, and despicable.

Her new life would start in a new land, a land of free Negroes, a land where she and Lawrence could live openly as husband and wife. Goodbye, she told her mother through the beating of her heart. I love you.

As the sky darkened, Claire and Elizabeth sat on the back steps, silently watching lightning bugs flicker. When the back door opened and Lawrence stepped out, Elizabeth got to her feet and, after touching Claire's head, went inside.

"I was worried about you," Lawrence said.

"I'm worried too."

From the kitchen window, Moses and Elizabeth watched Claire and Lawrence. When Lawrence put his arm across Claire's shoulders, Moses started for the door, but Elizabeth took his arm.

"Leave them be."

"They ain't need none of that."

"Come to bed."

"That young man best keep his hands to himself."

"Come to bed. Leave them be."

~

At dawn, Lawrence set his belongings on the front porch before he approached Claire's parents.

"Thank you for letting me stay here while I figured out what to do. I decided to go to sea. When I return, I'll be a man of the world with the means to provide for my child." He took Claire's hands. "Be brave."

Claire, Elizabeth, and Moses watched from the porch until Lawrence was out of sight.

"I hope he sends his parents a letter with the news," Moses said. "If Mr. Raymond asks, I'll tell him what I know."

After Elizabeth and Moses went inside, Mary wheeled Granny onto the porch, and set down a basket of mending. Claire threaded a needle, and began to repair grey flannel trousers split from the back to the crotch.

"Mary, you fit this family like a hand in a glove. You're a special package, Mary Baker. Go play with the girls down the alley. I'll finish the sewing," Claire said.

After Mary skipped away, Granny whispered, "You talk kind to that child. She been a comfort to me. Mary, she my arms and legs, but you my heart and soul."

"Granny," Claire swallowed and sighed. "Lawrence and I got married at church last week. Please don't tell Mama and Daddy until tomorrow evening. . . We booked passage on a ship for Haiti. It sails tomorrow."

"I knowed something not right. I feel in my bones you leaving me. You know Haiti ain't no heaven on Earth. A white man and black woman got no place in this world together 'less they master and slave, and you never be a slave, Claire."

"Felix's uncle lives in Haiti near a town called Jacmel. He needs help with his plantation. He'll give us work and a place to live – a place to raise our child. Felix says many people in Haiti are mulattoes, so our child won't stand out. He says Haiti is desperate for farmers, and Lawrence will be accepted once he proves himself."

Granny nodded and sighed. A song rose from deep in her throat.

I been rebuked and I been scorned, I been rebuked and I been scorned,

*children, I been rebuked and I been scorned, trying to make this
journey all alone.*

"Your journey ain't all alone, Child, because you and me share a heart.
I never saw no man carry a burden heavier than his woman do. Lawrence
still a boy, Claire. You soon have two children to raise. You got to be
strong."

When her grandmother's breathing settled into a soft snore, Claire
kissed her forehead and tiptoed away. But Granny waved Claire to come
close.

"Take the Wedgwood medallion Ben Franklin give your grandfather
after he fix his chimney. It's in the chest in my room. Hold it close and
remember who your family be."

"With you in my heart, I will always be brave," Claire said.

When the house was silent and Jupiter glowed in the night sky, Claire
crept downstairs and out the back door. She wore the Wedgwood medallion around her neck. As she stepped onto Germantown Road, she experi-
enced the sounds and sights of night – scuffling and grunting, silhouettes
behind fluttering curtains, coughs and laughter. Claire pulled her shawl
tight and clutched her small valise against her chest. The Deringer pistol
Lawrence gave her long ago weighed heavy at the bottom, under her
belongings.

Claire looked for Lawrence at the nearby bakery where they agreed to
meet for the walk to Felix's barber shop. After a few minutes and no sight
of Lawrence, she hurried down Germantown Road, afraid Moses would
discover her gone and come after her. The valise weighed heavy in her
arms. The baby pressed on her ribs. She panted, short of breath. Outside
the firehouse, men idled on the pavement. She lowered her head and
crossed the street toward storefronts on the other side.

"Hey, Nig," a coarse voice yelled. "Nig, I'm talking to you. Come over
here."

She dug for her gun without success. There was no time to load it in
any case.

"Dickie, that nig girl's ignoring you. I would say she's being
discourteous."

There was loud laughter.

"You off to do some rich man, are you?" Dickie's voice. "I'm talking to you, Nig. Long as you out walking the streets you can do me and my mates."

Claire broke into a run, her stride awkward from the pregnancy and the cumbersome valise. She prayed a warden would come along. When heavy steps drew close, she cried for help. A push from behind sent her sprawling to the ground. Fingers wrapped through her hair and pulled her to her knees. The filthy man Dickey unleashed his repulsive rod. He yanked her face into his groin.

"Do it, or I'll beat you bloody and you won't never do nothing to no one again. Do it."

The men circled her like a wolf pack. She cursed herself for packing away the gun. She'd shoot Dickie in a heartbeat. His britches dropped. He swung his stinking rod in her face.

"Now."

She blurted, "No matter the French pox sores?"

"Dickie, you hear that? She got the French pox. It'll make your prick fall off. Don't let her touch you."

Vomit splashed Claire's shoes. As if waking from sleep, Dickie tugged up his britches.

"You walk the streets to catty-bang us and give us the clap? I'll clap you good."

Dickie swung his right arm and socked Claire on the side of her head. She collapsed. His boot smashed her hip. Pain exploded, red and wretched. This is how I die, she thought. The pack surrounded her, laughing and goading each other on. A kick to the mouth split her lip and loosened her tooth. She rolled on her side and tucked up her knees, praying to protect her child.

A gunshot, louder than thunder, exploded. Claire covered her ears. Feet pounded over the street. Men grunted. A hand grasped Claire's shoulder. She raised her fists. She would fight.

"Claire?" Lawrence's voice. "Claire!" Louder now. He knelt by her face. "What have they done?"

Blood trickled down her throat. She gurgled a question.

"Did you kill him?"

Claire woke in an unfamiliar room, shivering under a quilt that smelled of lavender, tobacco, and men's bodies. Her mouth throbbed. She pressed her tongue against her gums, and discovered a gap where a tooth had been.

Everything hurt. She put her hands on her waist and felt the baby move. A damp cloth dabbed her forehead. Lantern light rippled. Men's voices flowed and ebbed.

"I think she's awake."

"Claire, you awake?"

"Her eyes are closed."

"Is she bleeding?"

"It stopped."

"Let me see."

She opened her eyes in a squint. In wavering light, Lawrence, Felix, and Samuel loomed over her.

"She back with us."

Kind arms surrounded her, helped her sit, and held the lantern so close she felt its heat. Her voice was raw.

"Did you kill him?"

"We ran them off," Felix said.

"I smack a rock on that boy's head," Samuel said.

"They knocked out my tooth."

"You didn't wait for me," Lawrence said in a shaky voice. "I was on the way to meet you when I heard the commotion. I wish you waited."

"Not as much as I do." Claire pressed his hand to her belly. "The baby's moving, thank God."

In the cool darkness before dawn, Claire and Lawrence hurried to the dock where the *Charlotte Corday* anchored. If Moses discovered their plan, he'd swim across the Atlantic Ocean to bring her home. She draped a lace veil over her face to hide the bruises and swelling. She felt nauseated, with the taste of blood on her tongue.

The ship's purser, a thin man with muttonchops and bad breath, confronted Lawrence.

"Your passage says you're Negro. There's been a mistake."

"There's no mistake," Lawrence said.

"You're no blacker than I am," the purser said. "All documents must be in order."

"My grandmother was a Negro slave, freed when the master's wife couldn't bear to look at the boy her husband put in Grandma's belly. That boy is my father, and my mother is white."

The purser studied Lawrence. "You're the whitest black I ever saw."

"Do you think I can pass?" Lawrence asked.

The purser huffed. "Go on with you."

Other Negro families, part of the group Jonathan Granville recruited, waited to board. As Claire and Lawrence lugged their bags up the gangplank, crew members stared at her covered face. A tall black man and his wife stood beside Claire while the boatswain advised Lawrence of their cabin assignment. The black man tugged Claire's arm.

"That white man beat you?"

"No. He's my husband. He saved me from a gang of rowdies."

"You have trouble, find me. We're done being scorned for the color of our skin. That's why we're going to Haiti."

"Thank you. Lawrence is a good man. We're going to Haiti to live as husband and wife and raise our child." Claire touched her belly as she surveyed the deck. "So many black families. I never imagined."

"All of us seeking a better life," the man said.

He escorted his wife, a full-figured woman with sad eyes, toward the ladder to the berth deck.

Lawrence returned, and led the way to a tiny room with narrow bunked beds. After he stowed their bags under the lower bunk, he took Claire's hand.

"I'd kiss your mouth if it wouldn't hurt you." He kissed her tummy instead, leaving his hand there. "The baby kicked."

"Those rowdy boys called me a streetwalker."

Lawrence flinched. "Those boys are the scum of the earth, and you're a beautiful married woman."

"And this ship to Haiti is our bridal tour. . . Did we do the right thing? Was Boston a better choice for our child?"

Lawrence reached into his bag and took out six large pouches. "Seeds, Claire. I never delivered these seeds to Otto Baumann. There's squash, beans, peas, peppers, lettuce, and pumpkin. I may know nothing about orange trees, but I know how to plant and grow these. Who knows how we'd fare in Boston? Haiti is warm. We'll live on a farm, with Felix's uncle to guide us."

Claire pressed the bags of seed to her chest. "May these be *the seed which the Lord has blessed.* You're smart to bring them, Lawrence." She returned them. "I'm tired but you should meet the other Africans. After we leave port, will you bring me a slosh bucket and a cup of tea?"

After the cabin door shut, Claire ran her fingers over her swollen lips. The gap from her missing tooth made her feel like a runaway. But she was no slave. As she relaxed into sleep, she envisioned her mother and father's faces once they learned she left for Haiti with Lawrence. Her father would be angry. He'd cover his eyes in the throes of a sick headache. Her mother would press her lips together and shake her head. Later, after Daddy took to bed, Mama would rock on the porch with Granny and wonder what she did wrong.

But Mama did nothing wrong. Only me. Only me.

PART 2

HAITI

1824 - 1834

CHAPTER TWENTY-NINE

PORT-AU-PRINCE SEPTEMBER 1824

After twenty days at sea they docked at Port-au-Prince. Lawrence paid a porter to carry their bags to shore. Claire felt unbalanced and queasy, frightened and disoriented. Everywhere – on the wharf, on the street, as far as she could see – the city buzzed with Negroes going about their business. The possibilities of a future in a country of free blacks touched something in her she didn't know existed.

As they followed the porter, smelly children tugged her skirts and grabbed her arms, chanting for handouts. A small yellow boy with large freckles and disturbing pale eyes raised his arms and cried, "Mami."

The children stared at Lawrence. A boy, slender and filthy, with flies buzzing around a wound on his head, yelled, '*Blanc*,' and kicked Lawrence's shin. The porter shooed the children. He dropped their bags near the Customs House and held out his hand for payment.

Completely perplexed, Lawrence turned in a circle. Black men, women, and children who disembarked with them milled around, equally confused and distraught.

After what seemed hours, someone called, "*Je cherche Monsieur Laurent Williams. Je cherche Madame Claire.*"

"*Je suis Laurent*," Lawrence shouted.

He grabbed their bags, and they hurried to the slender black man wearing a wide-brimmed straw hat.

"You are Felix's friends come to work on my land? I am Henri Renaud.

Come, come, this is no place to get acquainted. Too much noise and excitement."

With one hand over her mouth and the other against her waist, Claire stumbled behind Lawrence and Henri to a red donkey cart. Lawrence helped Claire make a seat among their luggage in the back, then joined Henri on the bench.

Port-Au-Prince was crowded with people and animals. Two-story brick buildings with balconies and balustrades lined both sides of the street. Feathery leaves dangled from branches of trees Henri called, palms. Colorful gardens surrounded most buildings. Music pulsated from an open square with a fountain, trees, and bright squawking birds, where two men beat cylindrical drums with their hands.

The streets hummed with shopping. On signs written in French, Claire identified a pharmacy, tobacconists, book sellers, tailors, and sellers of jewelry, scarves, and dresses. Outside one shop, two elderly men smoked corn-cob pipes and wove strips of straw into hats. A boy wearing only dingy white britches, carried a teetering tower of straw hats on his head. Henri motioned to him.

"Our sun is strong," Henri told Lawrence and Claire.

He chose a wide-brimmed hat like his own for Lawrence, then said something to the boy, and gestured. With the tower of hats swaying on his head, the boy hurried to the *Boutique de Chapeau*. He returned with a butter-colored straw hat wrapped with a bright yellow scarf. Henri nodded, and the boy presented it to Claire. She placed it on her head and tied the scarf under her chin.

"Thank you, Henri, I feel better," she said.

"Just so," he answered.

As the cart moved south, Claire thought the Haitian people flowed like water in the Wissahickon – unlike the rigid, self-aware movements of people in Philadelphia, always hurrying and vexed if someone wandered in their path. Here, people glided rather than walked. Women in French fashions called to each other from balconies. On the street, women in bright cotton dresses moved smoothly while baskets of fruit swayed on their heads. Most men – black, brown, or yellow like Felix – wore cotton shirts and trousers, but others could have stepped from the streets of Philadelphia in their tight pants and short coats. Still other men wore military uniforms, complete with gold buttons and epaulettes.

Claire expected Port-au-Prince to be smaller, with few buildings and little commerce. Instead, it bustled with shops, people, parrots, and palm trees. They passed the presidential palace, a large, low building painted white, and other magnificent houses and gardens Claire thought equal to the finest in Philadelphia.

~

Soon, the streets narrowed, and shabby, shirtless men lounged outside makeshift shacks where naked children chased dogs. Henri led the donkey to the back of a wood building the color of sand. The air smelled of salt and onions. Henri removed his hat and wiped his forehead.

"We eat here," he said.

Claire gathered her skirt, took Henri's hand, and dropped from the cart. Her vision dimmed. She weaved back and forth, then sat on the ground in a heap.

"Claire, are you ill?" Lawrence asked.

She took his arm and stumbled to scrub brush yards away, where she dropped to her knees and vomited. Insects buzzed around her face and settled on her lip.

"The cart, the flies, the heat," she said, to Lawrence's worried face. "I'm better, now."

Outside the small café, Henri tapped his foot and twirled his hat through his fingers. After they joined him, he called through the entry, "*Onè*."

A female voice answered, "*Respè*."

"Honor. Respect," he told Claire and Lawrence. "We honor and respect each other."

They entered a room brightened by sunlight from windows on each wall, and sat at one of four tables. A slender woman with large, dark eyes, in a red dress and red-print turban greeted them.

"*Bienvini*, welcome, welcome."

"Genevieve," Henri said, "these are Felix's friends from Philadelphia, Laurent and Claire, who have come to work on my land." He turned to Lawrence and Claire. "My sister, Genevieve."

"*Bon jour mes infants*." Genevieve stared at Claire's face and narrowed her eyes. "He beat you?"

"No, he saved me."

Genevieve rested her hand on Lawrence's head. "A man does not beat his woman, *n'est-ce pas si?*"

Lawrence looked confused. "Never. I love her."

"Ah, you love her." Genevieve kissed Claire's cheek and touched her belly. "*Enceinte*. I will bring good food for you and *le bébé*."

An elderly man with a dark face and white mustache sat with a younger man – his son, Claire thought – at the corner table.

"Henri," he called.

In words Claire didn't understand but with gestures she did, the man indicated that Lawrence didn't belong, not with Claire, not in this café, not on this island. Henri's answer was rapid and incomprehensible. The men stared and snickered. Henri returned to the table.

"Do not be concerned for their reproach. They do not forget the years of slavery and abuse from white planters. I assured them Laurent is no threat, and brings farming skills to my land. I told them you come to Haiti to escape bad treatment in Philadelphia. They laugh, because they have sons, daughters, brothers, and sisters who fled Haiti for Philadelphia. *Ils ont des araignées dans la tête,* they say, 'They have spiders in their heads.' That means, ah, you are crazy."

Claire walked over to the men who stared unabashedly. She pointed to her head, crossed her eyes, and stuck out her tongue.

"*Araignées,*" she said.

"*Araignées,*" they repeated and laughed. The old man took Claire's hand. "*Un bébé, non?*"

"Yes." She pointed to Lawrence. "Papa."

As Claire returned to the table, the men called something to Henri. She asked what they said.

"*Blanc* is a good breeder for one without whiskers."

Genevieve returned with three glasses of beer and a plate of bananas — a rare treat for Claire and Lawrence — and a large, smooth fruit that looked like a big pear. Lawrence and Claire finished their beer before Henri took a sip of his. They stared at the bananas and waited.

"Eat, eat," Henri said. "I told Genevieve you are hungry travelers. After the fruit, we will have soup."

While Claire and Lawrence ate the bananas, Henri divided the other fruit into pink-yellow cubes, then sat back and sipped his beer. Claire put a soft stringy piece in her mouth and chewed carefully. Her jaw still hurt from the beating. She liked the taste, like a peach or plum – sweet but not too sweet. Lawrence examined the slimy oval seed – smoother and longer than a peach seed.

"Mango. Like oranges, coconuts, bananas, and coffee, mangoes grow on my land without discipline, even as we, descendants of slaves who labored and died on those plantations, grow and flourish without the discipline of the whip. You, Laurent, will care for and nurture these fruits, tame them, and take their yield to market in a way that is . . . you know, according to . . ." Henri waved his hand.

"Crop management," Lawrence said.

"*Certainement*." Henri tapped his pipe.

For the first time since they stepped onto the ship to sail away from Philadelphia, Claire's stomach settled. She smiled at Lawrence, proud of him. These past weeks had been hard on him, a boy-man of seventeen.

From the kitchen came a strong, peppery smell that reminded Claire of Ruth's pepper pot soup and home. What are Mama and Daddy doing right now? What did they think when Granny told them I married Lawrence and sailed with him to Haiti? Don't think about that now, she told herself.

Genevieve placed a steaming pot filled with meat, onions, and potatoes in the center of the table. She went again to the kitchen, and returned with rice, beans. and sweet-smelling bread. Claire and Lawrence looked at each other.

"*Du griot*. Soup, or do you say, stew? Pig stew with spices and oranges from my land," Henri said.

Genevieve refilled their glasses with the pale drink that had little of the kick of Miss Anna's home-brewed beer. Still, it was refreshing.

Henri spooned *griot* over rice and beans, and passed steaming bowls to Claire and Lawrence, who ate like a starved man. Claire ate slowly. The stew tasted delicious, despite the peppers' sting on her lip and gums. The bread was as sweet as the *griot* was spicy, reminding her of the sweet rolls young Mary baked on holiday mornings. She took a breath and belched.

"The girl like my cooking." Genevieve smiled. "The spices are good for your milk. The child, he learn the taste of pepper. That is our way."

"Genevieve is the *sage-femme*. She will bring your baby into the world. She has many skills besides cooking," Henri said. "Genevieve is *Mambo*."

Claire, eyebrows raised, glanced at Lawrence, unsure what Henri's words meant. Genevieve ran her hand across Claire's waist.

"Your *bébé* will be here soon. I will travel to Jacmel as soon as my cousin, Chantal, arrives to work in the cafe. You will wait?"

"I will wait."

They drank tiny cups of sweet coffee, then Henri rose. He kissed Genevieve's cheeks.

"We must take our leave. *Orévwa*, Genevieve," he said.

"*Orévwa*," Claire said.

Lawrence muttered, "*Au revoir*."

Shortly after they resumed the trip, Claire fell asleep in the cart. Two hours later, she woke with pain in her gut that screamed urgency.

"Stop, stop!"

After Lawrence helped her out of the cart, she plunged into a thick growth of trees along the rocky mountain path.

"Stay away!"

She raised her skirts a second before what felt like her entire insides exploded onto the grainy soil of a Haitian mountain.

"Claire, do you need help?" Lawrence asked, from too nearby.

"Leave me alone," she croaked.

With soft moss, she cleaned herself, then backed away from her disgrace. She felt weak but better. The forest smelled green and damp. Carefully, she felt her womb. She feared the baby would spill out with the contents of her intestines, but a hard bump pressed her right side. When Lawrence helped her into the cart, the pain was gone.

That night, they slept in a small shelter stocked with blankets and dried fruits. Lawrence moaned and thrashed, then stumbled outside. Claire drifted back to sleep until his hand found hers.

"Lawrence?"

"Emptied my guts," he said.

In the morning, as they loaded the cart for the last leg of the journey, Henri smiled.

"Haitian purification."

Then he gave them bananas.

They made their way on narrow rocky trails. Brightly colored birds peered down from high branches, squawking as if warning them to stay away. Compared to the mountains and forests of Haiti, the trees and brush that rose in craggy ridges on both sides of the Wissahickon Creek seemed small.

Once out of the forest, they passed small farms and drove through villages where people gave them corn cakes, bananas, and the hard green balls that grew in clusters on palm trees — coconuts.

Henri used a cleaver-like knife called a *machete* to hack off the tops of coconuts. Watery juice sloshed inside.

"Drink," Henri said.

With both hands, Claire brought the coconut to her lips. The taste! The liquid slid down her throat, satisfying her thirst and leaving a sweet clean taste on her tongue. She smacked her lips. Lawrence grinned.

"This tastes like heaven. I've had coconut confections once or twice," he said, "but I never held one. I didn't realize they have such delicious juice," he said.

"You will learn of many magnificent fruits on this island," Henri said. "And you will make my orange trees *magnifique* — if you are the farmer Felix promised."

CHAPTER THIRTY

JACMEL SEPTEMBER 1824

A s they entered Jacmel, the sun hovered above cottony clouds. In Port-au-Prince, the sea smelled of dead fish and rotten eggs, but here, the indigo ocean sweetened the air. The shockingly blue sky was intoxicating. This beautiful city – elegant pastel buildings with delicate wrought iron balconies, brick sidewalks, and crushed rock streets – bustled with black people walking free, proud, and confident.

Palm trees with clusters of coconuts and feathery stalks lined the streets. As the donkey cart jostled back and forth, Claire let go of thought, and floated in colors. The sky bled so blue she wanted to soak in it. Brilliant clouds danced to breezes like blissful shouts — *You lead the way, you lead the way, you lead the way.* She bobbed her head to the silent but powerful rhythm.

When Henri clucked to the donkey to stop, Lawrence hopped down and gave Claire his hand. She stumbled onto the dusty road and inhaled the sea.

Lawrence scrunched his eyes and tipped his hat to shield the sun. Sweat beaded on his flushed face. He looked so young. Claire wanted to kiss him.

"*Une belle vue, n'est-ce pas?*" Henri asked. "Jacmel was once the most beautiful city in Saint Dominique. Although it bears scars from the War of Knives twenty years ago, it will soon regain its splendor."

Passersby looked upon Lawrence with suspicion. Claire heard the word *blanc* muttered. Glistening black men approached Henri with whispers and gestures. After Henri said, "A farmer, *le fermier*," the men embraced Lawrence. With Henri translating, they invited him to visit their plots. Claire felt proud.

Women examined Claire's swollen belly with smiles and whispers of, *le bébé.*

"Come, come," Henri said, "my plantation is up the hill."

The sun flared red like a torch. Claire and Lawrence walked alongside as the donkey pulled the cart up the rutted path to a battered two-story white house. Scorched pillars supported the roof of a porch that extended across the front and around the left side. The steps were thick but splintered. A white garden gazebo with peeling paint stood in a clearing, surrounded by ill tended flowering shrubs. Henri hitched the donkey, then swept his hand across the impressive vista.

"*L'Orangeraie.* Lemons, bananas, coconuts, sugar cane, and coffee beans grow nearby. You'll find chickens about and eggs underfoot. A few goats wander the land since the fences are in disrepair, but return to the site where outbuildings once stood to be fed and milked. I stable my horse and donkey behind the big house."

Claire followed Henri's gesture to the mishmash of trees in the distant orchard. White blossoms covered some trees' branches, with dots of green and orange fruit.

The disarray, so unlike the orderly orchards and fields of Wissahickon Farm, disoriented her. The baby moved and Claire grunted, supporting the protruding weight with her arms. Lawrence dropped their luggage and rushed to her side. She waved him away.

"No more than a kick under my ribs."

A dark, slender boy, nine-years-old, with tight curls and large brown eyes, hopped down the porch steps to join them. A red bandana across his forehead gave him a menacing look, like a miniature buccaneer. Claire noticed his britches needed mending.

"Henri," the boy said.

"Sebastien, did you tend the animals and fruit while I was gone?"

"Yes, Henri. Marie milked the goats and collected the eggs."

Henri and the boy spoke in french-sounding words, but Claire understood the gist of their conversation through their expressions and gestures.

Henri turned to the porch where a small delicate girl peeked from behind a pillar.

"Marie," Henri called, "*Viens, rencontrer ta mère.* Come, meet your mother." He spoke to Claire and Lawrence in English. "Sebastien and Marie are orphaned twins who were living under the porch when I acquired the abandoned plantation, barely surviving on fallen fruit. My sister, Genevieve, insisted I could not send them away, and so they stay. I am a busy man with no time for children. Now you are here, and I give them to you. Marie is a quiet girl, inclined to stealing, and can't be trusted. Sebastien is like a gale, twirling and lashing with great bursts of thunder, but kind in his heart. Care for the children, Claire, as Laurent will care for the trees."

Wide-eyed, Claire stared at Lawrence, who shrugged. The girl, eyes down, shuffled from the house. Her tangled hair smelled like a forgotten dishrag, and her scabby limbs were skeletal. She was small and feral, and looked no more than six-years-old, compared to Sebastien who was skinny but well-formed and exuded an air of competence. Claire wondered how twins, even different genders, could be so unalike.

"Marie, show Claire and Laurent the little house," Henri said. "Bring them fruit and eggs, a cooking pan, and show them the water pump." He turned to Lawrence. "Your dwelling needs work, I'm afraid. It's taken me nine months to make the big house habitable, and much more work remains. For almost thirty years after the revolution the house, buildings, and land were abandoned. With your help, I will restore the plantation's glory. Take freely from the trees — oranges, bananas, coconuts, whatever you desire. This evening, I have matters to attend to in Jacmel. Tomorrow, you will bring your skills to the orchards."

"Henri," Claire said, "please purchase bolts of cloth, needles, thread, and buttons when you're in Jacmel. Our infant will need swaddling, and the twin's clothes need mending, and . . ."

"Enough," he said. "I will buy these things, but I am not your uncle, I am your *patron.* I will record your expenses in the account book."

Claire's face burned. What precipitated the sudden change in Henri's attitude? She hadn't meant to be presumptuous.

"Yes, of course," she said. "Tomorrow, before Lawrence examines the orchards and I take on work, we must discuss payment for our services, terms of our employment, and living arrangements. After we agree, you and we will sign a contract."

Henri gave her a puzzled look, then climbed the porch steps and disappeared inside.

～

The sun hovered at the mountain's peak. Sebastien disappeared around the side of the house, but Marie re-appeared with a battered pan and a basket of filth-covered eggs. Without a word or gesture, she started down a narrow but well-worn path through bushes and ferns. They entered a clearing with one tiny ramshackle building surrounded by scorched wood and five demarcated foundations. A rusted iron wheel and blackened broken implements — an axe head, a rake, barrel staves, and unidentifiable detritus — littered the ground.

"There were outbuildings here," Lawrence said, scanning the area,"burned down in a fire."

Marie set the pan and egg basket on the ground. She tugged Claire's sleeve and grunted. Claire followed her through a clump of tall grass to the ancient cast iron pump hidden within it.

"Does the pump work? Is there fresh water?" Claire asked, but the filthy child ignored her and scurried away. "Come back," she called as Marie ducked out of sight behind thick ferns.

Lawrence dropped their belongings with a dull thud. They had very little – some clothing, a quilt Granny made, his flint box, knife, and pistol, Claire's small handgun, a powder flask, bags of seed. And the money pouch from Mr. Raymond. How much remained? Mr. Raymond taught Claire about money — about estimating costs and revenues, and recording transactions in a journal. She glanced at Lawrence who looked skeletal, with dark rings under his watery eyes, and dirt streaked on his face. He knew nothing of contracts and agreements. Tomorrow, she would bargain with Henri. Hunger pangs roiled her stomach. She followed Lawrence to what Henri called, *the little house.*

The structure listed left. A terrible smell hovered around it. The walls were built of pine boards stacked horizontally, covered by a peaked tin roof. In the dwindling light the building looked dismal and grey, like an abandoned rowboat Claire once found along the Wissahickon.

Lawrence stepped inside but backed out. He sank to the ground, head in his hands.

"It stinks. Chicken and rat shit, and who knows what else all over the floor. We can't sleep there."

Claire sat beside him, and put an arm around his shoulders.He'd been brave so long, he used up his courage. He leaned against her, and she kissed his forehead.

"We're married, Lawrence. We came to Haiti to be together. We didn't expect our lives here to be easy, but we expected better than this. At least it's warm and dry tonight, and we can sleep outside. Tomorrow, we'll tell Henri what we need to stay and work his plantation. He's no farmer, and your skills are essential."

"I'm starving," Lawrence said.

"See if you can get that old pump to work. I hear running water. There must be a stream nearby. I'll rinse the eggs and clean the pan, and we'll get a fire started. Where did the little girl go?"

Lawrence pushed through the grass to the pump, and Claire walked around the edge of the clearing.

"Marie, Marie, I need you."

The child crawled out from green shrubs thick with red berries. Her wide eyes bored into Claire's chest.

"Marie, gather bananas, oranges, and coconuts." Claire gestured as she spoke.

The child sauntered into the grove, and Claire followed the sound and scent of sweet-smelling water. A clear-running stream ran alongside the clearing. She splashed her face and arms, rinsed the eggs, and scoured the battered pan with gravel.

Back at the clearing, she collected rocks, set them in a ring for a fire pit, stacked dried wood in a pyramid and made a nest of dried grass. It would take Lawrence only moments to start a fire with his flint.

Marie dumped two coconuts, a bunch of bananas, and small green oranges at Claire's feet. The child glanced at Claire before she hurried to the path and disappeared. Claire sighed.

"Claire," Lawrence called, "I cleaned out the pipe, I think it might work now."

She pushed through tall grass to Lawrence and the pump. His cheeks flamed from exertion.

"I used banana peels to grease the fittings, and got the handle to move but nothing came out. Then, I forced a palm stem through the pipe to clear out mud and crud. I hope it works."

He pumped repeatedly to creaks and whines, but no water. His breathing grew rapid and sweat dropped on the ground.

"Stop, Lawrence. Tomorrow we'll tell Henri it's broken."

But Lawrence pumped harder, glowering like a mad man. Water gurgled underground, quietly, then louder. The pump gushed stinky brown water.

"I did it!"

He took a deep breath and puffed out his chest. His mouth curved in a smile. He pumped harder. The water turned from muddy brown to pale brown and finally ran clear. He thrust the handle one more time and ducked his head under the flow.

With sopping hair and wild eyes, he said, "It smells fresh, like the Wissahickon after a storm. I think we can drink it."

"It's wonderful, Lawrence, you're wonderful. But we've had enough Haitian purification. Marie left us fruit and coconuts. Tonight we'll drink coconut juice. Tomorrow we'll ask Henri if the pump water's safe to drink."

After Lawrence sparked the fire, and the pan got spit hot, Claire cracked their five eggs into it. As soon as the eggs cooked, they plucked out pieces without concern for burned fingers.

An hour later, stars illuminated the sky like a million candles. They lay down near the fire pit and covered themselves with Granny's quilt. Claire flailed at a mosquito that buzzed near her ear. Beside her, Lawrence, his skin hot, stroked her chest and belly. His hand dropped, and she listened to his sleeping breaths, shallow and regular like a child. He should be attending Harvard and living in Reuben's comfortable house. She should be rocking on the porch with Granny and studying the latest fashions from France to help Mama design clothes for wealthy clients. She slapped a mosquito and cried softly.

They woke to pink sunlight and the smell of coffee and citrus. A shadow loomed over them.

"Your accommodations did not suit you?" Henri asked, cheerful. "Come to the big house for breakfast, then we'll visit the groves and see what sort of farmer you are."

Lawrence rose eagerly. Claire knew he desired food above all else. He gave her a hand and helped her stand. She brushed dust from her face and straightened her rumpled traveling dress. When the baby came, she'd return to the comfort of britches. She needed to bathe.

"Before Lawrence examines your land, we must agree to the terms of our service. We won't work without a contract."

"You allow your wife to speak for you? That was not the way of white plantation owners," Henri said. "You are far too serious, Claire. All will be agreed upon. Did I not meet you at the wharf, transport you to this paradise, feed and shelter you?"

"You called a decrepit shit-filled chicken coop a little house, gave us a few eggs and fallen fruit, and told us to get water from a rusty pump that hasn't worked in decades."

Claire looked at Lawrence with surprise and pride.

"In Haiti, we do not expect to live in fine rooms with servants to do our bidding. You chose to come. Now you must learn our ways. After we eat, all will be decided."

Inside Henri's house, a modern, cast iron stove, much like one Felix and Samuel gave Claire's parents a year ago, took up the middle of the kitchen. Already, Claire missed her family. A pot of coffee, a pitcher of milk, bowls of rice and beans, oranges, and bananas spread across the middle of a long table. A jar of mango jam and a loaf of sweet-smelling bread sat on a buffet.

"Cassava bread," Henri said as he sliced a piece for Claire.

The bread's rich smell made Claire's mouth water. Despite concern about another attack of the flux, she felt weak from hunger and thirst. She poured goat milk into her coffee and dipped the dense bread in it. Lawrence scooped beans and rice into his mouth and belched.

"Did you prepare all this food?" Claire asked.

"Islande, my woman in Jacmel, sent it. *You must feed your guests well,* she told me."

After breakfast, Claire collected the dishes, rinsed them under the pump outside the kitchen, and stacked them to dry. She returned to the dining room where Henri puffed a pipe. Lawrence sucked the skin of an orange.

"The agreement," Claire said.

Henri nodded. "So."

"You're obligated to provide us with adequate food, shelter, and tools. That horrible decrepit chicken coop is not adequate. Lawrence will improve your orchards and coffee plants. He will maintain the equipment and farm buildings, but not your house. You will cover the cost of parts and supplies for the equipment and tools you own, as well as the cost of new or replacement equipment when needed. I'll tend to the livestock. Lawrence will build a paddock for the goats, and a coop and pen for the chickens. Once their numbers and yields increase, we can supply the big house with milk, eggs, and meat in amounts we will determine at that time. In addition, Lawrence requires the donkey and cart. I will feed Sebastien and Marie when they're on the plantation, but I can't be responsible for their whereabouts. I am not and will not be their mother. They're far too undisciplined to control. I know something of healing both people and animals, and will do what I can when I can. After Lawrence restores the orchards and crops, he'll bring the output to market with you, or on his own. Until the produce is market ready, perhaps six months, you will pay us ten American dollars a month. Once oranges and coffee are brought to market regularly, our payment will be twenty percent of the proceeds. The agreement must be written by a lawyer, signed by you, Lawrence, and me, and witnessed and sealed by the lawyer."

"Is that all?" Henri asked, eyebrows raised.

Lawrence nodded yes, but Claire said, "No. We can't live in that rundown coop. You must provide us with wood, nails, tools, and carpenters to help Lawrence build a cottage. Lawrence can build our furniture, but you must procure a cook stove, wash tub, and water barrel for us to meet your obligation to provide adequate shelter."

Henri glared at Claire. "You are mad! You Americans, you run to Haiti to escape hate and ill will, but demand to live like the French invaders who enslaved us. Do you think money grows on those neglected orange trees?"

Claire crossed her arms. "Money does grow on orange trees. If you want to harvest that money, there's no better man than Lawrence. From his first steps, he worked on his family's prosperous farm. I, too, worked on that farm since childhood. Lawrence will restore your orchards to the best on this island. I'll tend your goats, increase the herd, and collect high quality milk. Now your chickens wander aimlessly, easy prey for wild dogs. They lay eggs wherever and whenever. Most of those eggs are stepped on or lost. After Lawrence builds the new coop, I'll train the hens to lay eggs there, and we'll have wonderful eggs every day. But we must have a decent place to live. There's little risk to you. The cottage Lawrence builds will benefit your plantation for fifty years."

For a moment, Claire feared Henri might slap her. Instead, he turned to Lawrence.

"First, we walk the groves. You tell me how you will improve the orchard. If I am satisfied, I will take you to Jacmel to engage the advocate to write our contract – for fifteen percent, not twenty, of the proceeds. I will find men to help you build a cottage and I will pay for the materials. You, *Madame*, must make terms with the workmen and find the means to pay them. Come, Laurent."

When Henri and he crossed the room headed for the door, Lawrence flashed Claire a bemused smile. Alone in the empty house, she let out a breath and congratulated herself. She'd hoped Henri might agree to pay them ten percent of the proceeds.

You are not a slave, her mother's voice whispered.

CHAPTER THIRTY-ONE

JACMEL SEPTEMBER 1824

The smell of fresh wood and sweaty men drifted across the clearing where Claire and Marie draped clean, mended clothes over coffee bushes. The speed with which the cottage rose astonished Claire. It reminded her of the barn-raisings she witnessed at Wissahickon Farm.

By noon, Lawrence, with three men Henri enlisted, had placed heavy stones for the foundation and built a sturdy frame of pine. The lumber formed a rectangular, one-story house with a front porch, a sitting room, a bedroom for Claire and Lawrence, another small bedroom, and a kitchen.

Sweat glistened off black backs as the men laid floor planks and closed the walls. The men's initial mockery of Lawrence ceased once they recognized his skill.

The night before, Lawrence slaughtered an ancient nanny goat, and Claire soaked the meat in vinegar and orange juice. Early this morning, she boiled ground corn sweetened with sugar cane in a big pot. After it cooled, she added eggs, and made johnnycakes from the thick mush. She stirred the pot of goat meat, sweet potatoes, nuts, and beans while Marie added red peppers and onions.

By the time hammers banged nails into tin for the cottage's roof, Lawrence's back sizzled like bacon.

"The stew's ready," Claire called. "Stop to eat."

The men sat under palm trees to eat, and scooped the stew with johnny cakes.

"*Pas mal*," a man said. "But bland, like *Blanc*."

Lawrence offered a pail of watery beer to the men, who filled tin cups and drank in gulps. When he moved to the pump to fill the empty pail with water, Claire joined him.

"Lawrence, your back is beet red. You must wear a shirt."

"They'll think I'm a sissy."

"They'll think you're crazy if you don't cover up."

By evening the next day, a small wood cottage stood on flat ground next to the decrepit chicken coop. The smell of sawdust saturated the air. The cottage needed furniture, pots, pans, dishes. Nonetheless, tonight they would sleep in their home.

Claire had promised the workers shirts and trousers for their pay. When the men first arrived, she measured them, using her arm and a length of rope. Each man chose from the colorful cotton fabrics Henri acquired in town. If only the baby would wait until she finished sewing. She was tired, but thank God, their child would have a place to live.

At day's end, the men filled their tin cups with rum Henri supplied. A muscular man who reminded Claire of Samuel, with shining black skin, a long pink scar across his chest, and short legs, sat on the new porch steps. He squeezed an upside-down bucket between his knees and pounded it with his fingers in a festive beat. The rhythm resonated in Claire's chest, and the baby lightened.

Lawrence and the other men piled wood scraps and debris around the decrepit chicken coop and set it on fire. In minutes, flames licked the walls and crackled in accompaniment to the drum beat. The black men cheered. Lawrence's face glowed in the firelight.

The Haitians raised their voices in a song Claire didn't recognize, but Marie sang along. They beckoned Claire to join them in the cottage's front yard. Hand-in-hand with the men and Marie, Claire lost herself. The drum beat, the dancing, and the joy of moving in harmony with these people – her people – brought joy deep within where her soul resided. Marie's small hand clasped hers, and the child's eyes drew Claire into a dark, bottomless pool.

The acrid smoke from the coop's dilapidated timber curled in the air. When the sides caved in and the roof smashed on the ground, Claire felt better than she had since she first told Lawrence she was pregnant.

CHAPTER THIRTY-TWO

JACMEL SEPTEMBER 20, 1824

In the hour before dawn, Claire lay on her back next to Lawrence on the pallet bed he built. She pushed Granny's quilt below the bulge in her waist. She hadn't slept well for months, and now, in this foreign place, fatigue and misery enveloped her. Still, the smell of fresh-cut timber and the sound of Lawrence's soft breathing eased her mind.

Then, she was riding a wave – rising, cresting, and crashing to shore. With a swoosh, water gushed from her womb. Her belly collapsed into a sheath around the baby. A pain like a punch penetrated deep in her gut and made her gasp.

"Lawrence," she whispered and nudged him.

"What, what?"

"The baby's coming."

"Now? What do we do?"

How many births of animals had they witnessed and assisted? Yet neither had seen a child born.

"Has Genevieve come from Port-au-Prince?"

"I don't think so," Lawrence said. "Henri didn't say."

"We need rags. A cloth to wrap the baby. A knife to cut the cord. Bring the quilt outside. I'll birth the baby there."

Claire's womb contracted. She moaned, and leaned on Lawrence to move outside. He spread the quilt on the ground.

"Go ask Henri when Genevieve's expected."

Lawrence's eyes skittered side-to-side. "I'll be back," he said, and raced for the path to the big house.

Pain consumed her. She tucked her legs close to her body. The baby pressed against her ribs, stealing her breath.

I can do this, she told herself. Everyone comes into the world this way. Every woman births her children like this. Mama did, Granny did, even Miss Anna did. Claire rolled to hands and knees, and got to her feet, stooped over like Old Caesar. Walking eased the pain. She circled the yard where they danced only days ago. Drum beats played in her head as if they never stopped.

I'll make that area the garden, she decided. We'll build a proper coop over there with a fenced-in pen to protect the chickens from wild dogs. Another lingering cramp doubled her over. She gagged and vomited. She wanted Mama's cool hand on her brow, to hear her soft reassuring voice. Why did we leave? She needed her mother. She couldn't have this baby without her. Where is Lawrence? She screamed in fury and agony. Genevieve promised to be here. She lied. Pain brought her to her knees. The Philadelphia rowdy boys' punches and kicks were nothing compared to misery that built and built until she wanted to smash her head with a rock to make it stop.

When Claire could bear no more, the pain subsided. She stood straight and breathed clean sweet air. Dawn burst in pink and red ribbons above the mountains.

What's today's date? September 20th? She must write it down. The pain came again like the jaws of a vise, tight, tighter, tighter. The smell of coffee from the big house made her ill. Something trickled down her legs.

"Claire!"

Lawrence rushed down the path, swinging a bucket. As soon as he reached her, she collapsed against him. He dragged her to the quilt. After she sat down, he cooled her face with a clean rag from the bucket of water.

"I'll take you inside," he said. His lower lip quivered.

"It's too hot. What did Henri say? Where's Genevieve?"

Lawrence swallowed and stared toward the big house.

"He expected her two days ago."

As the sun ascended through cottony clouds, Claire writhed and moaned. Cramps came relentlessly, and eased only long enough for her to fear the next one. She wanted Mama, she wanted Granny, she wanted Molly, she wanted Miss Anna who despised her. Only women shared her agony. Lawrence's anxiety and solicitousness annoyed her. From behind a coffee bush that failed to hide her, Marie's owl eyes blinked each time Claire moaned.

"Water, Marie, *l'eau*," Claire called.

The child scurried to the pump, creaked the lever, and returned with an empty cup.

"Useless," Lawrence muttered.

He filled the cup and helped Claire drink. When she raised her arms, he helped her stand and supported her as they circled the cottage in short tortured steps.

"Our baby's a boy. No girl would cause this much trouble," she said.

Lawrence's smile was tight-lipped, his green eyes were sunken. Claire shook off his arm. With a gasp, she spit up the water. They returned to the quilt, where she lay on her side, legs tucked, eyes squeezed shut. A shadow passed over her, and the air cooled.

"Thank God," Lawrence whispered.

Claire opened her eyes to flashes of red and yellow. Genevieve loomed over her.

"I am here, *mon bébé*. A mighty boulder blocked the road through the mountains. I traveled the last twenty *kilomètres* on foot."

"I didn't think you'd come," Claire said.

Genevieve clicked her tongue. "*Bien sûr,* I will bring your *bébé* into the light."

She placed her hands on Claire's belly and closed her eyes, then turned to Lawrence.

"*Vas-y,* go, go. I will send for you when our work is done."

Lawrence kissed Claire. "Do you want me to stay?"

At Claire's grimace, he walked away, looking back before he disappeared on the path to the orange groves.

Claire lay back for Genevieve's examination, willing herself to stay still.

"Your body does not want to give up your *bébé*. The collar of your womb is buttoned tight. We must persuade it to unbutton so your package may be delivered to the world."

Even in distress, Claire perked up. On a tiny island in the Caribbean Sea, a black woman spoke the words used in her family's business. She smiled.

"You make fun at Genevieve? You think I have not seen the reluctant womb?"

"I don't laugh at Genevieve. I'm happy you're here."

"This oil softens the collar. Now, get up. You must walk."

Genevieve helped Claire stand. She held her arm and walked faster than Lawrence had. Each time Claire moaned, Genevieve pressed her hand against Claire's belly to feel the contraction.

"*Plus rapide*," Genevieve said, "walk faster."

Claire felt like the last child in a line playing whip, fearful she'd fly off and tumble to the ground. A strong cramp hit with the urgent need to force the baby out.

"Stop," she cried.

Genevieve ran her hand over Claire's belly and nodded. She led her to the porch, put Claire's hands on the railing, and handed her a wooden spoon.

"The spoon in your mouth gives the baby air. Lean forward and bend your knees. Hold onto the railing. When the pain comes again, push down. Your work is up here. My work is below."

Claire prayed and pushed, imagining herself as Star of Night delivering a foal. Pain flowed through her in never-ending waves. She heard a hundred screeching parrots and her throat ached. She realized the screeching was her own.

"*C'est bien*. Here is the baby's head."

Claire hated herself for screaming, but agony overwhelmed her. She was no longer Claire, no longer human, no longer anything but pain and fear. She screamed and pushed, desperate to end the suffering. A giant lump slid from her body. The cramps subsided. Every muscle quivered, and she collapsed, too exhausted to hold the rails. In one arm, Genevieve held a tiny blue baby face-down.

"Breathe, Little Man, breathe."

Genevieve tapped the infant's back and gunk dribbled from his mouth. She turned him upright to wipe mucus from his mouth and nose. Like Claire breathed for Star of Night's foal, Genevieve put her mouth on the baby's and puffed. Inspiration. The tiny boy lurched. His scrawny arms and legs flailed. Genevieve turned him face down and tapped again. He made a coughing choking noise. Genevieve cleared his mouth, and he uttered a strangled cry. When Genevieve placed her son in her arms, Claire sobbed.

As his color changed from blue to deep red, the baby opened his mouth and turned his face to Claire's chest. He was small, sticky, blood-streaked, and the most beautiful creature she ever saw. A thick, purple cord hung from his navel.

"Ah, the cord stopped beating."

Genevieve tied string in two places around the umbilical cord, and with a thick knife, cut it from below while Claire cradled her son.

"Will you call Lawrence?" Claire asked.

At the sound of Genevieve's voice, Lawrence raced from the orchard, tripped, rolled, brushed himself off, and launched himself to Claire's side. Tears filled his eyes.

"Can I hold him?"

"Wash yourself first," Genevieve said.

Lawrence raced to the pump. When he returned, he glanced at Genevieve who nodded. He took his son from Claire's arms, and kissed the baby's forehead.

"Look at his tiny fingers and toes. He's wonderful, Claire. Thank you."

Ten feet away, Marie, fingers in her mouth, silently stared.

"Claire must pass the afterbirth. Help her up," Genevieve said.

"I can't," Claire said.

"You must."

With the baby nestled in one arm, Lawrence offered his other to Claire. He helped her stand, and she reached for the railings.

"One push. Do not worry. The hard work is over."

Genevieve massaged Claire's stomach until the placenta dropped in a bloody gush. Genevieve caught it, examined it, and put it in a bamboo basket.

"I will bury the afterbirth under an orange tree to ensure good luck and good yields. Laurent, there is sweet rice and cold tea for Claire at the big house. Marie, stay at Henri's tonight."

After Lawrence and Marie started up the path, Genevieve wrapped the baby in a white cloth and took Claire's arm.

"Come, you will be more comfortable inside. After I clean you, the baby must suckle. When Laurent comes with food, you must eat and drink to make good milk."

"Thank you, Genevieve," Claire croaked. "I needed you and you came."

Genevieve collected her things and the basket with the placenta. Once Claire was settled, she waited until Lawrence returned.

"*Merci beaucoup*, Genevieve," he said.

"Claire and your son need you," Genevieve said, then headed for the orchard.

◞

"He looks like you," Claire whispered.

The baby boy had wide-set eyes. His skin was ruddy, much lighter than Claire's. She studied the baby's head, cheeks, chest, arms, and legs, and marveled at this fully formed human who dwelled inside her body an hour before.

Lawrence cleaned dried blood from the baby's head. He held both tiny feet in one hand. The child rooted against Claire's chest and found the nipple. They smiled.

"This is why we came to Haiti, to be our son's mother and father, together," Claire said.

"What shall we name him?"

"I like the name, Anthony, for Anthony Benezet, who loved Africans like brothers and sisters, and taught them to read and write. Do you like it?"

"I do. Can we give him the middle name, Raymond, for my father? Anthony Raymond Williams?"

"It's a beautiful name."

Claire fell asleep with the baby nestled on her chest.

Lawrence delicately touched his wife and child to make sure they were real. He cradled his body around them.

"I will love and protect you forever," he whispered, as his heart raced and tears filled his eyes.

CHAPTER THIRTY-THREE

Rotting oranges littered the ground and emitted a sweet cloying smell. In the months since they arrived, Lawrence spent days and weeks pulling weeds and clearing brush. To improve the fruit quality and yield, he pruned broken limbs and low-hanging branches.

In September when he explored the plantation, he discovered random lemon and lime trees beyond the orange grove's perimeter; blooming coffee bushes; and wild-growing green stalks he thought were corn but upon examination discovered were sugar canes. Throughout Henri's land, bunches of green bananas hung from trees with huge leaves, and palms bent with the weight of the woody-husked coconuts Claire loved.

In the days after Anthony's birth, Lawrence cleared the area around the cottage with a rusty machete. He dug up a portion of the yard for Claire's garden, and planted beans, squash, pumpkin, peas, peppers, and lettuce with seeds from Wissahickon Farm. On nearby farms, he bartered his labor for corn seeds, onions, cabbage, and sweet potatoes. His skin burned red until Genevieve showed Claire the spiny aloe plants that soothed burns. When he healed, his skin freckled and tanned.

The cottage withstood a great gale in October, with driving rain and winds that rattled their windows and terrified Claire. The storm tore off branches from most of the orange trees and downed the half-dead ones. But afterwards, the surviving trees produced more oranges. Better oranges. Lawrence and the orphan boy, Sebastien, picked and crated a cartful of ripe fruit they drove to Jacmel. The captain of a British sailing ship bought the entire lot. Lawrence was satisfied with his first sale, and confident he would improve both quality and yield with good agricultural practices.

Each day Lawrence rose early and carried his infant son outside while Claire cooked eggs from the hens she trained to lay in nesting boxes. He loved the dawn. The air was cool, and sunlight burst through clouds in shimmering gold. He loved returning to the cottage for breakfasts of eggs, corn cakes, and mango, with hot coffee from the plantation's bushes, thickened with fresh goat milk. He lingered until Claire settled in a rocking chair and put his son to her breast. Then, he headed to the grove. The work was hard, sometimes unbearably so. He found strength to go on because of love for his wife and child.

This day, Lawrence smiled at thoughts of his son, nearly three months old. Anthony had one blond curl on top of his head, large blue eyes, and skin the creamy hue of almond seeds. Even Henri said Anthony looked like him. Why did his parents question his relationship with Claire? If only they could see Anthony, they'd know he was their grandson.

Whenever Anthony cooed or smiled and kicked his legs, Lawrence's heart filled to bursting. No other child was as beautiful and brilliant. While he dragged away dead branches, he wished Papa and Mutti could see this wondrous child. With Christmas fast approaching, Lawrence thought he might write a letter to tell them of his and Claire's whereabouts and Anthony's birth.

He imagined Mutti was desperate for him to return home with his little family. But then he remembered her stinging words. She disowned him and wrongly accused Claire. Why should he write them a letter? Besides, days after Anthony's birth, Claire wrote to her family. His parents could learn of their grandson from the Pennimans, who never rejected Claire or the baby she carried.

As he hacked back overgrown vines, sweat dripped down his face, chest, and back. At the sound of footsteps, he lowered his blade. Claire waved from the path with Anthony in a sling on her back like an Indian papoose. These are the two I love, he thought. This is my family. Sweet citrus smells rose from the bundles of branches piled along the path.

"Some of those branches have oranges on them," Claire said when she reached him.

"Those branches have rotten oranges on them." Lawrence plucked one to show Claire. The fruit squished in his hand. "Henri will be angry when he sees the waste."

"You aren't accountable for the weather, Lawrence. The saplings you started are thriving. Will you have enough oranges for another trip to market?"

"Soon. Good oranges are ripening on the high branches. But I need to cut away more damaged branches, and burn this rubbish. There's work for a dozen men."

Claire's stomach rumbled. She thought of Wissahickon Farm, where the work was spread among many and the dinner bell called them to Molly's hardy meals. Claire could almost taste those sweet, buttery cinnamon rolls.

"Where's Sebastien? The boy is never nearby when I need him."

Lawrence took off his straw hat and ran his fingers through his sweat-soaked hair. His taut muscles glistened with sweat. Anthony bumped his head against Claire's back.

"You nursed an hour ago, Child," Claire said. "Wait while I help your father."

She re-tied her yellow scarf. White clouds formed a halo over mountains framed by an azure Haitian sky. She adjusted Anthony's sling, then helped Lawrence drag brush and branches to the path. The baby's whimpers became lusty cries.

"I hear you, Little Man. I'm hungry, too."

She shimmied Anthony out of the sling and sat with her back against a coconut palm. Anthony pressed his face to her breast, her milk flowed, and her heart filled with love.

Lawrence's cheeks flamed as he tied branches in bundles.

"Are you helping or sitting?" he called.

"I'm feeding Anthony."

Claire shook her head. As much as Lawrence loved Anthony, he expected Claire to put the baby aside whenever he needed or wanted her. Granny's words — 'You'll have two babies to care for' — rang true. If only she could talk to Granny right now. She steeled herself against tears. Still, she pitied Lawrence. He was a boy forced to be a man. A minute later he plopped next to her and handed her a banana.

With a pop and sigh, Anthony unlatched from her breast, asleep. She breathed her son's sweet baby smell. On soft leaves, she settled the sleeping child and covered him with her headscarf. A bead of sweat dropped from Claire's eyebrow. She felt exhausted and woozy.

Lawrence took her face in his hands, the scent of bananas and coconuts on his breath. His green eyes, bright in his tanned face, captivated her. The heat of his body leached the energy from hers. He helped her slip off her clothes. His shirt ripped when he pulled it over his head. Another thing to mend, she thought, as Lawrence filled her, his salty taste, his kisses and caresses, his boy's chest pressed against hers. Her breasts tingled. The insistence of his hips and her exhaustion and desire drove other thoughts from her mind.

"That was nice," he said.

"We could never be so free with each other at home. I love you," Claire said.

But even as she spoke the words, she felt a pang of something else – homesickness, regret.

"I miss you even when I know you're close. With so much work, we have little time for ourselves," he said.

Claire shimmied into her cotton trousers and blouse.

"I never expected you'd have to work so hard, and I never realized the amount of time it takes to care for a baby. Do you ever wish we stayed in Philadelphia?"

Overhead, clouds rolled across the sky, pushed by a breeze that ruffled the orange blossoms. Parrots squawked. Sweat stung her lips.

"Aren't you happy?" Lawrence asked.

Claire kissed him. "I'm happy we're together with our son. But I miss my family. I miss your family. And the farm. And Star of Night, and Inspiration, and Queen, and my goats. We're so far away. It's hard all the time."

"I don't think about that. I think about you and Anthony." Lawrence pulled on his pants. "I work and work and there's no time for fun. I'm doing my best for you, Claire."

She wondered if Lawrence really never thought of home, his family, or the farm. She sighed.

"No matter what, in Haiti we have each other. And we have Anthony," she said.

He leaned down and kissed the baby's head.

"We have Anthony."

CHAPTER THIRTY-FOUR

JACMEL 7 JANUARY 1825

D*ear Claire,*
Until your letter arrived, we lived in fear that we lost you forever. Even though Granny and later, Felix, told us of your marriage to Lawrence and your decision to sail to Haiti, with every footstep on the porch I rushed to welcome you home. With every breath, I blamed myself for driving you away. For that, darling Claire, I am eternally sorry. I never imagined the depth of your love for Lawrence and now, for your infant son. I was foolish to try to convince you otherwise.

We received your news with joy to learn of Anthony's birth, and sorrow to know you're too far away to share him with us. Only recently have I forgiven Felix for helping you run away. And yet, as much as we wish you were home working alongside me in the shop, being part of our everyday lives, I'm proud of your courage. When Granny told us you sailed to Haiti with Lawrence, she reminded us that the Lord watches over you – 'that you are no more strangers and foreigners, but of the household of God.'

Daddy sits across from me as I write. He loves you and wants you to know that whenever you come home, he will welcome your son and husband. You are ever beloved here. Granny starts and ends each day with a prayer – Lord, keep watch over Claire's going out and coming in, from this time to forever.

I shared your letter with Anna and Raymond. Anna is aloof and angry. She cannot look me in the eyes. And the loss of Lawrence diminished Raymond. While Anna sat with me in the front room, Raymond found your father and asked him to tell you he's sorry. If you return, he'll find a place for you to live, though not on the farm.

Raymond gave your father good terms on a young gelding named Buck, and a nanny goat with a white head and black stripe down her nose — one of yours descended from Queen, he said. Daddy named her Little Claire and lets no one tend her but himself.

Felix lent Samuel money to buy the building next to the barbershop, and Samuel does a fine business repairing harnesses, reins, and saddles. He helps your father with deliveries – of all kinds – and goes to Wissahickon Farm a few days each month. The cold and damp of winter pains Granny's rheumatiz. Mary takes classes at the church now and reads the bible to Granny each evening.

I know you'll be sad to learn Old Caesar died. The day after Christmas, Pretty Boy appeared at our back door, barking and whining. Daddy followed him to the shack, and there he found Caesar, cold and grey, sitting at the table with a cup of tea and a plate of bread and cheese set before him.

Felix tries to keep Pretty Boy at the barbershop, but every few days he goes back to the shack to look for Old Caesar.

Darling Claire, know that we think of you every day. We miss you and must rely on our imaginations to picture our little grandson, Anthony. Stay well, and remember your family loves you and longs for you to come home.

Your loving Mama, with Daddy and Granny's fond thoughts

CHAPTER THIRTY-FIVE

1 *5 April 1825*
 Dear Mutti and Papa,
 I have thought of you often, especially at Christmas. I find it difficult to write, knowing your feelings about my marriage and wondering if my letter will be received with delight or dismay. Despite my reticence, Claire urges me to contact you – she stands beside me now – so you might find peace of mind in knowing we are making a life for ourselves and our son, Anthony Raymond Williams.

 I know Claire's parents informed you of Anthony's birth. There is no question I am his father – his skin and hair are fair, and his eyes are blue and remind me of yours, Mutti. He is a remarkable boy and can already pull himself up to standing. He crawls everywhere and points to the birds in the sky. His two bottom teeth have come in, and he feeds himself bananas, and takes sips from our cups. Claire is a wonderful mother.

 It is hot in Haiti year round. Christmas without a chill in the air and snow on the ground seemed strange. In this country of colored men and women, I am the outsider, the 'blanc' who invites stares and comments, spoken in a sort of French I struggle to understand. Claire learned the local tongue far better than I, but thankfully the French I studied at the university helps me manage my business affairs. While white English, French, Spanish, and American sailors sometimes walk along the streets of Jacmel waiting to load their ships with bags of coffee and crates of oranges, the people who live and work here are of African blood or mulatto. Once they understand I am a farmer who works for Henri Renaud, and

I'm married to a black American, I am regarded without animosity – more often with curiosity.

Claire is accepted without reservation, especially by the women who love Anthony. Claire has formed a special friendship with Henri's sister, Genevieve, the midwife who delivered our son. Genevieve is a mambo – a healer and priestess in the tradition of Voodoo. Genevieve has taught Claire the healing properties of herbs and flowers that grow nearby, and Claire soothes my sunburned skin, lays poultices over our insect bites to calm the itching, and makes a bitter tea that helps with stomach upsets. It did not take long for people to learn of Claire's good hand to close wounds, even gaping ones, and she stitches up injured neighbors and their animals weekly. Her ability to read and write as well as cipher and keep accounts are much admired by the men and women here.

The Haitian sky and bay are violet-blue, and I sometimes wonder if the indigo shrubs which grow throughout the land create a miasma that rises from the pale purple blossoms to color the sea and sky. Anthony's eyes reflect the azure firmament.

The sun is falling and I find my eyes straining in the dim light. Tomorrow, I will rise early and work in the orange orchard, where I continue to clear away decades of neglect and coax the trees to share their bounty. Along with oranges, coffee, bananas, and coconuts grow on the plantation, although much grows wild since my efforts have been directed to restoring the orange orchard.

Claire helps with the trees and tends to the chickens, goats, and Anthony. She earns a bit of money making cotton shirts and short pants, dresses, and scarves for the market. She is well and strong. If you happen to see Moses and Elizabeth, please share this letter with them, and give our best regards to Molly, Hamish, and Duff. When next you write to Reuben and his family in Boston, please give him this news of Claire and me. We would be grateful for news about you and the farm.

My eighteenth birthday today makes me a man. I hope you will find it in your hearts to understand that my decision to marry Claire and migrate to Haiti was made with no intent to hurt you, but to recognize my responsibility to my child and Claire. I cannot imagine life without her.

With respect and regards,

Lawrence

CHAPTER THIRTY-SIX

The baskets of laundry wobbled as Claire and Marie strolled down the path to the river. The custom of balancing large loads on the head no longer seemed odd to Claire, and she felt proud she mastered this feat. On the streets of Jacmel, no sailor would identify her as American. In this country of blacks, Claire walked the narrow line between recognition and anonymity, where a stranger would not think her different, where the color of her clothing was more noticeable than the color of her skin. This sense of acceptance was a joy and a wonder to Claire. Still, it was a diluted joy – Haiti was not her home.

The sound of women's voices flowed and ebbed like the river itself. When Claire approached the women who laughed and gossiped while they did their laundry, she called, *"Oné."* A chorus of voices called back, *"Respé."*

With Anthony squirming to be freed from the pack on her back, Claire dropped her basket next to Marie's and unwound the chubby baby. When he crawled to a shallow pool to splash with other children, women touched his soft, yellow curls.

Nearby, a large woman with deep black skin and broad cheeks reached into a pouch and handed sun-bleached goat knuckles to a naked boy. A handful of children gathered to throw the bones in the air while Marie watched.

"Osslay," Marie said in a low voice. "Mami play *osslay* with Marie and Sebastien."

As Marie's brown hands pounded Lawrence's sweat-stained shirt, the smell of rotten eggs rose from her hair.

"After we wash the clothes, we will wash ourselves," Claire said. She paused, then continued. "What happened to your mami, Marie?"

"We lose Mami." A fly buzzed near the girl's eye.

"You lost your mother? And after you lost her, you slept under Henri's porch?"

"No, no," Marie looked to the sky as if searching for a memory. "Mami sick. We lose Mami. Go Yasmine *kay*, house. Yasmine fly. We walk. Then sleep under house of Henri."

Claire rubbed lye soap against Lawrence's britches, concerned that if she scrubbed hard enough to get out the stains, the fabric would shred.

Even on the river bank, the noontime heat sent trickles of sweat down Claire's brow and upper lip. The smells of water, shore, and damp greenery reminded Claire of the Wissahickon Creek, and Old Caesar cooking catfish on a stone grill. She mourned his death.

One by one, women gathered their children and clothing and bid Claire goodbye. In a shallow pool, Anthony sputtered when water went up his nose. Overhead, a black seabird with a long neck and yellow throat dove into river and rose with a fish squirming in its beak.

"Sebastien fly like bird," Marie said.

The girl confused Claire. Henri called her feeble-minded.

Claire spread their laundry over bushes to dry, then stripped off her clothes, swept up Anthony, removed his shirt and nappie, and waded with him into the river. She motioned for Marie to follow. The girl inched into the river and reached for Claire's hand. With Anthony in one arm, Claire dipped Marie's head under water to wet it, then soaped the girl and scrubbed her with a rag.

After they washed, Claire wanted to float with the current, head back and arms outstretched, like she and Lawrence used to do when the Wissahickon ran high from summer rains. But now Claire had Anthony and Marie, clothes to carry home, chores to complete, scarves, shirts, and dresses to make for sale in Jacmel, and meals to prepare. With a last dip under water to let cool river water run through her hair, Claire waded to the shore.

Once she settled Anthony, she lay on a flat rock to let the sun drink river water from her skin. The rock's heat rose through her core, and she smelled her body cooking, a sweet, meaty smell of coconut and spice. She covered her eyes with an arm and sensed Marie moving close.

The child stroked Claire's arm with surprisingly strong fingers, kneading her sore muscles like bread. Marie moved her hands to Claire's shoulders and slid them behind her neck. After a moment, the child shifted, then lay on top of Claire, hands caressing Claire's breasts like a lover.

"Stop!" Claire pushed the girl off. "I don't like that."

Marie tumbled onto the sand and knelt, covered in grit, gazing at Claire like a puppy, brown eyes bewildered. Claire dressed, tossed Marie her shift, and motioned for her to dress.

"Yasmine tell *òfelen*, orphans, make soft soft," Marie whispered, as if to herself.

"I don't understand," Claire said as she dressed Anthony and jiggled him into his sling. "Tell me about Yasmine while we walk."

After Claire balanced the laundry basket on her head, she helped Marie with the lighter one. As they walked, Claire's heart settled into a strong beat. She followed her shadow, a dark, stretched monster with muscular legs and an impossibly huge, barrel-shaped head. A smaller monster swayed alongside, like Grendel and his mother walking to their river lair.

Claire remembered the cold evening after final harvest when Miss Anna told the tale of *Beowulf*, the German hero who ripped off Grendel's arm and beheaded the monster's mother. That November night, stars dazzled in the dark sky while farm workers warmed their hands at the bonfire, and drank hot toddies. Lawrence, then ten years old, sat close to Claire and took her hand. They were fascinated and terrified. Marie has her own monsters, Claire thought.

As if reading Claire's mind, Marie kicked a pebble and took a breath.

"Mami *te mouri*, die. After Mami and Papi die, Yasmine take *les petits* to her shack. 'An empty sack can't stand up,' Yasmine say. 'I take care children, children take care Yasmine. You bring no food, you get no food.' We go to market, steal food for Yasmine. If *marchands* catch us, they beat us. Not catch me, never. Yasmine so *fatigué* from *les petits* she say rub her arms, back, *tetin, bounda*, soft soft so Yasmine sleep."

Claire's shoulders hurt. She stopped in the shade of a palm tree to shift the strap of Anthony's sling. Yasmine made the children rub her chest, her bottom? She shuddered.

"You stole food for Yasmine? You rubbed her at night?"

"*Oui.*"

"Sebastien too? Come along. We'll be home soon."

In a looping walk that took her from one side of the path to the other, Marie supported her basket with one hand and scratched a scab on her ear with the other.

"Sebastien fly. At *Bassin Bleu* he climb big stones way high. The *mons* give Sebastien *centimes*, sweet potato, and sugar cane to fly over falling water into pool. The *mons* say, '*Bravo, Flying Boy*.'"

"Marie, did Sebastien soft soft Yasmine?" Claire asked again, although she wasn't certain she wanted to know.

"*Pafwa* – sometime. When he say no, Yasmine beat him. Sebastien tell Marie, 'No more.' He tell Yasmine, 'Come watch Sebastien fly, watch Sebastien get *centimes* from the *mons, centimes* for Yasmine.'"

"Did Yasmine go to *Bassin Bleu* with Sebastien?"

"*Oui*. Sebastien say, 'Yasmine, you fly.' He *pouse* Yasmine to fly. Now, Yasmine sleep in deep water. And we sleep under house of Henri."

In sight of the orchard and the cottage, Marie dropped the basket and ran, heedless to Claire's call to come back. With Anthony heavy on her back and her shoulders burning, Claire picked up Marie's basket and lurched to the house.

"Marie," she called, "Sebastien."

But there was no response, not even the sight of dark eyes peeking from behind a bush.

Claire's upper lip jutted out, and her nose scrunched like she smelled something *degoutan* – disgusting. There was much she didn't understand about Marie, but today, what she learned made her ill. Did 'Yasmine sleep in deep water' mean what Claire thought? Did Sebastien push Yasmine off a cliff to drown in the pool below? It was too terrible to imagine.

The memory of the slave catcher straddling her hit Claire with a force that sent her to her knees. Anthony pulled her hair, and she set him down. Here, thousands of miles from home, two young children, and untold others, suffered terrible abuse at the hands of their caretaker. Sebastien, like Samuel, saved his sister. Her heart broke for the orphaned twins. No wonder they were hard to love.

Before going inside, Claire checked the chicks that hatched last month. Two developed combs – cockerels. One or both would be sold if they grew to be aggressive roosters. Claire scooped up Anthony and thought again about the twins who confused and frightened her. Still, she would not tell Lawrence what she learned. They were children, orphans, no matter what they'd done.

CHAPTER THIRTY-SEVEN

JACMEL MARCH 1827

As the sun rose over the mountains in ribbons of pink and gold, raindrops sparkled on glossy coffee leaves. In the pit behind the chicken coop, the rooster crowed. Flapping wings and Lawrence's voice rose above the clatter of chickens and goats.

Each day, Lawrence worked with an aggressive rooster he named Andrew Jackson. Claire found Lawrence's obsession with the bird bizarre, but he told her training the cock amused him, especially compared with his backbreaking work in the groves.

Claire carried bowls of porridge to the porch where Lawrence and Sebastien, both smelling of sweat and chicken shit, waited. Claire raised an eyebrow.

"You should wash up before you eat."

From inside, Anthony called, "Mami." A moment later, Marie led the toddler onto the porch, and Claire filled bowls for them.

While Anthony ate, Lawrence ran his fingers through the boy's curls. Frothy clouds crossed the sky. Claire tilted her head and considered Marie.

The girl worried her. Some days, smiling and talkative, she followed Claire like a gosling. Other days, she was remote and silent, refusing to respond. Every week or so, the girl disappeared and returned filthy, disheveled, and hungry. Sebastien, too, took off, often for days. Whenever Claire asked where he and Marie went, he'd say, 'The goat's business is not the sheep's business.' If she pressed for more, he'd say, 'You are not our mother. Be our friend.'

After two-and-a-half years, Claire's expectations for Marie were limited. Certainly, the girl was well fed, wore decent clothing, and bathed — when Claire dragged her to the wash tub. Sebastien grew tall and strong, and proved a quick learner, but Marie remained small, even withered, despite an inordinate appetite.

A glob of porridge splashed on Claire's foot. She turned too late to catch Anthony's bowl. It crashed and shattered.

"Oops," Anthony said.

"I'll clean him up." Lawrence carried the sturdy toddler to the pump as Claire picked up the sharp pieces of earthenware. Marie scooped up spilled porridge.

"Toss that porridge to the chickens," Claire said.

"Do you need anything in Jacmel?" Lawrence dropped Anthony in the front yard. "I have a delivery after morning chores."

"Fabric and thread."

The chickens squawked. Claire glanced at the coop to see Marie jam porridge in her mouth. The girl returned with gritty lips. Claire sighed.

A few hours later, Lawrence and Sebastien arranged crates of oranges and bags of coffee beans in the bed of the donkey cart.

A week ago, Claire and Marie picked red coffee cherries, and spread them in the wooden drying trough. Yesterday, they hulled the outer shells and packed the beans for market. The work demanded focus and quick hands. Coffee cherries had tough skin, but the white fruit under it tasted sweet and tangy. Claire loved the spicy smell, like cloves or sassafras. While they hulled the shells, Marie sang.

Yellow bird, up high in banana tree, yellow bird, you sit all alone like me.
  Black and yellow you, like banana too, you sit all alone like me. You
  can fly away, in the sky away, you're more lucky than me.

"That's a pretty song, Marie," Claire had said.

"Yasmine sing Yellow Bird," the girl responded.

"Tell me about Yasmine."

It had been over a year since Marie mentioned the woman. Whenever Claire tried to learn more, Marie ran away or pretended she didn't understand — until yesterday.

"After Mami gone, the *mons* take Marie and Sebastien to Yasmine shack – like chicken coop. Sleep on floor, no blanket. Many *ensek*, cockroach, bite Marie. Marie and Sebastien wake up, find food. We eat, give Yasmine *rès la,* the rest. Yasmine want all. Punch Marie, pow. Kick Sebastien. Sebastien say, no more."

"Did Yasmine fall into the waterfall?" Claire asked.

Marie's dark head bobbed and dipped. She danced around the trough before she answered.

"Sebastien *pouse* Yasmine. She fly down splash dark water," Marie whispered, so low, Claire barely heard. "Sebastien say no more Yasmine. We run fast. Sebastien find *zorang*, eggs. He find Henri house."

Claire wrapped her arms around the girl, ignoring the moldy smell of her hair. "You're safe now."

Marie jerked away and ran to the grove. When she returned hours later, she tugged Claire's sleeve to show her a tangle of grass and leaves, woven and tied.

"*Poupee*," Marie said, hugging the grass bundle against her chest. "My *bébé.*"

"A doll? My mother made me a rag doll when I was a little girl. Someday I'll make one for you," Claire told the child, and Marie had smiled.

Now, while Lawrence and Sebastien loaded the last bags in the cart, Anthony marched around the yard behind Marie, who swung her arms and sang — *You can fly away.*

Claire's thoughts flew away to Germantown. She wondered what her mother was doing this very instant. She tried to visualize Daddy, Granny, Mary, Samuel, and Felix going about their day.

A goat batted the paddock fence. Claire gazed at the fawn-colored doe. She thought of Queen, now six-years-old and surely the well-established herd matriarch. In Haiti, while she enjoyed caring for the goats, and hens, and the small donkey, she couldn't bring herself to name the animals.

"We're off, Claire," Lawrence called.

Claire turned as if awakened from a dream. Sebastien grinned, his cheeks broad and his skin shining. Lawrence tugged the reins to turn the donkey toward the road.

"Don't forget the fabric – bright colors, and ink and paper."

As the cart moved out of sight, Claire sighed. A light breeze ruffled the palm leaves. She collected eggs and picked fresh vegetables. On the porch steps, Anthony and Marie played patty-cake.

Claire felt lonely and bored. She shielded her eyes and gazed at the sky – the day would be fine. Why shouldn't they, too, go to town?

∾

Ruts from the donkey cart lined the dirt path that meandered through banana trees and thick, green bushes. Claire carried Anthony on her back and goaded Marie to keep moving.

On the outskirts of town, people squatted outside shanties and huts – talking, smoking, and braiding hair, while naked children kicked a dusty ball that landed at Claire's feet. Before she kicked it back, she saw the ball was a small skull stuffed with straw.

A lean woman in a thin shift, wearing a worn and faded green bandana, rose from her stoop to pet Anthony.

"*Bel ti bébé,*" she said. "*Joli bébé,* pretty."

"*Merci.*"

Claire untied her bright yellow bandana and offered it to the woman as barter — in trade for the woman's worn headscarf. The woman hesitated, then smiled from a toothless mouth and made the trade.

On Jacmel's main street, wealthy-looking dark people in European clothes drank tea and ate biscuits at tables outside cafes. The salty sea breeze complemented the grilled fish and fried banana smells. On both sides of the road, vendors plied their wares. Anthony squirmed to get down.

"Keep Anthony safe, Marie, *silvouplè,*" Claire said. She gave her a few *centimes.* "Buy coconut pudding and yam tarts for you and Anthony. Stay close."

After Marie took Anthony's hand and headed for the food sellers, Claire focused on the fabric booths.

"Here, Missy, best fabric, best price," a squat woman in a red turban called. Puffs of smoke rose from her cigar.

"This lot comes from France," an ancient man said. He looked as delicate as the cloth, as if a good breeze would send him flapping against a tree.

Each bolt of cloth told the story of its origin. Claire examined the fabrics with her fingers. She noted the texture, the weave's tightness, the weight, whether the color came off on her skin. Before she decided on a bolt of blue and a bolt of red, she tugged the fabrics to determine their give, and held them up to the sun to gauge their thickness.

"The blue, too thin," Claire said. "The red, too stiff. But I am desperate for these colors. I will take them off your hands for ten *centimes.*"

"*Non, non, Madame,* never," the squat woman said. "I sell the finest fabric in all Haiti. I make nothing at fifty *centimes.* For your desperation, I give you a gift at forty."

Other fabric vendors formed a half-circle around Claire and the squat woman to observe the dickering. A drop of Claire's sweat dampened the red cloth and the squat woman threw up her hands.

"Now, *Madame*, that cloth is no good. Take them, take them, you steal from me at twenty-five *centimes*."

Claire shook coins from a small purse and dropped them in the vendor's palm.

"It is fair," the squat woman said.

"It is fair," other vendors agreed.

"I will return for the bolts on the way back to the farm. *Merci*."

Marie wandered back with Anthony. Claire scooped up her sticky son.

"Come along. We'll find Lawrence and Sebastien and tell them to collect our cloth," Claire said.

Marie unmoving, stared at the bolts of fabric.

"Come, Marie, why do you wait?" Claire asked.

"You make *poupee*."

"Oh, Marie, that cloth is too good for a rag doll. When I have time, I'll make one from scraps. You must be patient. Let's look for Sebastien and Lawrence. By now, they must have sold the coffee and oranges."

While Marie ran ahead, Claire strolled along the street with Anthony's hand in hers. The Catholic cathedral loomed above the other buildings, with white-washed walls, arched doors outlined in blue, and copper crucifixes perched on the highest points of three cupolas.

She continued until she reached the far end of town. The air grew heavy with the smell of blood and dung. She sat Anthony under a palm tree and stared at the throng of men huddled around a pit.

A movement caught her eye — Marie, wild-eyed and running as if chased by a swarm of bees. In the blink of an eye, Sebastien burst into view, closing the distance between them. He reached out, grabbed Marie's shoulder, and threw her down. Claire gasped. She hurried over.

"Sebastien, what are you doing?"

Around the pit, men turned, frowning and shaking their heads. Sebastien put his finger to his lips. When Marie let out a wail, he covered her mouth and pinched her. He held up his hand to signal silence, and dragged Marie to the palm tree. Claire, dumbstruck, followed.

"*Bat kok*. Do not disturb a cock fight," Sebastien said.

"Cock fight? Where's Lawrence?" Claire's heart pounded. She stood tiptoe to see if he was near the pit.

"Men only. Stay here," Sebastien said.

A cheer rose from the men. Roosters crowed. Voices shouted, 'Fight! Get up! Kill him!"

While Anthony played in dirt, Marie twirled a stick and sang. Claire strained to see the action. As soon as one fight ended, another took place.

Finally, Lawrence, face ashen except for red cheeks, and Sebastien jogged from the pit to join them. Claire noticed Henri step outside the group of men and stare.

"Claire, what are you doing here?" Lawrence scooped up Anthony.

"I decided to walk to Jacmel to look at fabric and meet you. What are you doing here?"

"We sold the oranges and coffee as soon as we arrived, so we had time to watch the fights. All the men gather here. I get to talk with other farmers about crops and livestock and prices." Lawrence lowered his eyes but smiled. He spilled coins into Claire's hands. "I've been studying the fighting cocks to learn how to train Andrew Jackson. I learned how winners win. Today, I doubled our share from the coffee and oranges we sold. If I keep winning like this, we'll buy our own farm one day."

"When did you start gambling?" Claire's voice quivered. She felt a deep sense of dread.

"A few months ago. First I watched. Before I gambled, I kept track of how often I picked winners. When I almost always did, I bet a few *centimes*. Nothing really. I won some, lost some. Today, I won big. It's easy money."

"I don't like it," Claire said.

Lawrence kissed her. "Don't worry. I only wager a few pennies. If I lose them, I stop."

While Sebastien retrieved the donkey and cart, Claire shuddered. Something about Lawrence's guilty look and Sebastien's knowing one made her angry and fearful.

Lawrence set Anthony in the cart, then helped Marie climb in. As they walked toward the cloth sellers, Claire listened to Lawrence explain that cock fighting was an ancient sport and, although he never attended a cock fight in America, university students often traveled to Lancaster to bet on cocks. His young rooster, Andrew Jackson, showed every sign of being a strong fighter. Claire would see. He knew what he was doing. Hadn't he done wonders with the oranges? Didn't the seeds he brought for their garden prove hearty? When she pursed her lips and sighed, he said women don't understand the ways of men.

Claire thought of Granny's warning and decided it would be pointless to argue. She jingled the coins he gave her.

"Promise you won't wager more than fifty *centimes*, and if you lose them, you stop."

"I promise. Give me some coins for your ink and paper."

Down the road from the book store, they passed a stall with brightly painted toys.

"Wait here," Lawrence said.

He returned with a painted horse on a wheeled platform for Anthony. Marie leaned from the cart with arms outstretched towards a fat faceless rag doll on the shelf.

"*Poupee*," she cried.

"Not today," Claire said.

Before Lawrence led the donkey up the path to the farm, Sebastien had disappeared.

CHAPTER THIRTY-EIGHT

S unday fell on Lawrence's twentieth birthday. Outside, the early morning fog burned off and the sun glowed in the turquoise sky.

Claire stood at the stove stirring the pot of pumpkin soup, Lawrence's favorite. Later, she would bake a *kinderfest* cake and put a candle on top.

With Anthony napping, Marie out collecting eggs, and Sebastien wherever he disappeared to, Claire relished being alone with her husband. She wanted to discuss baptizing Anthony, and share the surprise. She was certain she conceived on the cool night in January when he pulled her close and she clung to him.

In the front room, Lawrence cleaned Claire's small pistol, set it aside, and picked up his long-barreled handgun. The peppery aroma from the pumpkin soup didn't offset the acrid smell of the old cooking grease Lawrence rubbed over the moving parts of his gun.

As Claire dropped red peppers in the pot, she thought of her mother's spicy oyster stew and the pepper pot soup Ruth sold on Germantown Avenue. A sob caught in her throat, but she would not cry. Instead, she wiped her hands and joined Lawrence.

"Genevieve says it's time she baptizes Anthony."

"There's baptism in Voodoo?"

"Haitians believe in God, and saints, and spirits like we do, but they call them different names. Anthony will be under the protection of *Papa Legba* because *Papa Legba* is like Saint Anthony. Genevieve's beliefs remind me of Molly's Catholic beliefs."

"I'm not certain I want my son to be a papist."

"I'm certain my parents and Granny would like him baptized, like I was at Mother Bethel."

Lawrence set aside his gun, and joined her. He inhaled the soup steam. Claire dipped in the wooden spoon and gave him a taste. He smiled.

"If that's what you want, I see no harm in it. Genevieve can baptize Anthony."

Now, Claire thought, is the perfect time to tell Lawrence about the baby. But Marie came through the door with a basket of eggs, and Claire swallowed the words. The girl smelled of dung and mildew. Straw and coffee blossoms clung to her hair. Her calico shift was torn and dirty.

"Did you fall in *la merde*?" Claire asked.

Marie said nothing. She stared as Lawrence wrapped both guns, checked his powder flask, and returned the weapons to the gun box. From the bedroom door she watched him set the metal box on a high shelf. Anthony whimpered. Lawrence pushed past Marie, and picked up Anthony who was drumming the floor with spoons.

"I'm taking Anthony outside. Marie stinks."

Marie stood silent, mouth open with a finger in her nose. Claire felt a rush of frustration. Now twelve-years-old, she acted much younger. She required constant reminders to feed the goats and chickens, and collect the eggs. As Henri warned their first day, Marie stole, lied, and often hid when Claire wanted her help. She never washed unless Claire insisted. Claire shook her head and sighed. At least, Marie loved Anthony. She always, surprisingly, took good care of him.

"Take off those clothes and wash yourself. Don't forget your hair." Claire tapped Marie's head. As the back door slammed, Claire called, "After you're clean, dress in the trousers and blouse on the clothesline."

As soon as Marie went outside, Lawrence came back in with Anthony.

"I don't like that girl. I don't understand why we're responsible for her. She's useless. At least Sebastien works . . . when I can find him."

He slapped a fly.

"Because she's an orphan and has no one else. She lost her mother and had to live with a terrible woman. She helps with Anthony," Claire said.

Lawrence shrugged and stroked Anthony's head.

"I plan to speak to Henri about sending her to Jacmel. She's twelve, old enough to find work at a hotel. We'll talk about it later. I have work in the grove. Ring the bell when dinner's ready."

Claire put Anthony down to nap in the stall-like cot Lawrence built. The sides were tall enough to keep him in while they slept or worked.

From the window, Claire watched Marie splash herself. The girl came inside naked and wet, but still smelling awful. Bits of debris wove through her hair, and her skin was etched with scratches. She must have fallen in briars. Claire turned her around and led her outside.

"Climb in the tub. I'll clean your hair, but you must do a better job washing yourself."

Claire doused Marie's head with water. She dipped her fingers in a pot of coconut oil and rubbed the soft, buttery cream through Marie's thick hair. Even clean and oiled, the girl's hair was almost impossible to comb. Claire shrugged and handed Marie a rag.

"Clean yourself all over. Chest, arms, belly, legs, and your bottom."

Marie's coffee-colored nipples topped small swells, and dark hair showed on her pubis. Whereas Sebastien had grown independent and manly, Marie was so small and childlike, the signs of puberty shocked Claire. It was time Marie learned about women's monthly courses. Claire decided to leave that discussion to Genevieve.

After Marie stepped out of the tub and dropped the rag on the ground, Claire glared until she retrieved it and flung it over the clothesline. While Claire watched, Marie tossed her filthy clothes in the laundry tub, then yanked the trousers and blouse off the clothesline and dressed. Claire bit her lip and sighed. She wanted to tell Lawrence she was pregnant today.

"You smell nice, like coconuts." Claire rested her hand on Marie's shoulder as they entered the house. "I set a plate of bread and cheese on the table for you. The soup's cooking, and Anthony's taking a nap. Will you stay in the cottage with Anthony while I help Lawrence in the orchard? I'll be back in an hour. Don't touch the pot, it's hot."

"*Oui*," Marie said, scratching her rump.

Claire crossed the yard, trotting past chickens in their chain link pen. In the paddock, the goats bleated. As soon as she reached the orchard path, the air smelled of citrus and coffee.

Soon, far from Philadelphia, they would have another child. Mama, she silently cried, and blinked back tears. She needed Lawrence to hold her, to remind her why they ran away. She visualized him as a little boy, silent and nervous, following her like a duckling.

Why did she nag him like he was still that little boy? He was man enough to father Anthony, man enough to start another life in her womb. Although nothing had been easy since they ran away, Lawrence loved her.

She was no beauty, with a missing tooth and stretch lines on her belly, but Lawrence loved her. Wanted her. And she wanted him.

The closer she got to the grove, the more the air smelled like Wissahickon Farm's orchards. When a coconut dropped in her path, she couldn't avoid it. Her ankle turned. She tumbled to the ground with a grunt.

"Claire," Lawrence called from a branch high up in the palm tree. "I'm sorry. I was picking coconuts and when I saw you, I dropped one for a joke. I thought you'd think it was manna from heaven. Are you hurt?"

He shimmied down. Claire beheld his anxious face and dandelion hair, and the sweat on his brow. She held out her arms. He fell to his knees and embraced her. She held him tight and thought how much she loved him. His green eyes absorbed her. She hugged him and laughed, and he laughed, a delighted but confused look on his face.

"I needed to see you and feel you," Claire said.

Lawrence crinkled his nose. "I'm right here."

She put his hand on her waist. "I have something to tell you, Papi."

Marie walked through the house, kicking her legs to swish her trousers. The clothes Claire made to sell in Jacmel were yellow like the sun, pink like the mountains, blue like the sky, green like waving palm fronds. Claire used pretty colors for buyers who swarmed the donkey cart to burrow through shirts, dresses, and trousers to find ones they liked. But Claire used fabric the color of mud for Marie's clothes. She is not my Mami, Marie thought. She lies like Yasmine. She promised to make me a *poupee*, a little doll, but *non*. And I do not like the *blanc*. He is mean to Marie.

From the front porch, Marie scanned the orchard path for Claire and the *blanc*. She heard a rustle.

"Claire, *où es-tu*?"

A parrot took to the air. Marie smiled. They weren't coming. She had time to explore. But, she must be careful. Claire always knew when Marie touched her things, and scolded her.

They never let Marie in their bedroom, but they weren't here. She walked around the room, then lay on the pallet bed, and covered herself with their quilt. She stared at the ceiling and the high shelf where the *blanc* put the metal box. She wanted that box.

After she kicked off the quilt, she climbed from the bed to the top of the chest where Claire and the *blanc* kept their clothes. On tiptoes, she reached for the gun box. Her fingers touched it, but pushed it farther back. She jumped onto the bed. The wooden frame cracked. Marie rushed to the front door and peered down the path. No Claire. No *blanc*. She returned to the bedroom and spread the quilt over the pallet. There. Who could say she broke it?

The smell of pumpkin soup made her mouth water. She was hungry, and devoured the bread and cheese. Claire's broom leaned against the dish cabinet. Now, she'd get that box.

Broom in hand, Marie climbed again to the chest top. She tapped the broom handle against the gun box. With two hands, she pushed the handle against the box with all her strength. Finally, it moved to the edge. Dust spilled down, and she coughed. She banged the box until it teetered and crashed on the floor. The guns, powder flask, and a handful of lead slugs spilled out.

Anthony whimpered and whined. Marie set down the broom and went to his cot. She stroked his back, cooing and humming until he quieted.

In the bedroom, she returned the guns, flask, and slugs to the box. But then the box was too heavy to lift. She ran to the porch to check for Claire and the *blanc*. The path was clear. She returned to study the little gun — it fit her hand just right. Anthony's cot rattled. With the Deringer in hand, she peeked into his room. His breaths were quiet and regular. She aimed.

"Boom, boom, boom."

She laughed. The little gun for me, the big one for Sebastien.

One at a time, she carried the guns and powder flask through the cottage and out the back door. She set them on the ground and covered them with a rag.

Back in the bedroom, she shoved the gun box under the bed, behind the *blanc's* boots. Hah, she thought, the *blanc* will never find it. She turned to the chest. She had to tug and tug the bottom drawer handle before it opened enough to reach in. She rummaged through Claire's aprons and blouses. In the corner, under Claire's night shift, she felt a package wrapped in paper, and smiled. She unwrapped a stoneware disk as big as her palm, with a picture of a kneeling black man in chains. A metal band twisted into a ring at the disk's top, and a thin leather necklace ran through the ring. A slave collar! She knew it. Claire was the *blanc's* slave. He made her hide the collar, and pretended to be her husband!

"*Kochon*! Pig!"

She draped the necklace over her head and caressed the black figure.

"When Sebastien sees this, the *blanc* will fly."

She checked Anthony. Asleep. She checked the orchard path. Clear.

Out back, she threw the rag off the guns and flask. She crawled under the cottage dragging the big gun, dug a hole, and shoved it in. She returned for the little gun and the flask. The hole wasn't big enough, so she dug more, piled the little gun and flask on top, and covered the hole with sandy soil. She was tired, but no one would find the guns. The poor black slave scraped the ground. She clawed in the dirt and buried the disk and necklace.

After she backed out of the crawl space, she noticed her clothes were smudged and dusty. She wagged her finger in imitation of Claire.

"Did you fall in *la merde*?"

Marie chuckled as she rounded the cottage to stare down the orchard path. Satisfied, she moved inside. Anthony was deep in sleep.

In the bedroom, the steamer trunk lid was propped open with a thick stick. Claire kept the bolts of pretty colored fabrics in the trunk. Marie stroked a bolt of red, the color of *Jezus'* sash in the stained-glass window of the cathedral. Anthony stirred and whimpered.

Marie ran to the porch and called, "Claire!"

No answer. She returned to the bolt of red fabric. Mami once wrapped a red scarf around Marie's head and called her *jolie*, pretty. Claire never called her *jolie*. She never let her touch the pretty fabrics. But Claire would never know. Marie shimmied the bolt to the edge, and pulled it with both hands. So heavy. So much hard work. She grit her teeth and groaned as she pulled. At last, the bolt tilted over the edge and dropped with a dull thunk.

Claire's sewing basket with scissors, needles, thread, and chalk was in the trunk, too. It was easy to lift. She set it beside the fabric bolt. Anthony farted and sighed, but didn't cry. Good.

Marie found a heavy coin pouch on the trunk bottom. As she hurried outside to bury the pouch with the guns and disk, she jingled the coins. I will buy bonbons, banana fritters, spicy pickles, and mango ice, she chanted.

Back inside, she dragged the bolt of red cloth and the sewing basket to the kitchen, then checked outside for Claire and the *blanc*.

On the floor near the stove, she unrolled the bolt three folds and smoothed the fabric. With Claire's chalk, she drew the *poupee*. As soon as she cut the cloth for her doll, she had to put the bolt back. Claire would come back soon.

Marie chopped the fabric with the scissors, but the cloth just folded into the blades. She'd watched Claire cut fabric with scissors many times. Why didn't it cut for her?

"*Merde, merde, merde.*"

Outside, a parrot screeched. Marie's heart raced. She dare not take time to check the orchard path. But Claire promised to make a *poupee.* Claire was bad. Marie had to make it herself. She had to cut cloth for her doll and put the fabric bolt back. If the *blanc* saw what she did, he'd put her in chains like the poor black man. Hurry, hurry, hurry.

A candle stub sat in a brass dish on the table, and an idea flicked through her mind. The pot of soup smelled of sweet pumpkin and onions. Her stomach rumbled. She set the candle on the floor, pulled a chair to the stove, and peered in the pot.

She dipped in her finger for a taste. Hot! When she yanked out her hand, she struck the pot's edge. It wobbled. Boiling soup spattered her, and she fell off the chair. Yellow broth seeped into the pine floorboards. With her burned finger in her mouth, she ran to the door, waving her scalded arm to cool it. No sign of Claire or the *blanc.*

Hurry! The red fabric lay crinkled and stained with soup. The scissors didn't cut. She had to get the bolt back so Claire wouldn't know what she did. But the *poupee*!

Marie grabbed the candle and held the wick to the fire under the pot. Wax burned her fingers, but finally, the wick caught. She held the flame against the tiny V she'd managed to cut. Anthony cried out. The cot squeaked from his rocking.

"*Attendez,*" she called. "Wait."

Tiny threads shriveled and blackened. The flame traveled along the crease, then jumped to the bolt and burned upwards. Her eyes teared, her hands burned. She pitched the candle stub into the flames.

She had to put out the fire before Claire and the *blanc* returned. Where was the water bucket? No time to go to the pump. She looked at the soup pot.

Marie righted the chair and climbed on. She yanked the pot to spill soup on the fire. A glob burned her chest, but when the pot crashed on the floor, it spread over the cloth.

"*Vwala!*" she shouted.

With a swoosh, the bolt exploded. The room crackled and flared like the *Carnival* bonfire. Each breath choked her. She must run away, *rapide, rapide*, before Claire returned, before Claire saw the burning fabric and discovered her missing purse.

"*C'était* Anthony," Marie would say. "Anthony pulled down the pot and started the fire."

Anthony's cot rocked. He screamed, "Mami, Papi, Mami."

"*Ton faute*, Anthony," Marie yelled back, "your fault."

Black smoke blinded her. She couldn't breathe. She must get outside. Where is the door? On scorched hands and knees she crawled into walls and furniture. She didn't know where she was.

"Marie! Marie!" Anthony cried in a strangled voice.

There is light, there is the door. Soup sputtered and snapped and stunk of seared pumpkin and burned meat. For just a moment to get a breath, she rested her head on her arm.

Since there was no work on Easter Sunday, Sebastien decided to visit Claire and enjoy pumpkin soup. He liked Claire. She talked to him, learned to speak French and Creole, and taught him and Marie English words. The *blanc* knew farming and worked hard in the orchard, but Sebastien remained wary of his motives. *Never trust the whites* had been drummed into his head for as long as he could remember. Many old men carried scars on their backs from whites' whips before the revolution. No one would ever whip Sebastien again. He could run faster and climb higher than any man.

Claire liked the *blanc* though. The little boy, Anthony, looked mostly white, and Sebastien loved him. When Anthony was an infant, he liked to suck Sebastien's finger. Now, whenever Sebastien visited, Anthony ran to him with arms raised.

He decided he would stay to work with the *blanc* tomorrow, maybe the next day, too. His clothes needed mending, and he'd enjoy Claire's good meals and sleeping under a roof. And he should see to Marie.

When Claire and the *blanc* arrived, Henri abandoned Marie to their care. Sebastien did too, despite his promise to their dying Mami, who told him, 'Your twin is *nerveuse*, with *san feb*, weak blood. You are the strong twin, the blessed one. You are the shoe that must know if the sock has a hole. Promise to care for her.'

Sebastien tried to look after Marie. He saved her from that wretched Yasmine. But Marie proved a miserable burden – too heavy for Sebastien's back. Sometimes he felt guilty. He hoped Henri or Genevieve would find Marie a husband soon, someone new to carry the burden, someone who wouldn't beat her.

As he trotted up the path, the air changed from the marshy green smell of the sea to the oily inland smell of palms and sugar cane. Overhead, parrots squawked their danger sound, and a flock of swifts raced across the sky. A salty smell of burned meat blew down the path as Sebastien's bare feet crunched over gravel and debris.

Something was wrong. His heart pounded. With a sick feeling, he stared in the direction of Claire's home. A pillar of smoke rose in the air like a demon. Without thought, he raced to Claire's.

Flames licked the kitchen side. Black smoke surged from the windows. He tried the door but heat and smoke forced him back.

Sebastien circled the cottage. A tiny cry came from the window on the side not yet devoured by flames. He grabbed the window frame and launched himself inside, headfirst. He landed on Anthony's cot. The cot, Anthony, and Sebastien crashed onto the burning wood floor. It was impossible to see through the smoke. Where was Anthony?

The toddler choked and whimpered. Sebastien tried to hold his breath. Another quiet cough and whimper. Sebastien swept his arm across the floor in a wide arc until he touched soft flesh. He grabbed a little leg, pulled it to him, then dropped Anthony out the window.

Sebastien's hands, knees, and feet burned, his eyes watered, his throat swelled. He wondered if he would die. He swung his leg onto the windowsill and spilled outside, desperate to escape the hell.

The moment Sebastien hit the ground, he grabbed the coughing child, and raced for the big house. When they reached the yard, Sebastien set Anthony down and slumped beside him. Anthony patted his face. They both gagged and coughed.

With a boom louder than thunder, red flames shot through the roof of Claire's house. Smoke blackened the sky.

As he rubbed soot off Anthony's mouth and nose, Sebastien wept.

The sky exploded. Lawrence and Claire fell to the ground, and Lawrence covered her with his body.

"What was that? It sounded like a cannon," Claire said.

"The cottage! Smoke from the cottage! Anthony!"

Lawrence took off running.

"I left him with Marie," Claire called, but Lawrence sprinted down the path without turning.

Claire followed, limping and lurching, heart banging like drumbeats. Her injured ankle shot bullets of pain through her brain. She ran, and hopped, and cursed.

Beyond the orchard, clouds of black smoke fouled the blue sky. When

Claire emerged from the trees, the air shimmered. Angry orange flames consumed their cottage, crackling and leaping into the sky. As she got closer, she saw chickens flapping against the chain-link fence, unable to escape. The donkey smacked into the post-and-rail fence, its braying like a human scream. Goats leapt out of the paddock and ran into the trees. The cottage was an inferno.

"Anthony! Anthony! Anthony! Anthony!"

She rushed toward the cottage, heedless to the heat stealing her breath and scorching her skin. Lawrence tackled her. His face was smudged, his eyes wide and frightened.

"Anthony's alive, Claire. Sebastien saved him. He's alive."

Lawrence took her hand, and they ran up the path to the big house. Sebastien held Anthony over his shoulder, patting his back. As soon as Claire arrived, Anthony held out his arms and she took him. The little boy pointed to his throat. "Cough."

Lawrence and Claire huddled over their child. They checked his eyes, nose, mouth. While Anthony whimpered, Claire removed his clothes, and they inspected every inch of him. The burns on his fists, legs, and chin were no worse than a bad sunburn. Claire wiped away the soot on his face with her blouse. She handed Anthony to Lawrence and hugged Sebastien.

"Tell me what happened. Did you get burned?"

Sebastien held out his blistered hands. Tears ran down his cheeks.

"I came up the path. I saw the fire. I heard Anthony crying, climbed in, and found him. I thought you were dead," Sebastien said.

Claire put her hands on his cheeks and kissed his forehead.

"You saved Anthony, you brave boy." She hesitated and frowned. "Marie. Where is your sister?"

Sebastien shrugged. Black mucus dripped from his nose. His eyes were red-rimmed and watery.

"*Je ne sais pas*. I didn't see her."

"Lawrence, find Marie," she shouted.

Lawrence handed over Anthony, and bolted to the cottage, but the heat drove him back. Flames roared throughout the structure. The donkey brayed. He unlatched the gate and smacked the donkey's rump. The animal ran for the trees.

Lawrence studied the fire. No one could survive the inferno. There was an earth-shaking roar, and the roof and sides caved in. He stumbled back. With orange licks and black, beastly breath, the fire devoured what remained. He cupped his mouth and shouted, "Marie!" Only the crackling flames responded.

He dropped his head, then raised it at the sharp, shrill cry from behind the house. He took a deep breath and rushed past the surging heat to the source of the cry. The piercing sound – now an ugly, gruff caw — was his rooster's crow.

Andrew Jackson attacked the fence around the pit. Lawrence climbed over and grabbed the rooster's legs. Sick and disoriented, he staggered back to Claire and Sebastien.

"Marie? Where's Marie?" Claire screamed, voice shrill.

Anthony wailed in fright.

Lawrence dropped the rooster and fell to his knees, coughing and spitting dark phlegm. He shook his head.

"The cottage collapsed. I couldn't get inside." He held his head in his hands.

Andrew Jackson flapped and screeched. Sebastien carried the rooster to a pen behind Henri's house. He returned as ashes floated down like leaves. Claire held out her hand to catch one. It crumpled into nothing.

Claire found Sebastien's hand, and held it to her heart.

CHAPTER THIRTY-NINE

JACMEL APRIL 1827

The night of the fire, driving rain turned the cottage's remains into a soggy mound of ashes and rubble. Two support beams, tops burned to ragged points, listed on the bedroom side of the house. The tin roof was buckled.

Later, after two days of sun, Lawrence left the abandoned slave quarters behind the big house — the ramshackle shelter Henri so *kindly* offered them — and walked down the path to inspect the damage. The donkey and goats emerged from the brush to meet him, braying and bleating for food and water. No chickens survived. Their charred feathers floated pitifully askance with each shallow breeze. He thought it a miracle he found Andrew Jackson in time.

Ashes blackened the pump handle and spout, but the pump and buckets were undamaged and water ran clear. He filled the water troughs and milked the goats before he stepped onto the cottage foundation.

Tears ran down his cheeks. The acrid odor of burnt wood stung his throat. His bare foot broke through a decrepit floor plank, and he screamed in rage and pain. He backed into the yard, planting drops of bright blood in the sandy soil. He would return later with a shovel and rake.

The tops of vegetables in Claire's garden were scorched, but the plants would recover. Lawrence raised his eyes to the sky in thanks that no flames leapt as far as the groves. Ashes blown there could stay — they were good for the soil.

On his return to Henri's, he gulped goat milk from the bucket. Since the fire, Claire hadn't left the dirty old slave shack. Today, she must get up, tend to Anthony, and help put things to order.

"Claire!" he called from the doorway.

She lay on her side on a quilt while Anthony chased cockroaches. When Lawrence walked in, the little boy jumped up and down.

"Papi!"

In a corner, tiny insects flew around Anthony's excrement. Lawrence took a breath and lifted the filthy child. He tossed Anthony's shirt aside, and rinsed him at Henri's pump. The child wiggled and whined. While Lawrence bent to wash blood off his foot, a stream of piss splashed on it.

"Anthony! Nasty. You're old enough to use the waste pit."

After he dressed Anthony, he sat the boy under a palm tree with a banana and a cup of goat milk. He ate three bananas himself. He wanted coffee. Anger gnawed as much as hunger. He tossed the banana peels into the garbage bucket.

"Claire, you need to come out and take care of Anthony. I have work to do," he called.

When Claire finally stumbled outdoors, her upper lip was swollen, and her hair stuck out in impossible disarray.

"You smell like death," he said.

"What do you know?"

She dropped to her knees and held out her arms for Anthony, who ran to her.

"I know you need to be outside and take care of our son. You need to clean yourself, eat, and help with the goats. When Henri comes back from Jacmel with fabric, needles, and thread, you need to make us new clothes. We can begin again, Claire, but I can't do it alone."

"No, you're too busy with your rooster."

Lawrence's breath caught in silent sobs. Anthony, wide-eyed, moved from Claire to Lawrence and back again, whimpering.

Claire sighed. "I can't begin again until we find Marie."

Lawrence took her hand. He led her to the pump, removed her stinking clothes, ran water over her, and rubbed her skin with a chunk of harsh soap.

Claire closed her eyes and imagined the spilling water came from the pump outside the Germantown house in the alley, where Granny's laundry flapped on the clothesline. The water stopped flowing.

"Wait here," Lawrence said.

He entered the big house and returned moments later with an old cotton shirt and short trousers.

"Henri gave me a trunk of old clothes we can wear until you make new ones. You need to eat. I brought bananas and milk. The donkey and goats are back, but the chickens are dead or gone. I asked Henri to buy four laying hens from our share of the orange and coffee sales. After I dig through the cottage ashes, I need to rebuild the paddock and pen. We need to work together, Claire."

"Find the trunk. Our money was in it."

"The coins must have melted, but they'll still have value."

Lawrence marched down the path to the cottage with a shovel and pitch fork perched on his shoulder like weapons. Sebastien appeared on the orchard path.

"Sebastien! Sebastien! *Aidez-moi!*"

They met at the edge of the ruination. Both hesitated, reluctant to climb over cinders into the burned-meat smell.

"Watch your feet, Sebastien, step carefully. The floor boards aren't sturdy."

Lawrence stepped onto the foundation, and motioned for Sebastien. Together, they shoved the warped tin roof to the side. They picked their way to the bedroom, where the steamer trunk skeleton, the charred chest of drawers, and the badly burned bed frame leered at them. Lawrence trembled when he examined the scorched pieces of wood that had been Anthony's cot.

"You saved our child," he told Sebastien. "I will always be grateful."

In the trunk, burned fabric crumbled into tiny chips of color incongruous in the ashes. Lawrence coughed. He covered his mouth and nose with a bandana and motioned for Sebastien to do so, too. The trunk's metal struts were black and crinkled, but the bottom slats withstood the fire. Lawrence filtered the ashes through his fingers, searching for Claire's coin pouch. He didn't find it. Silver coins might melt, but they wouldn't disappear.

Sebastien had been the last person in the house. Lawrence wondered for a moment if he stole the money. But the boy searched alongside him without a hint of culpability. And Sebastien saved Anthony's life.

"Look!"

Sebastien pulled the metal gun box from the rubble. The box lid was jammed and crooked. Lawrence shook it. It was light, too light. He pounded the box on the ground until it popped open. Nothing but molten lead slugs inside.

When he and Claire heard the cottage explode with a blast louder than a cannon's roar, he'd known his gunpowder had ignited. But where did the guns go? Even if the wood handles burned off, the barrels would survive.

Lawrence rethought his actions Easter morning, before the fire. He cleaned the pistols, set both guns in the box, and shoved it far back on the shelf. Then he returned to kitchen and tossed Anthony in the air. He definitely put the guns in the box, and put the box on the shelf. Definitely.

Sebastien sneezed. Lawrence tossed the gun box aside.

The kitchen stove was charred and dented but salvageable, along with the upside-down heavy cook pot. Charred cloth fluttered around a table leg. Lawrence dug through the debris with the pitchfork, and unearthed shattered dishes and Anthony's tin cup. Sebastien dug with the shovel along the front.

"*Au secours, ede*, help!"

Sebastien dropped the shovel. He covered his mouth with his hands. Lawrence swung around, aiming his pitchfork like a weapon.

"What? Tell me."

Sebastien choked, face frozen in terror. Lawrence put his arm around the boy's shoulders. Sebastien pointed to a black lump. Lawrence leaned close. He stared, then gasped. A skeleton. Marie's skeleton.

Her upper body lay twisted with her head thrown back and an arm raised as if to ward off a blow. With crusty patches of skin and tufts of wiry hair, Marie glowered at them from empty eye sockets, teeth bared like a street dog. Her remains lay a few feet from where the door had been. Why didn't she run outside?

Lawrence knelt at her side and brushed off ashes.

"Ahhh!"

He yanked his hand away. Blood seeped from a slice on his finger. His heart raced. Marie had slashed him.

"*La sang*, blood," Sebastien whimpered. "*Zombi*." The boy's face was taut, as if he were facing a strong wind. "*Arrêtez, Blanc*. Stop, stop."

Sebastien inched back as if he were afraid Marie would jump up and grab him.

Lawrence sucked his finger. He narrowed his eyes and jabbed with the pitchfork, probing for Marie's weapon. Metal claws jutted from the bones of Marie's hand. Scissors! Where did Marie get scissors? Dear God, what happened that day?

He followed Sebastien away from the ruins. His stomach heaved. He vomited under a coffee bush, its berries brown, roasted from the fire.

Sebastien called Marie a zombie. But nothing would bring that child back to life.

At the sound of footsteps, Lawrence raised his head to see Claire, ill-dressed in Henri's discards but clean and clear-eyed, walking toward the cottage. Anthony scurried behind. He rushed to stop her, but Sebastien reached her first.

"Did you find Marie?" She looked from Sebastien to Lawrence. "You found her. Show me."

Lawrence feared he might faint. He didn't want Claire to see the child's gruesome remains. But he recognized the determined look on her face, picked up Anthony, and stepped out of her way. No one stopped Claire when she set her mind.

Sebastien led her into the ashes and pointed. Claire knelt at Marie's side, touched the crusty meat of her arm, placed her hand on the child's skull, and kept it there. Sebastien put his hand on Claire's, and his warmth comforted her. She gazed into his eyes, then felt a shock, like a lightning strike. They pulled their hands away and stared at each other.

"*Savey-tu*?" Claire asked, eyes wild. "Did you see?"

Sebastien nodded. He returned his hand to his sister's skull, and Claire covered it with her own. A metallic taste filled her mouth. As if she were there, Claire saw Marie light the red fabric, flames shoot up, her attempt to smother the fire with pumpkin soup, her terror, and her final, hopeless breath a meter from the door and safety. The image burned in Claire's brain as powerfully as the fire burned the cottage.

Sebastien glanced at Claire. They removed their hands and moved away.

Claire and Lawrence carried Marie's body, as light as a fagot of straw, out of the ashes. They placed her corpse on a grassy patch under a tree by the stream. Marie looked like a bundle of burned wood. Sebastien, with Anthony in his arms, joined them.

"She set the fire," Claire said.

"How do you know?" Lawrence asked.

"She showed us when we touched her."

"That's impossible. She's dead."

"Her spirit abides in her body until we dance it to rest in the dark waters," Sebastien said.

"I don't believe that pagan Voodoo nonsense."

"It doesn't matter what you believe," Claire said.

"You spend too much time with Genevieve. The pot fell off the stove, started the fire, and Marie got trapped. Her spirit died when her body burned. I have work to do."

Sebastien caught Claire's eye.

"*Blanc,*" he whispered.

Henri returned from Jacmel with Genevieve and a cart loaded with food, cloth, and hens.

Lawrence helped Genevieve hop down from the cart.

"*Arriving and leaving, hoping and remembering, that's what life consists of,*" she said. "Sometimes paradise is no paradise. Henri told me of the fire and Marie. You found her, *n'est-ce pas?*"

"We found her body in the ashes, burned to bones. Claire and Sebastien cleaned her and wrapped her in a shroud. They've been praying for Marie and for your arrival."

"A terrible death. Too young. The child attracted a bad spirit. We will pray for seven days so Marie's *ti bon ange*, her soul, does not escape to cause mischief. Then, we will help Marie transition to the dark waters where her spirit will heal. Where is Sebastien? As her family leader, he must make arrangements."

Henri approached and handed Lawrence five coins.

"The oranges and coffee sold well. After I purchased your supplies, these remain. In an hour, come to the big house. Claire will help Genevieve prepare *griot* and cake for Marie's rituals. You will bring mangoes, oranges, and bananas. We will sacrifice a goat and chicken to encourage the spirits to welcome Marie to the dark waters."

Later, dressed in a white shirt and knee-length pants, with a white bandana on his head, Sebastien joined them.

Genevieve embraced him. "Sebastien, you are Marie's guiding light. Have you decided where she will enter the deep waters?"

"I have. Through *Bassin Bleu*."

Genevieve nodded. "The *loa* enjoy the three pools."

"*Oui*. She will enter the third pool, *Bassin Clare*."

"Ahh," Genevieve said. "It is fitting."

CHAPTER FORTY

The mourners made their way through the thick jungle, walking or riding donkeys and mules. Henri rode a white horse. Claire longed to feel Star of Night's chest heave under her legs. She hoped Duff took good care of Star and Inspiration. Regret consumed her – for Marie, for running away from her family, for Wissahickon Farm and the people on it, and for abandoning the horses and goats she loved.

Claire remembered Old Caesar asking, *Where my little child go?* Where did her childhood go? Who lived in her skin on this island far from home? In front of her, Lawrence and Anthony swayed on a mule. When did Lawrence's boyhood evanesce, replaced by the hardness and discontent of adulthood? Nothing felt like home, not the language, not the food, not the clothing, not the heat.

Only work bound her worlds together – the stitches she learned at Mama and Granny's knees, Lawrence's work in the groves, the kitchen garden, the squawking chickens, and the bleating goats. But it wasn't the same.

Lawrence slowed for Claire to ride beside him, and handed over Anthony. She smelled his sweaty head and calmed his wiggles. Children and their needs are the same, she thought, but I am not the same. She guided the donkey with her knees and peeled a banana for her son.

The thunderous sound of water cascading over rocks drowned out the clatter of hooves. A cacophony of human voices melded into a symphony of sadness when they approached *Bassin Clare*.

"Dismount," Henri called. "We leave the animals here, and climb down the rope ladder to the pool."

After they secured the animals in a flimsy shelter, Claire handed Anthony to Lawrence for the walk to the cliff and the ladder.

They followed the granite smell of rushing water. The rope ladder descended over craggy stone to a turquoise pool. Below them, white-garbed people congregated on a clearing rimmed by rocks and greenery. Smoke rose from a stone oven. Men set planks on logs to fashion tables. A small palm hut stood at the edge of the clearing. Genevieve touched Claire's shoulder and gestured.

"The temple."

"Who are these people?" Claire asked.

"They are believers, come to dance Marie home to heal in the dark water. They join us to honor the *loa*, the spirits. Thus, Marie's life force will be freed to renew itself."

Genevieve followed Henri down the rope ladder, and landed gracefully.

"I'll go first, with Anthony," Lawrence said. "Then you. Can you make it?"

Claire gazed at his green eyes and floppy hair, white from the sun. She nodded.

While Lawrence maneuvered down the ladder with Anthony, she inched to the edge of the cliff to look down. Flowing water spilled over the rocks in a winding path.

"Claire, Claire," Sebastien called from above.

The boy perched on a jagged overhang. Marie's words, 'Sebastien fly like bird,' echoed in Claire's head.

Sebastien whooped, "*Ici je vais,*" and leapt. With arms spread like wings, he flew over the turquoise water and disappeared under a ripple of white froth.

"Sebastien!"

Why didn't he surface? Claire couldn't lose him, too. Was this part of the ceremony? Because they were twins, must Sebastien join Marie in the dark waters?

After too long, Sebastien's head popped up. His dark face sparkled in the limpid pool. She trembled, then smiled.

"Fly, Claire!"

"Don't be stupid," Lawrence called from the beach. "Take the ladder and come down."

Bassin Clare's turquoise waters called her name. She climbed to the overhang, and gazed down. Claire felt exhilarated. Sebastien's smile, glistening black skin, and the ripples around him summoned her like freedom. She longed to plunge into the cold unknown and merge her essence with all souls who choose to embrace the abyss. Lawrence's disapproval drifted around her like smoke.

She stepped out of her white blouse and skirt, balled them, and tossed them to Lawrence. The waterfall's roar drowned out his voice. Sebastien beckoned her. Her breath caught in her throat. She raised her hand to salute Marie.

The rocky ledge, much like the ridges above the Wissahickon Creek, felt warm on her feet. She thought of the long-ago day when she, Felix, and Samuel threw the slave catcher over the ridge. Now she would feel what he felt, hurtling out of control to destiny.

Perhaps all eyes were on her, perhaps none. She felt only the eyes of Sebastien and the eyes of Marie. An incessant drumbeat became her heart's beat. Nothing existed but the rush of water and a spirit who called her name. Drops from the waterfall splashed her legs. She closed her eyes and opened her arms to embrace her family, Sebastien, and the bewildering orphan child, Marie.

"Claire, fly."

Sebastien's voice rose above the drumming. She heeded it, and plunged into air with nothing holding her back.

Yellow bird, up high in banana tree.
Yellow bird, you left all alone like me.

Marie's song flashed through her mind when her head broke the water's surface. Down, down she plunged. Her heart pounded, her lungs ached. Is this how I die? A hand found hers – Marie's, untouched by fire. Through wavering light, Claire gazed into Marie's penetrating brown eyes, and lost herself in the dark waters.

When her face broke the surface, she gasped for air. It was Sebastien's hand in hers, and Claire felt joy. Together, they swam to the beach. Lawrence embraced her.

"I thought you drowned." His voice sounded far away.

Lawrence helped Claire dress, then, hand-in-hand, they followed Sebastien and Anthony to the white-garbed people.

Lawrence appeared spectacularly white compared with the dark-skinned congregation. He stopped before they entered the temple.

"Come," Claire said. She bobbed to the drumbeat.

"Stay," Lawrence whispered. "Stay with me."

Claire frowned. "This is Marie's funeral. I want to honor the *loa* and send her spirit to the dark waters. It's why we came."

Lawrence dropped her hand and turned.

"Lawrence, come back."

But he stumbled towards the coconut palms at the edge of the jungle. Claire shook her head and muttered, "*Blanc.*"

Music from bamboo flutes wove through the drumbeats. Angel voices sang for Marie, sang for Claire, drawing her to the spicy, bitter scent of bodies moving to rhythms she knew before she was born. Lawrence diminished to a distant white specter, an albino ant, and was forgotten.

Claire joined the dance and fractured, shattered to pieces like a dropped porcelain cup. Powerful arms wrapped around her. A being mounted her back as if she were a horse. She bucked and kicked until the weight drove her to the ground. She closed her eyes and exchanged her heart for the beating drums.

Lawrence leaned against a palm tree and stared at the dancing throng. His parents spoke of the wild shouting and shaking that went on at Negro Sunday services, but this? He trembled with fear, as terrified as when the wild dogs attacked Wissahickon Farm's sheep. He lost Claire among the dancers, pulsating like a beating heart. His eyes welled with tears, but he wiped them away. These are not my people. This is not my land.

No one noticed him creep to a table and grab a jug. He returned to his tree and gulped dark rum until the jug was empty and his throat burned. He staggered to the edge of the crowd where he watched Claire jerk and pitch like she was having a fit. Someone gave her a thick cigar, and clouds of smoke drifted above her head. Lawrence's head swam, but he had to stop Claire's blasphemy. He lurched towards her.

"Claire!"

Her glazed eyes darted back and forth. She stared at him without recognition. His heart broke. But then she wrapped her arms around him, and rubbed her body against his in a dance so provocative his cheeks flushed. His heart pounded in anger and desire. What was she doing? She carried his baby in her womb.

Erzulie Dantor, someone shouted.

Lawrence slipped from her arms and turned away. But Claire came after him. From behind, she wrapped her arms around his chest, and nuzzled his back. Her hands dropped to his waist and caressed his thighs. He turned to face her, his desire painful, his mind blank. Together, they fell to their knees. The drumming stopped.

Claire's eyes were clear, and her breath sweet. He loved and feared her. Sweat glistened on her upper lip. He wanted to taste it. He wanted to consume her. A dark curtain clouded his vision, and he felt himself falling.

He opened his eyes to a circle of dark faces. In their midst, Claire looked like an angel. She took his hand and helped him rise.

"Where's Anthony?" she asked.

Genevieve held up the child. "We danced Marie's spirit into the dark waters so it might heal. Now, let us celebrate Anthony's life through baptism in the same pool."

As the people walked in procession to *Bassin Clare*, Anthony waved from Henri's shoulders. When they reached the lovely pool, Lawrence's head felt stuffed and foggy. Something fundamental had changed. He loved Claire and wanted her, but despite her hand in his, she had slipped from his grasp.

Genevieve carried Anthony into the pool. She blew in his face and dipped him under, then raised him dripping and sputtering.

"I baptize you, Anthony, in the name of the father, son, and holy ghost. Anthony, you are the intermediary between two worlds — the white world and black world, Haiti and America. Saint Anthony is the embodiment of *Papa Legba*, the spirit of the crossroads between life and death. Yellow is the color of those who serve *Papa Legba*, even as your skin is yellow."

Genevieve handed Anthony to Claire.

"Claire, you are *Erzulie*, this child's protector," Genevieve said. "You are a warrior, independent, yet loving. Your spirit's longing will be resolved only when you open your soul."

Genevieve turned to Lawrence. "You fear the *loa*, yet crave fulfillment. Be open. Be brave. I pray that one day you will welcome *Gan Bwa*, the spirit of all that grows. Care for your family. Give Claire your heart."

Finally, she spoke to Sebastien. "You are no longer a child, and must accept the weight of a man. Your twin passed to the great waters. Now, you must carry her life with yours."

Road weary and exhausted, Lawrence, Claire, and Anthony entered the slave quarters behind Henri's house.

Lawrence's skin burned. He stroked Claire's back and drew patterns on her skin. He kissed her shoulders and neck until she embraced him. They came together with urgency, hearts thrumming like beats of a drum.

CHAPTER FORTY-ONE

JACMEL OCTOBER 1827

For six months after the fire, Lawrence and Claire lived in the crumbling slave quarters. She knew her observations of Henri's comings and goings annoyed him. But whenever she tended the garden on the grounds where Marie died — and Anthony would have if not for Sebastien — her stomach reeled with disgust.

But the baby was due soon. She and Lawrence agreed they had to rebuild, and the only space Henri allotted was the site of the original cottage.

The fire had consumed the coins Claire carefully saved. The cost of replacing their supplies consumed most of what they earned since. Now, whenever she squirreled away a few coins from sales of bright cotton dresses, shirts, slacks, and headscarves, rodents fouled a crate of oranges or Lawrence broke a tool. With a sheepish look, he'd put out his hand and promise to repay after the next trip to Jacmel. When he returned, he'd report that prices were down, or no ships were in port, or he had to repay Henri for something or other. She missed their cottage, and their privacy.

After three years, Haiti still didn't feel like home. Each time she watched Anthony chase chickens or hug goats, she longed to share his exploits with her mother. Letters once or twice a year only increased her regret at running away.

Now, Anthony scampered ahead while Claire trudged down the path to their yard. Pregnancy weighed heavy. She panted and wiped her brow.

In an hour, Lawrence would return from the orchard hungry, sweaty, and silent. Since Marie's funeral and Anthony's baptism, he rarely spoke. But his work in the orange groves was Henri's pride, and local farmers often came to observe his techniques.

After those first months in Jacmel, he cleared debris and culled damaged trees. Then he tilled land beyond the existing trees and planted rows of orange saplings. For these, he took cuttings from the best trees and coaxed new roots in a slurry of rotting oranges, bananas, and coconuts. The trees from those saplings, nurtured by Lawrence's blood and sweat, grew strong and tall, but wouldn't yield fruit for years.

The relentless work sapped Lawrence's spirit. If he spoke, he complained of never having fun. A month after the fire, Lawrence packed the cart with oranges and coffee. Henri swung onto his white horse and rode along. That was the first night Lawrence didn't share their bed. The next morning, as the sun's rays illuminated the mountain tops, he stumbled into the slave quarters reeking of rum . . . and women. That was the first night. It wasn't the last.

Claire prayed that once they moved into a new cottage, Henri's influence would wane.

With Marie gone, Claire tended the chickens, goats, and garden, looked after Anthony, prepared the meals, and sewed clothing for sale into the dimming evening light. Haiti enslaved her. She thought often of Wissahickon Farm.

This morning, after she milked the goats, she lugged the steaming bucket to the stream to cool. In the garden, she picked beans, squash, and scallions, and boiled the vegetables with dried fish in a big pot on the outside grill.

The chickens squawked while Anthony collected eggs. Andrew Jackson crowed, then darted at the little boy. Claire dropped her cook spoon, raced to the pen, and grabbed the rooster's legs. She pitched the rooster over the fence into the training pit.

"Did he hurt you, Anthony?"

Anthony showed a bloody nick on his leg.

"Bad Andrew Jackson."

Claire kissed her son. She wanted to wring bad Andrew Jackson's neck.

When the sun hung high, Lawrence returned from the grove with oranges and bananas. After he rinsed his head under the pump, he scanned the chicken pen.

"Where's Andrew Jackson?"

"He attacked Anthony. I put him in the pit."

"What did Anthony do to him?"

"I didn't do nothing. Bad Andrew Jackson chased me and bit my leg. He needs to sit in the corner."

Lawrence picked up Anthony and swung him.

"Andrew Jackson's a fighting cock. I guess he thought you were another rooster."

"I'm going to throw rocks at him."

"No you aren't," Lawrence and Claire said simultaneously.

"The food's ready," Claire said.

Lawrence devoured the fish stew, and held out the bowl for more.

"It's good, Claire. Anthony, are you going to finish yours?"

Moments like this, when they sat together in peace, was a rare treasure.

"When will you start on the new cottage?" Claire asked.

Lawrence rested his eyes on the piles of planks and beams he cut and stacked in the months since the fire.

"I'm finished in the grove for today. I can start this afternoon. I stored the tools and hardware we've been buying in a cabinet in the coop. Shall I build the cottage like the first one?"

Claire raised her brows. He hadn't wasted all their money.

"I don't understand."

"I could build the new cottage in a square instead of a rectangle. It would be a bit different. Anthony's old enough to watch and learn."

"I want to help!"

Anthony leapt on Lawrence's lap. His copper-colored skin was darker than Lawrence's, and long blond curls covered his head. His wide eyes – blue, like the Haitian sky, like the striking eyes of his grandmother, Anna – drew stares and comments whenever they visited Jacmel.

Lawrence swatted a mosquito. He held Anthony's gaze.

"If you want to help, you can't act like a baby. Ask Mami to help you dress in long pants, and wear shoes so you don't cut your feet."

After they finished the meal, Claire dressed Anthony in cotton britches and palm sandals. Lawrence led him around the building site, and gave him a small hammer.

"Your job is to bring nails when I call for them."

Claire realized Lawrence had already prepared the foundation and dug holes for the corner posts. He made fast work of framing the walls. Each time she lugged a bucket of water from the pump, she noted progress.

Lawrence took a long drink. "I'll have it under roof tomorrow or the day after if Sebastien comes by."

"The kitchen will go there, the front room here, the bedrooms on that side," Claire said, voice high-pitched with excitement.

In the middle of the framed cottage, Anthony dug a hole in the sandy soil. He raked dirt out of the hole with the hammer's claw end, and heard a chink. He scraped deeper and struck something hard. He stared into the hole, saw a dark tip, and reached for it. His fingers circled a hard piece of metal.

"Papi!"

"Just a minute, Anthony."

Anthony lay on his stomach and dug with both hands. He slid his fingers around the metal, and wiggled it loose. He pulled it up, set it beside him, and brushed off the grit. A little gun!

"Papi, Mami, look what I found! It's mine."

Lawrence turned from aligning a wall board and gasped. He grabbed the Deringer and stepped into the yard.

"Claire! Look at this!"

Claire caught her breath when she recognized the rusty shape. Wide-eyed, she stared at Lawrence.

"Where? How?" she asked haltingly.

Lawrence took a breath. "I don't know. Anthony dug it up. Maybe the explosion buried it."

"It's so strange." Claire knit her brows. "Do you think anything else is buried?"

"I don't know, but we should poke around before I lay the floor. Perhaps . . ."

Together, they knelt next to Anthony.

"Show me where you found my Deringer," Claire said.

"Papa Legba told me to dig there," Anthony said.

"Papa Legba wants you to play in the yard now, while Mami and I make your hole bigger," Lawrence said.

"But I found the gun."

"It's wonderful you found the gun, Anthony. Play in the yard for a bit. That was good work," Claire said.

Dirt flew as Claire and Lawrence, on knees, burrowed into the earth around Anthony's hole. Belly against the ground, Claire's fingers detected something soft, damp, and slimy. She glanced over her shoulder at Lawrence, who focused on unearthing something else. She returned to digging out what she suspected was . . . There! She pulled it out and gasped. Tears welled in her eyes.

"Lawrence." Her voice came out a weak croak. Louder, "Lawrence."

"Did you find something?"

Coins jingled as the fabric disintegrated in her hand.

"My purse."

"The money survived the fire? I can't believe it," Lawrence said.

Claire nodded, unable to speak.

"Go sit in the shade with Anthony. I'll do the digging. You should rest." Lawrence took the coins, then handed them back. "I don't know what to think."

Claire's heart beat a wild rhythm, elated to find the coins, but nauseated from digging and the baby's weight. She gave Anthony a banana, and wiped sweat from her brow. As she stared at Lawrence, digging into the new foundation with fury, Marie's owl eyes and pissy smell filled her mind.

Anthony fell asleep in her lap, and Claire's eyes closed. Lawrence's sharp voice brought her to startled consciousness.

"Claire!"

He crossed the yard with his rusted long-barreled pistol, and dropped a dirt-spattered wicker basket on the ground. The basket smelled of ash and rotten meat.

"The thieving little bitch," he said.

Anthony squirmed and squinted.

"Watch your words, Lawrence."

"I'll say whatever I want about that devil child."

"Anthony, check on the chickens," Claire said.

"I don't want to."

Lawrence set Anthony on his feet and gave him a soft swat on the bottom.

"Check on the chickens, and wait for us," Lawrence said.

"My sewing basket." Claire brushed off dirt, and reached in. "Ouch."

A needle pierced her palm, and blood oozed around it.

"She's bedeviling us still, after all this time." Lawrence's eyes were narrow. "Your hand's filthy. Don't rummage through the basket until I'm back with clean water."

Chickens squawked. Feathers flew. Anthony's blond curls bobbed in the pen. Claire shook her hand. The pump creaked. Overhead, a red and green parrot flew from one coconut tree to another. Claire's mind returned to the moment her hand and Sebastien's joined on poor Marie's skull. The fabric, the fire, the desperate crawl for safety, the last burning breath. Lawrence was right, Marie was a thief and a sneak. She'd been alone in the cottage many times. What was she thinking the day of the fire? Claire understood why Marie stole her coin purse, but how did she reach the guns? Why did she bury them? And why on earth did she hide the sewing basket? The image of scissors clutched in Marie's hand when she took her last breath came to Claire's mind. Lawrence trotted back from the pump, water sloshing in a bucket. I almost understand, Marie, Claire said in her heart, almost.

Lawrence took Claire's hand and spilled water over it until it was clean. The needle prick was tiny and red. He shook his head. When Claire reached for the basket, he yanked it away, and emptied the contents on the ground — filthy ribbons, spools of thread, and needles.

"Marie stole our guns and money and buried them under the house. You know I'm right," he said.

"I know."

Claire felt guilty, as if she were the thief.

"I'll dig a bit more, see if anything else turns up," Lawrence said.

Claire, hands on hips, watched him unearth pieces of the exploded powder flask. He rubbed something on his britches, glanced at Claire, and sauntered to her side.

"Look at this. Granny's medallion. You made yourself sick grieving for that girl. She's an ungrateful wretch who stole from us and set our cottage on fire. She could have killed Anthony." Lawrence cradled his gun. He held out his hand. "Give me the coins. I'll hire men to finish the cottage."

As Lawrence stomped away, Claire brought the medallion to her lips.

"What did you do, Marie?"

∾

A few days later, in the middle of night, Claire woke in agony to rolling waves of pain that drifted and surged.

"Lawrence!"

She needed him, but he hadn't returned from Jacmel. She clenched her fists and buried her face to smother the moans. Genevieve wouldn't arrive for a week, but this baby was coming tonight. Another cramp intensified until she cried out in desperation and fear. Anthony awoke.

"Mami, what's wrong?"

Claire rolled off the pallet and pushed herself up. She had to move against the pain.

"Our baby is coming. Walk with me."

"Where's Papi?"

"He'll meet us at the new cottage." She didn't believe her own words.

Palm fronds swayed in the breeze, and the full moon cast an ethereal glow as they walked hand-in-hand away from the slave quarters toward the cottage. That morning, Lawrence and the hired men attached the tin roof to the rafters. Soon, they would enclose the walls. In moonlight, the beams and rafters, joists and posts shone white like bones. Another cramp drove her to her knees. She struggled to breathe as if she were under water.

"Mami, Mami, Mami!"

Anthony's anxious voice pulled her to her feet. The skeleton house beckoned. After another cramp hit and subsided, Claire and Anthony climbed the wooden stile and inched across the foundation to the completed section of floor. Anthony dropped the quilt on the plank floor and crawled across to spread it flat. A great gush of water drenched Claire's night shift.

"Oh no! Mami, you wet yourself."

"Anthony, you must catch our baby like I catch baby goats when they're born. You're Mami's big boy."

In the dim light, the little boy's face took on a brave and resolute look, and Claire cried at the knowledge this would steal his childhood. The urge to push, push, push this baby out overwhelmed her. She lost herself in the pain and the need, lost Anthony, lost Lawrence, and descended into the dark waters where she sought Marie. From far away, she heard Marie's deep, awful scream. They reached for one another.

"Marie!"

The instant Marie's fingers touched hers, the pain stopped. Then

Anthony's insistent voice penetrated the dark waters. She kicked to the surface and opened her eyes. Anthony cradled a bloody ball attached to a ghostly cord.

"Mami! I catched the baby."

Claire took the child, a tiny girl, and unwrapped the cord from her neck. She placed the infant head-down over her arm and patted her back. The tiny body squirmed and mewed. She turned the baby face up and cleared mucus from her nose and mouth. The newborn wailed. Anthony cried too, his body pressed against Claire.

"Anthony, you brought your sister into the world. Now, I need you to do something important. Run to the quarters and get my sewing basket. We need to cut her cord."

As dawn broke in a ribbon of gold, Lawrence, disheveled and drunk, staggered down the path from the big house. The last coins they found in the rubble jingled in the purses of other cockfight gamblers. Today, Lawrence would spend an extra hour training Andrew Jackson. Soon the rooster would win back their money.

"Claire, where are you?" he shouted, angry with the expectation she'd make him explain what he did with the money.

Anthony burst from the half-built cottage and met Lawrence as he lurched past the chicken coop. The boy looked at Lawrence with all the accusation and righteousness a three-year-old could muster.

"You weren't here. Mami screamed all night. I catched the baby. She was bloody, but Mami said babies come out that way."

"The baby? Where's Mami?"

Anthony led Lawrence to Claire, asleep on the plank floor while the baby suckled at her breast.

"Jolie's my baby, not yours," Anthony said.

"Jolie? Her name is, *Pretty*?"

Lawrence knelt and touched the baby's head. Claire stirred and woke.

"I needed you," she said, cradling the baby girl.

"I'm sorry. What can I get you? Tea? Bananas? Did you give Jolie a middle name?"

Claire pushed herself to her elbows and stared at Lawrence with his red eyes and beaten expression. She wondered when she lost the boy she once loved.

"I thought we might name her, Jolie Claire, because the best I can hope for this little girl is she grows up to be like you," Lawrence said.

When he reached for the child, Claire gave her up and lay back in exhaustion. Lawrence carried his daughter outside. He sat on the ground with the child soft against his chest, and inhaled the sweet scent of new life.

"Jolie," he whispered, "my pretty girl. Your father is an ugly man."

CHAPTER FORTY-TWO

I n the terrible gale, palm fronds darted like errant kites. Lawrence dodged wind-whipped branches to open the paddock gate so the goats and donkey could escape. A corner of the chicken coop roof clanged like a sprung saw. After the storm subsided, he'd have to tack that down. Though the coop would be soggy and the cottage damp, at least the land was high above the flooding sea.

Rain stung his face, and wind tore open his shirt. To return to the cottage, he leaned into the wind, as powerful as ocean waves. The sky turned grey-yellow, and debris – branches, leaves, and unidentifiable shards – danced across the yard like drunks at *Carnival*. He nailed the gale shutters closed, then slid through the door and pulled it shut. In a nest of quilts under the table, Claire huddled with Anthony and Jolie. Something thumped against the house, and eleven-month-old Jolie whimpered.

"At last you're back," Claire said, "dry off and sit with us."

"I opened the paddock gate. The animals will fare better on their own. Wind loosened the coop roof. If it doesn't blow off, the chickens will weather the storm. Where's Andrew Jackson? I sent Sebastien to bring the cock inside."

"Sebastien's in the storm?"

Claire crawled from under the table, handed Jolie to Lawrence, and peered out through the back shutter. Rain stabbed through the slats. She opened the back door a few inches, but a gust of wind yanked it from her grip and blew it wide open.

"I'll find Sebastien," Lawrence shouted, but Claire stepped outside and disappeared.

Blinded by rain, she stumbled toward the training pit. She shouted for Sebastien, but the wind smothered all sound. With one hand extended as if to ward off an attack and the other shielding her eyes, Claire pressed forward until she splashed into roiling water at the edge of the pit.

"Sebastien!"

Her bandana blew off. Something struck her leg like a bullet, but she turned and let the wind push her eastward toward the coffee bushes.

A distant form jerked and lurched. Claire made her way toward it. The wind tossed her like a low-flying kite. When the form materialized into Sebastien, naked, clutching Lawrence's damned rooster to his chest, her heart broke. Together, they fought the wind back to the cottage. Muddy water swirled around their legs. The rooster pecked at Sebastien's chest.

Finally, they reached the cottage. Outside the door, Claire fell to her knees, exhausted, and Sebastien knelt beside her. The sun broke through the clouds, and the wind let up for an eerie minute. Lawrence leapt down the steps and gathered Claire in his arms. With Sebastien following, they stumbled into the cottage before the gale winds blew again.

Lawrence handed Sebastien a blanket, and Claire found clothes for the naked boy. While Andrew Jackson pecked at crumbs on the floor, Sebastien reported that before he reached the training pit, the rooster flew past on a gust of wind. He found the rooster entangled in coffee bushes. By the time Claire reached him, he was heading back, clothes ripped off by the wind.

Claire spread aloe salve on Sebastien's chest, and dabbed a wound above her ankle. Lawrence caged the rooster in a fruit crate, then served bananas and coconut milk to them all. Claire kept silent.

Later, while Lawrence played *osslay* with Anthony and Sebastien, Jolie crawled into Claire's arms and fell asleep

By night, the storm passed. Stars and planets beamed in the inky sky, and the air felt cool and clean. Overhead, Lawrence's hammer rapped, *bang, bang, bang.* Claire visualized him with nails in his mouth as he repaired a leak in the cottage roof before he fixed the chicken-coop.

Her heart pulsed with exhilaration. Though the gale frightened her, she reveled in the aftermath of being blown about in the storm, finding Sebastien, and leading him to safety. While life in Haiti was rife with challenges, she missed adventure, especially from the family business. She longed for problems that required clever solutions, where she'd consider different possibilities and decide the best approach.

Somehow during these four years in Haiti, while Lawrence managed the groves, Claire became like Molly – cook, seamstress, house servant. The children were her greatest joy, but even they failed to fill the gap in her soul.

When she'd entered the storm, Claire felt like herself. But she hated the rooster that drew Sebastien into the storm, and she hated Lawrence for caring so much about his damned cock.

∾

When Lawrence lay on the bed beside her, Claire stirred from light sleep.

"The cottage fared well in the storm. Only minor damage," he said.

"What about the damage to Sebastien?"

Silence, then a sigh. "His scratches will heal. Thank the Lord I didn't lose Andrew Jackson."

"You care more about that rooster than the children and me."

Lawrence rolled to his side. After a moment, he rested his head between her shoulder blades and stroked her arm.

"I care about the rooster because of you. You can't imagine the money that passes hands in cock fights. Andrew Jackson will be ready soon. You'll see. When he wins, we'll have enough money to live wherever we want."

Claire wanted to live on Wissahickon Farm, but no amount of winnings would change Miss Anna's heart.

CHAPTER FORTY-THREE

JACMEL FEBRUARY 1829

Lawrence, sweat beading on his forehead, stared from the edge of the grove. Sebastien sat on a porch step drumming a raucous rhythm – loud, fast, and joyful — while Claire, sparkling like he hadn't seen for years, danced with Anthony and Jolie. He stood rooted like a statue, unable and unwilling to join them. Claire's primitive display embarrassed him. Why had Claire so attracted him all those years ago? How could she embrace Genevieve and the frenetic Voodoo dances that accompanied her visits? In this remote and foreign place, Lawrence lost something fundamental – order; rules; seasons, for God's sake.

Heat, like drumbeats, resonated in waves. Lawrence yearned for cool breezes, autumn, winter. He needed winter, the long, cold season when fields lay fallow with short days devoted to fixing, building, and creating. Silent and dark, like a fetus growing under the cover of a mother's skin, winter gave land and the men on it time for rest and renewal, time to linger under a blanket of snow until heeding the sun's summons to begin life anew.

Here, rest and renewal came only for the dead. He swatted a fly on his shoulder, spat, and jogged up the path to Henri's for a jug of rum to get him through the day.

~

Claire's laughter rode the hot current.

"Ashes, ashes, we all fall down," she sang and tumbled to the ground with her children.

From there, Claire watched two parrots, bright green except for white around their beaks and red on their guts, swoop clumsily towards Lawrence's head before they perched on a palm. He'll be drunk when he comes home – if he comes home. She took Sebastien's hand to stand up.

In the evening after the children fell asleep, Claire rocked on the porch, inhaling hot, salty air and watching the fiery sun sink below the mountains in ribbons of red, purple, and gold. She set aside her sewing and closed her eyes. What did they gain by running away to Haiti? What did they lose?

In an invisible journal, Claire listed the gains – Anthony and Jolie first, of course, then living in a country of free blacks, then Genevieve, Sebastien, the sea, the mountains, the oranges. Last she listed, marriage to Lawrence.

On the cost column, Claire listed — leaving Mama, Daddy, Granny, and Samuel; then Felix, Mary, Jonah, Ruth, and James; then Wissahickon Farm, and Mr. Raymond, Molly, Hamish, Duff, Star of Night and Inspiration, Queen and the other goats, books, and yes, she included leaving Miss Anna. She sighed, went inside, took her purse from behind the cook pot, and shook out the coins. Not nearly enough for passage home.

Yet at home she'd have faced life with a half-white child, and life without Lawrence. Jolie wouldn't have been born. She loved Lawrence, she did, but Haiti was hard, hot, and foreign. Marie's soul rested in the dark waters. Claire's own soul felt lost, wandering through this paradise of loneliness while Lawrence's soul struggled to rise above a cesspit of damnation.

Of all Claire lost when they ran away from home, her greatest loss was Lawrence.

CHAPTER FORTY-FOUR

JACMEL NOVEMBER 1831

C laire walked down the path from Henri's, smelled the salty air, and longed for the fresh scent of wheat fields, alfalfa, and the Wissahickon Creek. At the big house, she'd cleaned and stitched a little Haitian girl's wound, but still worried the deep cut would fester and poison the child's blood. The child, who ripped open her heel on a broken conch shell, was the daughter of one of Henri's friends. It was an ugly wound – ragged, dirty, open to the bone – with little flesh to stitch together.

The girl screamed and flailed until her father spooned rum in her mouth and held her still. Claire doused the wound with vinegar, cleaned out what sand and grit she could, pinched the skin with her left hand, and stitched with her right. In fear and rage, the child defecated on herself and Claire. The filth threatened to contaminate the injury. Will the child live? How long before the stitches tear apart? Will she ever run without a limp? Claire sighed.

Now that the wound was closed and wrapped, Claire wanted to douse herself under the pump, wash away the child's blood and shit, rinse away her own pungent sweat, dress in fresh clothes, and sit with a cup of tea.

There's nothing looks as bad from the far side of a cuppa tae, Claire remembered Molly saying so long ago. Claire would tell Lawrence how Molly's words came to her, and remind him how angry she was the day he told her she looked like a boy – *but for the brown duckies peeking from your vest –*

and thank him again for saving Queen from the pit. Together, they'd laugh. They needed to laugh. Claire needed to laugh.

After she washed up, she joined Jolie in the front yard, where the little girl drew on the ground with a stick. At four, the child was smart and sassy, talked constantly, and relished the responsibility of collecting eggs and feeding chickens. She was quick to tell Anthony what he should and should not do. While Anthony's blue eyes were stunning against skin the color of ripe oats, Jolie's eyes, amber like a cat, flashed gold against her dark skin. Like a cat, some days Jolie cuddled and purred. But other days, she hissed and scratched. Today, Jolie happily formed letters in the dirt.

"Where's Papi?" Claire asked.

"Jacmel," Jolie said and squinted. "With Andrew Jackson."

Claire caught her breath. "Where's Anthony?"

"Oh, he's in the garden. I told him to weed and pick onions and beans for soup."

Despite her rage, Claire smiled. She met Jolie's eyes.

"Anthony doesn't like you telling him what to do. After I have a cup of tea, we'll ask Anthony to work with us on letters and sums."

Andrew Jackson won the first fight, but sustained head wounds and a torn hock. Lawrence held the rooster proudly while Claire stitched its leg. Since the win, Lawrence made special feed for the rooster. For hours each day he chased the cock and pitched it on its back, training it to immediately roll to its feet. Each morning when it crowed them awake, Claire wanted to wring its neck and serve it for supper.

Now, even though oranges were ready for harvest, and coffee cherries had dried in the trough, Lawrence left for an entire day to enter the bird in a fight. She was sick of it.

She spooned tea leaves in a mug and poured in boiling water. Then, she rocked on the porch and watched her children play. Lawrence bringing his damned cock to Jacmel looked every bit *as bad from the far side of this cuppa tae*. Enough. She would go to Jacmel and insist he come home.

"Mami, Anthony peed on my letters," Jolie said.

"Put on shirts and hats. We're going to town."

"Good. I want to see Andrew Jackson fight," Anthony said. "Hurry."

Claire raised her eyebrow. Lawrence already contaminated Anthony with his cockfight nonsense. After she helped Jolie dress, she reached behind the cook pot for her purse. Not a *centime* remained. Every hard-earned coin she saved now jingled in the hands of the bookmaker. She shook with fury, but controlled herself for the children.

As they walked down the path to Jacmel, Jolie's babbling filled the silence of Claire's wrath. Anthony ran ahead. He pitched stones at parrots and hid behind rocks, leaping out to make Jolie scream.

The scents of sea, fish, and seaweed enveloped them. When they reached *Rue de Commerce*, Claire ignored the vendors who called out their wares. She shook her head when Jolie begged for fried plantains. She marched through the street like a soldier – focused, leaning forward, slowing only when they approached the cockfights. She led the children to a hill above the pit to watch.

"I want to be with Papi," Anthony said.

"Stay here." Claire's voice was harsh. "Do not leave this hill for any reason. Anthony, you're responsible for Jolie. I'll be watching you."

Anthony glared at his mother with fear and resentment but stayed with his sister when Claire headed for the pit.

All around the pit, men with wild eyes shouted and gestured. Claire gagged from the stench of sweat, bird shit, and fancy women's cheap perfume. A tall mulatto woman dressed in the French fashion stood behind Lawrence with her arms around his waist and her forehead against the back of his neck. Her hair was wrapped in a bright yellow headscarf — one Claire made last week. A shout erupted and Lawrence stood tall.

A handler carried Andrew Jackson into the pit. Another brought in a black gamecock. When the roosters, still in handlers' arms, were held face-to-face, the black one pecked at Andrew Jackson. Lawrence's bird pecked back. The moment the handlers dropped the cocks they leapt at each other — feathers flapping, heads butting, beaks pecking, hackles rising like old-fashioned ruffs.

The black cock pinned Andrew Jackson. A handler separated the birds. Immediately, the black cock drove his beak into Andrew Jackson's neck. Lawrence's rooster lay limp, weakly flapping its wings. A handler pulled the black cock off.

Outside the ring of men, Claire watched Lawrence, eyes glazed, inch toward the pit. She glanced up the hill. Her children sat where she left them. Anthony shook his fists, and yelled for Andrew Jackson to get up and fight.

A loud shout drew her attention. A man in a white cotton shirt raised the black cock high above his head. Andrew Jackson sprawled on the ground in a yellow heap. The fight was over.

Lawrence glanced side-to-side, color drained from his face. Laughter and the word, *blanc,* rose from the crowd like a chant. One of the handlers, a boy of eleven or twelve, scooped up Andrew Jackson and delivered him to Lawrence. The woman who wore Claire's yellow headscarf put her hands on Lawrence's face, kissed his cheeks, and walked away chuckling.

Gamblers surrounded a slender man with tight white hair and a cigar hanging from his mouth. He counted out coins to the winning bettors.

"*Blanc, Blanc*, next time leave the chicken and bring your cock," someone shouted.

Claire gasped when Henri, wearing a fedora, accepted a fistful of coins from the money man. The man whose daughter she stitched that morning received a handful of coins, too. Claire narrowed her eyes. Next time, she'd charge for taking care of Henri's friends.

The crowd turned to the next fight. Lawrence slinked away. Andrew Jackson's blood blossomed on his shirt. When Claire stepped into his path, he looked drunk and confused. She tugged his sleeve.

"You took my money. Did you lose it all?"

With the rooster cradled in his arms, Lawrence collapsed against a tree. A muted croak came from Andrew Jackson.

"Who was that woman?" Claire's voice was like iron.

"Celeste? Where did she go?" Lawrence looked dumbly at Claire and held out the bleeding rooster. "Fix him."

"Let Celeste fix him. You don't even know me. And I don't know you." Her upper lip curled in a sneer.

Lawrence hadn't spoken Claire's name, but he named the other woman — Celeste. He gambled away all her money. She hated him. She shook with fury. She turned to the hill and gestured for her children.

Anthony and Jolie ran to keep up with Claire's frantic pace. At a table outside a café, Celeste sat with her arm around a man's shoulder.

"Walk on," Claire ordered the children. "I'll catch up."

After Anthony and Jolie disappeared up the road, Claire stepped to the table and ripped the headscarf off Celeste.

"Hey, what is this?" Celeste's face showed surprise and anger.

"I'm taking what's mine." Claire spat on the scarf and ground it in dirt with her heel. "It's as worthless as you."

Fists clenched, Celeste moved toward Claire, but the man held her back.

"*Non*, Celeste, don't fight the American. She suffers enough in marriage to the *blanc*. Let her go in peace."

Celeste snorted. "Keep your white cock and his chicken."

When darkness fell, Claire sat on the porch steps, listening to the hum of insects, the sound of the sea, and her children's even, sleepy breaths. Scuffling footsteps came down the path, and a silhouette framed in moonlight appeared. Sebastien. He sat with Claire and took her hand.

"*Blanc*," he said sadly.

Claire sat silent, wondering how it had come to this.

CHAPTER FORTY-FIVE

B askets filled with tobacco, bananas, yams, beans, rice, coconut, and cassava bread balanced on the heads of Genevieve and a dozen women who arrived at the big house to celebrate the new year.

"*Bon jour, bon jour.*" Genevieve's ample breasts bobbed under a bright print dress. Her beaded necklace chinked.

At the cottage, Claire heard Genevieve's voice – a joyful song carried by the breeze – and identified her in the crowd of women by her red turban. Thank God, Claire thought. Genevieve's visits – vibrant, days-long celebrations with dances and special foods – provided welcome respite from everyday monotony and loneliness. How did more than seven years pass since they left home and family? She and Lawrence spoke to each other only to exchange information about the children or chores.

She followed Anthony and Jolie up the path to the big house.

Genevieve greeted them with open arms. "*Mes enfants.*"

In the cushion of Genevieve's body, Claire inhaled the essence of coconut and hot spice. Her anxiety dissipated like salt in soup. Around the small temple that Henri built for Genevieve's ceremonies, women bustled, covering tables with fruit, popped corn, cinnamon-dusted rice pudding, yams, and sweet potato dumplings. Alongside the food, women placed thick cigars, bowls of coffee beans, and bottles of rum. Later, the men would bring their drums, reed flutes, and lute-like instruments called *strum-strum*.

Genevieve pulled Jolie onto her lap. The girl stared at Genevieve from a solemn face surrounded by cascades of dark hair.

"Let Genevieve look at you. You have grown so much, *ma chérie*. Smile for *Tante* Genevieve."

The four-year-old hugged Genevieve, then squirmed down, and Anthony stepped forward for his hug and inspection.

"Anthony," Genevieve said, running her hands along his arms, "I feel your strong muscles. You work hard, *non?*"

Anthony bent his arms to show his biceps. Genevieve squeezed one and nodded.

"And so, Anthony of the strong arms, what must you do with your strength?"

"Work," he said.

When Genevieve continued to look at him expectantly, he thought for a moment.

"Protect my mother and sister . . . and you, *Tante* Genevieve."

"What is your color, protector of mother, sister, and *tante?*"

"Yellow, for *Papa Legba.*"

"*Oui, Antoine, oui.*"

Beating drums announced the evening celebration. After Claire washed herself, she pulled on a freshly laundered white cotton dress and wrapped a white bandana around her hair. Anthony leapt into the room, hair dripping, in a white shirt and short white trousers.

"Can I go now, Mami?" he asked, shaking water from his head and dancing in tight little steps.

"Go," Claire said, laughing.

She helped Jolie into a white pinafore dress, and tied a white scarf with blue flowers around the child's head.

"Jolie, you're as pretty as your name. Run now, I'll come soon."

Claire joined Lawrence on the porch to watch Jolie skip up the path to the festivities. When Lawrence moved to the steps, sat down, and drew in the dirt with a stick, she sat beside him. His matted hair smelled like overripe onions. Drops of sweat cut paths through dirt on his chest.

"I put your clean shirt and trousers on the bed. Wash up and come with us. There's food, music, and dancing. It's good for us to be with people and have fun."

"I won't go, and I don't want you to. Genevieve's mumbo jumbo is a bad influence on the children. We are Christian people, not wild Voodoo dancers."

The peppery smell of tomato sauce and simmering chicken made Claire's mouth water. The salty, meaty scent mingled with sweet smells of fried plantains, cocoa, and cinnamon. Anthony had, no doubt, served himself molasses brittle and mango juice. Claire hoped he helped Jolie get food and drink. Her foot tapped to the drum beat. She'd seen Sebastien lug his drums up the path. He played them well, hands moving with lives of their own in rhythms joyful and provocative.

"I'm lonely, Lawrence. Christian, Voodoo, what does it matter? I want to laugh with the women, drink rum, eat special food, and dance. Come with us. Everyone expects you. I'll help you clean up. I'll wash your hair and braid it."

"You have no idea what it means to be a white man on this island. You think those people accept me. They don't. They see me as an intruder. You'll never understand. Go dance with your *negs*. *Blanc* will stay here."

Claire jerked back. "How dare you say I don't understand. You think whites in Philadelphia accepted me? To hell with you."

She wanted to scream. She wanted to punch him. She had to walk away.

As she headed up the path, she felt his eyes burrow into the back of her head. When she turned, he stood in the doorway, then disappeared inside.

The next morning, Claire woke to cotton in her brain and sour grit in her mouth. She didn't remember returning to the cottage. Lawrence loomed over her.

"Henri wants me to deliver oranges to a ship in port."

"Where are the children?"

"Anthony's milking the goats."

He plopped Jolie on the bed. The little girl smelled like bananas.

"I fed them. I have to load the cart."

Claire raised herself on an elbow. Each time Lawrence went to Jacmel, the image of Celeste's arms wrapped around him burned in her heart and mind.

"We'll go with you. I have clothes to deliver. I want to look at fabric and see if the *Librairie* has any new books in English."

"Not today." His tone was harsh.

"You're angry because I went to the big house last night, and now you won't bring us to town with you."

"For God's sake, Claire, I need to go alone. You have plenty of work here."

"Will you deliver the suits and bring back the full payment? Anthony needs a hat."

She pressed her lips together, smothering other words — no gambling, no women, no throwing our money away. Those words would infuriate him. But Lawrence looked scraggly and beaten, and she had no will to fight.

"Fine. Give me the soap. I'll wash up before I go."

Claire rolled out of bed, and sent Jolie to work in the garden with Anthony. Then she followed Lawrence.

After he stripped off his filthy clothes, his buttocks shone as white as his dandelion hair, but his arms, chest, and back were tanned and ruddy. He scrubbed himself under the pump.

"I'll wash your back," she said.

He stood silent while Claire scrubbed his shoulders and down his spine. Perhaps, she thought, I've been too angry and lonely to tend to him, and he's too exhausted to care. Work, the children, money that never accumulated, the heat that sapped their strength, her loneliness, and his frustration turned him into a silent specter – a phantasmal semblance of the boy she once loved.

In the early months, after they arrived and she healed from Anthony's birth, Lawrence had been a gentle lover, sweet in his need, and concerned for her pleasure. Later, love became a duty, with stolen moments of gratification between fieldwork and Anthony's claim on her body. She longed for those days.

Lawrence left for the oranges at dawn, often before she woke. He cut trees for lumber, nurtured sprouts from seed, harvested and packed oranges and coffee for sale. But even before Andrew Jackson died, at day's end he returned from the groves listless and distant.

He spent evenings with Henri in the big house or rode with him to Jacmel, returning hungover and marked with the scent of women's perfume. Something dark came over Lawrence then, like a storm that blackened the sky and whipped up great hurtling winds. On those nights, he fell on her in a rage, face sullen and mean as she lay hurt and defiled. She'd choke back tears, think about her wedding vows, and long for the gentle boy she married. He was in there, somewhere. She wanted to find him.

Now, at the pump, she knelt to wash his calves, and rubbed the washrag inside his thighs.

"Don't. I have business."

His words pierced her heart with venomous fangs. Soon his poison would flow through her blood and transform her into a tarantula who would eat her mate but protect her young. She dropped the rag.

"Go take care of your *business*," she said.

After the donkey cart swayed down the path, Claire, Anthony, and Jolie walked to the big house, enticed by the smell of corn cakes, coffee, and fried plantains. Despite the bitter taste in her mouth – from Lawrence or the rum, she wasn't certain – Claire felt hungry. Anthony brought a pot of goat milk to share, and Jolie carried a basket of eggs.

In the dining room, Genevieve, Henri, and Sebastien, now a young man of eighteen, drank sweet-smelling coffee. Claire craved a cup. Sebastien jumped up and offered her his seat.

"Ah, *bon jour, mes enfants*," Genevieve said. "Sit, sit. Where is Lawrence?"

"On the road to Jacmel to deliver oranges to a ship," Claire said, "for Henri."

Henri nodded but Claire thought he looked surprised.

"*Bien*," Henri said.

Claire poured a cup of coffee, added brown sugar and goat milk, and watched it swirl through the dark, bitter drink.

"Genevieve," she said, suddenly desperate to be alone, "I want to go to the sea and collect conch to make stew. My mother makes the most wonderful oyster stew, and I have a taste for it. Will you care for Jolie today? And Anthony? Although he can take care of himself."

Genevieve smiled. "My pleasure."

CHAPTER FORTY-SIX

JANUARY 1832

The best parts of Haiti, Claire thought, are the blue sea and the green mountains. As she trotted through the jungle, palms and pines reminded her of the cool, lovely woods and rocky ridges along the Wissahickon Creek. A bead of sweat fell from her eyebrow, flashed before her eye, and left a salty taste on her lips. Here, heat became breath. Insects buzzed always in her ears and eyes, now a rarely acknowledged nuisance. Her net bag flopped on her back.

The sea smell cheered her. When she reached the white sand, she lay face down, absorbing its warmth. After a few minutes, she turned onto her back and covered her face with her bandana. Sweat trickled between her breasts like tears. A soft breeze fluttered her blouse. She struggled toward the absence of thought and fell asleep.

Waves lapped against the shore, leaving their signatures in uneven strokes. Claire woke and seeing no one, stepped out of her clothes and into the sea. The current pulled on her legs, a seductive invitation to go deeper and deeper until Haiti disappeared. Salty water stung where a thorn scratched her knee, but it was good pain, specific and numbing.

She sifted her hands through the water, gazed out to sea, and let her thoughts drift to oysters tapping in a boiling pot, and Granny fussing over bean plants rabbits nibbled.

A rush of water swooshed through her legs, driving her backwards off her feet, pitching her under. She fought to the surface, gasping for breath, heart racing.

She heard Sebastien's laugh, deep and full of song, before her eyes focused on his glistening face. She swung her fist and punched his arm.

"Ow. Who taught you to fight?"

"What are you doing here?"

"I couldn't let a fine woman travel to the sea without protection."

"Who will protect me from you?"

"Do you need protection?"

He wrapped his long arms around her and drew her close. The sea's movement pressed their bodies together in a provocative rhythm.

"Sebastien, I . . ."

He covered Claire's mouth with his, their kiss salty and sweet. Claire gasped with desire. Fear and doubt floated away in her need to be held and cherished. Sebastien's hands explored her body with tender touches that tingled her flesh. Her fingers found the grooves of his muscles, ran down his spine, and outlined his eyebrows, nose, and lips.

In the current's gentle sway, Claire clung to him and yielded with passion she'd thought extinguished. When he released her, she kissed him, tasting mango and coconut. They stumbled to shore, breathless and peaceful.

"Now you and Haiti are one," Sebastien said.

Claire sat on the beach while the sun drew salty swirls of white on her skin. Her brain buzzed like a bee's nest. She wondered what Lawrence was doing in Jacmel.

Down the shoreline, Sebastien scampered in shallow water, dipping and bobbing, sea spray glistening like crystals on his back. Behind him, mountain tops pierced the clouds. Palms and mangroves swayed, keeping secrets in their dense greens and warm browns.

Claire no longer knew who she was, but she felt young, and free, and loved. She ran her tongue over her lips, tasting Sebastien. She wanted to float across the ocean as an offering to *Agwe*, the god of the sea, all the way home.

"*Voila!*" Sebastien called, "*lambi.*"

He splashed through shallow water, arms cradling three large conches, and gestured for Claire. He dropped the spiral-shelled mollusks and opened his arms. She raced to his embrace. They made love without regard for waves lapping their legs or sea foam capping their hair.

Sebastien raised himself on his elbows and smiled. Claire wept. They rose only when a wave broke over their heads.

Afterwards, confused and self-conscious, Claire pulled on her blouse, the dusty color of the cottage's walls, and stepped into trousers that flapped around her ankles like waves lapped the shore. She felt troubled but righteous. She didn't come to the sea in search of gratification. Sebastien pursued her. Sebastien loved her, wanted to protect her. Now, he presented her with a conch.

"*Merci*," she said.

The mottled shell's open pink lips swirled to a cathedral-like spire. I came to the sea for conch, she remembered. As she turned the shell, the snail inside retracted.

"He is hiding," Sebastien said. "Watch and learn."

He tapped the shell, then with a flick of his knife, cut off the tip of the spire.

"Now, he cannot hold."

He tugged the conch's foot and slid it out. After he trimmed off the inedible parts, he cut the rest in pieces. The rubbery meat tasted salty but bland. Later, Claire would pound the conch to soften it, and simmer it with onions, peppers, and tomatoes, like Mama's oyster stew.

Sebastien dug a watery hole to store the other conches, then cleaned the first shell in the sea. He blew through the hole in the spire, and drops of water sprayed Claire's face. She threw wet sand at him.

"Wait, wait," he said.

He stood tall, licked his lips, inhaled, then blew. The deep tone rose slowly, and echoed against the mountains. The long, plaintive cry resonated with sounds of lowing cows, howling wolves, and keening wails of lamentation.

Sebastien caught his breath and handed Claire the shell. She put it to her lips, and caused a sound like a horse fart. Sebastien laughed. He turned Claire to face the sea.

"Look."

A long-necked, long-beaked pelican glided over the water.

"No, under the surface."

Hand-in-hand, they waded in a few feet. A huge shadowy mass, like submerged boulders, moved languidly under water. Claire drew back, but Sebastien held her hand tight. When the mass came close, she counted five huge water beasts. A thick head rose above the water to breathe. She gasped.

"What are they?"

"*Manatee*."

Other snouts broke the surface then submerged again.

"Are they animals or fish?"

"They are called sea cows, and so they are both."

The *manatees* had pig-like snouts. Their flat stubby tails moved gracefully up-and-down to propel them. They were so big, Claire thought they should be called water elephants. Her father liked to tell the story of the April day in 1798 when he watched a huge elephant named Old Bet walk along Philadelphia streets on the way to an exhibition in the old part of the city. She sighed, wishing Daddy could see these *manatees*.

The sun crept across the mountains, casting a golden glow on the sea. It was time to go home. Claire's eyes filled with tears. Shame burned her cheeks. What had she done?

"My children are waiting, and Lawrence may be home from Jacmel. I have to go."

Sebastien put his hands on her waist and drew her close. He raised her face to his and kissed her. She turned away. He narrowed his eyes.

"You love me. We share spirits. I am a better man than the *blanc*. The *blanc* shares nothing."

"He shares our children. I'm sorry, Sebastien, I was wrong to love you. This can never happen again."

"*Blanc* does not know you. He does not see your pain and your glory. He leaves you to buy women in Jacmel. What woman stays with such a man?"

Claire took his hands. Tears spilled down her cheeks.

"My spirit weeps, but Lawrence is my children's father. I will never forget the joy you gave me this day."

Sebastien shook his head. He retrieved the conches and put them in Claire's bag. They ascended the rocky path from the beach, neither speaking.

Jubilant drumbeats greeted their approach to Henri's house and the cottage. Sebastien embraced Claire, then pushed her away.

"Never trust whites."

With a last sorrowful look, he left her.

Claire's knees buckled. She leaned against a palm tree, hand on her throat. She'd been calm and happy with Sebastien. He made her feel human, desirable, and worthy.

Marriage put nooses around her neck and Lawrence's. She strangled him as much as he strangled her. But they entered life in Haiti together, and together they must go on — until Claire saved enough money to go home.

Images of sunlight shimmering on the sea, swimming elephants, and Sebastien's warmth filled her mind. As she ran through the groves to the cottage, her step was light. Sebastien extracted the long-lost Claire Penniman as easily as he extracted the conch. That Claire didn't hide in the dark. That Claire was strong, smart, and independent. That Claire would find a way to go home.

Later, when Genevieve brought the children to the cottage, the pot simmered with succulent stew.

"You found conch?" Genevieve's brows were raised.

"I did. Will you stay to eat?"

"*Merci, non, bébé.* I leave for Port-au-Prince at dawn. There is much to do."

Genevieve hugged Claire and looked into her eyes.

"Haitian conch is a pleasure, a special treat, a delight to savor always."

Anthony and Jolie kicked the table legs while Claire filled their bowls with conch stew.

"Your grandmother, Elizabeth, makes delicious oyster stew, with milk, butter, and onions. We ate it with rye bread and green beans from Granny's garden. It's the best food I ever tasted. Perhaps tomorrow we can make sweet buns, like Molly did, if Papi brings rice flour from Jacmel."

Jolie dipped a piece of cassava bread into her stew and sucked the broth.

"Tell us about the Wissahickon, about Queen, and Star of Night, and Inspiration," Anthony said.

Claire's heart filled with pleasure. Her children loved her stories of home.

"Once upon a time, Mami and Papi lived across the sea, in a big city in America called Philadelphia. We worked on a farm with cows and chickens, goats and pigs, and beautiful race horses. Summers were as hot as Haiti but winters were so cold, rain froze in the air and turned to snow. Snow covers the ground like a giant white blanket — a cold white blanket. Papi and I loved the snow. We pulled a sled — a little bench on metal runners — up the highest hill, then rode it to the bottom as fast as water falls into *Bassin Clare.* I had a goat named Queen who was black and white and quite a nuisance. Once she fell into the cesspit, and Papi jumped in to save her. Papi saved me too, when I went into the Wissahickon Creek in a gale. Your Papi was a brave little boy when we lived on Wissahickon Farm."

Claire sighed and gazed at the fading light.

"Tell us more, Mami," Jolie said. "Tell us about Molly, and Hamish, and Duff."

"That's all for now. You both need to go to bed, and I need to sew."

Anthony yawned. "Will Papi be home soon?"

"I hope so."

CHAPTER FORTY-SEVEN

JANUARY 1832

The sun rose pink in the eastern sky. Claire watched Anthony milk a nanny goat.

"Let me try," Jolie said.

Anthony responded by squirting her. Jolie wailed.

"Don't waste milk, Anthony," Claire said.

The donkey's bray reached them before the cart pulled into sight.

"Papi's home," Jolie shouted and raced to meet Lawrence.

"Go on," Claire told Anthony.

She took his place on the stool and finished milking. She kept her eyes on the goat, but listened to the children chatter with Lawrence.

"After I talk to your mother, I'll show you what I brought from Jacmel."

~

Lawrence's shadow passed over her.

"Claire."

She turned to face him, and caught her breath. His eyes were clear, his face clean shaven, and his hair cut short. He looked like a boy. He smelled like donkey and oranges, with no hint of cheap perfume. At least not this time.

"I bought your thread and fabric, and I put the money from the suits on the table."

Claire nodded. Lawrence swallowed.

"There was a farmers meeting yesterday evening, so I stayed overnight. There are plans to make Jacmel a major market for citrus fruits and coffee, and to sell hats and other handicrafts at the port. We could sell your bandanas, even shirts and trousers there, without Henri taking a share of the earnings."

"That took all night?"

Lawrence's animated expression faded to sullen.

"I thought you'd be pleased."

"You thought I'd be pleased with Andrew Jackson's winnings. That didn't turn out well."

The *blanc* needed more than one sober trip to Jacmel to convince Claire he changed his ways. He'd shattered her, leaving her to mend herself. Now, he kicked the ground and turned away.

Claire carried the milk bucket to the cottage. Without a word, she crossed the porch where Lawrence rocked with Jolie on his lap. The child cuddled a new rag doll with a black face and wooly hair.

She hated the tears welling in her eyes.

CHAPTER FORTY-EIGHT

A lmost ten years after they landed in Haiti, in the mirror Claire faced a dark-skinned woman with a drawn face and sunken eyes. A raised pink scar from the Philadelphia rowdy boys ran from her nose to her mouth. She suspected that Lawrence, lean and muscular as he approached twenty-seven, with a thin mustache and fair hair, found her ugly. Not that he would say. Not that he would say anything.

For two weeks, both children suffered with fever, chills, coughs, runny noses, and the mottled rash of measles. There had been a run of it in Jacmel, and Claire felt certain Anthony picked it up when he delivered oranges with Lawrence. Anthony, a sturdy nine-year-old, had a terrible time of it. His right ear ached mercilessly until it burst and pus spilled onto his pillow. In the past two days, though, he felt better. But Jolie, only six, still slept poorly and coughed like a barking dog.

Lawrence continued to manage Henri's groves without interference, leaving Henri free to entertain women in the big house, or visit them in Jacmel. Lawrence spent his free time with Henri. Some days, Claire became so angry she wished he'd stay in town. Other times, she felt so lonely, she daydreamed about their childhood games, their first kiss, and the night Inspiration was born. Many nights she dreamt of being swept into the Wissahickon in the gale, reaching for Lawrence, and watching him walk away.

While she milked the goats or worked in the garden, Claire hummed, *Yellow bird, up high in banana tree,* and thought of Marie. But whenever she heard the joyous rhythm of distant drumbeats, Sebastien's image consumed her – his smile, his smell, his touch, his taste. She sacrificed Sebastien's love for Lawrence, who didn't love her. When she rejected Sebastien as a lover, she assumed they'd still be friends. But after that day at the sea, he never visited to sit with her on the porch, hold her hand, or console her about the *blanc*. Claire asked Genevieve about Sebastien, and learned he had a woman in Jacmel.

Outside the cottage, boots crunched on gravel. Anthony spoke enthusiastically with a man whose accent Claire struggled to place. American in a way, but with a touch of . . . Irish, she thought, or Scottish.

She carried Jolie onto the porch and stared at a white lad in a blue sweat-darkened shirt and wide white pants, with a sailor cap on his head. When the sailor spied Claire, his face broke into a familiar smile. She didn't remember anyone being so happy to see her, not even her children, in a very long time. The sailor removed his hat.

"Miss Penniman?"

Penniman? No called her that for almost ten years. She stared at the sixteen or seventeen-year-old boy.

"I'm Claire Williams."

"Don't I know the very thing? Do you remember me?"

Claire took in the ruddy freckled face and tousled red hair. There was something about the smile.

"It's Donal," he said, and pushed hair off his forehead. "You sewed my eyebrow when I was a wee lad. I told the captain you knew me, so I should deliver the letter."

"Donal? Of course, I remember you. How in the name of Jesus did you end up in Jacmel, Haiti, on this farm?"

Claire sat on a step with Jolie, limp with fever, on her lap.

"After my mother died, I shipped out as soon as a captain would take me. I sailed to England, Spain, and France. When we docked at Philadelphia a month ago, a black man approached Captain Cousins, inquiring if the ship was soon bound for Haiti. When the captain told him the *Ocean Queen's* next port was indeed Haiti, the man paid him five dollars to deliver this letter to Lawrence Williams who grows oranges in Jacmel. The black man said Mr. Williams was a white man married to Claire Penniman, a black woman from Germantown. I told the Captain, as I'd been listening to the whole transaction, I happen to know Mr. Williams and Claire Penniman. I'll take responsibility for getting this letter to him as soon as we dock. And here I am and here it is. I've done my duty and must return to the ship tomorrow before they shove off and leave me."

Claire held the letter against her lips. "What does it say?"

"I wouldn't be one to break the seal, Miss Claire. Have you a drink for a thirsty sailor?"

Jolie stirred, sat up, and stared at Donal. "Papi?"

"No, my darling, Donal is an old friend from home. Donal, it's so good to see you and hear your voice. I'm sorry, the children have been ill. I need to put Jolie down to sleep, but Anthony's over the worst of it. He'll show you the pump where you can cool off and quench your thirst. I'll be back in a few minutes."

After Claire settled Jolie, she held the letter to the light. The envelope was too thick to discern anything. She dare not open it. The letter was addressed to Lawrence from Miss Anna.

She stepped outside to the boys' chatter and laughter, like songs she forgot how to sing. Anthony waved, then trotted toward the groves. Donal, dripping, pulled on his shirt as he hurried to the porch. He smelled like the sea.

"Tell me the news of home," Claire said.

"You wouldn't recognize the city. They've made great progress building the railroad. Steamships travel up and down the Delaware River. Everywhere it's hurry, hurry, and bustle, bustle. The Fairmount Water-works are a sight – clean running water comes to more houses every day. It's the modern age, Miss Claire. Ah, Molly made me promise to give you a message. At last, she found her sister, Bridget, and that same Bridget was my mother. When Mam died of consumption, my father took Molly for his wife. She's now both my aunt and mother."

The news hit Claire like a brick to the head.

"Why, I can hardly take it in. Is she fine then?"

"Indeed she is. After two Sullivan women, my da's calmed down. He bought the Black Horse Tavern on Bethlehem Pike, not far from Wissahickon Farm. Trade is good, and he's thankful for Molly's good cooking." Donal gazed into the distance. "The mountains are wonderful here, but it's god-awful hot and your bug bites are vicious. Now tell me of your life here. Molly will tweak my ear if I don't return with news of you and Mr. Williams."

"We've made a life here, Donal. Lawrence increased the yields of the orange trees by scores. The seedlings he planted when we first arrived are growing and make beautiful blossoms. Most of them bear fruit. But the truth is, I miss my home. Is there word of my family?"

"Molly tells me your mother's dress shop does good business. When I happen to be in Philadelphia, I sometimes see your father making deliveries across the city." He paused. "There's street fighting here and there. It's best to go about your business and avoid the ruffians."

Some things never change, Claire thought, but her longing for home was keen. She gazed at the mountains and smelled the sea. A stunning country. Still, each time her children took sick she was certain they'd die without ever knowing her family. Donal's visit felt like an omen.

She heard Anthony's voice. Lawrence and he appeared from the groves. When they reached the porch, Lawrence, hair flat and sweat dripping from his blond beard onto his naked chest, stared at Donal from green reptilian eyes.

Donal offered his hand. "Gone native, I see, Mr. Williams. Did the boy tell you my name and my business?"

"He did. You're the child who split open his brow in Germantown years ago?"

"I am."

"What a strange reunion."

Lawrence spat. Claire handed him the letter. He stared at it a few moments, then handed it back.

"You read it." He turned to Donal. "I've fruit to harvest. If you're still here when I return for supper, I'll speak with you then."

Claire tried to steady her hands as Lawrence splashed himself at the pump, then trotted back to the grove.

Anthony lugged a basket of oranges to the porch and peeled one for Donal. The young man must be starving, Claire thought. I should be a better hostess. From inside, Jolie whimpered.

"Let me get the lass," Donal said. "I've no fear of a baby's fever."

"Thank you. After I read the letter, I'll introduce you to cassava bread, *griot*, and mangoes."

Donal returned with Jolie, and he and Anthony took the child to the water pump to cool off.

Claire broke the letter's seal.

25 December 1833

Dear Lawrence,

It's with heavy heart I write this. Your father succumbed today. He's been poorly since November with a great hacking cough – pneumonia, Reuben said. Your father longed for you these many years. Each time a carriage or wagon drove up to the farm, he stopped whatever he was doing and watched to see if it was you.

Reuben has made a life in Boston, with a wife, five children, and another on the way. He writes weekly and returns at harvest time, but he has his physician's life and hospital work, and I cannot ask him to move kith and kin to the farm despite your father's passing.

And so, Son, here it is. I find I cannot manage the farm alone. I don't want to sell the property that has been in your father's family since William Penn first granted Cyrus Williams 500 acres. Hamish died a few months before your father, but Young Hamish and his Indian wife, Sky Blue, returned to the stables to work with Duff. The Negroes, Jonah and Ruth Chestnut, have proven themselves hard workers. Raymond couldn't have kept up the farm without them. Molly married a man, Seamus Reilly, who lives nearby in the village of Flourtown. She comes to the the farm most days but also helps Seamus with their business, the Black Horse Tavern. I remember well how hard my parents worked to run the Hansel and Gretel Inn.

Will you come home, Lawrence? It's almost spring, and the fields must be prepared for planting. Your father's dying wish was that you return to inherit the Wissahickon Farm of your blood. I have enclosed a guarantee for the cost of passage to Philadelphia for you and yours.

I await your return with hope and regard,

Mother

~

Claire's face burned. Mr. Raymond dead. Hamish dead. Not a word to acknowledge Claire or her children except, you and yours. Claire wrote letters to Mama and Daddy a few times each year, and Mama shared those letters with Miss Anna and Mr. Raymond. But even after ten years, Miss Anna couldn't acknowledge Claire by name. She'd wasted no ink offering to accommodate Claire and the children.

But she guaranteed the cost of their passage. Finally, they could go home. Claire wanted to go home.

~

At the sound of Donal's sweet voice singing to Jolie — *The Last Rose of Summer* — Claire raised her head. Molly often sang that song.

> *When true hearts lie withered and fond ones are flown, oh who would inhabit this bleak world alone?*

Grief for Mr. Raymond withered Claire's heart. She and Lawrence had flown away from their fond ones. They'd inhabited this bleak world for too long. After a thoughtful look at Donal, Jolie, and Anthony, she went inside to prepare the meal.

In her heart, Claire believed Mr. Raymond always cared about her, and longed to meet his grandchildren. Her children would never know his love and kindness. She visualized him in the happy years, standing in the front yard with a scarf flapping around his neck, handing out Christmas gifts to thank workers for their loyal service.

She remembered a day soon after she came to the farm. She'd thrown sticks in the Wissahickon Creek to watch them float like boats, but slipped on a mossy rock. She fell down hard, scraped skin off her palms and gouged her knee. She wailed for Daddy until Mr. Raymond raced to her side, and carried her to the house. While Molly cleaned her cuts and bound her knee, Mr. Raymond told jolly stories to make her laugh. Now, as she filled bowls with rice and *griot*, she found herself weeping. It was time to go home.

Donal and the children finished eating before Lawrence returned.

"Can I show Donal the big house?" Anthony asked.

Claire glanced at Donal.

"There's no place I'd rather see," Donal said. "We'll bring Jolie. The walk might perk her up."

The sweet sight of Anthony skipping up the path followed by Donal with Jolie in his arms turned bitter. The pump handle creaked. Water splashed. Claire retrieved the letter and waited while Lawrence washed himself. He swung his filthy clothes over his shoulder and strolled to the porch.

"Where's your friend? Where are the children?"

"Anthony's showing Donal the big house."

Claire's hand trembled when she handed him his mother's letter. Still naked, he stood like a weather-beaten statue as he read. His sweat smelled like rum. Claire felt every nerve in her body. Without a word, he returned the letter and moved to the door.

"We're going home," Claire said.

He stopped in the doorway but didn't face her.

"It's time, Lawrence. Your mother needs you, and I need my mother. Haiti isn't our home."

"You and your brown children will be reviled in Philadelphia, like I'm reviled here."

Claire shook her head and curled her lip.

"Me and my brown children? They're your children, too."

"My work is here."

"Lawrence, your work is to honor your father's legacy, Wissahickon Farm . . . I want to go home."

"And if I want to stay?"

Claire took a breath. "Tomorrow, the children and I are leaving with Donal."

"No surprise. You like your lads young and white."

Claire gasped and stared, wide-eyed. Then she flew at him, pummeling his chest and arms. She punched until he grabbed her wrists and held them so tight they hurt.

"Let go of me!," she screamed. "What would your father think of you?"

"My father's dead."

When he released her, Claire saw tears in his eyes. She hated him. But he'd come with them. The children were all the *blanc* had in Haiti, other than oranges, and oranges left on their own soon rotted.

There was little of their lives in Haiti to bring home. Claire draped her grandmother's medallion around her neck. She shoved clothes for herself and the children in a carpet bag, along with drinking cups, spoons, and blunt knives. She tucked her Deringer pistol and the few remaining coins into a purse she tied around her waist. She strapped blankets on the children's backs, and wore Granny's tattered quilt around her shoulders like a cape.

"Donal! Donal's here!" Anthony called.

Claire watched Donal drive the carriage he leased in Jacmel across the yard. She walked through the cottage one last time. No future tenants would experience the unbearable conditions she and Lawrence, young and frightened, had. Whoever Henri hired were were welcome to it. We're going home.

As if she conjured him with her thoughts, Henri's angry voice shattered her contentment.

"You cannot leave! You are bound to me!"

"No provision in our contract binds us to you or the land. We came freely, and we will leave freely. I've done everything you asked and more. Your groves produce the best tasting oranges and highest yields in Haiti, and sales of coffee increase every season. The cottage, chicken coop, and fences I built are sturdy and well maintained. Fresh water flows from the pump. The animals are healthy, the hens' eggs are abundant, and good vegetables grow in the garden. Pay me, Henri, what you owe." Lawrence's voice was hoarse.

"There is no money to pay you," Henri said.

"Of course there's money. We sell oranges every week."

"Ah, but your share of the money is gone. All to cover your debts."

"What debts?" Lawrence flushed.

"Gambling, *Monsieur*, rum, and women. Do you think we forgive your losses at cards? At dice? At the cockfights? Do you think rum and women come without cost to honor your white face? Oh no, *Monsieur*. You spent your share. Do you dispute it?"

"You son of a devil!" Lawrence raised his fist.

"Lawrence, you're scaring the children." Claire took his arm, and felt him tremble.

"I'll kill him."

As she dragged Lawrence to the carriage, Henri laughed.

"You will kill no one. If you harmed me, you would not make it one kilometer before you, your wife, and your mulatto children dangled by your necks from the orange trees."

On the carriage bench, Donal, a pistol clutched in his hand, watched Henri while the children, Claire, and Lawrence climbed aboard. Henri's glare burned in Claire's brain. She didn't look back.

As the carriage rocked down the path to the Jacmel wharf, the loud, low call of a conch trumpet followed them, sounding a last lament.

PART 3

**GERMANTOWN
WISSAHICKON FARM**

1834 – 1836

CHAPTER FORTY-NINE

GERMANTOWN FEBRUARY 1834

When the ship entered the Delaware River from the Atlantic Ocean, a putrid smell rose from the cold, swirling water. Claire inhaled the rank air of industry with joy. Snow flurries speckled the children's eyelashes and melted on their tongues.

Claire held Anthony's hand, and Lawrence carried Jolie. On wobbly legs they stumbled down the plank to the Philadelphia dock in early morning. Icy snow tortured their sandaled feet. The winter wind bit through the thin cloth jackets Donal bought from the ship's purser. Donal's blue cap covered Anthony's head. Claire's purse held their entire fortune, a handful of coins. On the voyage, Granny's medallion disappeared. Claire suspected Lawrence sold it to buy rum.

When they stepped onto the wharves, sailors and merchants stared as if they were circus freaks. We look like stowaways, Claire thought, penniless immigrants hoping for a better life in America. The bitter cold stunned her. They were ill-prepared for winter arrival. Donal put his hand on her shoulder.

"Claire, this way."

He led the family to the Custom House. The clerk raised his right eyebrow and asked for their names.

"Lawrence Williams, Anthony Williams, and Jolie Williams." After he spoke, he averted his eyes.

"White?"

"Yes."

The clerk stared at Jolie. "The children?"

"White."

"American?"

"Yes. We're returning from Haiti. I was hired to improve orange groves there."

"Address?"

"Wissahickon Farm in Whitemarsh Township."

"This woman is your nursemaid?"

"Yes." Lawrence answered without hesitation.

Claire reeled as if he punched her. She opened her mouth to refute him, but Anthony's icy hand in hers stopped her. The lie would protect the children and improve their chances for entering Philadelphia unimpeded. Foreign born black children might be sent to an orphanage while authorities decided what to do with them. To hell with Lawrence and the presumptuous clerk. She'd soon be with her family in Germantown.

"Name?"

"Claire Penniman."

"African?"

The clerk scratched a sore on his nose.

"I'm an American Negro, born free in Germantown."

"Will you accompany Mr. William and his children to Wissahickon Farm?"

"I will return to my family home in Germantown. My parents are Moses and Elizabeth Penniman."

The clerk wrote the information in his book.

"Move along."

"Where do I find a hackney?" Lawrence asked. "The children are freezing."

The clerk pointed. "You can see them from here."

Puffs of steam rose from the nostrils of a dirty white horse attached to the nearest hackney. While Lawrence hustled the children to the carriage, Claire turned to Donal, whose cheeks shone red in the cold.

"Who would think the day you split your eyebrow would become my lucky day? You've proven to be a real friend, Donal. Please tell Molly she has a wonderful son."

Claire shivered and crossed her arms.

"I was brave." He smiled.

"You were and are. Brave and kind and good."

"We'll meet again, Claire Penniman," Donal said.

Claire wanted to hug him, but thought better of it. She approached the carriage, relieved to see the driver was black.

"The Penniman home," she called. "Up Germantown Road."

"I know Moses, and Samuel, and Felix. You the daughter run away to Haiti?" the driver asked.

"Yes. I'm Claire."

She climbed in the carriage door. Inside, Lawrence blew on his fingers, then covered Anthony and Jolie's hands with his. Claire shivered, desperate to warm the children. Her feet ached with dreadful pain. She put Anthony's feet on her lap and rubbed them. He snuggled closer. Jolie stared from Lawrence's lap, as if her little eyes had frozen open. Claire glanced at Lawrence, then dropped her eyes.

"The children will stay with me in Germantown."

"For now," he said.

As the hackney rumbled north over cobbled streets, Claire felt disoriented. Wood and brick buildings that lined the streets ten years ago were gone, replaced by huge granite and marble structures.

Lawrence stared out the window. Bearded and dirty, his skin had faded to sallow yellow during their sea voyage. They drove past shops that seemed familiar, though Claire wasn't certain where in the city they were.

"Stop!" Lawrence called to the driver. "Stop here."

"But," Claire said.

The sign outside a red brick building read — *City Tavern Fine Food and Drinks.*

"I'm getting out here." Lawrence glared at Claire. "I need money."

Claire saved a few coins for the hackney fare, and handed him the purse.

"Why?"

"That's my business."

After he kissed Anthony and Jolie's heads, he hopped out, wrapped in a filthy blanket. As the carriage pulled away, Lawrence entered City Tavern. Good riddance, Claire thought, but Anthony and Jolie stared, bewildered.

"Why did Papi leave?" Jolie asked.

Claire patted her daughter's knee. "He has business there. But we're going to Germantown. You'll meet your grandparents soon."

The grey sky smelled of snow and tar, as welcome as the scent of fresh bread. Now midday, Germantown Road was strangely quiet, with few people making their way through the snow.

The driver drove the hackney into the alley and stopped at the Penniman house. No one appeared at the door. After the man set their bags on the porch, Claire offered the coins.

"Keep it for the children, Miss." He tipped his hat and hurried to the hackney

As she hustled the children inside, she called, "Mama? Daddy? Granny?"

No reply. The house smelled of biscuits, salty soup, tobacco. Where could they be?

She swallowed her alarm when she observed the worn settee, her father's chair, and the round rag rug on the sitting room floor. Tears ran down her face, from relief, from pain, from Lawrence's humiliating denial of their marriage, from the hackney driver's kindness.

Jolie whimpered, and Anthony shivered. Claire hustled them to the kitchen where warmth emanated from red embers nesting in the base of the Franklin stove. After she pulled off their wet clothes, she wrapped Jolie in Elizabeth's apron and Anthony in a wool shirt hanging on a chair back. The children looked bedraggled and miserable. They huddled together close to the stove until their shivering subsided. Claire found a loaf of bread in the bin. The children ate ravenously.

"I can't imagine where your grandparents are, but they wouldn't leave a fire unless they planned to be back soon. Anthony, don't let Jolie get any closer to the stove. I'll find blankets and dry clothes."

Her parents' main-floor bedroom looked entirely different with Granny's quilt spread across the mattress. A walking stick leaned against a side table, with a white chamber pot underneath. A bonnet and nightdress hung from a hook on the door. A lace cloth covered the oak chest. The room smelled of linen and witch hazel liniment. Her parents had moved Granny to this room.

She bounded up the steps, and hesitated at the door to her room. In place of her wood bed, a mattress covered a low pallet. Neat piles of clothing and fabric were stacked against one wall. Nothing of her remained.

Next door, her parents' bedroom furniture filled Granny's old room. In the closet, she found a worn brown cotton dress to change into and a shawl to cover her children.

When she returned to the kitchen, Anthony and Jolie slept huddled together like puppies. She spread the shawl over them. This is your real home, she told them silently.

Claire's hands and feet were numb from cold, and her heart was numb from Lawrence. She lay next to her children and let herself cry — for now, not forever.

Before she gave in to sleep, she whispered, "I'm brave, I'm strong, and I'm free. This is my home with my people."

"Claire, Claire, is it you? Is it really you? Moses, it's Claire! Come see. Look at these children, asleep on the floor like vagrants."

Claire opened her eyes to her mother's voice and her father's deep brown eyes. She reached for her father's hands. Her sleepy children woke in fear and confusion with their faces pressed against Elizabeth's snow-splattered coat. Moses' rough hands held Claire's. His tobacco smell thrilled and comforted her.

Behind her father, a sturdily built young woman Claire knew was Mary, navigated tiny, wrinkled, white-haired Granny's wheeled chair close. Claire could hardly speak for crying.

"Granny."

A voice ancient as Earth, whispered, "Child, child."

Claire knelt before her grandmother, put her head in Granny's lap, and felt the touch, light as a bird's feather, of quivering fingers.

"I knowed you coming home," Granny croaked. "Today at church, I pray to Jesus and Hallelujah, Jesus answer my prayer. My child come home to me afore I die."

Claire raised her head to look into Granny's bespectacled eyes.

"Your child is home with her children," Claire said. "Praise the Lord, we're home."

Samuel and Felix stood back. When Jolie glanced up from Elizabeth's arms, Samuel knelt to hug her. Anthony put his hand on Samuel's shoulder.

"We your people. This where you belong," Samuel said.

CHAPTER FIFTY

GERMANTOWN APRIL 1834

E ven on warm sunny days, Claire and the children suffered from the cold. Church members had been generous, offering their worn winter clothing. Finally, in the middle of April, trees budded, grass turned green, and early peas sprouted in Granny's vegetable patch.

In the back room of Elizabeth's dress shop, Claire worked on a fancy lace collar. After she finished the collar, she'd add puff sleeves to the green satin dress, let out the waist, and flounce the skirt. Mrs. Shipman's daughter, Margaret, demanded that the gown 'swell like a balloon when I twirl.' Claire feared Margaret Shipman would burst like a balloon when she twirled.

Dressed in a blue calico dress, Jolie sat at Claire's feet. As the little girl pressed the slate pencil on a writing slate, her tongue stuck out. Each time Claire named a letter, Jolie repeated it and drew it on the slate.

"W," Claire said.

"W," Jolie repeated. "That's hard to mark."

"W is for Williams, your last name. And W is for Wissahickon, the creek we like to explore. Now try X."

For now, Claire taught Jolie herself. Anthony attended the Free School for African Children, funded by the Quakers and the Abolition Society.

Last month, when Claire went to the school to register Anthony, the Quaker woman stared at her and her son.

"The child is white," the woman said.

"His father is white. I'm his mother. He's named for Anthony Benezet."

"Ah," the woman said, "our revered friend. The boy is welcome."

On Anthony's first day, his schoolmates kept their distance until one boy touched Anthony's hair.

"Smooth as Chinese silk," the boy said.

Later, Moses arrived to walk Anthony home, and the issue of heritage vanished. Now, Anthony monopolized dinner table conversations with accounts of all he learned.

Claire set aside her needle and gazed at Jolie. While Anthony's skin was the color of a Palomino, Jolie was bronze like a sorrel horse. Her complexion was lighter than Claire's, but she wouldn't be mistaken for white. At six, she remained oblivious to stares, but clung to Moses if the curious came too close.

The doorbell jingled. Claire set the collar on the table, darted her needle into a piece of soap, straightened her dress, and entered the front sales room. She stopped short.

"My goodness, Claire, I wouldn't recognize you except you look so much like your mother," Miss Anna said.

Lawrence stood in the doorway dressed like a dandy, with high-waisted buff trousers, a white shirt, a violet waistcoat, and a brown velveteen jacket. His blonde hair was parted in the middle and cut in the modern style. Scrawny sideburns ran to his chin. In the months since they parted, his face filled out. His expression was nonchalant, even soft. Claire thought he looked quite handsome.

She smoothed down her hair. In contrast to Lawrence, Claire wore a tattered hand-me-down dress. Why did they come without notice? She found her voice.

"Good day, Miss Anna. Hello, Lawrence. I trust all is well."

Her voice quivered. This was awkward. She and Lawrence met each other's eyes shyly. Jolie burst into the room.

"Papi, Papi!"

Lawrence looked truly happy. He held out his arms.

"Papi, why did you leave us? I needed you, but you didn't come."

Lawrence swept up the child, holding her tight against his chest. He kissed her forehead and twirled her around until she squealed. He turned to Anna.

"This is Jolie, my daughter." His voice was filled with pride.

Miss Anna's eyes flitted from Lawrence to Jolie. She sighed and turned to Claire.

"May I sit?"

Claire indicated a blue upholstered chair. Miss Anna wore her downy white hair in a bun. Her blue eyes were bright, but the skin around her eyes sagged. Nevertheless, she held herself in an imposing manner. Claire's eye twitched.

Jolie wiggled out of Lawrence's arms and lunged to Claire. From behind her mother's knees, she glared at Miss Anna. When she peeked out, Lawrence made a silly face. She rushed to him and leapt into his arms again. He set her down in front of Miss Anna.

"This is your grandmother," he said.

"I live with my grandmother. She's not my grandmother, she's white."

"I am certainly your grandmother, young lady. Your father is my son." Anna stared at Jolie as if taking inventory. She glanced at Lawrence with an eyebrow raised. "I don't see much of you in the child."

Claire knew exactly what Miss Anna implied. Lawrence caught her eye and shrugged. Miss Anna gestured to Jolie.

"You're a skinny little thing, aren't you?"

"I know my ABCs."

"Let me hear them."

"Shall I?" Jolie looked at Claire. "May I say them for the white lady?" Claire nodded. Jolie climbed on Lawrence's lap.

"A, B, C, D, E, F, G, H, I, J, K, L, M, N, O, P, Q, R, S, T, U, V, W for Williams and Wissahickon, X, Y, and Z."

"Nicely done. You've been well taught." Miss Anna glanced at Claire, then spoke to Jolie. "Your mother was my best student. You take after her."

Jolie retrieved her slate and drew letters for Lawrence to admire. Claire caught her breath, and spoke.

"I was shocked and sorry to learn of Mr. Raymond's death. He was a great man. The lessons he instilled helped Lawrence become the best farmer in Haiti. I'm glad he returned in time to prepare and plant the fields."

"He's been a godsend. I only wish Raymond lived long enough to welcome him home." Miss Anna cleared her throat. "Is your mother nearby?"

"She's doing fittings at Mrs. Shipman's for the wedding."

The awkwardness of speaking with Miss Anna was assuaged by a clean and sober Lawrence, who sat on the floor with Jolie.

"Where is the boy? Lawrence tells me he was a great help with the oranges."

"Anthony's at school."

"Which school is that?"

"The Free School for African Children."

Miss Anna gasped. "Did you know about this, Lawrence?"

"I haven't seen the children since we disembarked."

"Today's Lawrence's birthday, though I'm suppose you didn't remember. He wanted to see his children and introduce them to me. I'd like to meet the boy."

The bell jingled. Elizabeth entered the room in a bustle.

"Good afternoon. Has my daughter, Claire, addressed your needs?" Elizabeth put a hand over her mouth. "Miss Anna? Lawrence? It's been so long."

"Hello, Elizabeth. At last, our children are home. I only wish Raymond lived to see Lawrence return."

"I suspect Mr. Raymond shouted, *Hallelujah*, from the heavens when Lawrence returned to Wissahickon Farm. How are you managing?"

"Thanks to Lawrence, the fields are plowed and seeded. We sell as much meat, butter, and cheese as we bring to market. Lawrence plans to expand the orchards. Two weeks ago, he traveled to Lancaster and brought back a fine bull."

"What of Star of Night? She's over twenty, now," Claire blurted. "And Inspiration?"

"Star of Night is long gone," Anna said. "She broke a leg in a gopher hole soon after you left, and Raymond put her out of her misery. Inspiration hasn't been raced for a few years, but she's well. She spends her days in the pasture."

Claire shuddered. Star of Night, dead. In Haiti, thoughts of the lovely mare helped her through many tough times. She'd imagine riding Star, their hearts beating in time, with wind in their faces and freedom in their souls.

She had a million questions. How did Hamish die? Tell me about Duff, Jonah, Ruth, and little James. How did you feel when Molly married? When did Young Hamish and his wife, Sky Blue, come to the farm? Have any horses proven winners? Claire's foot tapped a nervous beat.

Lawrence bounced Jolie on his knee and avoided Claire's eyes. She hardly breathed while her mother conversed with Miss Anna.

"Lawrence and I would like to spend time with his son," Miss Anna said.

"Anthony arrives home by 5:00 each day. Would you care to take dinner with us?" Elizabeth asked, to Claire's surprise.

"I think not, Elizabeth, thank you. Lawrence and I will stay at the Mansion Inn tonight. We'll come for Anthony tomorrow morning at 9:00. Lawrence wants to show his son the University of Pennsylvania where he and Reuben studied. Then we'll all sup at the City Tavern, as we have business there."

"Anthony is expected to attend his classes tomorrow," Claire said, trying to calm her voice.

"Claire, it's one day," Lawrence said. "I miss Anthony, and I know he misses me. I'm not going to steal him away, but I want to spend time with my children. Soon, I want them to visit the farm."

The next morning, Claire watched Anthony skip down the steps. She stayed awake all night to stitch yellow corduroy knickers with a matching jacket and cap so Miss Anna wouldn't think her son poorly dressed. She'd struggled to explain to both children why Lawrence suddenly appeared with his white mother.

When Lawrence came to the door, Anthony rushed to him. Claire looked hard at Lawrence. His eyes were sunken, and his breath smelled of rum, as it had in Haiti.

"Are you drinking again?"

"Don't start. I'm a grown man. I had business with men." Lawrence rubbed Anthony's head. "You've grown. Your grandmother is anxious to meet you."

"I live with my grandmother here, Papi."

"My mother, Anna, is your grandmother, too."

Anthony threw a guilty glance at Claire before he took Lawrence's hand and went down the porch steps to the waiting carriage.

At the dress shop, Claire repaired the lining of a gentleman's frock coat. She poked her finger with a needle.

"Damn it."

"Claire, it's not like you to use such language, especially in front of Jolie." Elizabeth took Claire's hand. "You knew sooner or later Lawrence would come to see the children."

"I didn't expect Miss Anna. She acts like I'm the children's nursemaid.

She'll never acknowledge I'm Lawrence's wife, and the mother of his children."

"Anna's pride is her curse. It wasn't easy for her to face you in order to meet Anthony and Jolie."

"They're my children."

"They're Lawrence's children, too. He loves them, and they ask for him daily. They thought he abandoned them."

"He abandoned me before we ever left that island."

"Did you tell him how you felt?"

"I tried, at first. But I couldn't bear fighting with him. You and Daddy were right. I should have stayed with you and raised Anthony in Germantown. Lawrence should have gone to Boston. How different our lives would be!"

"We missed you terribly, Claire. Your father blamed us for indenturing you so young. He said you didn't know who you were. Samuel fared better, perhaps because he was a boy. Then again, perhaps he didn't. He hasn't taken a wife. He spends all his free time with Felix. We did our best, but it wasn't best for you."

"No crying. No crying." Jolie went from Claire to Elizabeth, holding up her hand to tell them to stop.

Claire pulled Jolie close. "We're crying about the years we weren't together. We're happy now."

Jolie's chin sunk to her chest. "Like I cry because we aren't together with Papi."

Anthony returned late afternoon, dressed in a blue sailor suit and fancy boots.

"Lawrence registered Anthony at Germantown Academy, and paid his tuition." Miss Anna handed Claire money tucked in an envelope. "For the children."

Claire tried to return it, but Miss Anna clucked her tongue.

"Don't be foolish, Claire."

Lawrence glanced at Claire, took a deep breath, and handed Jolie a brown-paper-wrapped package.

"I bought this for you."

Jolie opened the paper to reveal a blue yoke dress with a white pinafore, a blue cape with a matching bonnet, and a small purse filled with jingling pennies. She flung the cape over her shoulders and twirled. Miss Anna watched with folded arms.

"Come, Mutti, I'd like to be back at the farm before dark."

Before he followed Miss Anna to the carriage, Lawrence knelt to hug the children.

Anthony called after Miss Anna, "Good bye, Granna, thanks for my new clothes."

Claire wanted to rip them from his body.

CHAPTER FIFTY-ONE

In mid-July, when Philadelphians complained about the heat and humidity, Claire and the children finally felt comfortable.

Mornings and evenings during the withering heat, Anthony carried buckets of water to Granny's vegetable patch. Yesterday, he instructed Moses on the proper time of day and appropriate amount of water for the garden during the children's visit to Wissahickon Farm. Moses' serious expression in response to Anthony's orders made Claire turn away so neither saw her smile.

As she dusted furniture and swept the floor, she felt empty. The children's upcoming visit to Wissahickon Farm meant two weeks without her children. Except for Anthony's school days and the children's short visits with Lawrence, she'd never been apart from them.

A few weeks ago, Lawrence and Anthony attended the play, *The Gladiator*, by Robert Bird, Lawrence's classmate from the University of Pennsylvania. Since then, Anthony strutted through the house brandishing a stick and spouting lines about tyranny.

Lawrence proved more circumspect with Jolie. He took her for walks along the Wissahickon Creek, bought her candy and rag dolls, but avoided center city and popular places where her deep skin tone set her apart.

Jolie thrilled at each visit, but Claire agonized over the limited time Lawrence spent with her. He insisted it was because of her age, but Claire knew he favored his light-skinned son over his dark-skinned daughter.

The visit to Wissahickon Farm would be good for the children, Elizabeth told Claire. Whatever Claire's differences with her, Miss Anna always treated people fairly. Jolie would be as well cared for as Anthony. Molly, Duff, Jonah, and Ruth would watch over Jolie, too.

Anthony and Jolie dashed up and down the alley, each wanting to be first to see Lawrence and the wagon.

The front door slammed. Jolie's voice echoed into the house.

"Papi's here!"

Claire leaned the broom against the wall and walked outside. Lawrence, dressed in denim overalls and a short-sleeved cotton shirt, waited on the porch. He smelled of dirt, hay, and cows, like the boy she once loved.

"I'll be taking them, then," he said with a shy smile.

"I hate for them to leave me, Lawrence. I haven't been away from them a single night of their lives."

She pressed her lips together to hide her missing tooth and willed her tears away. A current of stifling air ruffled her blouse.

"Then you know how I feel. Country air is good for them. You were Jolie's age when you first came to the farm."

Claire had a hundred things to remind Lawrence – Jolie likes her curtains drawn at night but Anthony likes his open. Jolie won't eat turnips, is afraid of loud noises, and if she gets a coughing spell, must be held upright to sleep. But before she had the chance, the children leapt off the porch, and climbed onto the wagon. She pitched their canvas valises in the back.

"Be good, mind your manners, learn your chores, and do them well." Claire touched Jolie's cheeks, then Anthony's. "I'll think of you every minute. Give Molly, Duff, Jonah, and Ruth my fond regards. I love you." Before she stepped away, she asked, "Do you have the tablecloth Granny Elizabeth embroidered for Miss Anna?"

When the carriage crunched toward Germantown Road, Claire wished she was a bobolink. She'd fly over her children in the day and sing them to sleep at night.

CHAPTER FIFTY-TWO

WISSAHICKON FARM JULY 1834

Along Germantown Road, the carriage passed fine stone buildings – new businesses and homes built in the years Lawrence and Claire had been in Haiti. Soon, Jolie fell asleep. Lawrence handed the reins to Anthony.

"You drive for a while."

"Why did we leave Mami?" Anthony asked.

"Mami didn't want to come."

"She did," Anthony said. "She talks about Wissahickon Farm every day."

"Mami didn't want to come with *me*. When we married and left for Haiti, we were children. We didn't have time to grow up, and somehow we forgot how to be friends. I don't know why."

"Is it because of me and Jolie? Is it my fault?"

Lawrence patted Anthony's knee. "You and Jolie are the best things that ever happened to us. No, it's my fault. I was too young to be a man, and now I regret it. Your mother tried her best."

"Will you ever come back and live with us?"

"Someday, I hope we'll all live together on Wissahickon Farm."

The sun blazed in the cloudless sky. In the garden, Anna knelt by the tomato plants, pleased at their firm red flesh. She wiped sweat from her forehead, ran her fingers through the rich black soil, and plucked a fat green bug off a leaf. She must remind Jonah to make the men drink plenty of water in this heat.

Where is Lawrence with the children? The boy, Anthony, was the spitting image of her son, handsome and smart – a charmer, more self-assured than Lawrence as a child. But Anna felt little affection for the girl, Jolie – what a silly name. She found herself calling her, Jolly. Clearly the child, brassy and distant, took after Claire. Anna wondered if Claire carried on in Haiti. No mentioning it to Lawrence, though. He loves her like she's his own.

The crunch of wheels brought Anna to her feet. She rose quickly and swayed, a black curtain shimmering in her eyes.

"Sure and Claire herself came home to Molly," she heard Molly cry.

Anna, wiping her hands on her apron, hurried to the front of the house to see the girl in Molly's arms. Molly set her down and kissed the child's cheeks.

"Ah, Miss Anna, there you are. Isn't she the image of young Claire? Wait until Duff sees her."

Anna turned her attention to the boy. "Anthony, how was your trip? What do you think of your family farm?"

Anthony turned in a circle. "It's bigger than I imagined, bigger than the orange groves."

"Williams have owned Wissahickon Farm since 1697," Anna said. "It's your legacy."

"Do you get to sleep in the big house, Papi?" Jolie asked.

"Yes, and so will you. It's our house – Granna's, mine, Anthony's, yours, and my brother, Reuben's family, too, if he were to come home."

"It's my house? And that lady's?" Jolie nodded at Molly.

"Ah, my darling, it is not my house, though I have a room in it. When your mama was your age, she shared my room. Will you come and see it then? And you, young Anthony, aren't you the lick of your father? It's a happy day when our children come home."

"Anthony, you'll sleep in your father's boyhood room," Anna said.

"And I'll sleep in Mami's," Jolie said.

Lawrence, Anna, and Molly glanced at each other.

"Mami slept in Molly's room, next to the kitchen," Lawrence said, voice husky. "But it's too crowded now."

"Then I want that room." Jolie pointed to the last dormer window on the right. "I can see the animals from there."

Lawrence turned to Anna, who nodded.

"And that's where you'll sleep," he said.

"We'll have a grand time, my darling. Will I show you inside?" Molly offered her hand and Jolie took it.

Anna pursed her lips but held her tongue. Molly acts the fool, she thought, fussing over the dark little girl.

At the dining table, Anna sat at the head with Lawrence to her right. Anthony sat on her left, and Jolie – she'd never grow accustomed to that name – sat to Lawrence's right. Anna invited Jonah and his eleven-year-old son, James, to join them. They sat at the opposite end of the table. Ruth, Jonah's wife, helped Molly serve. A gangly dark-haired man slid into the seat next to Jonah.

"Duff?" Jolie whispered to Lawrence, who nodded.

"Sister Claire raised two fine-looking children," Ruth said.

Anna frowned. Lawrence cleared his throat.

"Bless this food, Lord we pray, that we may prosper day by day."

"Amen," Jolie responded.

With undue enthusiasm, Anna noted. Ruth handed Lawrence a platter of cold meat pasties, then passed plates of barley with mushrooms, dilly carrots, and peas. Molly filled glasses with cold mint tea.

Anthony stared at his plate. When Lawrence caught his eye, he gingerly put a dilly carrot in his mouth and tucked it in his cheek. Finally, he chewed and swallowed. It was good, acidic yet sweet, and crunchy.

Jolie nibbled a meat pasty and bit into a dilly carrot. She wrinkled her nose and snuck the carrot out of her mouth. She pushed her plate aside.

"It's sinful to waste good food with so many starving people," Anna said.

"The starving people can eat my dinner."

Molly coughed and left the room in a rush. Anna glared at Lawrence.

"I'm shocked you allow this behavior. Anthony enjoyed his meal, didn't you, Young Man?"

"Yes, Granna." He glanced at Jolie and raised his eyebrows.

"Aren't you hungry, Jolie?" Lawrence asked.

"I'm hungry, but not enough to eat food I don't like."

Anna pursed her lips. "What food do you like, Missy?"

"I like cassava bread, and Granny Elizabeth's sweet potato bread. I like mangoes, and bananas, and coconut milk, and *griot,* and pumpkin soup, and boiled eggs. I like beans and rice in spicy sauce, and goat milk cheese."

"It's time you learn to eat American food, Missy. For now, Molly will bring you two boiled eggs. I think you'll find that Molly and Ruth make excellent goat milk cheese. But you should know bananas and coconuts don't grow in Pennsylvania," Anna said.

"But we grow peaches, plums, and apples in the orchard," Lawrence said.

"Beg your pardon, Miss Anna," Ruth said as she cleared the plates. "I sure could make pepper pot soup for the childrens. West Indian coloreds in Germantown came round my pot every day. They love my spicy cooking."

"That won't be necessary," Anna said.

Lawrence put his hand on his mother's wrist. "Ruth, I would especially like that. Mutti, you should try it. We rarely had a head cold in Haiti. Henri's sister, Genevieve, told us hot peppers clear the head and gut. She was the midwife who helped Claire with Anthony's birth."

"Do as you like then," Anna huffed, "but serve normal food for the rest of us."

"Yes, indeed." Ruth smiled. "Indeed I will."

While Molly and Ruth cleared the table, Jonah and James took their leave. The dark-haired man approached the family, and knelt by Jolie.

"Do you know who I am, Miss?"

"You're Duff! Mami's friend," Jolie said.

"Did your mami tell you about me?"

"She told us everything about Wissahickon Farm," Anthony said.

"How is your mami? Why hasn't she visited us?"

"She's busy with the dress shop," Lawrence said.

"Duff, bring the horses to the first paddock. There's more shade there. Make sure the water trough is filled," Anna said.

Duff put his hand on Jolie's head. "I'll be gone then. Come visit the stables, your mother's favorite place. There's something special there."

"Today I'll show you the farm," Lawrence said when they stepped outside. "Tomorrow you'll have chores, and Granna will start your lessons."

"Mami does my lessons," Jolie said. "I want to see the horses."

As Lawrence and the children started across the yard, Anna ran after them, waving a wide-rimmed felt hat.

"Anthony, here's your grandfather's hat! No need to get sun burned."

"Did you bring a hat for Jolie?" Lawrence asked.

"I didn't think she needs one with her dark skin. I'll ask Molly to make her a bonnet," Anna said.

Lawrence put his hat on Jolie. The little girl crossed the yard, arms out and spinning, until she collapsed from dizziness.

"How many fields are yours, Papi? I've never seen so many cows. Why do some have white faces?" Anthony asked.

"The land as far as you can see is Wissahickon Farm. Years ago your grandfather, Raymond, bought twelve white-faced cows and three bulls from England called Hereford cattle, and now they're almost half of our herd. The others are Devon cattle. They originated in England, too. We grow wheat, barley, rye, and corn in the fields."

Anthony ran ahead, then waited for Lawrence and Jolie to catch up.

"Why don't you start an orange grove here, Papi? There's so much land."

Jolie picked a dandelion, and brushed it against Anthony's cheek.

"The weather's too cold in Pennsylvania for oranges. We have to buy them at the market. Some oranges that come by ship from Haiti may be oranges from our groves," Lawrence said. "I'd like to grow oranges again. There are some places in America warm enough — like the Florida territory and Louisiana."

"You'll grow oranges again, Papi." Jolie stroked his face.

Anthony adjusted his hat. "Where are the horses?"

"The stables are across the creek, over the stone bridge. See the long white building?"

Anthony, bare feet turning green, raced Lawrence across the bridge. Jolie ran after them but stopped to look over the bridge wall. Catfish darted through ripples, their shadows wavering on submerged rocks. A butterfly floated drunkenly over the water. Lawrence came back, and dangled Jolie over the wall. When she squealed, he set her down.

"Is this Mami's creek?"

Jolie didn't notice Lawrence's smile fade.

"This is the Wissahickon Creek. Mami brought you to the creek, didn't she?"

"Sometimes we walk to Old Caesar's creek."

Lawrence knelt and embraced her. "Yes, this is Mami's creek. It belongs

to her and everyone who loves it. It's Old Caesar's creek, too. It runs from
here all the way to Old Caesar's shack and farther still until it meets the
Schuylkill River. See if you can make this stone skip."

Lawrence carried Jolie on his shoulders the rest of the way to the stables.
The horsy smell of sweat, piss, and worn leather hit him when they
reached Anthony and Duff.

A slender fair-haired man with ruddy cheeks and blue eyes, and a
striking Indian woman with shiny black hair and black eyes, waited, too.

"Jolie, this is Young Hamish and his wife, Sky Blue," Lawrence said.
"They live behind the stables, like Duff does. Like your Uncle Samuel did.
They have a little boy named Eddie."

Jolie, hands on hips, studied them. "Mami said Hamish died."

"It's almost a year since my da died," Young Hamish said. "Did your
mother tell you she saved his leg when she was no more than a girl?"

"She told us he was a great man who taught her everything about horses," Anthony said.

"He thought your Mami was a great soul, and great with the horses,"
Sky Blue said. "I wish he lived long enough to welcome her home."

"Me, too," Jolie said. "Where's your little boy?"

"He's reading," Sky Blue said. "You'll meet him later."

"Duff, will you show the children their surprises?" Lawrence asked.

"Nice to meet you," Young Hamish said.

"We've plenty to do," Sky Blue said, and they turned away.

Duff entered the stable and returned leading a small Palomino and a
piebald pony. Jolie jumped and clapped. Anthony stroked the horse's neck
while it snorted and nudged him.

"The Palomino's yours, Anthony. I bought him for you in Lancaster
two weeks ago."

"He's my horse, my own? He's beautiful, Papi," Anthony said. "What's
his name?

"We call him Goldy, but you can give him a new name if you like,"
Lawrence said.

Anthony rubbed his chin in a gesture reminiscent of Moses. The boy
walked around the horse.

"Mami's horse was Star of Night. I want to name my horse, North Star. Mami told us the north star shines like a beacon to freedom."

"The perfect name," Lawrence said.

Star of Night and Inspiration, too, had been Claire's horses more than they were his father's. How she'd love to see the children with their first horses. I robbed her of that joy, Lawrence realized. Next time, I'll invite her, and insist she come along. Mutti would let her visit the farm, but she'd have to spend the nights at the Black Horse Tavern with Molly and Reds. He thought she wouldn't mind.

Jolie tugged Lawrence's sleeve. "What about me?"

"This is your own special pony," Lawrence said. "A horse man in Lancaster bought four Shetland ponies from Scotland to haul anthracite. This is the first foal born to a pair of them. The man didn't want to part with it, but I charmed him into reconsidering."

The pony's head was black, his body white with black patches. His legs were black with white socks. His mane grew away from his face, giving him a surprised expression. He stamped in the dirt.

"I love him."

"Duff calls the pony, Patches. Do you like the name?"

Lawrence and Duff shared smiles as Jolie stroked the pony's neck.

"Patches is a dog's name. My pony hates it. He said his name is Eclipse, like the day Mami was born."

His children's deep love for Claire astounded Lawrence. She influenced their thoughts and their lives. She was there for them when he was not. He proved to be a selfish, sometimes cruel husband. Had he been a good father? If he was, it was because of Claire. She carried the burden of raising the children. She cared for them in sickness. She taught them manners along with reading, writing, and arithmetic. She bathed them, clothed them, fed them, and soothed their wounds. He looked after them only when it suited him, and sent them back to Claire as soon as their needs or demands annoyed him. Why had he followed Henri so desperately — drinking, gambling, and buying women's company? How could he reject the person he most loved? He lost himself in Haiti, he knew that now. Even worse, he lost Claire.

"Papi!" Jolie tugged his sleeve.

"Eclipse is a fine name. Duff will help you ride Eclipse while Anthony and I inspect the farm."

Duff helped Anthony mount, and Lawrence and Anthony rode off. After they crossed the stone bridge, Duff turned to Jolie.

"Your pony is Scottish, like me. We're feisty, but faithful. You need to be as headstrong as he is. Are you ready to ride?"

~

The horses crossed the bridge. Lawrence hopped down to open the cow pasture gate. Red Devon cattle lazed on the hill while white-faced Herefords flapped their tails at green flies. The air smelled of clover and cow dung. Anthony swayed in the saddle and stroked North Star's neck.

"Your farm is as big as all of Haiti."

"Far from it, but it feels that way when we plow, plant, and harvest."

"And when you gather fruit from the orchards?"

"Yes, then too. But the truth is, your grandmother hires day workers to prune, pick, and pack the fruit. I'm glad Mutti called me home, but she didn't really need my help. Jonah Chestnut knows the farm as well as I do. Life is much easier here, but I liked working the orange groves, being my own man, with production and harvest depending on me."

They rode in silence. Every inch of land reminded Lawrence of Claire – Sheep Hill where they bundled together on the sleigh; their first kiss; the places along the Wissahickon Creek where they swam, or fished, or skipped flat stones. He halted his horse when Anthony spoke.

"Sometimes I miss Haiti. But I learn so many things at Germantown Academy, and I like the city – especially the theatre and play-acting. I like living with Granny Elizabeth, and Pops, and Granny. I like Mary Baker too, and Samuel, and Felix. Why can't you live with us?"

"Perhaps some day, I hope."

Black and brown sheep and white lambs spread across a hill, their wool oily smelling. In the sky, a red-tailed hawk circled the fields in wide, unhurried loops, gliding on outstretched wings. Lawrence's horse turned in a circle. He pulled the reins and said, "Whoa." Then, he faced his son.

"I met a man in Lancaster who bought a plantation in Louisiana where he plans to grow sugar cane. Louisiana weather is like Haiti's. In fact, many Haitian people settled there. The man told me he's looking for a good man to manage his farm. If I took the job, he'd let me establish orange groves on his land."

Heat shimmered the air like ripples in *Bassin Clare*.

"You have this land, Papi."

Anthony slipped to the side of the saddle and shimmied back into place.

"Yes, this is wonderful land. Still, it's interesting to think about growing oranges in Louisiana. Do you think your sister has worn out Duff and her little pony by now?"

Sunday afternoon, the day before Anthony and Jolie returned to German-town, the Williams family and their farmhands gathered for a picnic under shade trees along the Wissahickon Creek. In the cook pit, the pig roasting over hickory wood crackled and spit. Anna, Molly, and Ruth tucked ears of unhusked corn under stones at the edge of the pit and placed pans of diced turnips, sweet potatoes, and onions on the grill top.

In the farmhouse kitchen, strawberries soaking in sugar waited to be layered with thick cream on shortcakes. Barrels of beer, cisterns of cider, and jugs of mint tea cooled in the Wissahickon. On level land across the creek, Lawrence, Duff, and Molly's stepson, Donal used Anna's good potholders as 'bases' on corners of a large diamond-shaped playing field. The game, Town Ball, was all the rage, though Anna thought it much like cricket.

Shrieking and shouting, Jolie and Eddie Lightfoot, the five-year-old son of Young Hamish and Sky Blue, played in the creek. To the children's delight, Duff splashed with them. Anna sighed and leaned back in her chair. Anthony and James – Jonah and Ruth's sturdy son – begged a rope from Young Hamish and tied it to a branch of a giant poplar. They took turns swinging across the creek.

At the cook pit, Molly's husband, Reds Reilly, poked and prodded the roasting pig, his face growing redder each minute. Smoke blew across Anna's face, smothering the fresh scents of daisies, and grass, and well-kept animals.

Anna wondered what Molly saw in the hardscrabble Irishman. It must be the connection to Bridget. It was sheer luck that Molly came across her sister at a papist Mass in the city, especially since Bridget died from consumption a year after their reunion. No one was more surprised than Anna when a blushing Molly reported she agreed to marry Reds, and live with him at the Black Horse Tavern in Flourtown. In the past month, Molly's face and waist filled out considerably, and Anna suspected she was pregnant.

Across the creek, the young men gathered for their Town Ball game. Anna rose, dizzy with those damned black spots again. Last time Reuben was home, he told her to rise slowly and drink plenty of water, especially in summer, as such dizziness came from a lack of fluid in the body. Otherwise, Reuben said her health was good, though she might eat less cake and more apples. She substituted apple pie for cake, and felt vindicated. Before she moved to the edge of the creek to watch the game, she waited for her vision to clear.

The crack of a hickory bat against a leather ball and shouts of beer-filled men echoed through the fields. The game was something to see. Lawrence threw the ball at the player holding the bat. That player tried to strike the ball as it flew past. If the player managed to hit it, he or she ran like blazes to Anna's potholders. If the ball got past the batter, Donal, who squatted behind the batter, caught it and threw it back to Lawrence.

Duff was the next batter. He swung at and missed two balls. The next throw, he hit the ball over the heads of the players supposed to catch it. He ran to each potholder, and returned to the start while his teammates cheered.

When Sky Blue, Young Hamish's Indian wife, picked up the hickory bat, Anna studied her. Like Claire so long ago, Sky Blue wore britches and worked as hard as any man. Yet, she moved with a woman's grace and spoke with a woman's voice. Times were changing.

The first ball Lawrence threw bounced on the ground and rolled over Sky Blue's foot to Donal. The second skewed to the right and landed in the creek. Anthony jumped into the water, retrieved the sodden ball, and tossed it to his father. Lawrence rolled the ball in his shirt to dry, stared at Sky Blue, nodded to Donal, and threw.

With the bat held high over her shoulder, Sky Blue stepped forward, swung, and slammed the ball so hard, water sprayed out. The ball curved past Lawrence's head and over the post-and-rail fence into the cow pasture. A startled beast uttered a loud moo and trotted away.

Anna feared the dumb cow might start a stampede, but she and the other cows simply milled away from the humans and plopped down farther from the fence. Like a shot, Jolie scrambled out of the creek, shimmied under the fence rail, and grabbed the ball. On her way back, she slipped in a slimy mess of cow dung, while Sky Blue, like Duff, stepped on each potholder, and returned to the start.

"Pork's done," Reds called from the cook pit.

Jolie crawled under the fence, handed Lawrence the ball, and put up her arms for him to carry her.

"Not likely, Miss Cow Pod," Lawrence said. "You're covered in it. You stink."

After Jolie, crying, crossed the creek to the farm side, Anna took her hand.

"Stop crying. You can't live on a farm without getting covered in dung from time-to-time. Your father should tell you about the time he jumped in the cesspit. Come along, I'll help you clean up and dress in fresh clothes. We'll be back lickety-split."

"I want Mami. I miss my mami. I want to go home."

"Tomorrow, Jonah will drive you and Anthony to Germantown. Wissahickon Farm is your home, too, Jolie, your home with your father."

Anna led Jolie to the pump outside the farmhouse kitchen.

"Why can't Mami come to the farm?"

"Perhaps another time. Here, step out of those clothes."

As Anna pumped and water gushed over Jolie, the child jiggled under the spigot, singing —

Frère Jacques, Frère Jacques,
Dormez-vous? Dormez-vous?
Sonnez les matines! Sonnez les matines!
Din, dan, don. Din, dan, don.

On the clothesline, the children's laundry hung stiff and dry, ready to be packed for their Tuesday return to Germantown. Anna plucked off blue-check cotton pantalets and a matching blouse with short sleeves. In the bright clothing, the child looked handsome despite her brown skin. It was obvious Claire shared Elizabeth's good hand with a needle. Jolie's thick hair refused to be tamed, but Anna tied it back with a blue bandana.

"There now, you look pretty. Do you hear that? The pork and corn are calling us," Anna said.

Anna put out her hand, but the child lunged for her with a wide-armed hug.

"Thank you, Granna. I like you now."

Anna thought her heart would burst. This was the first time Jolie called her Granna. She wrapped her arms around her granddaughter, astonished to realize the depth of her affection for the little brown child. The girl has spunk and spirit — like me, she thought.

Later, after the leftovers were wrapped and stored in the cellar, people sat in quiet conversation or dozed on blankets. Jolie napped with her head on Lawrence's thigh. When he eased her onto the blanket and headed to the stables to bring in the horses, Anna stroked the sleeping child's hair.

Alongside the serving table, Anthony and James turned tin buckets upside down. They drummed on them with wooden spoons. The frenetic beat both annoyed and stimulated Anna. She found her foot tapping and her shoulders swaying. Jolie stirred, got to her feet, and swayed her hips in a joyful dance Anna considered risqué for a young girl. After a moment, Sky Blue joined Jolie. Anna thought they danced like wild Indians.

Young Hamish put his fiddle to his shoulder and accompanied the drummers, while Donal made tinny music with a mouth organ. Jolie skipped to Duff, took his hands, and begged him to dance with her and Sky Blue.

At first Duff moved stiffly, but then he placed his hands on his hips, hopped from one leg to the other, and twirled in circles with a hand raised to the sky. His obvious mastery of whatever dance this was surprised Anna.

Anna let go of her inhibitions and clapped to the primitive music. From who knew where, Molly flew into what became the dance ring, pulling along Reds. With arms at their sides, they hopped and tapped in practiced movements. When Jonah and Ruth joined the dancers, they moved their hips in ways Anna found erotic. Yet the dancers were joyful and having fun. Anna couldn't remember the last time she had fun. Jolie took her hand.

"Dance with me, Granna, s'il tu plait."

"Oh, no, I haven't danced in ages."

The drunken farmhands shouted for Miss Anna to dance. Lawrence, back from the stables, leaned against a tree with a strange expression Anna read as melancholy. He'd miss the children when they returned to Germantown.

"Dance, Granna, dance," Anthony shouted above the din.

Anna smiled nervously but moved to the beat. After a few moments, her feet remembered the German dances of her youth. She raised her skirt above her ankles, and Jolie imitated her. Shouts, claps, and stomping feet echoed across the farm.

Jolie took Anna's hand, and they twirled among the other dancers. Anna's legs felt as light as they had fifty years ago, when it was Raymond's hand in hers, Raymond dancing with her. She visualized him watching, clapping his hands, and admiring her moves. Raymond's soul touched her then. She felt his relief to see her happy, dancing with their granddaughter while their grandson joyfully beat on a battered bucket, and she knew she set his soul free. Yet when she glanced at Lawrence, a wave of sadness washed over her.

"Granna, why aren't you dancing?" Jolie asked.

Against her dark complexion, her granddaughter's amber eyes glinted gold like a mountain lion's. Anna saw love and acceptance in the child's eyes, love and acceptance Anna denied Claire, and almost denied this darling child. She wondered what poison hardened her heart.

When the drumming stopped and the dancers flocked to the beer barrel, Anna wiped sweat from her brow. Jolie and Eddie Lightfoot ran circles around Anthony and James.

Exhausted, but sensing Raymond's approval, Anna turned to Lawrence with a smile to honor him and his children. But he wasn't there. Tomorrow, they must talk. They must talk about Claire.

When she trudged up the hill to the farmhouse, Anna's breathing was labored, and her legs weighed a ton. But, oh, she would do it again in a heartbeat.

Before dawn, Jolie woke to the sound of horse hooves. She peered out the window. In the haze of breaking day, she watched her father ride across the stone bridge.

"Papi," she called, but not so loud as to wake Granna.

Her blue-checked pantalets and blouse lay on the floor where she dropped them last night. She slipped off her nightgown and pulled on her clothes, tiptoed downstairs, and creaked open the front door.

"Papi," she called, "Papi!"

He must be at the stables, she thought. She ran as fast as she could, certain her father would see her and stop.

The entire time they'd been at the farm, Papi let Anthony work with him. He taught Anthony about the new plows and harvesting equipment, let him ride race horses around the track, and took long walks along the Wissahickon Creek – without her.

Jolie had dumb jobs like collecting eggs, feeding the hens, picking strawberries, fetching things for Ruth, and sitting for lessons at the dining table. The best time each day was when Granna let her run to the stables. Duff helped her mount Eclipse, and led the pony around the paddock. Duff was nice, and funny. Young Hamish, Sky Blue, and Eddie Lightfoot were nice, too, and Molly, Ruth, James, and Jonah. But most of all, she wanted to be with Papi.

"Papi!"

Jolie yelled as loud as she could, but she didn't know which way Papi went. The cook pit smelled like burned grease and onions. She found two apples in a basket, and bit one. It was crisp and tart, but sweet. Eclipse loved apples. She decided to go to the stable to give Eclipse an apple. Then Duff would carry her on his shoulders back to the farmhouse for breakfast. Ruth promised sweet potato bread today.

As she approached the stone bridge, she passed burly white sheep chomping onion grass, while lambs romped nearby.

The air felt heavy. Sweat beaded on her forehead. Philadelphia heat was different from heat in Haiti – 'It boils rather than bakes you,' Mami said.

Inside the stables, horses shuffled. The doors were locked. Jolie's fingertips reached the door latch, but she was too small to lift it. Eclipse whinnied. Jolie jumped as high as she could, and pushed the latch over the catch.

"I did it!'

Inside, the agitated horses stamped, ready for pasture. The grey dawn cast little light in the dim stable, but Jolie's eyes adjusted. When she approached Eclipse's stall, the pony nickered and kicked. After she led him outside, she couldn't secure the latch, so she pressed a rock against the bottom to keep it mostly shut. Eclipse snorted.

"I have an apple for you."

With a loud crunch, the pony bit the apple, moving his jaws side-to-side. He ate the whole apple, seeds and all.

"Duff?" Jolie called, but not too loud in case he was asleep.

Across the eastern horizon, a band of shimmering gold illuminated streaky grey clouds. Duff should wake up soon. Eclipse nudged her.

"You want to go for a ride, Eclipse?"

Jolie only ever mounted the pony with Duff or Lawrence's help. But today or tomorrow, she wasn't sure, she and Anthony were going home to Germantown. When Mami was at Wissahickon Farm, she rode horses by herself. Anthony rode by himself. I'm big enough to ride my pony by myself, if I can mount him. She scanned the area.

A big bucket sat alongside the water trough. She dragged it to Eclipse's left side, the side Duff said she must mount from. With a hand on Eclipse's neck, she stepped on the bucket, and launched herself onto his back. The pony kept still while she settled. She wrapped her fingers in his mane. Duff will be amazed to see me riding Eclipse by myself, she thought.

Eclipse started a slow walk on the familiar path around the paddock.

Jolie used her knees to balance, but without the saddle, she slid a little. The pony's coat felt scratchy and warm on her legs. She stroked Eclipse's neck.

After a few minutes, Jolie felt confident. The sun rose higher and glowed orange and pink. A blue jay screeched from a maple tree. A mosquito buzzed near her ear. When she slapped it, she lurched forward, and Eclipse began to trot. Frightened at first, she relaxed to the motion. But when she rested her chest against Eclipse's neck, the pony started to canter, too fast. She bounced and almost lost her grip. She wanted Duff. She wanted Papi.

"Stop, Eclipse, slow down. Whoa. Please."

Sky Blue joined Duff outside the stable.

"Did you let her ride alone?" Sky Blue asked.

"I dinna. I don't see her father. I don't know who put her up to it."

Sky Blue pointed out the water bucket. She and Duff shared a knowing look.

"Her bum's out the window, and it's making me sick," Duff said.

"*Ayee.*"

They watched the pony round the far end of the paddock where sweet-smelling honeysuckle vines laced the fence.

"They're coming back in one piece," Duff said.

A grey ruffled grouse burst from underbrush along the fence, beating its wings.

Eclipse shied left, and Jolie tumbled off right, landing hard. Jolie curled into a ball, moaning, while the pony galloped back to the stable.

Sky Blue reached her first and turned her on her back.

"Are you hurt?"

"Eclipse broke my arm."

Sky Blue ran her fingers along Jolie's arm.

"It's a little break, not so bad. You will survive."

"Is she hurt?" Duff called, short of breath. "What happened, Jolie?"

"Eclipse wanted me to ride him, but a bird jumped out and scared him, and I fell and my arm broke."

"Sure, aren't all birds trouble?" Duff said.

"You are so young, Jolie, your bone will heal before summer's end," Sky Blue said. "I will take care of it."

In Duff's arms, Jolie cried with her face pressed against his shoulder. When they reached the farmhouse, Anna hurried to meet them.

"What happened? Where's your father? I thought he took you for an early morning walk along the Wissahickon."

"Jolie took a tumble off her pony," Sky Blue said.

"I'm sorry," Duff said.

"It's my fault. I didn't wait for Duff," Jolie said. "Papi rode away, Granna. I called him, but he didn't come back."

After they settled Jolie in her bedroom, Anthony watched Sky Blue and Granna tend to his sister. The Indian woman massaged Jolie's arm to make certain the bone was in place, covered it with linen, fit a curved piece of bark around it, then wrapped it tight with cotton cloth. Anna fashioned a sling from a silk scarf.

"Move your fingers for me. Good," Sky Blue said. "Your mami will check your arm and rewrap it. You can do whatever you wish as long as you keep your arm in the sling and promise not to fall off any horses."

"It's the bad bird's fault. I rode Eclipse fine. He's still my pony, right Anthony?"

"He's your pony," Anthony said and touched Jolie's cheek.

Anna concentrated on slowing her breaths to control her pounding heart. If the child had been badly hurt. . . She never imagined Jolie was capable of getting the pony from the locked stable, mounting it, and riding it. What will Claire think? Will she blame me for Jolie's broken arm? Will she let the children return to Wissahickon Farm ever again? And where did Lawrence go before dawn? The clatter of dishes rose up the stairs. Anna sighed.

"Perhaps we should eat breakfast before you dream up more mischief, Jolie. Are you hungry for Ruth's sweet potato bread?"

"I'm sorry, Granna. I'm hungry."

"There's no need to apologize. We had some terrible injuries over the years, and your mother had a great hand for healing, like Sky Blue."

Anna took Jolie's good hand to help her walk down the steps. The children had fine appetites for Ruth's cooking. The farm felt so alive with them here. She would sorely miss them. Where on Earth is Lawrence?

After breakfast, Anna found the letter perched against her bedroom mirror.

After the wagon, packed with vegetables, fruit, and a leg of lamb wrapped in brown paper, disappeared over the bridge, Anna rocked in her chair on the porch. Ruth and James decided to join Jonah on the ride to Germantown, and the absence of human voices disoriented her. Still, quiet lows and random bleats reassured her of the closeness of living creatures with their warmth and their needs. Green corn stalks waved in the dry breeze. Cows and sheep lolled in the pastures. When she listened well, she heard the Wissahickon Creek, running high, splashing over rocks. She inhaled air imbued by rich earth, growing grain, and healthy animals.

The happiness Anna felt these past two weeks was an illusion. She admitted her self-deception and surrendered to melancholy. Lawrence's note was brief.

Dear Mutti,

I will be gone to Louisiana for a time to try my hand at growing oranges. I know my decision will be difficult for you. All my life I followed my heart, and my heart is Claire. During these months of separation from her, my heart – hardened by years of toil on another man's land – has shattered. Without Claire, I'm not a man. I don't know what I am or who I am. All those years ago, I believed that by marrying against your will, fathering children, and abandoning the comfort of this land, I made myself a man at seventeen. Yet now, ten years later, I live as a child at my mother's hearth, having failed the woman I love.

I'm satisfied that the farm is in good hands, with little need for me. Jonah Chestnut impresses me with his knowledge and good sense. I offer nothing more.

The children enjoyed their visit. I hope they'll spend many more weeks here even while I'm away.

I'm sorry to disappoint you. I disappoint myself. I want to be a better man, a man with courage to hold the hand of the woman he loves for all to see. When I return, it will be as a man with a heart I shall give to Claire if she will have it. My greatest hope is that you will find it in your heart to embrace Claire as you embraced our children.

With fondness and love,

Lawrence

Lawrence's departure stunned her as much as her attachment to the little girl had. 'Jolie means pretty,' she told Anna early in her visit. The child proved to be a rascal so much like her mother, Anna had to catch herself from calling her, Claire. Raymond so enjoyed Claire at that age and, truth be told, Anna had as well.

Anna thought back, aiming to pinpoint her change in feelings toward Claire. It was after Lawrence almost died in the cesspit. Anna never got over that. And she couldn't forgive Lawrence for choosing Claire over her, his father, and this land. Those were Lawrence's decisions, not Claire's, but she blamed Claire. She wished they'd come up with a decent solution all those years ago, but she knew she'd been too angry, bitter, and ashamed to consider anything other than rejection.

Raymond would love Anthony and Jolie. It took his death to bring Lawrence home. Now, after only six months, Lawrence left her again.

Anna wanted the best for her sons, and to keep Raymond's farm in the Williams' name. Yet each son rejected the farm and their legacy. They rejected Raymond. They rejected her.

She rocked until the sun began its descent and the cows needed milking.

CHAPTER FIFTY-THREE

GERMANTOWN AUGUST 1834

Claire pricked her finger, and a drop of blood beaded on the tip. It tasted like the waves that lapped Jacmel's shore, and her heart beat to a song of the brilliant Haitian sun, the gentle sea, Sebastien's taste, his embrace. She forced away the indelicate thoughts and returned to the lace trim for Miss Allen's ball gown. Today her children were coming home.

At noon, Claire left her sewing and walked up Germantown Road, headed home. *Pepper pot piping hot.* She smiled at the pepper pot woman as she rounded the side road and strolled down the alley.

On the porch, Felix and Samuel waited with Granny. Moses and Elizabeth would return in a few hours, after their deliveries.

Wagon wheels crunched behind her. Her heart raced at the sound of Jolie's voice.

"Mami!"

Jonah pulled over the wagon, and the children climbed out. Jolie rushed to embrace Claire, but Anthony stood back, silent and shy. At the sight of the sling, Claire's eyes widened. She hugged Jolie gently.

"I missed you both so much. I want to hear everything about the farm, but first, tell me how you hurt your arm."

"I fell off Eclipse. It wasn't Duff's fault. Sky Blue fixed it. She said you should rewrap it."

"Sky Blue? Young Hamish's wife?"

Jolie nodded.

"You met Duff, then. What is Eclipse?"

"My pony. He's Scottish, like Duff. I had to leave him at Wissahickon Farm, but he's mine. Papi bought him for me. Duff promised to take care of him until we come back."

"Papi bought you a pony? That's special."

"Molly said I look just like you. Her hair is orange, but she says it's red. Donal and Reds came to the picnic. Everyone was there. I played with Eddie Lightfoot. He's Young Hamish and Sky Blue's boy. Anthony played with James."

Claire suffered a twinge of jealousy. Everyone was at Miss Anna's picnic but her. She turned her thoughts to Molly and Duff. She longed to see them, to learn all she could about the past ten years.

Ruth hopped out the wagon. She and James joined them.

"Seem like Anthony and James knowed each other all their lives. Look at my boy, taller than his mama," Ruth said.

"Ruth, oh I missed you! You look wonderful. And this tall young man is James? The last time I saw you, you just started to walk."

"I remember you," James said in a low voice.

"We leave you to your children," Ruth said. "Miss Anna gave us a list. We be back to visit afore we go to the farm."

Jonah unhitched the mare and led her to the back yard to water and graze. Then, the Chestnut family, swinging satchels and baskets, walked to the cut-through to Germantown Road.

Claire reached out to Anthony. With downcast eyes, he shuffled to her side. She wrapped her arms around his shoulders. He'd grown during the two weeks at the farm.

"I missed you, Anthony. I'm so happy to have my young man back. Did Papi show you the livestock? Did you visit the stables and meet Duff?"

"Papi bought him a horse, a golden horse. He named him North Star!" Jolie reported enthusiastically.

"What a beautiful name, Anthony, so thoughtful and meaningful to Papi's heritage and mine."

Anthony shrugged, unable to suppress a smile. "I rode North Star with Papi when he showed me the farm." He glanced at Jolie. "Mami, I want to live at Wissahickon Farm. It's my birthright."

Claire's heart ached. She took a breath and hugged him again. "Wissahickon Farm is in your blood, Anthony. Papi and I need you to live with Pops, Granny Elizabeth, and me while you complete your studies at Germantown Academy, like he did. But I'll tell Papi you want to spend more time with him at Wissahickon Farm. I'm sure he'll be pleased."

There, she did it. She set her beloved son free. She felt empty, but resigned. He had years of schooling before he'd leave her for good, but for now he needed to know she honored and respected him. Anthony looked away.

"You can't speak to Papi. He rode away on his horse and didn't come back," Jolie said, tearfully.

"Where did Papi go, Anthony?"

Anthony stared at the ground, but Jolie took Claire's hand.

"Granna said he had business."

"What business?"

Anthony kicked a stick. He smelled of onions and horses, like Lawrence. He held out his palms.

"Papi left without telling us, but the day we got to the farm, he told me he met a man who asked him to work on his land in Louisiana. Papi said oranges would grow there."

Claire swallowed. Surely, the children misunderstood. Lawrence wouldn't go off and leave his mother, the farm, or his children.

"I know Papi loves you both. I'm sure he'll be back. Go say hello to Granny, Samuel, and Felix. They've been waiting."

Claire stood back while the children greeted Granny, who stroked Anthony's hand, then Jolie's.

"Old King Solomon say, *Grandchildren the crown of the aged,* and I sure did miss my crowns."

"Granna sent sweet potatoes, apples, and peaches for you, Granny, and a leg of lamb I helped butcher," Anthony said.

"That fine." Granny closed her eyes.

Samuel set aside the leather harness he was working on, while Felix finished binding a quilt. Anthony regaled them with talk of North Star and Eclipse. Claire sat on a step with Jolie.

"Can I look at your arm?"

"Sky Blue said you would change the dressing. Granna said you had a great hand for healing."

Claire blinked. That was unexpected. She assumed Miss Anna had no good words to say about her. She unbound Jolie's arm and observed a purple bruise the size of a silver dollar above the wrist.

"Can you move your fingers?"

"Sky Blue asked me that, too. I can." Jolie wiggled her fingers as proof.

"I never saw a bark brace before, but it fits your arm just right. I hope to meet Sky Blue some day to thank her."

"She's nice." Jolie yawned.

Samuel scooped her up. "Hungry? Felix made eggs and peppers."

"I'm hungry," Anthony said.

~

The sound of happy conversation announced Ruth, Jonah, and James' return. Claire stepped from the kitchen to the back yard. James whistled for the mare.

"James and me be loading the wagon," Jonah said. He glanced at Ruth, then Claire. "You and Mr. Lawrence make fine children. I never see Miss Anna happy before. . . We soon ready to go, Ruth."

When they were alone, Claire took Ruth's arm, and led her away from the house.

"What happened with Lawrence? What's going on?"

"Mr. Lawrence so proud have his children at the farm. He showed Anthony and Jolie the fields, the animals, the stables, and give them horses. He tell me, Ruth, make spicy food the children like. Miss Anna, she funny about Jolie. Seem she didn't take to her, then, Jolie her favorite."

"They told me Lawrence rode away, and didn't even say goodbye."

"I been scared to tell you. He left afore sun up."

"Was he drinking?"

"He done powerful drinking when he first come back, but slow down. Miss Anna say Mr. Lawrence turn to drink because he miss his children. She right. He took nary a drop when they at the farm. Mr. Lawrence and Anthony ride horses all over and work the fields alongside Jonah. Little Jolie love her pony, and Duff. Near the end, she even love Miss Anna."

"I don't understand why Lawrence left? Is he coming back? What did he tell Miss Anna? Anthony thinks he's headed for Louisiana."

Ruth lowered her head and her voice. "After Jonah loaded the wagon, the childrens say goodbye to everyone but Miss Anna. She weren't in the kitchen or library. I look upstairs and find her in the bedroom, sick looking, holding a letter. I tell her the children waiting. She say, 'Lawrence left me to grow oranges. He won't be back.' Then she drop the letter, come outside, and tell the children they always have a home on Wissahickon Farm. She sad, Claire."

"She's devastated, I'm sure. I understand her pain. Please tell her the children loved their visit, and came home happy and healthy. Jolie's injury is nothing to worry about. . . Tell her I'm sorry Lawrence left."

"Poor ole Miss Anna, alone again," Ruth said.

"Come 'long, Ruth. Miss Anna be waiting," Jonah called.

Ruth hugged Claire, then hurried to the wagon.

Claire rocked on the porch while Samuel and Felix played jacks with the children. She remembered Marie playing *osslay*. What happened to Lawrence in Haiti? Both of them changed, but now she was content on the porch of her family's home, while Lawrence headed to Louisiana — *a slave state* — to recreate his life in Haiti growing oranges. Nothing made sense.

CHAPTER FIFTY-FOUR

AUGUST 1834

Mary Baker stepped into the kitchen where a pot of *griot* bubbled on the stove

"Smells good, spicy," Mary said. "Haiti food?"

"I promised Felix. Tell me about the meeting," Claire said.

Since last December when the Forten women — Charlotte and her daughters, Margaretta, Sarah, and Harriet — along with Quaker Lucretia Mott founded the Female Antislavery Committee, Mary attended meetings.

"Our school for black children will open in November. We voted to politic for city jobs for Africans."

"The school will serve so many families, and especially black girls. I can only teach Jolie so much while I'm dressmaking at Mama's shop."

"How's Granny? She's finicky when I'm not here."

"She gets bored when you're not here to read the bible to her, bring her news, and listen to her stories. You're a wonderful addition to this family, Mary."

"This family's been good to me."

"Granny told me you met a fine strong man," Claire said.

Mary dipped a spoon in the pot and sipped. She hung her shoulder bag on the back of a chair and sat down. Her smile was shy.

"Billy Carpenter. He moved into Old Caesar's shack after Moses found Caesar's dead body. God rest his soul. The shack needed work. Billy put a new wood shingle roof on it, with a thick glass window in the middle for light. He replaced the rotting siding with fresh wide planks and painted them brown. Billy says he made the shack a cabin. You can't hardly see it unless you know it's there. He hung a new door, too, with an iron latch. You can believe Pretty Boy was happy when Billy moved in, and he had another man to take care of."

"Pretty Boy took Old Caesar's death hard, Daddy said. I'm glad he belongs to Billy now."

"So many changes while you were in Haiti. Must be hard," Mary said. "I best tell Granny I'm home, or she'll be worrying."

Felix stooped so Jolie, riding on his shoulders, wouldn't bang her head on the door frame. Samuel followed him into the kitchen.

"*Bon jour*, Claire. Did you add pepper to the pot? I will soon see what you learned about cooking in Haiti." Felix dropped Jolie onto a chair. "This little spider is hungry and tired."

Samuel glanced at Felix, then touched Claire's arm.

"You raising Anthony white or black? 'Cause the boy think he white."

"*Non*," Jolie said. "Anthony's mulatto, like me. Not white, not black."

"How does a little girl know such a big word?" Felix asked.

"Anthony knows his race," Claire said. "He's not the only fair-skinned black man in Philadelphia. Look at Felix."

"*Monsieur, Madame, Mademoiselle*, at your service, Felix Bonnet, the chameleon. One day he is white, the next, he is black." He bowed.

"That boy telling folk he own Wissahickon Farm."

Claire raised her eyebrows. "He might some day."

Samuel snorted.

"I miss Eclipse, Mama. I want to ride him again. Duff says he's the perfect size for me. Can we go tomorrow?"

The spicy smell of hot peppers saturated the kitchen.

"It's not a good time. Your Grandmother, Anna, expected Papi to help with the farm. Since he left, she has her hands full. Besides, no horse riding until your arm's fully healed."

Samuel put his hand on Jolie's head. "I know a horse you can ride – a flying horse."

"Horses can't fly!" Anthony burst through the door. It slammed shut behind him.

"We rode flying horses when you were at Wissahickon Farm," Felix said.

"I'm hungry. Felix and Samuel made me walk all the way to the big rock in the creek, and we didn't even catch any fish." Anthony dipped a chunk of bread into the *griot*. He wiped broth off his chin with his sleeve and turned to Samuel. "You didn't ride flying horses."

"Today we eat your mami's Haiti food. Next week, we show you the flying horses, Doubting Anthony," Samuel said.

"*Bien sur*," Felix said.

Claire tasted the *griot*. "Spicy. It's ready."

"Woman, you are an immigrant Haitian. I am native born. I enjoyed spicy foods at my mother's breast. Show me your spicy dish, and I will laugh at it."

Felix carried the steaming bowls to the table. After a few spoonfuls, he guzzled a glass of water.

"Children, see how Haitians laugh at spicy dishes?" Claire said.

She dipped her spoon in the *griot* and ate with a smile.

That night, unable to sleep, Claire lit a candle, went downstairs, and sat at the kitchen table. Her heart pounded, and her mind raced. Lawrence enraged her. How dare he drink himself stupid, make his children fall in love with the farm, then slink away to Louisiana? Of all places, a slave state! How could he abandon them? What happened to his love – for her, Anthony, Jolie? For his mother? The candle's flame flickered. Tendrils of smoke spiraled in the air.

Since their return from Haiti, most days she wondered how they could have left Philadelphia. Other times, she longed for the tranquility of life in a country of blacks. How awkward it must have been for Lawrence. His need for approval and acceptance made him appear childish and weak. He made a fool of himself, chasing after Henri. They were so young when they fled America. Then, after ten years, when Claire decided to leave Haiti, Lawrence argued against it, but she knew he'd return to Philadelphia with them. He was a follower, incapable of making big decisions. Until now. He made the decision to forsake his family and his farm to work on another man's land. It made no sense.

Claire didn't force Lawrence to marry her, just as he never forced her into intimacy. They made adult decisions with adult consequences when they were children. Perhaps if Lawrence reached adulthood under his father's influence instead of Henri's, he'd have become the man Claire envisioned him to be.

She was fortunate to have Genevieve's friendship and guidance. Claire regretted leaving Haiti without thanking Genevieve or saying goodbye. A month after she and the children settled in Germantown, she wrote to Genevieve, but received no reply. Now Haiti was a diaphanous memory.

Here, Claire had the comfort of her mother's touch, the smell of her father's pipe, Granny's wisdom, and the Wissahickon Creek. Fair-skinned Anthony attended the finest school for boys in Germantown and would grow to be a scholar. In November, she'd register Jolie for the new school for African children.

But the streets of Germantown and Philadelphia throbbed with rage, both concealed and conspicuous. Not a week passed without whispered slurs and barred doors.

Claire sighed. With Lawrence gone, she'd never be welcome at Wissahickon Farm. She'd hoped the children's visit would open the portal for her longed-for return. And what did Lawrence long for? Oranges?

CHAPTER FIFTY-FIVE

GERMANTOWN AND PHILADELPHIA AUGUST 1834

They were a wonder, the flying horses. With real horsehair manes and tails, carved saddles, and leather reins, six wooden horses galloped in the air on long poles attached to a thick center pillar. When two men stationed at the pillar turned a crank, the horses flew in a wide circle.

Claire and her children stood in line with Felix and Samuel in the stifling building. Excited squeals rose from the flying horse riders. In both the white and black lines, people fanned themselves against the relentless August heat. Outside, people picnicked on the lawn where a group of rough-looking youths played tug-of-war.

Jolie, arm free of the sling, sat between the lines, drawing with a stick, and singing to herself. A little white girl slipped out of her father's hand, and sat beside Jolie.

Mary had a little lamb, little lamb, little lamb, Mary had a little lamb, its fleece was white as snow.

Jolie drew a lamb in the dirt. "I have my own little lambs at Granna's farm."

The white girl scoffed. "You don't have no lambs."

"I have a pony named Eclipse."

"Niggers don't have ponies."

Felix picked up Jolie and stepped back into line.

"We'll have our turn soon," he said.

"Why your daddy white when you black?" the girl asked.

The white girl's father turned from his conversation and stared at Felix.

"I'm mulatto," Jolie said from Felix's arms.

Claire frowned at Jolie. "Hush."

Anthony moved next to Felix and puffed out his chest.

"She's my sister, and our farm has lambs, horses, goats, cows, and chickens."

"White boys can't have black sisters," the little girl said.

The girl's father reached for her. "I don't want your type bothering my daughter."

"Why are they allowed to ride the Flying Horses anyway?" the girl's mother grumbled.

"Next." The Flying Horse man nodded to the white line.

Claire tugged Samuel's sleeve. "We should go."

"You promised." Anthony stood on tiptoes to watch white riders fly through the air.

Jolie looked at Claire with a furrowed brow. "Please, Mama. I won't talk to no more white girls."

"Ain't nothing we can do about what they say, but our money good as theirs. We take our ride, then go back home," Samuel said.

Felix nodded. "Let the children ride."

"Next," the Flying Horse man called. "Six Negroes."

Anthony ran to a dappled grey horse. "Only Negroes this ride, Young Man."

"He's my son. His father's white. Please let him ride with us." Claire dropped an extra nickel in the man's hand.

The man muttered, "He don't look like a nigger boy," but let Anthony stay.

Claire sat on a white horse. She held on tight when the ride started. Anthony sat up straight with a serious expression — the same expression he assumed when he play-acted Spartacus after he saw *The Gladiator* with Lawrence at the Arch Street theatre. Jolie squealed, and shook the reins as if she were riding Eclipse. Felix and Samuel rode with blank faces, but Claire smiled at the thrill of each circle and the delight in Jolie's voice. The ride ended much sooner than it had for whites, but the children enjoyed it.

"Thank you," Claire said when she hopped off with Jolie. "It was wonderful."

As she turned to collect Anthony and rejoin Samuel and Felix, a wet wad struck her face. Claire looked skyward thinking a bird fouled her. Another wet glob splattered her leg. Spit! She shielded Jolie with her body.

A man with a harsh voice shouted, "Look at them nigs, acting proud, like they as good as us."

"Anthony! Where's Anthony?" Claire turned in a circle, searching for her son.

A gang of white youths rushed the building. A band of black men and boys blocked them. Shouts and jeers terrified Claire. Two white ruffians held torches to the flying horses' tails, and clouds of acrid smoke spread through the building.

Whites cheered and shouted, "No nigs allowed!"

A black man yelled, "Go back to Ireland, Bog-trotters!"

As flames erupted, smoke drove everyone outside. Whites and blacks formed groups. Whites hurled rocks, bottles, and bricks. Blacks picked up the missiles and hurled them back.

"Claire, Felix gone to find Anthony. We got to get Jolie out of here. Anthony and Felix look white, they be all right." Samuel's wide eyes looked wild. He grabbed Jolie and called, "Run!"

Claire raced behind, holding onto Samuel's shirt, looking over her shoulder again and again for Anthony. She couldn't believe her eyes.

Moments earlier the quiet park was filled with people tossing balls, picking flowers, and waiting their turn on the Flying Horses. Now, white and black families ran in every direction, clutching their children. Dozens of white rowdies appeared as if conjured, far outnumbering the black men and boys. A blow to the center of her back left Claire gasping, but she ran on blindly, hanging on Samuel's shirt tail.

At a church down the street, they stopped to catch their breath. Jolie whimpered and clung to Samuel. The air throbbed with angry shouts and the crackling of burning wood.

Where is Anthony? Claire imagined him searching for her among the crowd and being pummeled by blacks or swept away by the white mob. He was almost ten-years-old and cocky. Claire prayed no one would harm a little boy, that he'd have sense enough to run from a fight, that Felix would find him. Claire followed Samuel to the main road, praying for God to protect Anthony and Felix.

"This way," a white woman called from the second-floor window of a brick house. "It's safe here."

When the door opened, Claire, Samuel, and Jolie slipped inside. The woman led them to the second floor where they watched the fracas with the woman's husband and two daughters.

"Let me take the little girl," a daughter said.

She took Jolie's hand and led her away from the window.

Bloodied stragglers of both races lurched to the periphery of the mayhem. This is like war, with my son trapped in the middle, Claire thought. She scanned the crowd for a light-skinned boy in a blue cap, and a slim yellow man wearing a top hat.

"My son is out there," Claire gasped.

The woman put a hand on Claire's shoulder. "We'll pray for him."

Finally, the fighting lulled.

"We should take a hack to Felix shop. He know to find us there. Don't worry, Claire. He won't stop looking until he find Anthony," Samuel said.

"Where can we find a hackney?" Claire asked the woman.

"The African drivers wait on Broad Street," the woman said. She took Claire's hand. "We're not all like them."

Before she followed Samuel and Jolie out the back door, Claire hugged the woman who saved them.

When word of the riot reached Germantown, Moses and Elizabeth rushed to the barbershop. They were there when the hackney arrived, and ushered Samuel, Claire, and Jolie inside. Elizabeth gave them cups of tea and biscuits with bacon.

Passersby poked their heads in the shop with news.

"They're burning Africans' houses."

"They beat up James Forten's boy, beat him bad."

"I hear whites stealing our silver, burning furniture."

"We fighting back. Our boys breaking heads."

By midnight, Claire had nodded off in a chair. Jolie slept at her feet. The doorbell jingled. Claire leapt up, almost tripping over the little girl.

"Mami," Anthony croaked.

Claire gathered him in her arms. In the dark, she saw only his figure, but her fingers found crusty scratches on his face and arms. He winced when she touched his soft puffy eye. A lump as big as an egg bulged from his forehead.

When Felix stumbled through the doorway, Samuel caught him. Moses and Elizabeth went from Anthony to Felix and back again. Mercifully, Jolie stayed asleep.

"The lamp," Claire said.

In the flickering light she examined Anthony, head to toe, front and back.

"Tell me your name," she said.

"Anthony Raymond Williams. I'm nine-years-old."

"Where do you live?"

"Germantown. And Wissahickon Farm."

"Mama," Claire turned to Elizabeth, "what do you think?"

"He's right banged up. Anthony, Granny Elizabeth needs you to pee. Go on, right outside the door is fine."

Anthony limped to the door. He managed a few squirts and returned.

"Did that hurt? Was the pee dark or light?" Elizabeth asked.

"I couldn't see, but it didn't hurt."

Elizabeth glanced at Claire. "He has his wits about him. He'll have a black eye, and that knot on his head will take days to come down. Better it came out than went in. Anthony, you'll be sore for a few days, but good as new after that."

Moses held out his arms and Anthony climbed on his lap. In a moment, he was asleep.

Samuel and Claire helped Felix move to the settee. Elizabeth held the lamp, and Samuel inspected Felix's wounds.

"His hand bleeding," Samuel said, voice husky.

"Hold the lamp, Samuel, so Claire and I can look."

Elizabeth pushed Felix's crusty hair off his brow. Cuts and bruises darkened his face. A gash ran down the inside of the fourth finger of his right hand. His blouse was torn and bloody, and Claire worked it off. His chest was scratched, but those wounds weren't deep.

"Felix ain't no fighter, but he fought to get Anthony home." Samuel rubbed his eyes and sighed.

"Felix, we need to sew your finger. It will hurt," Elizabeth said.

"Fix it, please, I must be able to wield my scissors."

Samuel brought Elizabeth clean rags and a pot of warm water, then slid behind Felix and held him. Claire dipped Felix's injured hand in the water. She pried open his fist. After she washed away the blood and dirt, she propped Felix's hand on a small table, and pinched his skin for her mother's stitches.

"I'm sorry, Felix," Elizabeth whispered as she drove her needle through his flesh.

Before she tied the first stitch, Felix moaned. His head lolled back.

"He's unconscious. Better for him," Elizabeth said.

The only sound in the dim room came from Moses' foot tapping. Claire dabbed Felix's wound while Elizabeth focused on making close, neat stitches the length of the finger. When she finished, she let out a breath.

"We need to splint it so it doesn't heal crooked."

When they finished, Samuel lay Felix on the settee. He helped Claire and Elizabeth strip away the rest of Felix's tattered clothing. The flickering candle showed black and blue fist-sized circles on his arms and legs.

Claire remembered the day Felix first entered the Penniman home, a delicate young man, bruised and bloody, back crisscrossed from a whip. She glanced at her mother and brother and saw the same memory in their eyes. This battered beautiful man entered their lives and stole their hearts.

From the moment they met, Felix offered himself, body and soul, to her family. He, as much as Samuel, was her beloved brother. She struggled to keep from sobbing as she examined his wounds and saw what he sacrificed to save her son.

Later, as the sun rose orange in the eastern sky, Elizabeth brewed tea in the back room of Felix's shop. On the steps outside, Moses sat with Anthony and Jolie, repeating the oft-told tale of the British soldier who collapsed in the front yard when Moses was a boy. Samuel came from the bakery with a loaf of fresh bread and six sweet rolls. Anthony followed Samuel inside.

"I'm starving," the boy said, reaching for a roll. Felix sat up and squinted, and Anthony pulled back his hand. "Felix eats first."

Felix turned to Claire. "You have a brave son."

While Claire filled teacups, newsboys' shrill voices echoed down the street – *Mob Sends Horses Flying. Read all about it!*

Felix held up his hand. "Is the finger fixed? Will it work?"

"It will." Claire smiled.

"Turn the shop sign to CLOSED," Felix said.

He accepted Claire's hand to stand and moved to a chair. Anthony sat at his feet. The family gathered around. Before Felix spoke, he took a deep breath.

"The park was chaos, like Haiti when I was younger than Jolie. That is what I remembered while I searched for Anthony – the smell of burning wood and the sound of people running and screaming. I pushed through the crowd to the white side and took a cuff to my head. An elderly Negro man writhed on the ground, flailing his cane while young white men kicked him. When I came to his aid the mob turned on me. 'He's old, he's harmless!' I screamed as I helped the frail fellow to his feet. He could hardly toddle away. Two black women hazarded the crowd and dragged him away from the fighting. 'Send them to Africa,' someone shouted. 'You there, whose side you on?' Rocks and bottles sailed past my head. One sailed into my head. I dodged punches and brickbats while calling Anthony's name. Smoke filled the air. I feared I'd never find him. When I could no longer breathe, I took refuge under a chestnut tree, away from the worst of it. I sat but a moment before a chestnut dropped on my head. Then another and another. I became enraged and glared up into the branches. And there I saw Anthony." Felix stroked the boy's hair. "Time for a haircut, Anthony. You'll be first when I can hold the scissors again."

"I climbed down and fell into Felix's arms. I was so scared until he found me. Then we ran fast as we could," Anthony said.

"You ran like a deer. But I, clumsy oaf, tripped on the legs of a white vagrant who lay drunk on the ground. When I rose to follow Anthony, the pig grabbed my leg and yanked me down. Most of my bruises came then. He beat me with a staff, laughing with each strike. I thought I would die. I covered my face with my hands, expecting more clubbing, but the drunk collapsed."

Tears welled in Felix's eyes. He looked from person to person, then shrugged and smiled.

"I hit the drunk like Spartacus, leader of the slave revolt. When I realized Felix wasn't behind me, I ran back and saw the man beating him. His bottle of rum lay on the ground. I snuck up and *BAM!* bashed his head with the bottle. Then I kicked him in the balls. He screamed, and four white boys came running," Anthony said.

"Ah, but we ran faster than they did."

"We ran like horses, like North Star, like Star of Night. We ran until we couldn't breathe. Then Felix led me home in the dark," Anthony said.

Samuel trembled. Moses took his son's hand and unclenched his fist. Claire found herself sobbing. She knelt next to Anthony and hugged him. Then she gently wrapped her arms around Felix. Jolie, finally waking, climbed on Elizabeth's lap.

"And here we found our family waiting," Felix said.

CHAPTER FIFTY-SIX

WISSAHICKON FARM AUGUST 1834

News of rioting reached Wissahickon Farm by way of a peddler who drove his grey mule and wagon up the path to the house.

"Tinware, needles and thread, brushes and brooms, brass buttons, wood buttons, bone buttons," the peddler chanted.

Molly came off the porch to look at his wares.

"Do you have those new brushes for teeth?"

"I do. Did you hear the news?" the peddler asked.

"Well how could I know if I heard the news if I don't know the news you're asking about?" Molly said.

"City boys are hunting the nigs. A big to-do started two nights ago at the Flying Horses ride. It's about time blacks learn their place. Africans think they can go wherever, and do whatever, no matter Philadelphia's a white city. Niggers so whoopty-do fancy nowadays. They steal our jobs for lower pay, call themselves *colored*, and go to the park to ride the same Flying Horses as whites. About time the boys show them what's what. Last night they burned down half the houses in nigger town. Moving up to Germantown tonight. Gonna burn out more jigs. Send the rest back to Africa."

"Germantown? Burning out Negro families? Stay here," Molly said.

The man rolled a cigarette, spit out a bit of tobacco, arranged his wares on a shelf, looked at the sky, whistled.

Anna Williams dashed from the house, hair askew, apron cockeyed.

"Tell me the news from Philadelphia."

"Like I told your girl, the boys been hunting the nigs going on two days now. Bunch of them heading to Germantown tonight. Blacks been getting too high and mighty, you might say. Only way to get rid of them is to burn them out. Now looky here, I see you're a woman what likes to cook. I got pots and pans from New England, finest made in America."

The peddler tapped his foot. Anna folded her arms, pursed her lips, and controlled her breath to stop trembling. She glanced over her shoulder to Jonah, pitchfork in hand, who watched from the barn. She gestured for him. Only when Jonah stood beside her did she speak.

"This man oversees Wissahickon Farm. I'd be lost without him. Tell him what you told me."

Ruth and Molly came from the house, carrying cast iron pans. James moved behind his father. The boy tapped Raymond's hickory cane on the ground.

The peddler raised his hands. "I don't want no trouble. I'm reporting the news is all. It's city blacks stealing jobs, working for next to nothing, not African farm workers. How you manage your farm ain't no business of mine." He wiped the back of his neck with a kerchief.

Duff trotted up the hill. Young Hamish and Sky Blue followed close behind.

The peddler backed up and secured his wares. He turned his mule to the gravel road.

"Didn't mean no harm. Just reporting the news. You folk stay clear of the city. There's no end to the trouble."

~

After the peddler crossed the stone bridge, Anna turned to her people.

"The man said white mobs have been attacking negroes for two days, burning them out. Tonight, the mob is headed to Germantown."

"He said they were *hunting the nigs.* Hunting! What kind of people are they?" Molly asked.

"Claire and her family live in Germantown," Duff, wild-eyed, said. "Can we bring them here, Miss Anna?"

"There isn't time. Jonah, hitch up the carriage. I'm going to Germantown."

"I coming, Miss Anna," Jonah said.

"I'll come. I'll come. I'll come."

Each person volunteered, and Anna's heart filled with gratitude.

"Jonah, I can't risk you getting caught up in that mess. Bring me

Raymond's rifle and make sure it's loaded. Everyone, please go about your business. No one will stop an old white women. I'll get to the Penniman's house better alone."

Anna marched into the house and returned in minutes wearing a green cotton dress with her hair tucked into a matching bonnet. She felt younger and taller.

Jonah offered his hand to help her into the the carriage.

"Be careful, Miss."

"Thank you, Jonah."

She propped the rifle against the bench seat and took the reins.

CHAPTER FIFTY-SEVEN

GERMANTOWN AUGUST 1834

For two days, white gangs rampaged black neighborhoods, burning and ransacking houses and churches, and attacking negroes who dared cross their paths. Outnumbered, city constables did little to suppress the violence.

Around noon, a young black man from down the alley told the Pennimans to run.

"White people crazy. This morning, me and men from church was walking along Germantown Road, hoping to keep peace. Here come a gang of raggedy chimney sweeps, no bigger than spit, poles and brushes on their shoulders like soldiers. 'Go along, boys,' we say, 'no one want trouble.' One of them scalawags yell, 'Get the niggers!' Then the white boys come at us swinging the poles like to bop us. I say, 'Go home afore you get hurt.' You think they stop swinging? They don't stop. We grab the poles, turn the boys around, and send them home with smacks on their bottoms. They go off shouting, 'Niggers beat us, niggers beat us.' I ain't know much, but I know those boys bring trouble tonight."

"This is our home for a hundred years, before those rowdies were born, before they landed in Philadelphia," Moses said.

But he sent Mary Baker to Billy Carpenter's cabin with Granny, Jolie, and Anthony.

∾

At dusk, the alley was silent — devoid of the usual clatter of people returning from work. Moses, Elizabeth, Samuel, Felix, and Claire huddled in Claire's second floor room, watching from the window. Claire checked her gun, the Deringer Lawrence gave her long ago. It was effective only at close range, but if the rioters came near, she'd shoot. Felix's gun, his trophy from the slave catcher, was powerful. His injured finger got in his way when he tried to load. Samuel, face grim, loaded it for him.

Moses poured powder into the ancient musket the British soldier left during the Battle of Germantown, and dropped a ball down the barrel. Claire feared the ancient firearm would backfire. She prayed no white mob found its way to the alley. The house Jack Penniman built was sturdy, and bricks didn't burn, but her heart pounded when she thought of what could happen if the rowdies got inside.

Samuel continued making brickbats — stockings filled with broken bricks and rocks. Claire organized piles of rocks and stones under each window. Elizabeth whittled a pike from a chestnut branch, then hammered nails through the flat end of her longest baking peel. The nails extended an inch and more. They'd rake through skin and leave nasty wounds. Her admiration for her gentle, accommodating mother grew immeasurably. Elizabeth wore a hard look, and she recognized her mother's strength and resolve. Claire too, would stand and fight for her family.

The smell of burning tar befouled the air. Black smoke wavered in the sky. Shouts came from Germantown Road. Claire knelt between Samuel and Felix at one window. Moses and Elizabeth watched from the other, scanning the alley for signs of the mob, then ducking out of sight.

The cart horse squealed from the back shed, and Claire cursed herself. She forgot to release it. She visualized the horse rearing in fear of the smoke.

A negro family with three children rushed by, headed for the Wissahickon Creek.

"Maybe we should run to the woods," Claire whispered.

"No paddies gonna drive me from my home," Moses answered, eyes red-rimmed, nostrils flared.

Running steps crunched outside. Custis Brown, a black man who rented a room down the alley, ran past. He glanced over his shoulder, then raced for the woods. Four brutes, with flat-rimmed caps, blue knickers, and loose-fitting shirts chased after him, hollering and laughing. As they approached the Penniman house, a cap flew off and lodged in the mulberry bush.

"Wait a goddamned second, the lot of ye, while I get me cap."

"Sure and we lost him," another said.

"Keep down," Felix whispered.

A dozen boys and men, one in a top hat, followed the first four onto the alley. They gathered across from the Penniman's house, voices rising and ebbing like mules in a pasture.

"Where's the nig?"

"In the woods. We won't get him now."

"I mean to break more heads before this night's over."

A man with stringy hair and a thick beard led Moses' horse from the backyard.

"Looky here, I always wanted a pony. I'll take that cart too, can I get it hitched."

"All them niggers ran off. None here no more. Let's find a grog shop. Rioting and burning makes a man thirsty."

"Ho now!" The man with Moses' horse yelled.

A sharp slap, and the horse squealed. Claire peeked out the window. Samuel tugged her arm, but she saw the rioters moving away.

"They're leaving," she whispered.

She took another look. A fair-haired man with wide shoulders stared at the window. He tipped his top hat and smiled.

"Not all the nigs went to the woods. One's in that window."

Men moved toward the house.

"Here they come," Claire said.

Samuel shoved her aside, stared down at the gang, aimed Felix's gun, and fired. The top hat flew off the fair-haired man's head.

"The black devil shot me! I'll kill him me-self."

While Samuel reloaded the gun, Moses aimed the old musket.

"Careful," Felix said.

The musket roared. A pike shattered in a boy's hand. The boy screamed and raised his bloody fist. Another boy pulled him toward Germantown Road.

"Burn them out," the fair-haired man yelled.

Samuel's brickbat struck the man's chest, and he stumbled backwards, cursing.

"Bring the torches!"

The mob hurled stones through the first floor windows, and pitched lit torches inside. Moses fired again. The musket boomed but the ball struck no mark. Claire and Felix threw brickbats while Samuel and Moses loaded the guns and fired. The rabble backed out of range.

Smoke rose up the stairs. Elizabeth grabbed the nail-studded peel, covered her mouth with a kerchief, and stepped down the stairs. Claire followed.

A torch smoldered on the settee. Claire tossed it in the fireplace. The fair-haired man watched through the ragged glass of a broken window. He threw himself against the bolted front door. The mob shouted, banged pikes, pelted stones. The door frame cracked. Claire cocked the Deringer, ready to fire when the man broke through. It might be the last thing she did in life, she knew, and she must do it well.

The hinges groaned. At the next blow they'd break. Elizabeth moved alongside the door, holding the nail-studded board like a Town Ball bat. The mob grew louder.

From down the alley came the sharp crack of a rifle. Horse hooves pounded nearer. Constables? More rioters? Claire brandished her Deringer.

"What the —?" someone yelled.

"He's coming at us, and he ain't stopping. Move back. Move back!"

Another rifle shot. The door gave way. The fair-haired man's face was beet red. His tobacco-brown teeth were bared in a sneer. He wielded a pike. Claire looked him in the eyes and fired. Blood erupted from his left shoulder. He grunted.

"I'll kill you, you black devil!"

Elizabeth slammed the peel on his head. He wobbled. Blood streamed down his face. He staggered backwards . . . into a rifle barrel.

"Run for your life," Anna ordered.

The man tumbled down the steps. On the porch, Anna faced the mob, rifle aimed and ready. With eyes fixed on her, two men inched forward, grabbed the fair-haired man's belt, and dragged him away. In the doorway, Claire and Elizabeth stared at each other.

Weapons drawn, Samuel, Moses, and Felix joined Anna on the porch, facing the white men who remained. Elizabeth threw two more torches into the fireplace, while Claire poured water on scorched floor planks. They stepped onto the porch together, Claire with her empty Deringer pistol, Elizabeth clutching the nail-studded peel.

Bonnet gone, white hair windblown, blue eyes wild, Anna looked like a madwoman. She aimed at the man holding the reins of Moses' horse.

"You won't shoot your own kind," he yelled.

Anna balanced her rifle with one arm and put her other arm around Claire's shoulders.

"You're not my kind, these people are. I'll shoot you here and now unless you and your ruffians remove yourselves and never return. And leave the horse."

Anna fired a shot in the air.

"Leave the horse."

CHAPTER FIFTY-EIGHT

WISSAHICKON FARM APRIL 1836

T he sun gleamed gold in a cloudless sky on the Friday of Lawrence's twenty-ninth birthday. As Claire and Anna worked in the vegetable garden, the date weighed heavy on their minds. Each knelt in her own row, planting peas, beets, lettuce, and onions. It had been a miserable winter with months of snow and eight-foot drifts. But today, the bitter winter was a memory as fleeting as a cloud sailing across the sun.

Lawrence's letter arrived December 31st. Claire read it repeatedly during the short, cold winter days — after they cleared snow from the paddocks so the animals could move outside.

8 December 1835

Dear Mutti,

I read your letter with gratitude and joy to learn Claire and the children moved to the farm. Even now, more than a year later, I smile with glee to imagine your wild ride to Germantown brandishing Papa's rifle. No reconciliation in all of history can compare with yours and Claire's. I would not want to be the man on whom you fixed your weapon, nor among the men who threatened Claire and her family. Cads and ruffians be forewarned – Take Williams women for granted at your peril. The two of you together are a force to be reckoned with.

I regret my time apart from you, but it's been time well spent. I realize now it takes an exceptional man like my father to align his life with an exceptional woman like you, like Claire. I know I fell short of exceptional. I'd like to blame my youth, the shock of Anthony's conception, and living in a foreign country far from home. Claire's life was so much harder – yet she made her way without bitterness, meanness, or despair. When I was my most selfish and cruel, she asked what my father would think of me. That was when my hard heart began to crack, but I was too proud to ask her forgiveness and beg for another chance. No longer will I play the self-righteous weakling. Henceforth, I strive to be an exceptional man of whom my father would be proud. My greatest hope is that Anthony will prove to be such a man and Jolie, such a woman.

Still, I fear for my children's safety. News of other city riots like the Flying Horse incident reaches us even deep within Louisiana. Each time I hear ignorant men speak of the degeneracy of the Negro, my fists clench, and I realize how unenlightened I was to travel to Louisiana to establish orange groves for a man who, I'm ashamed to admit, owns slaves. As I became mindful of the mistreatment of enslaved workers, I fell out of favor because I refused to overwork or punish slaves. A phrase from Matthew has been running through my mind – Do not throw your pearls before swine.

I am taking those words to heart. As soon as I complete the terms of my agreement, my pearls and I will leave this employ. The seedlings I planted are thriving, but it will be a decade before they bear fruit. I will not be here to pluck a single orange.

Before I return in the spring, I plan to accompany my only friend on this plantation, a man from Texas, to visit his family's farm. He's been like a brother. I want to honor our friendship before our paths separate forever. But oh, how I long for the Wissahickon and my home.

I've been away too long. My place is on our farm. I know that now. I know, too, that the measure of a man is reckoned by the way he loves and provides for the people, creatures, and land in his care. If Claire allows me to give her my heart, I believe she will agree I now meet that measure. My fondest dream is to walk arm-in-arm with Claire and our children down the streets of Philadelphia, proud that she chose me for her husband, proud to proclaim for all to see the children we created together.

I can see them now. Anthony Raymond, growing tall and strong, his heart filled with my father's kindness. And Jolie Claire, Pretty Claire, smart and brave like her mother and grandmothers. My soul, separated from all I love, flounders in a cesspit of despair. It's time to come home.

With love to you, Anthony, Jolie, and my dearest Claire,

Lawrence

∼

The women worked silently and efficiently, intending to finish by the time Jonah returned from Germantown with Anthony and James. Fetch, the spotted terrier, barked like he cornered a fox. Horse hooves crunched on gravel. Claire raised her soil-blackened hands to wipe sweat from her brow and left a streak on her cheek that smelled of onions.

Anna turned to her. "Is Jonah back so soon from Germantown?"

Claire's heart pounded so loud she felt certain Anna heard it. Could the rider be Lawrence, returned at last?

"It may be Jonah, or perhaps a peddler. I'll see who's come."

"When I finish this row, I'll join you." Anna returned to the soil.

Claire hurried to the farmhouse, eager to see Anthony after his month away at school, but more eager to see Lawrence. Since returning to the farm, she encountered Lawrence in every room, on every stalk of grain, and blade of grass. She heard his voice in the caws of crows, horses' whinnies, lowing cows, and the rippling creek. Most nights, a young Lawrence spun through her dreams. She took a deep breath to calm herself and shielded her eyes from the sun's glare. Neither Lawrence nor the farm cart crossed the yard. Instead, two men in military garb approached on huge, panting horses.

They must be coming for Jonah and Ruth, Claire thought. Did someone inform on them? She prayed for their safety. Ruth and Jolie had gone to the sheep pasture to check on the new lambs. Jonah, Claire hoped, still sat with Moses and Elizabeth in Germantown, enjoying a meal before bringing the boys home. Dust followed the horses' hooves like shadows.

"Is this Williams Wissahickon Farm?" one blue-clad soldier asked.

The brim of his military hat shadowed his eyes. He ran his fingers through a thick handlebar mustache. Sun glinted off his coat's shiny brass buttons. In the warmth of the sunny day, the soldiers' meaty odor blanketed the grainy farm smells.

"Yes," Claire said. "May I ask your business?"

Anna arrived from the garden, wiping her hands in her apron, her face ruddy, and her eyes suspicious.

"I'm Captain Robert Logan and this is Sergeant Yocom. We have a message for Mrs. Williams."

"I'm Mrs. Williams," Claire and Anna answered together.

The Captain looked from one woman to the other.

"What is it, Captain? Please, give us the news," Anna said.

The soldiers swung down from their saddles, tethered the horses on the hitching post, and removed their hats. They stood at attention in front of Anna. The captain spoke first.

"I'm afraid I'm the bearer of sad news, Mrs. Williams. The Secretary of War directed me to extend his deepest sympathy in the loss of your son, Lawrence Williams, during the defense of the Alamo in Texas. Lawrence died on the sixth of March, along with every fighting American man in that fort. A dozen Pennsylvania men fought and died courageously there. My sincere sympathy, Ma'am."

Anna collapsed. Sergeant Yocom leapt to her side. Claire, rocking on her heels, stared at the soldiers. Her head buzzed like a nest of a thousand wasps. Overhead, a peregrine falcon drifted, its slate-gray wings wide-spread, its underbody ribboned black and white. A harsh *aak-aak* echoed through the sky. The raptor tucked its wings and dove behind the trees along the creek, out of sight. Claire helped Anna stand.

The captain reached in his saddlebag. "Our fighting men knew the odds against them. Many sent final letters and packages with couriers before the assault. This is Lawrence Williams' knapsack. A card tucked inside directed that it be delivered to Wissahickon Farm near Philadelphia in the event he did not appear to claim it."

Anna took the canvas pack. "What of his remains?" she asked in a quivering whisper.

"Ma'am, the Mexicans burned the bodies of the fallen. There are no remains."

Claire watched Ruth and Jolie cross the bridge from the pasture. Jolie raced toward the soldiers.

"Mami, Mami, why are soldiers here? Why is Granna crying?"

Claire took the child in her arms, and smelled sheep.

"The soldiers came to give us a message. It made Granna sad." Claire turned to the men. "Water your horses at the trough and cool your necks at the pump around back. I'll ask Ruth to prepare food for your return to the fort."

Anna stumbled to the porch and collapsed in a chair. She rocked back and forth, holding the knapsack to her chest. Claire wanted to snatch the pack from her arms. She wanted to rest her head against the canvas that rested against Lawrence. Instead, she told Jolie to fill a basket with mulberries, then she led the soldiers to the pump.

"Lawrence wasn't a soldier. We read newspaper accounts of American lives lost at the Alamo," Claire said. "His name was not included on the roster. If the Mexicans burned the bodies, how can you be certain he died there?"

"Travelers entered the fort regularly. Besides his knapsack, Mrs. Dickinson, one of the few survivors, reported she met Lawrence when he arrived with a group led by Senator David Crockett. It was with those men he died." Captain Logan's eyes filled. "On the last day of fighting, Americans and Mexicans engaged in brutal, hand-to-hand combat. Americans fought with their hands and hearts, and never surrendered. Every fighting American was slaughtered."

Claire clutched her throat and, through the cloudy lenses of brimming eyes, envisioned Lawrence — dirt-caked hair tied back with a leather strap, aiming his rifle, firing, striking his marks with precision, like he shot leaves off branches below Sheep Hill years ago.

She beheld the Mexican army swarming the fort. Lawrence, powder flask empty, with no rock or room for refuge, stood his ground, smashing the attackers' swarthy faces with the butt of his rifle. His knife, clutched in his left hand, pierced the underbelly of the soldier whose bayonet killed him, opening the Mexican's gut like a pig's.

With his strong heart pumping out his lifeblood, Claire imagined Lawrence rising up on his elbow, gazing skyward, and with his final breath, whispering the names of his beloveds – Anthony, Jolie, and Claire.

All the while, Claire, safe and sound, waited for him on the farm. Somehow, she should have known. She should have shared his soul, felt his resolve . . . and his agony. Her spirit should have been with him to comfort him, to kiss him, soft and sweet like the first time, to tell him she always loved him, and to rest her hand on his chest while his heartbeat grew feeble.

"I love you, Lawrence," she whispered.

Blinded by tears, Claire made her way to the Wissahickon Creek. For hours, she sat on the bank and skipped stones, commending Lawrence's soul to heal under the running water. As the sun descended, she felt his soul hover then rise, at last content.

The day after the soldiers brought news of Lawrence's death, darkness lingered in a morning sky layered with grey clouds. Heavy rain had fallen all night, and water puddled on the porch. Jolie spread a quilt on the porch floor. Anthony brought a cushion from the settee for Anna, then sat across from Claire. All four stared at the knapsack.

"You're the man of the family, Anthony," Anna said. "Open your father's pack."

After Anthony spilled the contents onto the quilt, Anna sorted through the few items. Claire and Anna's hands met when they reached for a piece of coarse brown paper marked, *Return to Wissahickon Farm, near Philadelphia,* in Lawrence's small neat handwriting. Anna removed her hand, and Claire traced the letters with her fingers. When he put this note in his knapsack, did he expect to die?

"There must be a letter," Anna said, voice quivering. A blush burned on her cheeks. Her eyes, blue and watery, skittered side-to-side. She peered in the knapsack, then returned it to Anthony. "If Lawrence wrote a letter, it didn't make it home."

Her deep sigh wavered in the damp air. Jolie shimmied over and put her hands on Anna's cheeks.

"Papi sent us the knapsack, Granna. That's like a letter."

Anna took the child's hands and kissed them. With sad eyes, she smiled at Claire and Anthony.

"What would I do without you?"

A pistol, one Claire didn't recognize, lay on the quilt. An intricate swirling pattern decorated its single barrel and curved wooden handle.

"Do you think Papi sent this for me?" Anthony stroked the engraving before he handed the gun to Claire.

Along with the odors of gunpowder and grease, Claire searched for Lawrence's essence. Lawrence's hands held this pistol. She felt his hand touch hers.

"I'm certain Papi sent this for you, Anthony. Remember the day you found our buried guns? You were too young then. Now you're older. Papi trusts you to take care of his pistol, and use it to protect your family. I know he's as proud of you as I am."

"I'll take care of it, Mami. I'll protect you, and Jolie, and Granna." Anthony held the gun to his heart. "I'll always make Papi proud."

A small, pocket-sized book with a dusty, brown leather cover had landed close to Claire. She realized it was an old, school edition bible, the pages dog-eared.

"Lawrence's bible. I'm certain he'd want you to have it, Anna."

Anna's hands trembled. She let the book fall open, then read from Ecclesiastes —

Two are better than one because they have a good reward for their labor. For if they fall, the one will lift up the other. But woe to him that is alone when he falleth for he hath not another to help him up. Again, if two lie together, then they have heat, but how can one be warm alone?

She closed the bible softly and pressed it against her cheek.

"Lawrence intended to come home to you, Claire. He read those verses, over and over, thinking only of you."

The air was still. In the silence, Anna took Claire's hand. Claire reached for Anthony's, who took Jolie's. When Jolie joined her hand with Anna's, the circle was complete. Tears streamed down their faces.

Jolie sobbed, "Papi, Papi, Papi."

A palm-sized disk wrapped in a leather strap lay on the quilt. Claire unwound it and gasped — Granny's pendant, the Wedgwood medallion.

She fingered the engraving along the edge — *Am I Not A Man And A Brother?* Claire lost the pendant on the voyage home from Haiti. But it wasn't lost. Lawrence had it all this time. She realized he took it to keep part of her close to his heart. Claire pulled Jolie close and draped the medallion around her neck.

"Papi sent this for you. It's very special, and honors our African ancestry. Papi wants you to wear this and remember that though we're born free, many Africans are slaves. Slave or free, we must treat all people like sisters and brothers."

Jolie gazed at the pendant. A determined look came over her face. She stood and held the pendant to the sky.

"I'll treat all animals like brothers and sisters, too, Papi."

Claire and Anna smiled through tears.

"There's nothing left for you, Mami," Anthony whispered. "You can have the pistol."

"Papi wanted me to have his knapsack," Claire said. "So I can hold him close and carry on."

When Anthony tossed the knapsack to Claire, a tiny stone dropped out — a baby tooth. Anthony's or Jolie's? Anna held out her hand, and Claire dropped it in her palm. Anna moved her hand up and down, as if weighing the tiny tooth. A smile came over her face and she shook her head in disbelief.

"Do you remember when you lost your first tooth, Claire? You gave it to Lawrence, and he put it under his pillow. He kept it always, a part of you he couldn't let go." Anna's smile turned sorrowful. She wiped her eyes and took Claire's hands. "I'm sorry. I blamed you for stealing him from me. But he wasn't mine. Lawrence always followed his heart, and you are his heart."

CHAPTER FIFTY-NINE

The air hung heavy with the smell of ripe peaches. Claire leaned over the stone bridge wall, dropping pebbles in the creek. She turned at the sound of footsteps. Anna joined her.

"Do you know what today is, Claire?"

"Saturday. Duff took the trotter to the Hunting Park race course. I think we have a good chance of winning."

"Oh, it's more than that." Anna panted and fanned her face. "Twenty-four years ago today, you made your mark on your indenture agreement – a C inside a circle. How long ago that was, and yet it seems like yesterday. Those were my happiest years. Raymond was strong and hearty, Reuben and Lawrence knew every inch of the farm, Hamish and Molly were like family, and Samuel and you came into our lives. Raymond rarely laughed before you arrived. 'That Claire's smart as a whip,' he'd say. After you and Lawrence sailed to Haiti, Raymond often said, 'People live, people leave, people die, but the land is our legacy. Our lives are seasons to germinate and grow. Once winter comes, and our yields wither on the vine, it's time to lay fallow while fresh seeds take root.' I thought Lawrence returned to take root on Wissahickon Farm. But I failed my son when he needed me most."

"If I never signed the indenture agreement, it would be Lawrence standing with you, tossing pebbles in the creek. I think of that often," Claire said.

"He loved you from the moment he laid eyes on you, but all I saw was a sassy black girl who didn't know her place. I failed you, too."

"I loved him even more than I realized, but my love for Lawrence was interwoven with my love for this land. He understood, but that's how I failed him. . . In Haiti, when people honor the spirits of the dead, they feel their souls' presence. I feel Lawrence's soul every day, finally at peace because his family continues on this land. Perhaps we didn't fail him."

"Last week when I traveled to Philadelphia, I visited our attorney. Upon my death, Anthony and Jolie will inherit Wissahickon Farm. I designated you as property administrator for life." Anna took Claire's hands. "I set the attorney straight when he dared question me about the childrens' race. What darkness in our souls convinces us skin color is reason to hate?"

Claire gazed at the clouds, then into Anna's eyes.

"I've come to believe blindness causes hate. When we see people only for the color of their skin, we're blinded to the beauty of their souls. If we looked inside each other, we'd find the path to love and acceptance. Lawrence was never blind, but the world dropped a veil between us. I'm forever grateful he tore down that veil and proved love is stronger than hate, stronger even than death. Our love lives on in our children and will continue in our grandchildren, great-grandchildren, and evermore."

Claire found Lawrence in Anna's eyes, and felt light and happy. Joined together by love, the women gazed down from the bridge.

The Wissahickon Creek flowed over the rocks, through the land and across their lives. Their reflections wavered in the ripples and disappeared with the splash of a stone.

ACKNOWLEDGMENTS

Family and friends offered encouragement throughout my journey with this novel. I'm especially grateful for the support of Susan Shreve and the George Mason University community of writers. K. Clodfelter, an outstanding writer and friend, edited the novel with a keen eye. The 2014 and 2017 versions of *Wissahickon Souls* were published by Meredith Eaton.

This story evolved after months of research into the lives of white and black Philadelphians in the early 19th century. The idea to cast Claire as a freeborn African American indentured to a white family developed after reading *Forging Freedom* by Gary Nash. I recommend his many wonderful books of history. David Contosta and Carol Franklin's four volume masterpiece, *Philadelphia's Wissahickon Valley 1620-2020 Metropolitan Paradise* provided context for my research. Madison Smartt Bell's three novels about the Haitian Revolution offered rich details. Scores of other books, articles, and web visits helped me imagine 19th century life along the Wissahickon Creek. Wissahickon Farm was created from childhood memories of Erdenheim Farm. A scene where characters enjoy out-of-season oranges was inspired by the lovely BBC television series, *Cranford*.

Sadly, the people most responsible for the genesis of this novel, Mike and Peg Jeffers, my parents, are no longer alive. In 1954, they made our home in an old house on W. Wissahickon Avenue in Flourtown, Pennsylvania, where they shared the magic of the Wissahickon Creek with my brothers, sister, and me, and set us free.

ABOUT THE AUTHOR

PJ Devlin grew up in Flourtown, PA, near the Wissahickon Creek. She wrote her first book at six-years-old and has been writing ever since — except for a thirty-year break to earn a PhD in economics, serve as a civilian manager in the Fairfax County Fire and Rescue Department, and raise four children with her husband, John. PJ studied creative writing at George Mason University in Fairfax, VA.

    Wissahickon Souls, Becoming Jonika, and her short story collection, *Wishes, Sins, and the Wissahickon Creek* have won numerous awards in the independent publishing world.

Visit *PJ Devlin Author* on Facebook, or contact the author at benezetstreet-press@gmail.com.

    If you enjoy *Wissahickon Souls,* please consider posting a review on Amazon and Goodreads.

BOOK CLUB DISCUSSION QUESTIONS

1. What is the significance of the title, *Wissahickon Souls?*

2. Setting and Time Period
   - Was the setting authentic?
   - Did you feel swept into the place and time?
   - What role does the Wissahickon Creek play?
   - What is the impact of early 19th century Philadelphia culture?

3. Themes: Race, regret, and reconciliation
   - What is Claire's motivation? How does that influence her choices?
   - How did Claire and Lawrence's decision to run away to Haiti reflect these themes?

4. Plot
   - What incidents surprised you most?
   - Discuss Anna's emotional journey.
   - How did Lawrence's death impact the story's end?
   - Were socioeconomic factors realistically portrayed?

5. Characters
   Discuss various characters' personality traits, motivations, inner-qualities. Who did you like best, least? Which characters change most?

6. Dynamics of power between characters
- Claire and Anna
- Claire and Raymond
- Claire and Lawrence
- Lawrence and Anna
- Lawrence and Raymond
- Lawrence and Henri
- Anna and Jolie, Anna and Anthony

7. The Ending
- What factors led to Claire and Anna's reconciliation?
- How did Lawrence's death impact the story's end?
- Did your understanding about life in antebellum America change?
- What does the future hold for Claire?

www.ingramcontent.com/pod-product-compliance
Lightning Source LLC
Chambersburg PA
CBHW070358260626
47161CB00001B/188